WHATEVER IT TAKES
By Sarah Hanks

PRAISE FOR
WHATEVER IT TAKES

As a historic fiction author and avid Civil War fan, I started reading *Whatever It Takes* for the sake of the historical timeline, but Everly and Ivy's story in the contemporary line quickly engaged my interest and my heart. Before I knew it, I was eagerly turning the pages, as deeply invested in the story of the two sisters as I was in Henrietta fighting for her life on the battlefields in order to provide for her sisters. I highly recommend Hanks's story. And amongst the pages, I discovered a heartfelt romance and a swoon-worthy hero that filled my romantic heart with joy.

~Sherry Shindelar, Author of *Texas Forsaken*

Whatever It Takes is an engrossing tale of sisters who will go to great lengths to keep their promises and care for the loved ones God has given them. I'm amazed by Hanks's ability to portray women both on the giving and receiving end of a modern-day surrogate pregnancy as well as undercover female Civil War soldiers to the extent that we can feel what they feel and see the world through their eyes. But best of all is the way she speaks to our own deep-seated fears and struggles through the vehicle of story, weaving truth and encouragement into the pages and reminding us that only by surrendering control to a sovereign, loving God can we lay down our burdens and find peace. I was entertained, encouraged, and fascinated by this story and know you will be too.

~Heather Wood, Author of the Finding Home Series

Whatever It Takes is a riveting dual timeline story of heartbreak, hope, courage, and love between realistic and down to earth sisters during the Civil War and present day. Author Sarah
Hanks expertly weaves a tapestry of characters and plot with a unique flair. A poignant saga of grief and suspense, the story wraps up with resolutions focusing on faith, family, and love, ultimately connecting both generations through the discovery of old family letters. This unforgettable story will stay with you long after you've read the last page.

~Becky Van Vleet, Award-winning author of
Unintended Hero

Split time novels aren't my first choice for reading for pleasure, so I wasn't entirely sure what I was getting myself into. *Whatever It Takes* took me by surprise! I LOVED THIS NOVEL! Sarah seamlessly handles two different time periods and very different situations and ties them together neatly—a must for me. I thoroughly enjoyed this book.

~Erma M. Ullrey, Elk Lake Author

Is there anything you wouldn't sacrifice for those you love most?

In this work, Sarah Hanks takes on the issues of cancer, adoption, In Vitro Fertilization (IVF), and surrogacy along with poverty and the horrors of the American Civil War, and she does so unflinchingly with her personal understanding of family dynamics.

Both modern-day Everly and her ancestor, Henrietta, are the responsible elder siblings in their grief-stricken families, placed in situations that will require more from them than should ever be asked. In this tale, Hanks blends beautifully the stories of two women, one who must tackle the horrors of 19th century combat as a Confederate soldier, the other confronting the ghosts of her past and the struggles of the many faces of motherhood. Despite the hardships, the two are willing to do 'whatever it takes,' all for the love of their sisters.

~Jenny Powell MD, Family physician and soon-to-be
Winged Publications author

Every time I read a Sarah Hanks novel, I know I'm in for a special experience, and *Whatever It Takes* was no exception. Hanks has a way of creating a large cast of characters with very different personalities and making every one of them feel real and unique. And the internal struggles in this book were so beautifully captured, I found myself fully immersed in each of their lives, rooting for them to find purpose, acceptance, and peace that can only come through surrendering every part of their lives to Jesus. This is an exceptional book.

~ Sarah Everest, Author of the Darkening Dragons
trilogy

Edited by Janice Boekhoff

ISBN 979-8-9854789-7-6

ACKNOWLEDGEMENTS

Books are often referred to as "babies," thus it's only appropriate to thank the "midwives" who helped bring this story into the world.

Thank you to Kristine Delano, Sherry Shindelar, Heather Wood, and Jenny Powell for your assistance with perfecting this story. Thanks to the Scribes critique group, as well as Erma Urley, Jack Cunningham, Becky VanBleet, Patti Shene, Kathy McKinsey, and Shaen Layle for your assistance. Much love to the Christian Mommy Writers and my local St. Louis ACFW chapter.

To my editor, Janice Boekhoff, thank you. You've taught me so much, and you always work magic on my manuscripts.

And thank you to my ultra-supportive husband who is forever in my corner and my children who encourage me (and also roast me) daily.

And to Jesus, who walks beside me every step of the way, much love and gratitude.

May you, dear reader, enjoy this story, and may it lead you closer to Him.

Chapter 1

Suburb of Wilmington, North Carolina
Present Day

"Smile, Everly. It's not a funeral." Ivy's cheery tone masks the lapse of judgment in choosing her words. No, *this* isn't a funeral. We've already checked that one off our list for the month.

The handles of the blue paper bag weigh heavy in my hand as I fidget beside Ivy. Can I drop off the gift and leave? Snuggling on my sofa with Zach and watching a good documentary would prove far more pleasant than torturing myself like this. But my sister and I came together. And she drove.

Like a spring breeze, her hand flutters to the doorbell. A chipper sound follows.

The door swings open, and our cousin Jessica's glowing face greets us. "Everly, Ivy, hello." She steps back and gestures for us to enter. "You could have just come in."

She speaks of a familiarity that does not exist. I haven't seen Jessica in half a decade, if not more. I've never *not* rung the bell.

We're three steps inside when I thrust the bag toward her like it's a dirty diaper she needs to trash. The sooner I can rid myself of it, the better, but Jessica makes no move to alleviate my burden.

Ivy shifts beside me. "Where do we put the gifts?" She waggles a narrow box in front of her. The pristine wrapping and perfectly placed bow fit my sister in every way.

"Oh." Jessica waves the presents off as if there was no need to bring gifts to her baby shower. "There's a table over there." She nods to the corner where a blue-boxed pyramid stands.

"Thanks. You look beautiful, by the way." Ivy leans in and kisses Jessica on the cheek.

Manners. Of course. It's hard to think with the whooshing in my ears. I shouldn't have come. I'm in no state to make polite conversation, much less participate in this celebration. Will there be games? *Oh, Lord. Please, no games.*

I suck in a breath and force out the expected words. "Yes, beautiful. How are you feeling?"

She chuckles. "Oh, you know, pregnant."

Ivy laughs. The words *you know* swirl in my gut like dirty water down a drain. I can't make myself laugh, but I manage not to wince. Where are the refreshments? I need something to wash down all the words I'll never say.

Jessica walks with us to the gift table. The bag I brought snags on my ring as I set it down. It clings to me, and the whole table rustles as I attempt to shake it free. Heads swivel in my direction. Great. I'm making a scene.

Ivy gently twists the bag's ribbon handle, rendering my hand weightless. Her eyes say, *Really, Everly?* She doesn't understand. She can't. I hope she never will.

I spy the kitchen island laden with snacks. A tower of cups stands on the counter behind it. I take a step in that direction, except Jessica lays a hand on my arm before I can escape. "I'm sorry to hear about your father." Her gaze includes both my sister and me. "I was out of town for work or I would have made the funeral."

"Thank you," we say in unison, as if rehearsed. Or perhaps as if we were telepathic twins instead of sisters born ten years apart. We've had plenty of practice syncing our responses over the past couple of weeks.

Jessica's tone brightens as she angles toward Ivy. It's obvious what's coming. I can safely slip away. Their conversation floats behind me as I do. "I hear we'll be having a shower for you soon. When's the big day?"

While Ivy gushes about her upcoming wedding, I down a full glass of lemonade and a refill. Sugary lemonade, likely with additives and dyes. This is what I've been reduced to. I murmur greetings to distant relatives and people I've never met while loading my plate with every snack option available. Not only the typical veggies, but crackers, chips, dip, meatballs, and pigs in a blanket. Ridiculous. I'll never eat this much, even if doing so would prevent me from having to engage for the full duration of this shower. And I think this is processed cheese dip instead of homemade. Ew.

With my plate so full it's on the verge of collapse, I edge through a thickening crowd back to my sister. She hasn't budged. I nibble on a raw carrot.

"Who knows?" Ivy rubs her flat stomach. "Maybe we'll get lucky and have a honeymoon baby."

Shards of carrot shoot from my mouth as I sputter a cough.

Jessica's eyes go wide. "You okay?"

Ivy pats my back harder than necessary.

The plate wobbles in my shaky hand, and I nod while attempting to tamp down my cough. "Fine. Wrong pipe." I swig lemonade, and my throat relaxes. My eyes search for the carrot bits I spewed, but they're nowhere to be seen. Hopefully, they didn't end up in someone's hair. Gross. My cheeks flame.

"Anyway," Ivy continues when all settles.

Only I can't let her statement go. "Slow down, Iv. What's the rush to start a family?" Of course, she and Austin will eventually have kids, but so soon?

She lifts a brow. "It's been my dream since I was little."

My voice sounds otherworldly as I say, "Dreams change."
"Not mine." Her eyes narrow in a familiar challenge.
Not here.

I let my gaze drift to the rest of the room as I slide an olive into my mouth. Yes, this is how I should spend the afternoon. Observing. Not engaging. Definitely not speaking. Who knows what might spill out?

A brunette with tattoos adorning both arms nears. "Are you Everly? Jess mentioned you're a chiropractor."

I nod, and for the first time since we arrived, a genuine smile teases my lips.

"I have daily headaches. Docs can't figure out why. They only want to prescribe meds, but I wonder … Could it be an alignment issue?"

My shoulders relax. A safe subject. "For sure."

I ask clarifying questions and explain how the spine relates. Within five minutes, I'm transformed. I feel it in my posture, my breathing, my tone of voice. When she walks away, a card for Moore Chiropractic protrudes from her back pocket.

"Attention, everyone," a blonde with a high ponytail calls from the center of the room. "It's time for games."

Ugh.

Energy saps from me in an instant as cheers erupt all around. Ivy settles on a couch and pats the space next to her. I make a beeline for it. Perhaps the safest place for me here is next to my pining-for-a-baby little sister. Once I set my plate on a side table, I'm able to push the pressure point between my thumb and index finger. Hard.

A ball of yarn comes around, and I'm told to cut off a piece to guess how large Jessica's belly is. This lack of originality makes me fear we might be tasting baby food or smelling candy bars melted into diapers. Why did I come again?

My sister's leg pressed against mine on the narrow sofa reminds me of the reason. She's all I have left in the world. Well, she and these distant cousins I barely know. Okay, I have Zach. Always my hubby Zach. But Ivy's my sister, and if she asks me to do just about anything, I'll do it. Even if it nearly kills me. When have I not? After all, I promised Mom. I twirl the ring on my finger. Some people might take promises lightly. Not me.

I unwind a length of string and snip, not bothering to hold it out and strategize. As Ivy takes the ball, her phone buzzes in the pocket of her skinny jeans. Game forgotten, she pulls it out. Her brow scrunches as she reads. She leaps up, sending the ball of yarn tumbling to the floor. A distracted "Sorry" falls from her lips, but she doesn't bend to retrieve the yarn. "I've got to make a call."

I attempt to question her with my gaze, but she doesn't even glance at me as she rushes away.

~~

Ivy Alexander twisted the bathroom lock and leaned against the wall. With trembling fingers, she dialed her doctor's number. Boisterous laughter drifted under the doorjamb. She plugged her other ear with her finger.

"Radiant Health after-hours line. How can I help you?" The operator's matter-of-fact tone eased her racing pulse. Everything was fine. Typical of her to jump to conclusions.

She wrapped her free arm around herself. "This is Ivy Alexander. I received a text requesting me to call and schedule a face-to-face appointment. I'm concerned."

"I see. You'll need to call Monday morning to make that appointment."

Her chin quivered. "Could someone contact me today to let me know what this is about?" Though it was easy to guess. But maybe it was standard to meet even if the test results showed nothing amiss. *Oh, Lord. Help.*

"I'm sorry, ma'am, but our policy is—"

"Please." Her voice quaked. "I'm worried."

A pause. "What's your date of birth?"

Keys clicked as Ivy confirmed basic information. Would this operator see Ivy's call history? Because this wasn't the first time she'd contacted the after-hours number. And yes, "nothing to be concerned about" seemed to be the basic consensus. What if they'd flagged her as a hypochondriac and she found herself in a boy-who-cried-wolf situation?

More clicking. "Okay, I'm pulling up your information."

Ivy's insides churned like Mom's old washing machine. The piece of junk had scooted across the basement floor with every wash cycle, shaking as if at the epicenter of an earthquake. At least that's how it had seemed to Ivy's five-year-old self. She'd always been called overdramatic. She probably *was* overreacting, but what if—

"Ms. Alexander, I see a note here. I'll have a doctor give you a call as soon as possible."

"O-okay." Did that mean …?

"You'll hear from someone soon. Hang tight."

The line went dead.

Heavens, something was very wrong. Dying. She had to be dying. Why else would the operator have reacted that way? She was supposed to be getting married. Her throat burned as she pictured Austin at the front of a church for her funeral instead of their wedding.

"Breathe, Ivy. Breathe." She had to talk herself down from this ledge before she embarrassed herself and ruined Jessica's baby shower. "Stupid anxiety. I hate you."

On the back of the toilet sat a can of lavender-scented air freshener. Perfect. Lavender had a calming effect, right? Everly touted the benefits of it often. Ivy sprayed liberally and dragged in a deep breath. She gagged. Wouldn't be the first time Ev's methods didn't work for her.

Experience told her a return call could take time. She couldn't remain holed up in the bathroom much longer before her sister would bang down the door and demand an explanation. She had nothing to explain, not yet. Best to try and forget she was waiting for a possible life-altering call. Three minutes of deep breathing and she'd readied herself to face the room of jovial women. Shoulders back. Smile in place. She could do this.

Dodging eye contact with Everly, she wove her way back to the couch. Her sister's rigid posture proved her discomfort. Maybe she shouldn't have pushed for Ev to come, but when her sister had said she'd moved on, Ivy had believed her. It was so long ago. Was Ev truly so apprehensive about babies?

The string game must have finished. Ladies were hunched over pieces of paper, pens scribbling wildly. She plopped next to Everly and peeked at the blank paper in front of her sister proclaiming *How Many Words Can You Make Out of "Celebrating Our Baby Boy"?* Everly tapped a pen on her knee and stared into the distance.

Ivy nudged her. "Ray. Bay. Or."

"Huh?" Everly startled. "Oh." She wrote Ivy's suggestions. "What was that about?"

"Nothing. Yay. Y-a-y is a word, right?"

Everly added it to the list without comment. "This isn't supposed to be a partner game. What do you mean, nothing? It was obviously something."

"If we win, I get the prize since I'm doing all the work." Ivy pointed to the list. "Rate. Tale. Brat. Grate."

"Oh." Everly's eyes lit. "Bra."

"Great contribution." She rolled her eyes. "Table. Role. Oh, just give me the pen. You're too slow."

Everly leaned close to her ear. "Cable. Stop avoiding the question."

"I'm not. We're in the middle of a game."

Jessica's voice invaded their bubble. "Ivy, there you are."

She turned to find the mother-to-be beaming at her from in front of a piano. How could she not have noticed that beauty? "I was hoping you could help with *Name That Tune*. Shelby was supposed to do it, but she couldn't make it. The flu." She held up a handful of paper. "I have the sheet music right here."

"Yes. Of course." She scrambled to her feet, pen dangling from her hand.

"Go ahead." Everly scoffed and snatched the pen. "Leave me to suffer alone with this game."

Now who was being overdramatic? "You'll be fine."

Music called to her. How long had it been since she'd played a real piano? Her electronic keyboard couldn't compare. She ran her finger over the keys, eliciting a soft plink on E and G.

Jessica placed the sheet music on the stand. "The game's simple. Each song has the word *baby* in it. Everyone tries to guess the title and artist."

Ivy sat on the bench and stretched her fingers, then wiggled them.

"Ivy on the ivories. Fitting." Jessica chuckled.

Though Ivy had heard that line dozens of times before, she grinned. "It does fit, doesn't it?" She fit here, in this place her mom had so often occupied. Everly might have gotten Mom's ring, but Ivy had received Mom's gift for music. "Can I play something to warm up? None of these." She pointed to the papers in front of her. "Wouldn't want to ruin the game."

"Sure. Play whatever you'd like while we finish the word scramble."

What an invitation. What should she play? Beethoven? Tchaikovsky? Her fingers fluttered into formation and danced of their own accord. Her eyes drifted closed. The corners of her mouth twitched upward even as the corners of her eyes burned.

"Our song." Everly's voice lapped at her shoulders like a wave threatening to sweep her under. "It's been a long time." Her sister scooted next to her on the bench and hummed "Ebony and Ivory" as Ivy played.

When the chorus came, they sang together. "Everly, Ivy, living in perfect harmony."

The room erupted in applause. Ivy's hands flew to her warm cheeks. "I didn't know everyone was listening." A strand of hair, loose from its topknot, tickled her face.

Everly tucked it behind her ear. "Don't be surprised. You deserve to be noticed."

Whatever. They could have just as well been clapping for Ev's vocals.

Jessica announced the objective of *Name That Baby Tune*, and all eyes turned to Ivy. She shuffled the music and started playing "Baby I Need Your Loving." When she got to the part of the song that included the word *baby*, Beethoven's Twelfth belted from her back pocket.

The doctor. How could she have forgotten? Her fingers faltered, splintering the air with dissonant chords.

Blasted music. It always made her forget what she needed to remember. And remember what she should forget.

She jumped to her feet, scraping the backs of her legs against the piano bench. "Sorry. I have to take this." Every eye stared as she fumbled to answer her phone. "Hello, this is Ivy Alexander." She rushed toward the bathroom.

"Hello, it's Dr. Anderson. I'm calling regarding the colposcopy performed yesterday."

"Yes?" She stepped into the bathroom and attempted to close the door, but Everly's foot blocked the way. She scowled as her sister followed her in, then closed and locked the door behind them.

Apparently, they were in this together

Everly's face scrunched as she whispered, "What's that smell?"

Ivy pointed to the air freshener. Her sister cringed. Seriously? Not the time.

Ivy put her phone on speaker but punched down the volume button to avoid any eavesdroppers.

"Ms. Alexander, I'm not supposed to discuss results over the phone, but I understand your concern. And unfortunately, it's warranted."

As Dr. Anderson continued, laughter filtered in from the other room like a noxious gas. Ivy's vision clouded with moisture. Everly's arms wrapped around her, holding her upright while her world crumbled. Again.

Chapter 2

HOW GLADLY WOULD I WASH OUT WITH MY TEARS
EVERY LITTLE SPOT UPON YOUR HAPPINESS, AND
STRUGGLE WITH ALL THE MISFORTUNE OF THIS
WORLD, TO SHIELD YOU AND MY CHILDREN FROM
HARM. BUT I CANNOT.

JULY 14, 1861, LETTER FROM MAJ. SULLIVAN BALLOU TO
WIFE SARAH

Outside of Warsaw, North Carolina
February 1861

The sun crested over the plain, bringing with it a blinding brilliance that paled in comparison to Henrietta Frontenac's overwhelming desperation. Loreen's hopelessness seemed to beg for her intervention. Henrietta lowered her gaze to the task at hand, the washbasin where they both scrubbed. Far better to focus on Mrs. Middleton's skirt than her younger sister's haunted expression or the way Loreen's ribs showed through her threadbare blouse.

A train whistle bellowed in the distance. A reminder that a larger city with greater opportunities was only a few hours away by rail.

She took a breath and infused hope into her voice. "Perhaps you could find work in Wilmington." At seventeen, her sister was a prime age for employment.

A lonely tear crept down Loreen's cheek as she scrubbed. "Not without shoes. Can't afford shoes."

"We'll take in extra washing." Even as the words escaped her mouth, they fell to the ground, as useless as dirt. They already laundered for everyone in the area who could justify the luxury, trekking back and forth to both of the nearby towns, Warsaw and Faison. And they all went to bed with hunger gnawing their bellies. Of course, Henrietta and Loreen, the oldest two, gave larger portions to Gretchen, Beatrice, Charlotte, and Mildred. It pained something fierce to see the young'uns cry for more when there was none. How much could a person water down soup before it didn't satisfy one lick?

Loreen huffed. "It won't be enough, and you know it. There's not one job afforded a woman that would be enough to keep us afloat."

Henrietta's mouth twisted as she bit back a retort. Loreen was right, after all. *Girls.* Why'd Ma and Pa have to bear six girls without one boy in the lot of them? Poor Ma, gone to heaven after birthing baby Mildred six years prior. She'd hoped for a son. Lot of good hope did her. Another mouth to feed without any offspring to help bring in a decent wage.

She glanced at where Pa sat in his coarse wooden chair on the front porch. Her gaze settled on his bum leg before she abruptly shifted her focus back to the sudsy water. Pa had made a livable income at the railway until the accident. Now, he spent most days in that same chair, staring into the distance. Acres of farmland he couldn't farm surrounded them. It belonged to the neighbors, anyhow. All they had to their name was a measly plot of land, a dilapidated one-room farmhouse, and a minuscule garden.

Indignation swirled in Henrietta's belly even as an idea she'd pondered earlier spun in her mind. It was ludicrous. Her family would laugh her into the next county. There had to be another way. One that allowed her to stick close to home, near the people who meant everything to her.

But as she hung a shirtwaist on the clothesline, her mouth parted, and words rushed out. "I heard some men talking 'bout how roustabouts at the docks get paid a handsome sum."

Loreen sighed without lifting her gaze from the murky water. "Too bad you're not a man."

"Yeah, too bad." She plunged another blouse under and scrubbed it against the washboard. But what if …? No. She'd find another solution.

The sun-bleached porch door banged shut, and both girls turned toward it. Gretchen rushed past Pa and down the rickety steps to where they stood in the yard, her sweat-dampened brow creased in concern.

Henrietta took Gretchen's hands in her soapy ones. "What's wrong?" She scanned the horizon. No sign of Charlotte or Beatrice. They must still be out searching for wild greens.

"It's Mildred." Her lip wobbled.

Henrietta winced. "Her cough has worsened." It wasn't a question. And to think Henrietta had been optimistic that morning. Sweet little Millie. As if she didn't have enough to battle against with the teasing over her deformity. Now pesky name-calling was the least of her worries. "What of the fever?"

"Worse." Gretchen's hands trembled. "Should we fetch the doctor?"

Oh dear. If her sister was considering spending money on a physician, it must be dismal indeed. Henrietta dried her hands, snatched Ma's ring from the pouch cinched at her waist, and slid it back on her finger. In times like these, the heirloom brought strength and purpose. She must fulfill her promise.

"Let me see her." Picking up her patched skirts, she rushed inside, Loreen and Gretchen in her wake.

The sight on the mattress in the corner pummeled her. Little Millie, already but a waif, seemed to have dwindled even over the last few hours. Gaunt, colorless cheeks sagged against bone. Her body racked with a cough, the sound clawing at Henrietta's soul.

Oh, Lord in heaven. Are You there? Do You see? Do You care? Doubtful. He'd abandoned them long ago. Still, something within wouldn't allow her to untether from her mother's faith entirely. Prayers she never expected Him to answer lifted from her lips in desperate moments. Many such prayers lately.

What should they do? Gretchen's consideration to call for the doctor was rational, even if they lacked funds.

Henrietta knelt by her youngest sister and smoothed dingy strands of brown hair from the girl's hot forehead. "Hi, Mill Moo. I'm sorry you're not feeling well." Millie's glassy eyes barely registered Henrietta's presence. "It's going to be okay. We're going to get you better. Don't worry."

But worry churned Henrietta's middle. Forcing a smile, she stood and motioned to Loreen and Gretchen to follow her back outside. They stepped onto the porch. Pa remained in his chair, seemingly oblivious to the storm brewing around him, his eyes as empty as Millie's. Though the girls stood inches away from him, there was no use including him in the conversation.

Gretchen took the lead. "We should fetch the doctor."

Henrietta shook her head. "If we do, we'll owe all we brought in this week. We'll have nothing but wild greens to eat. How will Millie recover without proper nutrition? She'll fare a better chance with a full belly than with the doctor's tonics." After all, those tonics hadn't saved Ma. Best not to put trust in doctors.

"A full belly?" Loreen's laugh held no humor. "Since when have any of us had that?"

Gretchen fidgeted. "We must fetch the doctor. What if she—"

Henrietta stuck out her hand. "Don't say it." Millie couldn't die. Not their sweet ray of sunshine. She shook the possibility from her mind. Unthinkable. "The doctor won't come on credit. Not anymore." His mercy had limits, and they'd reached them.

Her stomach growled as if to remind her of the point she'd made. Food. They all needed it, but right now, Millie needed it most. If they gave their portions to her, perhaps she stood a chance.

Gretchen cast a glance at their father. "Let's ask Pa."

Henrietta rolled her eyes but complied. She knelt in front of their old man and explained the situation to him.

His long, brown beard quivered with his sigh. "What does it matter what we do? The Lord is against us. If He aims to take her, there ain't nothin' we can do to keep her here."

Henrietta slumped forward, inhaling slowly to strengthen her resolve. Pa wasn't about to lead this family. The job fell to her, and she had no choice but to rise to the task. If one day her father awoke from his despondency, she'd gladly relinquish the role. For now, though, she'd do what had to be done.

She squared her shoulders and stood, meeting each sister's eye. "I'll take care of it."

~~

Draped in inky darkness, Henrietta sneaked back into their home, careful of the squeaky floorboard. She set her sack by the front door and inched it closed.

"Where were you?" Loreen's whisper sent a shiver up her neck.

Her hand flew to her chest. "Don't scare me like that."

Her sister stood inches away, arms crossed. From the corner, Millie sputtered a cough. Henrietta cringed at the sound.

Loreen toed the sack. "What's in the bag?"

"Chickens. Two of 'em."

"What? Where'd you get them?"

"Don't ask."

"You stole them, didn't you?"

Blasted Loreen. Why couldn't she mind her own business? "I said, don't ask."

"Henrietta!"

"Sh." A finger to the mouth silenced her sister's protests.

If only Henrietta's conscience could be lulled so easily. But why should she feel guilty for doing what was necessary? It wasn't her fault they were starving. Plus, the Rielys had plenty of fowl. What else was she supposed to do? Taking the moral high road could leave a little girl dead. Is that what God wanted? Far be it from her to allow that to happen without a fight.

She couldn't afford morals.

Only … what would she do the next time hunger gnawed or sickness threatened? A life of petty thievery disgusted her. What if she was caught? Jailed? And all for a couple of measly chickens. No. This wasn't a long-term solution.

But there *was* a solution.

She grabbed a lantern, took her sister by the arm, and led her outside. On the porch, she set the lantern down and turned to her sister in the dim light.

Loreen guffawed. "What's this about?"

"Remember when we were younger and we put on plays for the folks? Who always played the gentleman part?"

Loreen raised a furrowed brow. "You, of course. What are you getting at?"

"What if"—Henrietta bit her lip, then loosed a tentative smile—"I performed for a wider audience?"

Loreen stilled. "Excuse me?"

"What if I set off for the docks dressed as a gent?"

Loreen's hands flew to her hips. "Henrietta, you're off your rocker!"

"Hear me out. I could get double what I make laundering. Perhaps triple. Send it straight home to you. With decent clothing and shoes, you'd stand a chance to gain finer employment yourself."

Loreen's blue eyes flashed in the duskiness. While the rest of them had inherited Pa's brown orbs, Loreen's took after Ma's piercing ones. "But impersonating a man is illegal."

"Only if someone catches you."

"You'll need shoes yourself and train fare to Wilmington. How do you suppose to scrounge that up?"

Infernal negativity. Why'd her sister have to ask questions she wasn't prepared to answer? They had nothing of value to sell. Unless … Henrietta spun Ma's ring on her finger. She could get a mighty fine price for such an heirloom. She nibbled her lip. No. She couldn't part with it, not for good. She'd rather beg like Old Man Meager. She shivered at the memory of the ragged man rattling his tin cup.

Her sister raised a brow.

"Don't ask." If she needed to steal more than chickens, that's what she'd do. It would be worth it if it got her family out of the steel trap poverty had caged them in.

Loreen frowned but let the comment pass. "You won't be around to plant the garden or harvest it."

True. Harvesting their garden was a bright spot in their dull lives. Memories of Loreen digging up potatoes and tossing them to Henrietta to catch in her apron swirled. They made a mighty fine team. Now Loreen would need to take the lead.

Her sister tugged at the end of Henrietta's braid. "Would you truly cut your gorgeous hair? It's just like Ma's."

Henrietta pulled out the ribbon, threaded her fingers through her hair, and loosened her braid. Auburn locks fell around her shoulders like waves and reached halfway down her back. Like Ma's had. Her heart twisted. She clenched her jaw. "Hair will grow back." She cupped her sister's chin. "My family is far more important."

Tears leaked from Loreen's eyes and moistened Henrietta's palm. Loreen's voice came out in a broken whisper. "You'd do that for us?"

"Of course." Henrietta kissed her forehead. "I'd do anything for my sisters. You mean everything to me."

Loreen wrapped her arms around Henrietta and squeezed. "I think you'll make a fantastic boy." She giggled. "You never were very ladylike."

Henrietta pulled back and let her jaw drop in mock offense. "I beg your pardon?"

Loreen's grin—the first in a long while—rivaled a brilliant moonbeam. "But you've always been the best sister."

~~

Henrietta winced as Loreen brought the scissors close. She had to repeat to herself what she'd told her sisters multiple times: *Hair will grow back*. Nothing Loreen did would be irreversible, yet a solemnity hung in the air as the rest of the girls watched from the rough-cut bench seat in the middle of their home. After this, there'd be no changing her mind. Her heartbeat thundered against her ribs. Shorn hair would seal her fate, at least for a while.

At Henrietta's right side, Loreen took deep breaths that did little to steady her nerves, if her trembling hands were any indication. The cool metal blade slid along the base of her neck.

But her wait for hair to fall away was in vain.

"I can't do it." Loreen's voice held a mixture of apology and frustration.

Henrietta worked to keep her voice calm. Soothing. "Of course, you can."

The blade lifted from her neck. "No, I can't." Loreen blubbered watery words that were past deciphering. Something about Ma interspersed with what might have been an apology. Hard to tell with her carrying on.

Henrietta stood and wrapped her sister in her arms. Loreen's shoulders shook. She'd always been the most emotional Frontenac girl.

Henrietta patted her back. "It's okay." She took Loreen's face into her hands and swiped her sister's cheeks with her thumbs. "Don't worry. Someone else can do it."

"Oh, me! Me." Charlotte jumped up from the bench. "I can do it." She lunged for the scissors in Loreen's hand.

Henrietta snatched them first and held them above her head. "No, thank you, Little Miss." Anyone who'd dive for a sharp object in such a reckless manner had no business near her head.

A cough erupted from the mat in the corner. Millie stirred but didn't wake. Was it her imagination or had the sweet girl gained a bit of strength from the nourishing game? A full belly allowed her to sleep soundly now. Thank heavens. Rest would do wonders to restore her. It had better.

Charlotte planted her hands on her hips and scowled. "I'm not little anymore, 'Etta. I'm almost ten years old."

Henrietta sucked in her bottom lip to hide her smile. That girl would give any man a challenge when she was old enough to wed. "Even so, you may *not* cut my hair."

Beatrice raised her hand. "I will."

Oh, sweet Bea. Henrietta shook her head. "Not you either."

"I'll cut it." Gretchen marched to her and held out her hand for the scissors. At fourteen, she was a mite better choice than the younger ones. Still, her carelessness with the garden proved her to be easily distracted. One wrong snip could ruin Henrietta's chances of being taken for a respectable gent. No, she couldn't trust Gretchen either. In fact, not one of the sisters knew a thing about a man's haircut.

But someone in their family did.

"Thanks, but no." She offered Gretchen a conciliatory smile, then swept out the weather-worn door, scissors still raised high. Her sisters followed. Pa neglected to turn their way. His hair nearly brushed his shoulders. He must not have trimmed it in a long while. Still, if he knew how to cut his own hair, surely he could do the same for her.

"Pa?" She knelt before him and implored him with her eyes to snap out of whatever daydream he'd wandered into. Recognition dawned with his slow blink. He heard her. Saw her. She held the scissors in his line of sight. "I need you to cut my hair."

He wheezed out a breath but didn't respond. He'd listened when she'd told of her plans, hadn't he? He hadn't objected. Neither had he agreed. She wouldn't wait for a blessing that might never come.

"Pa?" She waggled the handle of the scissors in front of him.

He shook his head, his frown pronounced. "It's come to this, has it?"

Was that disappointment in his gaze? If he thought she should be able to take care of the family without resorting to such measures, he must be dismayed. But she wasn't the one who had failed their family. Not yet, anyway. "It's our only chance."

His jaw firmed. "I won't stop you, but I'll not aid this foolhardy plan."

So, he wouldn't do anything. No surprise there.

As she stared back at the shell of a man who had once been a loving father, a vine of tenacity wound around her core. Her hand clenched the scissors. "Fine. I'll do it myself."

It's what she should have done in the first place. No use depending on anyone else. She was the only one she could count on. It had been that way since God stormed out of their lives.

"I'll grab the mirror." Gretchen rushed inside.

"I'll hold it for you." Beatrice's chest puffed out.

Charlotte nudged her. "No, me."

Henrietta scolded them with a look. "You can take turns."

When she finally perched in the chair, her sisters gathered around, and she had to dig deep to find courage. She'd touted that there was no other way. Was it true? Of course, it was. They'd tried everything else they knew to do for years. If she didn't go through with this, a life of thievery was the brightest option available. Far better than her—or worse yet, Loreen—selling her body for sustenance. The very thought breathed bravery into her.

She took a strand of brittle auburn hair in one hand and opened the scissors with the other. She refused to wince as she snipped, sending the lock cascading to the floor.

Loreen gasped. Charlotte giggled, and the tarnished hand mirror wobbled in her grasp.

Beatrice clapped. "Do it again!"

And Henrietta did. Chunk by chunk until her auburn hair splayed on the dull wooden floor around her feet. By the time she finished, a somberness had replaced all gaiety. The girls stared at the tendrils in silence. Henrietta scooped up a strand and fingered it, her heart sinking to her toes.

"Can I touch it?" Bea held out a finger and leaned close.

"Of course." Henrietta held the lock out to her. "It's only hair. It won't bite."

Bea stroked it gently.

Charlotte's frown deepened. "You look strange."

Henrietta puffed out her cheeks. She needed to lighten the mood. The girls acted as if the world were ending. She couldn't leave them like this, full of trepidation.

She stood and brushed off her skirt. "Charlotte and Bea, go gather five sticks, please."

Though Loreen quirked a brow, the younger ones rushed off to do her bidding with nary a question or protest. When they returned minutes later, Henrietta tied locks of hair to the base of every stick. "There. You can pretend they're ribbons and dance with them like the Chinese." Ma's home education had done them good. She'd exposed them to many things through books. Though they'd had to sell those books after Pa's accident, their memories remained.

The younger girls giggled and raced out the door with their new toys.

The edges of Loreen's mouth ticked upward. "How do you do it?"

"Do what?"

"Turn things around. Bathe everything in peace like—" Her voice caught. "Like Ma used to."

Henrietta shrugged. Air tickled the nape of her neck.

Loreen fiddled with the end of her braid. "I fear I won't do nearly as well holding this family together in your absence."

Henrietta cast a glare toward the front porch. "You shouldn't have to." If only Pa would step up. What a burden that would take from them.

"We do what we must." Loreen reached out and looped her pinky finger around Henrietta's. Their show of solidarity.

Oh! The ring. How could she have forgotten? Her chest tightened as she slipped Ma's ring off her finger. "Keep this safe for me. Wear it until I return."

She'd garnered strength from the heirloom and how it connected her to Ma. Her hand shook as she placed the treasure in Loreen's palm. Hopefully, Loreen couldn't feel the tremor. Bravado proved essential to this plan. If her sister sensed her fear, she might beg her not to go through with it, and Loreen's pleas were a force to be reckoned with. To embark on this endeavor, Henrietta needed to stomp out any uncertain thoughts about what this new path might require of her.

Chapter 3

Suburb of Wilmington, North Carolina
Present Day

Ivy's knees wobbled as the elevator rose to the tenth floor. Austin gripped her left hand and Everly her right. With support like this, surely everything would be all right, wouldn't it? Her stomach lurched as the elevator came to a stop. Her experience as a medical transcriptionist had taught her that *not* everything turned out well, not by a long shot. Accidents happened regularly. People got sick every day. People died.

Would she be next?

She bit her lip. No. She couldn't allow her mind to go down that road.

Everly squeezed Ivy's fingers. Mom's ring bit into her flesh. "Cervical cancer is entirely treatable. Prognoses are good."

Ivy mumbled, "I know," as she had the previous dozen times her sister had spouted such reassurances. A simple Google search had told her that much, at least when the cancer was caught early. But was hers caught early enough? They'd yet to find out whether the cancerous cells had spread throughout her pelvic area. If they had … Oh, why had she brought this on herself? If only she hadn't gone rogue as a teen. Her wild streak had come back to taunt her. Would the consequences of her actions devour her future?

"Don't think about it." Austin moved his hand to her back, grounding her. "Don't allow your thoughts to rush ahead. One step at a time."

They arrived at the gynecologist's office. She needed a little nudge to cross the threshold. Austin placed gentle pressure to the small of her back, guiding her into the office and to the front desk.

Everly spoke close to her ear. "You can do this. I'm right beside you."

Ivy's teeth chattered as she signed in and waited for a nurse to call her back. Why'd they have to make hospitals so cold?

Austin's brow furrowed. "Do you want me to run out to the car and get your sweater?"

Before he'd even finished the question, Everly was removing hers. "No need. Take mine."

"Ms. Alexander?" Ivy would give anything to not have to walk through the door the nurse held open. But seeing as she had no choice, she stood, sending her stomach tumbling to her feet. It had never taken such effort to force one foot in front of the other. "Come on back." The nurse waved her through.

Everly nearly stepped on her heels. "I'm her sister. I'm coming with her." Ev's tone didn't leave room for argument.

The nurse's brows shot up, but she waved Everly through as well. Thank God. She couldn't imagine doing this alone, but it would be mortifying for Austin to see her in such a state. She could rest in the assurance that he'd be praying for her the entire time.

After a mandatory but unnecessary pregnancy test, the nurse ushered them into an exam room. Ivy's gaze settled on a painting of a rowboat in the middle of a peaceful lake. If only she could transport herself into that picture. Row away from this nightmare. Numbness spread through her mind as she answered routine health questions.

The nurse pointed to a paper gown on the exam table. "Nothing on from the waist down. The doctor will be in shortly."

The soft click of the door sent another shudder through her. Trapped. She was trapped.

"Whoa," Everly soothed. "Breathe with me." She trailed gentle fingers up and down Ivy's arm. Up for inhale. Down for exhale.

Ivy followed her sister's lead. One step at a time. She could do this.

"Ready to change into that stylish dress?" Everly teased.

"Ready as I'll ever be."

Minutes after she'd donned the gown and taken her place on the table, Dr. Bingford entered. He pulled spectacles onto the tip of his nose and consulted his computer. A sad, obligatory smile pulled his lips upward a fraction. "Hello, Ms. Alexander." Abandoning the chart, he rubbed his hands together. "You're here for a Loop Electrosurgical Excision Procedure or LEEP. Do you understand what that is?"

Her throat tightened. Not even a simple answer squeaked out.

Everly jumped in. "You'll insert a wire loop into her cervix and pass an electrical current through it to remove any abnormal cells, right?"

Dr. Bingford tilted his head. "Sort of. The wire loop excises, or cuts out, abnormal tissue, and the electric current cauterizes the cervix to prevent bleeding." He focused his gaze on Ivy. "Beforehand, I'll put a bit of iodine on your cervix to make it easier to see the abnormal tissue as I look at it through a special microscope called a colposcope. Then, I'll numb the area before beginning the procedure." He stood and snapped on blue latex gloves. "Any questions?"

Only the one that had consumed her waking hours since she'd heard about this next step. "What if it doesn't work?"

He placed a headlamp onto his graying head. "A cone biopsy would be the next step. Let's not get ahead of ourselves, though."

She was tempted to laugh. Not get ahead of herself? This doctor obviously didn't know her.

But Everly did. And she held tightly to Ivy's hand, humming "Ebony and Ivory" over and over again as the scent of burning flesh filled the room.

~~

I wait while Mrs. Livingston turns onto her left side. My fingers trail her spine until I find the culprit causing her pain—T12. I situate her leg and hip properly, then apply the needed pressure. Her body moves in the way it's supposed to. She sighs with relief.

"That should feel better." I pat her shoulder. "Now, let's look at that neck. Onto your back."

I've been going through the motions all day, adjusting client after client, but my heart is miles away. When Ivy's LEEP had shown cells of significant concern, they'd scheduled her for an immediate cone biopsy. She should receive the results today. My ears stand as sentinels, waiting for her call.

I trace my patient's neck muscles, turning her head gently to the side to stretch where it's tight.

The older lady moans. "Your fingers are like warm butter. You should have been a masseuse."

I grin at the odd compliment. "Well, I am taking classes in massage therapy, but only because it's connected to acupressure, which is what I want to specialize in."

I'm so close. Only fifty training hours and one licensing exam to go, and I'll achieve my long-held dream of certification. I'll be satisfied then, won't I? This high school dropout will have achieved an impressive level of success. Major props to me. Now, if I could only learn to garden, I'd be able to completely silence the feeling of failure that nips at my heels.

"You'll be adding that service, then?"

I swiftly twist her neck with a gentle movement. A sound like popcorn rewards me. "Eventually. Acupressure and perhaps acupuncture. My husband will still focus solely on chiropractic."

"That's nice. You make a great team." She takes hold of my extended hand, and I pull her to standing.

"We sure do." My smile comes easily, like most things involving Zach. I hit the jackpot with Mr. Tall, Blond, and Handsome. From the day we met in foods class our sophomore year of college, Zach and I have fit together like raw milk and local honey.

Finishing each other's sentences, communicating whole paragraphs with a single look. After the poor choices I'd made in the past, he was my first choice for a beautiful future.

"Thanks so much. I'll see you next week." Mrs. Livingston grabs her purse and heads for the door, her movements far less stiff than when she waddled in.

Behind Zach's closed office door, a phone rings. I strain to listen.

"Hi. Yes." The heaviness in his voice roots me in place. "I'll get her. She's been waiting for your call."

Goodness, no. It's Ivy or Austin. Has to be. And judging from Zach's tone, the news isn't good. I dig my fingers into my palms.

Zach's office door swings open, and he captures my gaze. He mouths, *Austin*, and points to the phone. The desire to flee itches my legs, as if I could outrun this nightmare. Panic must be evident in my expression because Zach brings his hands up like he's approaching a frightened deer.

He says nothing as he comes to me with slow steps. He takes my hand and leads me toward his office. Steady. Calm.

Controlled. His serene presence gives my feet courage to follow. One step at a time.

Once inside his office, he reaches behind me and shuts the door. Then he presses the speaker button and says, "She's here. We're both listening."

"It's not good." I doubt Austin's ever cried in his life, but he sounds as if he's teetering on the edge of doing so now. "They detected cancer near the margins of the cervix, near the edge of the uterus. The tumor is about two centimeters."

My throat burns as I picture the monster that's invaded my sister's body.

"Stage three adenocarcinoma cervical cancer."

My eyes slam shut. How could such horrible words be coming out of Austin's mouth? I lost my mother. Then my father. Don't tell me I might lose my sister too.

No. Not on my watch.

I blink my eyes open and widen my stance. "How do we fight it?"

Zach's frown deepens. Does he disapprove of my use of "we"? Maybe I'm reading into things.

"The new doctor wants to do a radical hysterectomy. He said removing the uterus and cervix, as well as the lymph nodes in the pelvic area, will give her the best chance."

My chest tightens. Zach nods as if that's completely reasonable. And of course, it is. Saving Ivy's life is most important. But … My throat constricts. They want to cut out her womb right before she gets married? My sweet sister who's dreamed of a house full of children as long as I can remember.

"How's Ivy taking it?" I hear my voice ask the question, but it's as if I'm floating outside of my body. I listen for the sound of rapid keyboard playing, Ivy's go-to when she's stressed but not panicked. There's no music. This is severe.

Austin clears his throat. "About as well as you can imagine."

What I imagine is her hyperventilating on the floor. The poor girl did such a great job keeping anxiety at bay when she got news of an abnormal pap smear. She confessed that she knew false abnormalities were common, and since she'd never had any issues before, she didn't spiral. Not then. Not until she got the colposcopy results at the baby shower.

But now? I cannot conceive of Ivy currently upright. She's horizontal somewhere, most likely in the fetal position. There's no way she can win the battle against this level of anxiety.

Oh, me of little faith. You can do anything, Lord. Carry her through this.

Once again, Zach's eyes lock onto mine, and he nods. He's giving me permission to go to my sister, to comfort her the way only I can.

"I'll be over in twenty," I say.

"Thanks." Austin's voice chokes with emotion.

As soon as Zach hangs up, he reassures me that he'll juggle the rest of my clients as well as his. How he'll manage is anyone's guess. I don't have the mental capacity to worry about it now. Ivy needs me.

~~

Ivy sat sandwiched between Austin and Everly in the consult office. Two days ago, Everly had literally picked her up off the floor to comfort her. She and Austin had been holding Ivy together ever since. Meeting with the doctor threatened to be more reality than she could handle, but she forced herself to focus. She had questions. The first one had burned inside her since she'd found out the proposed treatment plan.

"Isn't there another way?" She scooted to the edge of her seat, propelled by threadbare hope.

"There is." The doctor's tone indicated that anything he said next would be a bad idea. Still, she held her breath.

Perhaps this was the answer to prayer. "We could do a radical trachelectomy instead, which would preserve the uterus, but"—he clicked his tongue—"it's risky. Your cancer has spread fast. This option would mean a greater chance for recurrence." He studied the papers in front of him with a frown. "There's not much listed as far as family history."

"Is that a problem?" She'd left most of the section blank because she was clueless about her extended family's history. Mom and Dad were the only ones she had any idea about.

"It would be helpful to know more." He scrubbed his jaw. "But we'll proceed with the information we have." He tented his fingers together. "You have my recommendation."

Austin placed a hand on her bobbing knee. "We'll follow whatever your recommendations are to save Ivy's life."

Ivy's wide eyes flashed to Austin, then back to the doctor. "I'll never be able to have children?" It should have been a statement. Obviously, no womb, no babies. But as if desperately searching for a pinprick of light in a dark cavern, her sentence lilted as a question.

Lines extended from the doctor's frown. He must have been accustomed to sharing bad news. "You'd have no uterus, so you'd have no means of carrying a child. But with the transposition of your ovaries, you'll still be able to produce eggs."

Yeah, okay. What good were eggs if they had nowhere to go? Darkness threatened to swallow her. She opened her mouth to beg for option B, the one where she could keep her womb, but Austin's voice broke in. Confident. Assured.

"We'll do whatever we need to do to save her life. If you recommend a radical hysterectomy, that's what we'll do."

The doctor folded his hands on his desk. "That's my strong recommendation due to the size and position of the tumor."

Everly tucked a strand of hair behind Ivy's ear. "We need you, Iv. There are other ways to be a mother."

After everything Everly had lost, who could blame her for not wanting to risk the one Alexander she had left? Her sister and her fiancé needed her. She was valuable, even without a womb. She must do this for the people she loved.

Ivy crossed her legs as she considered. Her foot bounced so fast, the heel of her flat slipped off. "How long do I have? Before you'd need to do the surgery?"

"I recommend having the hysterectomy as soon as possible."

Her mind thumbed through her calendar for the next few months. Preparations for their upcoming wedding consumed nearly all non-work hours. How could she fit a life-changing surgery into the mix? Before or after the cake tasting?

"We're getting married in three months. Can it wait until after?" She worried her lip.

"Not if you want to walk down that aisle."

His words tore the breath from her lungs. Her limbs numbed.

Stillness settled in the room like a fog. Ivy glanced to her sister, then her fiancé. All color had drained from their faces.

"We'll push the wedding back." Austin sounded as if someone had punched him in the stomach.

Back? If she was going to trudge through this nightmare, she wanted a husband by her side.

"Or up." She leaned forward. "What if we moved the wedding up? Could we do the surgery in a month?"

"Ivy—"

She threw a hand up to stop Austin's protests. No doubt he was filing through all the practical reasons that wouldn't work. They'd have to find a different reception venue, scramble for fittings and flowers. It would mess up his wedding prep spreadsheet. But she needed to know if it was possible.

The doctor looked from Austin to Ivy and shifted in his chair. "No longer than six weeks."

Six weeks. She could marry Austin as a whole woman, with every body part God put inside of her. Even go on a honeymoon. Then they could suit up for battle as man and wife. Her eyes welled as she turned to Austin. "Please, honey. Let's move up the wedding."

His mouth twitched as his gaze roamed her face, probably battling with his answer. She was asking him to marry a woman with stage three cancer. Too much to ask? Maybe he wanted a guarantee she'd make it through this before he said his vows. He deserved more than this, a better life than pledging loyalty to a death-risk. Perhaps she should release him from the engagement. Set him free to find someone else. Someone healthy and whole. Except she couldn't summon herself to suggest it. Selfish or not, she wanted him next to her through it all.

Austin pulled his gaze away from her to peer at the doctor. "Waiting six weeks won't endanger her?"

The doctor gave a thoughtful head tilt. "No one can predict the future."

Didn't she know it. Who could have predicted this?

"But I'm fairly confident if we do the surgery no longer than six weeks from now and follow it with radiation, there's a good chance we can eradicate all traces of cancer."

Austin nodded. "Schedule it for four weeks, to be safe." He took Ivy's hand and squeezed. "You'll be doing surgery on Ivy Hartgrove, not Ivy Alexander."

Ivy's heart swelled. He was choosing her. To marry her still, to walk beside her through all of it. To throw his careful preparations to the wind and embrace a bout of spontaneity. They could marry in a courthouse for all she cared. She'd never been so assured of his love for her. She flung her arms around his neck.

Everly rubbed her back as Ivy and Austin embraced. "We have our work cut out for us." Her soft chuckle was out of place in the somberness of the room.

The doctor made a note, then stood. "I'll have my staff book you for surgery in one month." He shook each of their hands. "I wish you the best on your upcoming nuptials." Then he opened the door and ushered them out of his office into a future of unknowns.

Chapter 4

FEB. 26, 1862, JAMES B. GRIFFIN

Outside of Warsaw, North Carolina
February 1861

Henrietta recited her last line and bowed, sweeping the hat from her head with the motion. Applause filled the farmhouse.

Bea jumped up and down. "Bravo, 'Etta!"

Henrietta hiked Pa's old trousers higher on her waist. She needed to tighten the rope holding them up. Blasted things. How did men get any work done in them?

Loreen lifted her off her feet and twirled her in a circle. "That was splendid. Thank you for obliging."

She tucked her shirt back in where it had flounced loose in the back. "Of course." The girls had begged her to put on one last theatrical performance before she left for the docks. She couldn't deny them. Their rosy cheeks, flushed from excitement, made it well worth her while. Looking at them now, she'd almost do another production if it would prolong the inevitable goodbye. How would she leave these dear ones? They were part of her. The loss of their presence would maim her.

Gretchen squeezed her arm. "You're going to fool everyone for sure."

"Fool them! Fool them!" Charlotte chanted, then Bea chimed along.

Loreen silenced them with a glare. Perhaps she'd excel as the leader of the home after all. Her countenance smoothed as she turned back to Henrietta. "You'll make a better boy than the boys."

Henrietta scoffed. Doubtful, but she'd blend in as much as she could.

Bea tapped her bare feet together. "You're gonna get lots of money, then we'll all get shoes and beautiful dresses."

Charlotte rubbed her belly. "And we'll eat piles of bacon and corned beef and biscuits and gingerbread."

"And we'll drink so much milk we'll fall over." Bea's eyes sparkled.

Gretchen joined in. "We're going to live like queens."

"Queens!" The girls grasped hands and spun in a circle.

The sight made Henrietta dizzy, or maybe it was the pressure. Such grand dreams depended on her. What if she fumbled and her femininity snuck through? What if she couldn't convince the men at the docks she was one of them? What if her sisters' simple dreams of full tummies crashed like a dead carcass at her feet?

A slight tic in the muscle of Loreen's left cheek indicated similar reservations. But Henrietta couldn't have her sister worrying about the plan at the docks. There was enough to concern herself with on the home front.

Mustering as much bravado as possible, she poked her younger sisters' bellies. "You forgot butter and honey for your biscuits. I'm going to get you so much of it, you'll go to bed greasy and sticky."

They giggled.

Millie's soft voice came from her perch in the corner, but a cough garbled her words. Color filled her cheeks, thank goodness. She grew stronger hour by hour. No doubt when Henrietta returned, Millie would be running around with the rest of them.

Henrietta drew closer to Millie, her finger itching to trace around the red-patched beauty mark marring her sister's right cheek. The mark she labeled a rose petal's kiss, but other children pointed to with sniggers and whispers, declaring Millie a monster. "What'd you say, Mill Moo?"

Millie's gap-toothed smile beamed up at her. "Thank you for saving us, 'Etta."

The gentle praise pierced her heart like an arrow. Saving them. That's what they expected her to do. What she *must* do. The future of these precious souls depended on her.

Her throat burned. "I'd do anything for you girls. You know that, right?" Her voice cracked on the last word.

Millie nodded, eyes wide and solemn.

Enough of that. She needed to go before she broke down and wept. Or before she lost her gumption and refused to leave.

"All of you come here and hug me farewell." She waved her sisters to her.

As each pressed close, cloaking her with their love and appreciation, she tucked the scent and feel of them deep within. She studied each of their faces, committing every detail to memory. These beautiful ones would be the fuel that would keep her going.

~~

Three weeks later, Henrietta paused from brushing cotton off her trousers to wave to a young boy who watched from the steamer's deck. Black puffs of smoke belched from the boat's stacks. Men in suits and women in fancy dresses peppered the deck, some observing the town or the roustabouts as they finished loading cargo, some lounging in chairs.

"Look, Mama." The boy tugged on his mother's skirt. She bent and followed the direction of his chubby finger to where Henrietta stood on the docks. "That man looks like a sheep."

Henrietta chortled. She probably did look like a barn animal after unloading twelve barrels of cotton. The blasted stuff stuck like a leech. The mother's eyes widened, and she hurried the boy off. Did she think he'd embarrassed her? Henrietta loved seeing children at the docks. They reminded her of home.

Work finished, she stretched her aching back before settling on a bale of hay and breathing deep of the pungent air. Every muscle in her body hurt, but at least she'd get to send her pay home. Loreen should be able to afford shoes and food. With her eyes closed, she listened to the water lap the dock and to the whistles in the distance. Gulls sang their songs.

"Hey, Henry." Samuel, a fellow roustabout, stood tall and snapped his suspenders. "The next steamer won't dock for an hour, and several of us is off to Paddy's Hollow. Join us?"

Henrietta forced a smile. As much as she needed to appear to be one of the fellas, she couldn't waste her pay at a pub. "Maybe next time."

He rolled his eyes but didn't niggle her. She needed a good story about her temperance, or she should go with them occasionally to avoid suspicion. Her main goal was to blend in. Her constant avoidance of the pub only made her stand out. What kind of gossip had that produced? Spending six cents here and there on ale might be worth it if it helped to keep her guise. But the thought of enjoying such a luxury while her sisters went to bed without sustenance caused bile to climb up her throat.

Once Samuel ambled down the street, Henrietta relaxed against the hay bale. She'd keep her eye out for anything entertaining to report to her sisters in an upcoming letter. Never having ventured from the homestead, they devoured gossip. To them, she lived in a strange and adventurous world.

Of course, a slight embellishment here and there aided in that perception. She had to do what she could to add some color to their drab lives.

Three negro women in colorful headscarves sold fish and oysters to sailors returning from a voyage. A couple of others washed clothes in a vat farther down the way. As if they could ever truly rid the fishy smell from the clothes of those who worked on the water. Several chaps gathered around a uniformed man on a horse. A trader paraded a line of slaves toward the courthouse, their chains scraping the street. Men repairing a nearby schooner jested back and forth, using language that would burn through the paper if she dared to write it.

There was that old beggar again. Henrietta shuddered. With holes worn clean through parts of her clothing and a face streaked with dirt, the woman reminded her of Old Man Meager. She walked the street, rattling a tin cup. The very sound induced nightmares of the bum who'd accosted children with his demands. Henrietta would leave her out of the letter home.

A soft whistle alerted Henrietta to someone else's approach. She craned her neck to see a boy shuffling toward the button factory. He couldn't be much older than Gretchen, as his bare face attested, yet he walked with a resoluteness that proved he'd lived a lot of life in those years. But it wasn't his lighthearted tune that drew her gaze to him each day, nor was it his scuffed shoes and threadbare attire. It was the red mark marring the side of his neck and chin, one that resembled Millie's rose petal's kiss.

Did others tease him because of it? Shun him? His countenance gave no indication of ridicule. Perhaps he'd found acceptance and joy despite the disfigurement. It would do Henrietta's heart good to believe so, to see in him a picture of what Millie's future could be. Her sweet sister would be able to find a suitable husband one day, wouldn't she? Surely, the right man could overlook the blemish and see the beauty that bloomed inside.

Two gents strolled directly toward the boy. Fellow roustabouts, one with fiery red hair, the other dark-headed. Samuel's friends. Perhaps they were headed for the pub too. Henrietta had never interacted with them before, but she'd seen the three of them together.

Instead of sidestepping the boy, they nearly barreled into him. "Clarence, you have something on your face." The red-haired one shoved the kid's shoulder, and he stumbled.

No, not gents. Scoundrels.

"Go home, mongrel." The black-haired one jeered.

Henrietta jumped to her feet. The tips of her ears burned. In five long strides, she had entered the fray. "You're the one who'd better leave, or I'll sock you." She brought fisted hands up and clenched her jaw.

Clarence scrambled away.

The redheaded roustabout scoffed at her, apparently not intimidated. "Why are you defending that no-good wretch?"

"I won't abide scallywags. Be off with you."

Red's eyes narrowed as he studied her.

She jutted out her jaw lest the uneasiness show. "I said, go." A step toward him didn't force him to back off. Instead, he squinted at her.

"There's something funny about you."

Her insides quivered at his perusal, but she dared not show it. She spit on the ground near his shoe. "The only thing funny's gonna be your nose after I break it."

The black-haired fellow cast longing looks down the street toward the pub. "C'mon, Nathan. This shrimp ain't worth the trouble."

Shrimp? She glowered at them. Her frame had to have grown more muscular over the past few weeks of hefting crates and barrels. She felt stronger, at least. But of course, no amount of bluster could make up for what she lacked in stature.

Nathan sneered. "You'd better watch your back."

He and his cohort swaggered away, leaving Henrietta to fume in their wake. A glance down the street showed Clarence must have ducked into the factory already, with nary a word of thanks to his rescuer.

Now that imminent danger had passed, Henrietta's limbs shook. What had she been thinking? Couldn't she leave well enough alone? They were on to her. A few more minutes under their scrutiny and they might have unearthed her secret. Then what? She swallowed. Jail, most likely.

No. She couldn't let that happen. She had a family to feed. Maybe she could relocate to another maritime city. Would a swift departure arouse suspicions even more? If they sent the law after her, she might not be able to evade them. Making her way back to the hay bale, she sifted through her choices. If only Ma were alive to counsel her.

The whinny of a horse startled her from her internal debate. Before her stood a chestnut gelding with a gentleman in full gray uniform sitting atop. The man smiled down at her, and his bushy black mustache lifted. "Hello, young man."

Henrietta blinked up at him, then glanced over her shoulder. Who was he talking to? No one stood behind her. When her gaze returned to the gent, his focus zeroed in on her. Would she ever get used to being addressed as a man?

The man chuckled as he dismounted. "Allow me to introduce myself. Patrick Summerland, at your service." He stuck out a hand to Henrietta. She shook it warily. "I come on behalf of the Confederate army. I'm recruiting a brigade of North Carolinians to fight in the war against Northern tyranny." He doffed his cap, revealing slicked black hair, and stared into the horizon as if he could see a battle raging there.

After a few seconds, he gave a slight shake of the head and settled his gaze back on Henrietta. "You look like a strong, intelligent buck. I could use the likes of you in my regiment."

She nearly snorted. A strong, intelligent *buck*? If she looked like a man at all, it was a gangly, fresh-faced boy who would hardly be old enough to shoulder a gun. Some days, she thought her plan intelligent indeed, but other days, it seemed downright foolish. She was always one mistake away from ending up in jail. Surely, a wiser person could have found a better way to feed the family.

"You want me to fight for the Rebs?" She raised a brow. North Carolina wasn't even part of the Confederacy. President Lincoln had called for their state's troops to help put down the rebellion. Sure, she'd heard talk about secession, but despite murmurings, her state still belonged to the Union.

"Sure do. Need you to, in fact."

"But we're not Confederate."

"We will be. Our secession convention is set for May 20. Mark my words, we'll join."

"I don't know …" It was one thing to play the part of a roustabout, breaking her back on the docks each day. Quite another to join up as a soldier. What did she think about this war anyway? Each day, she awoke with the image of her sisters and Pa in her mind. Feeding and clothing them was all that mattered to her. Let others settle the squabble between the states. If she were to die in battle, who would care for her kin? "I make a good income here at the docks. I need that money." She brushed a piece of hay from her trousers.

"Son, come soldier for the army, and we'll pay you double what you're getting at the docks, plus I'm giving a hundred-dollar signing bonus."

Henrietta's jaw dropped. "Pardon?"

His mustache twitched as he chuckled again. "That's right. Eleven dollars a month, plus a one-hundred-dollar bonus for signing on."

She opened her mouth to claim eleven dollars wasn't exactly double what they were paying her, but he spoke first.

"Keep in mind, in the army, your meals are included. Not a penny out of your pay will go for food or lodging. Can't say that currently, can you?"

No, she could not. Eleven dollars a month straight to her family. One hundred dollars right away. What could they purchase with one hundred dollars? She salivated thinking of a feast of roasted beef and sweet potatoes. That would fatten the lot of them up something good. The young'uns would sleep soundly with bellies full to bursting. Why, they might even need new dresses as they shot up a foot with such nourishment. She bit back a smile.

"You're serious?" She eyed the man for a hint of guile.

"Sure am."

But could she do it? Keep the guise as she tented with men day and night? Shoot and kill? She might excel at acting, but war was a different matter. She could be the one injured or … killed. What would that mean for her family? She fought the urge to bite her lip. Too feminine.

Angry voices echoed from down the street. She chanced a glance at the source of the commotion. Nathan headed up a throng of a dozen men stomping in her direction, faces tight and fists clenched.

"I'm telling ya, something was off about him. I bet if we swing a few punches, we'll find out what." Nathan slammed his fist into his palm as they passed by without a glance her way.

Her scalp tingled. She had to get out of there. Now, before they turned around. She'd figure out the rest later.

With a deep breath, she pushed all hesitation down under her toes and extended her hand. "Sign me up, sir."

Chapter 5

Suburb of Wilmington, North Carolina
Present Day

Tears coursed down Ivy's cheeks as she walked down the aisle to her groom. Not an aisle, really. A path in the grass between rows of white folding chairs in Everly and Zach's backyard. Church friends had decorated the modest gazebo with white lace and twinkle lights, which shimmered despite the daytime hour.

Austin beamed at her, but sadness swam in his eyes. It wasn't pity, was it? She'd wilt if the prevailing emotion today proved to be pity instead of celebration. Maybe it was only a realization of how fragile life was and how happy he was to spend it with her, however long that might be. He'd said as much. She'd tried to believe him.

Everly looked stunning. Her lavender dress complemented her complexion. Her hair curled over one shoulder. Ev, too, gazed at her with an odd mesh of emotions playing on her face. She looked like she might leave her position up front as the maid of honor to run to Ivy and smother her with a hug.

On both sides, family members and friends watched. Pleasant whispers floated to her ears. Oohs and aahs and "Isn't she beautiful?" In the midst of the praise, a comment from an older lady—a great aunt, maybe?—snuck through. "Make sure you get good pictures. We'll want them in case … well, you know."

Ivy's cheeks flamed. In case she died? Is that what she meant? They'll want good pictures of her to display at her funeral. Her pulse kicked up a notch. She'd tried not to imagine the cancer gobbling her body, but every time she pushed it from her mind, it reemerged. A panther ready to pounce.

"It doesn't even look like there's anything wrong with her," someone behind her whispered.

Her step faltered, and she stumbled but regained her balance. Salty tears leaked into the corner of her mouth.

Wrong with her. There was something wrong with her.

Another whisper met her ears. "Isn't cervical cancer caused by an STI?"

Her breath snagged. How dare they? Desire to spin around and lash out at the guest churned, but shame followed on its heels. She couldn't deny the accusation and implications. How would she be able to face her church group if the rumor spread? *Sweet Ivy has a sour past.* No one would look at her the same.

Austin. She must focus on Austin.

She locked eyes with him, and his steady gaze ushered her forward until she stood next to him. There would be no "Who gives this woman?" There was no one to give her away. Not unless her sister took that role. But the Bible said to forsake father and mother and be joined to her husband. Good thing it said nothing about forsaking her sister. She would not leave one to have the other. They were both hers.

She handed off her bouquet to Everly and took Austin's waiting hands. Together, they formed a formidable force. The power of it tingled up her arms. They could weather anything if they had each other.

Austin's gaze contained so much love her knees weakened, as if she were walking on three-inch heels and hit an uneven patch in the sidewalk. She swayed slightly to her left, but Austin righted her with a gentle tug back to center.

The corner of his mouth twitched as if he wanted to laugh but held it back. Completely inappropriate as their pastor spoke of the sanctity of marriage. A giggle escaped her. She attempted to disguise it with a small cough.

She forced herself to look from Austin to the pastor. If she didn't, she might burst into laughter. All in attendance would then think her crazy in addition to being sick.

Cancer. For those brief, precious moments, she'd forgotten. Could she make herself forget again? Cancer might steal her womb, but it shouldn't steal her wedding day.

There would be no live music in the ceremony. Though Ivy had played the piano and sung at Everly's wedding, her sister declined to reciprocate with a song. She'd said she wouldn't be able to hold it together enough to grace them with her vocals. Was that the cancer's fault too? Doubtful Ev would be so emotional without it. Ivy had only seen her sister cry four times.

Austin's best man—a friend from college—handed the pastor the rings.

"Austin, repeat after me."

She shut out everything except for Austin's pure voice.

"I, Austin Hartgrove, take you, Ivy Alexander, as my lawful wife. To have and to hold from this day forward, for better or for worse, for richer or for poorer—"

He swallowed. When he spoke again, his voice thickened, and his eyes filled with unshed tears. "In sickness and in health, to love and to cherish, until death do us part."

Oh, gracious. She loved this man. His vows flooded her heart with affection. Her handsome banker had counted the cost and deemed her worthy of the price. When her turn came to pledge herself forever to him, she did it with a grateful heart.

~~

As they wheel my sister back for surgery, my heart plummets. The doctor assured us there's little risk from the procedure itself. Still, I feel like I'm saying goodbye. Maybe I am. Ivy will emerge from this changed. The version of Ivy I've known all my life will die on that table. What will the new version be like?

Oh, Lord, strengthen her. Don't let her harden. Keep her heart soft.

If only I could collapse into Mom's arms. Or Dad's. When Mom died, she took a piece of him with her. He never returned to normal. It was as if we'd played a game of hide and seek with him for the past two decades, glimpsing a foot peeking out from under a curtain or an arm sticking out from under a table, but never fully seeing him. I doubt he would have been much comfort in this situation. But it would be nice to sink into his embrace.

Instead, I settle for a side hug from Austin. This newbie to our family has been a rock during this crisis. He's a godsend for my sister. The jealousy that clawed at me when Ivy first started seriously dating him has dissipated. He won't take my sister from me.

Zach will come by after work. He's holding down the fort at the office again so I can be here. Nothing but supportive. I have a rock of a man too.

Austin and I settle into stiff chairs to wait. Soft sounds emanate from a mounted television as a sitcom rerun plays. Muted background noises of phone calls and beeping monitors pepper the room. A few seats from me, an elderly man with an oxygen tank, the only other person in the area, stares blankly ahead. Awkward silence swirls around us. I should say something, but what? I hardly know my brother-in-law.

He speaks first. "You two make me wish I had a brother."

"Oh yeah." I massage my left hand with my right, hitting the pressure points. "You're an only child, right?"

"Yep." He lets out a resigned sigh. "Your bond fascinates me."

"Really? Zach's an only child too, and I think he's mostly annoyed that Ivy and I are so close."

"Annoyed?" He quirks a brow. "Jealous, more likely."

Should I tell him Zach's nickname for Ivy? Will he think it funny or offensive? I'd better stay silent since I'm clueless. But he's right. Jealousy must play a factor.

I study the serious man in front of me. "You're good for her." Ivy is breath and life. Austin is the ground beneath her feet. "With you, she forgets to be anxious."

A humorless laugh spills from him. "Oh, she's pretty anxious."

I tilt my head, considering. "Less so."

"It used to be worse?"

I nod. "She flitted through life as a young girl. Then when Mom … well, you know, the panic attacks started. Night terrors. It got better, then worse. Considering everything, I'm surprised she's doing as good as she is."

He shakes his head. "I wish I could free her of the worry. The cancer. All of it."

"Don't we all. But that's too massive of a job for us puny humans, isn't it? We've got to leave it to the Lord." Wow. I spouted that off well. As if the truth were cemented inside of me. In reality, my ability to let go shifts from day to day. Today, as my sister undergoes surgery to save her life, I'm struggling.

A noncommittal noise emanates from his throat. Perhaps he, too, knows the truth of my statement but struggles with walking it out.

Silence stretches between us like taffy. Voices murmur from down the hall. Computer keys clack. Distant beeping hints at patients receiving care behind the closed double doors. Have they started on Ivy yet? What's going on in the operating room?

My mind wanders to the ancestry search I've begun. Ever since the doctor spoke of the family history we're clueless about, the desire to learn more has risen within me. Ivy seemed curious, too, though less convinced it matters. If I can find a link to relatives who've battled similar cancers and came out victorious, relief will wash over me. I'm sure of it. It will be clear that Ivy can beat this thing.

A confession swirls in my mouth. I press my lips together to hold it back, but it persists. "I feel like this is my fault."

Oh, goodness. I don't know this man well enough to bare my soul to him. Yet the empty chairs around us signal there's no one better. No one else.

His forehead puckers. "How so?"

"My rebellious streak as a teen. I was supposed to set a good example for her, and instead, I went off the deep end. Perhaps that's why she went a little wild at the same age."

We've never spoken about how Ivy's cervical cancer was likely caused by HPV, a sexually transmitted infection. Thinking of my sister now, so pure and upright, it seems ludicrous. Why does she have to pay for a season of life that is far passed? She turned her life around much faster than I did. She's spent years walking the narrow road only to have the past smack her in the face.

Austin leans forward, propping his elbows on his knees. He tents his fingers together and meets my gaze. "Ivy's choices are her own. You're not to blame."

"Yeah, but—"

"No buts. We all have a past. The important thing is that Ivy didn't let hers define her. She turned to the Lord, and He's washed her conscience clean. Sometimes, there are practical consequences, but He's going to walk her through this."

I nod. Theoretically, I agree. Something inside me, however, isn't convinced. If I had held it together after Mom's death, would Ivy have followed suit when I left her for Zach? I'll never know, and pondering the what-ifs only causes stress to pool in my gut.

~~

Ivy stepped out of her car and into the hospital parking lot, heading for her daily radiation treatment. Why had she told Austin not to accompany her anymore? Her steps dragged. Everything in her wanted to turn around and go home.

"Only two more weeks. Three down. Two to go. You can do this." Her pep talk did little to hasten her pace. Who could blame her for not racing to poison her body with radiation?

Austin had accompanied her to her daily treatment every day prior, but she needed to buck up and do it herself now. No more clinging. She was tired of appearing weak and pathetic. She could be strong and independent.

She'd held it together fairly well through her half days at work. Having something to take her mind off her circumstances helped. After her daily radiation treatment, she'd go home and sleep the rest of the day. A welcome escape.

Her phone rang. Everly calling for her daily check in. Ivy tried to infuse lightness into her voice. "Hey."

"Hi, sis. You at the hospital?"

The automatic doors swooshed with her entrance. "Walking in now."

"How are you doing today?"

She tried to push the word "fine" out, but the lie wouldn't come. What if she answered honestly for once? "Struggling," she choked out.

"Want me to come keep you company?"

"No." She needed to do this herself. Be strong like Mom. Like Everly. "I'll be okay."

"It's okay to not be." Ev's voice sounded motherly.

If only Ivy could burrow inside it. Instead, she pressed the elevator button. "Remind me again that I'm not frying my ovaries." The only womanly organs she had left.

"They're safely tucked under your ribs, thanks to the transposition."

The doors swooshed open. Ivy stepped inside the crowded elevator and pressed the button for the third floor. "I feel like a bus ran me over. I don't know if I can keep doing this."

A woman in a pantsuit cast her a side-eyed glance.

Everly's voice soothed. "Everything you're feeling is normal. You're almost done. You can do it."

Yes, extreme mood swings were common with a hysterectomy. Fatigue was common with radiation. Grief was common when losing the ability to bear children. None of that offered much comfort. She needed a beam of hope.

"The flowers Bridget got you are gorgeous. I loved the picture."

"Yeah." She sighed. Her coworker's kind gesture had done little to brighten her day. Still, she'd tried. "Thoughtful of her."

The doors slid open, and she stepped onto the cancer floor. How good it would be to ring the bell and leave this place once and for all. Move on with her life. What would that look like? She'd never envisioned a childless existence. Nearly impossible to picture happiness within.

"I'm almost there. Better let you go." The signal weakened around the next corner.

"All right. Call me later and tell me▨" Her sister's voice cut out.

No one to talk to now, except God. *Lord, help me out here. I don't want to drown in depression. I know You are all I need, but I'm over my head in grief. Give me a sliver of hope.*

She heard no voice. Felt no arms embrace her. Nothing but emptiness stretched before her, threatening to undo the tightly woven threads of her faith.

Chapter 6

Warrenton, North Carolina
May 1861

Dearest Loreen,

Oh, sweet sister. How I miss you. How do you all fare? Use the enclosed money to purchase shoes for yourself and Gretchen, if you haven't already, and the plumpest hen you can find.

I have good news. At least, I hope you'll find it so. I'll be sending you a fair amount of money soon. I wish I could see your faces when you gaze on the amount. I want you to stock up on all the food you can in case money becomes tight again. Please do that before paying back the doctor. I can't stand the thought of y'all ending back where we started.

How I'm arriving at this money is the part you may not be too keen on, but don't be cross with me. I'm doing it for you. For all of you.

I've signed up for the Confederate army. I'll be mustered into service tomorrow here at the Warrenton racetrack.

Don't fret over my welfare. This will be a quick war and an easy victory for the South. For as long as it lasts, my belly will remain full, and my ample pay will go straight to y'all. This is the best solution. Trust me.

I'll send word of where you can write back.
Yours truly,
Henry

Henrietta nearly growled as she folded the letter. How it irked her to sign a missive to her dear sister with anything other than her true name. But if someone were to rummage through the mail, she couldn't risk them discovering her secret. Best to continue playing the part. To always keep her disguise in place. But oh, how it rankled. How could she have anticipated the weight pretending would place on her? And the act had likely only begun. How long until she could be known as her true self again?

Best not to think on it. Such selfish thoughts would not avail her.

She stood and stretched, looking out across the racetrack teeming with men eager to fight. So many men. Hundreds? Over a thousand? Surely enough to whip the Federals. The smell of so many sweating bodies amassed in one place turned her stomach. Might as well get used to it. Who knew when she'd revel in the scent of clean country air, fresh herbs, or jasmine soap again?

As the men moseyed around the track, dust swirled in the air. It coated the roof of her mouth. No wonder those around her kept spitting. It didn't seem like a right terrible idea. Still, she couldn't quite bring herself to do it. Not yet.

Her agenda remained the same. Blend in. Be one of the boys. Avoid anything that would disclose her feminine nature. She placed her letter into her haversack, then sauntered to a group engaged in a game of cards. A square of wood rested on top of a barrel, creating a tabletop to hold the cards. With the game already underway, she had an excuse to watch and learn how to play lest her ignorance betray her.

"Hiya, fellas." She hoisted herself onto an empty barrel, careful not to cross her ankles. "Who's winnin' this hand?"

"Davey here." A guy with a head full of curly black hair pointed with his cigarette, raining ashes on their makeshift table. "But I ain't convinced he's not swindlin' us."

The burly chap in question huffed. "I play fair. Ron's dimwitted."

When the five other men laughed at his retort, Henrietta did too. She peered over Ron's shoulder and tried to decipher the rules of whatever game this was. Was the objective to win as many chips as possible or cause everyone else to fold? Perhaps both.

A low whistle drew her attention away from the game and toward a crowd forming outside the track. What was the commotion about?

"Pretty lady, wanna come here and play me a hand?" someone yelled.

Lady? Were there other women here? She hopped down and hustled toward the growing mob.

Another whistle sounded, and its suggestive nature made her skin prickle.

"Show me a little leg, honey."

"Why don't you give this hungry soldier something to feast on?"

Smooching sounds and catcalls rose around her as she shoved her way to the front. Three women scampered past. Their raised parasols failed to hide their flushed faces. Properly attired from covered head to booted foot, nothing about them hinted at immodesty. They'd likely been curious as to the large gathering in town, had wanted a closer peek, and had gotten more than they'd bargained for.

Henrietta's face heated too, but for an entirely different reason. She'd bet money none of these buffoons would dare talk in such a crude way if their wives, mothers, or sisters stood within hearing distance. Who did they think they were, embarrassing those poor women? "Stop it, the lot of you." She used the sternest, gruffest voice she could muster. "Quit harassing those women."

The circle around her hushed as heads pivoted her way. Some men huffed. Some sneered. Others had the decency to lower their eyes.

"What would your families think if they heard you carrying on that way? I'd like to think decent menfolk make up this regiment." She shook her head in disgust, then stomped away.

Murmurs and taunts trailed her.

"Who does that runt think he is?"

Her pulse thrummed in her ears. What had she done? She'd set out to blend in, and instead, she'd set herself apart.

A baseball pummeled her in the back, sending a jolt of pain up her spine. She winced. Everything in her called for her to turn around and confront the culprit. She clenched her teeth. No, she couldn't react. Last thing she needed was a fistfight with a throng of burly men. She'd better garner self-control or she'd never make it. If her stunt made her an object of ridicule, so be it. As long as no one inspected her too closely. She hadn't even been mustered into service yet. She couldn't allow her impulsivity to ruin her chance so soon.

She strode forward as if nothing had happened. As if she didn't hear the jeers. She crossed the track and found a place to sit. Alone. A sinking feeling in the hollow of her chest whispered that loneliness would be her lot from now on.

~~

Dear Henry,

We can't thank you enough. The money you sent has been like manna from heaven. We've eaten better this past month than in years. Gretchen and I purchased shoes from the store. My feet barely know what to do with the comfort. I've been training Gretchen to tend to the house and garden so she can run the household when I find work in town. Soon, I shall clean myself up and hunt for a job. Do you think I'd be a good nanny?

We are fretful over how you've put yourself in harm's way. Reports of the war buzz around town like hornets. I fear we might be stung next. Stay safe. Do whatever you can to survive and return to us. Don't take unnecessary risks. You have too many people who depend on you.

I also worry you're sending us too much of your pay. Do you have all you need? Are you still faring well? It seems everyone in town has family fighting for the Southern cause. They brag about how heroic their men are, and I wish I could speak of your courage as well. The grocer's wife asked after you, and I said you'd gone to Wilmington to find work. It wasn't a lie, and it must have sufficed as she didn't pry further.

Now, entertain us with tales from the front. How do you occupy your time? Have you met many interesting people? You were always the best at making up delightful stories. Now, it seems you're living one.

Write back soon.
Yours truly,
Loreen

Army life suited Henrietta fine, especially since they hadn't seen a lick of combat. Drilling was the extent of the excitement. That and the occasional prank. Some of the men she'd rankled at the racetrack labeled her a prude and smoked out her tent.

She reciprocated by catching two garter snakes and placing them in their tents. A yelp after lights out signaled that her prank had succeeded. At breakfast the next morning, everyone had a good laugh at Grant's story of how he'd nearly fallen asleep when something slithered over his leg. Finally, she'd earned some respect, though the mark of a prude remained.

Well and good. No one blanched when she claimed the camp latrines were too filthy to use and opted for the woods. Being called a prude was a far cry better than being discovered as a woman.

What a splendid break from the constant pressures she'd faced at home. While some of the men complained about the simple fare, she rejoiced in regular meals. At least for now, she could send money to her family without risking life and limb. Filling her lungs with fresh air, she returned from using the necessary in the woods.

"Hey, Henry." Duke held a cigarette out to her as he lounged against a tree, cap low over his brow. "Want a smoke?"

She couldn't be sure, but he was probably the one who'd thrown the baseball at her at the track. Had she earned his respect yet?

"Nah." Henrietta waved him off and continued walking. Duke was trouble. He took the men's money through gambling and offered favors like cigs only to demand repayment later. Best to stay clear.

Duke shifted and smirked at her. "You don't smoke. You don't drink. Are you afraid someone will write your mama and report bad behavior?"

Raising her hands up, she backed away from him. A metallic taste filled her mouth from where she'd bit her tongue to hold back a retort. She could not make an enemy of this wretch any more than she already had. "Staying focused is all." She turned her back to him and put another step between them.

"Pretty high and mighty for a freckle-faced boy who's too young to shave."

She took a deep breath and continued walking.

His derisive laugh crawled under her skin. "People usually regret walking away from me."

She stopped and angled herself in his direction. "I mean no disrespect. Thank you for the offer of a smoke, but I must decline."

"Ooh." Laughter rolled through him until he doubled over in a coughing fit. She blinked back at him. He waved a hand in front of his face as his coughs subsided. "So polite. Almost like a lady."

At his pronouncement, an icy ripple crept up her spine. She straightened with every nerve taut. Should she challenge him? Yell that she was far from a lady? Or would he sense the anxiety that snaked through her every word? Surely, if she spoke, her voice would tremble. She shook her head as if disgusted and continued, tuning out his laugh and the sound of him spitting behind her.

Her hands shook as she stoked the fire that night. She could nearly see Loreen's gaunt face in the flames, looking at her with wide eyes, asking, "How could you, Henrietta? How could you lose such an opportunity when we're depending on you?" They might be faring better, but one slip up and they'd be right back where they started.

She threw another log on the fire and blinked. Her sister would never berate her. Not when she'd tried her best. Not after all she'd done—or tried to do—to take care of her family. But if she got caught, would they jail her? And if she was free to go, how could she face trudging up the hill with the news that she'd failed? A pang lodged itself in between her ribs. She couldn't. There was no way she'd let those girls down. Life—

God, perhaps—had done enough of that to them already. It was time for someone to come through. That someone had to be her. Failure wasn't an option.

~~

Old Man Meager haunted her dreams that night. She shivered at the vision of his gaunt cheeks and sunken eyes. He stumbled toward her, wearing threadbare clothing, gray trousers with the knees worn through, and a shirt that should have been white but instead resembled the color of ash. She gagged at the putrid stench emanating from him.

He pointed a bony finger in her face. "You. I won't let you rest, no matter where you go. I'll find you. I'll bring you down to the dust with me."

She shook her head and tried to back up, but her legs were rooted in place. "No. You're gone. You're gone."

"Who's gone?" Another voice broke through, louder. Closer. Riley, her tentmate? She opened her eyes to find him propped on his elbow facing her, brow furrowed.

"What?" She rubbed her eyes. "Bad dream."

"I figured as much." He lay back down. "Still want to know who's gone."

No way she'd take that bait. A man wouldn't fear an old beggar, would he? No, admitting to as much would peg her as a woman for sure. "Don't worry about it."

"If you say so. Your voice sounded funny. How old are you anyway?"

Had she cried out like a girl in her sleep? She bit her lip. "Eighteen."

"Naw. Tell me the truth. I'll keep your secret."

Her secret? He couldn't possibly know, though if she avoided his questions, he might suspect.

"I'm guessing you're sixteen. Am I right?"

An out. She could confess to something and appear as if she were coming clean. Acknowledging to corn, as soldiers liked to say. "Yes," she mumbled as if irritated at being caught.

"Ha. I knew it. You're far from the only one. Lots of boys here, some younger than you, set out for a chance to whip Yanks."

She angled her face away, so he couldn't see her eye roll. Yanks or Rebs. What did that matter? Her sisters were what moved her.

But she played along. "Don't tell." As if it mattered. The Confederacy had no minimum recruiting age. They weren't likely to turn away willing recruits for much of any reason. Unless that reason had to do with their sex. The only thing she risked by letting them think her younger was a little teasing. That, she could bear.

As long as she didn't unknowingly give her true secret away.

Old Man Meager was after her, and she had a feeling Duke was too.

~~

Henrietta looked both ways before slinking off to the woods. No one had noticed her, right? It was easy enough to avoid Duke during the daytime, which was filled with drills. Much harder as the sun sank on the horizon. But nature called, and she couldn't remain in her stuffy tent a moment longer.

"Henrenna, where are you off to?" She froze at Duke's voice behind her. Henrenna? Was the man so daft as to not figure out the female counterpart of Henry?

She snorted, then turned. "What do you want?"

A smug smile plastered his face. "Can you catch?" His chin tilted in challenge.

Was he referring to the baseball he'd lobbed at her? She crossed her arms. "Sure."

"Then catch this." Faster than she could blink, he whipped something from behind his back—a potato—and hurtled it in her direction.

Instinct took over. She swooped down and grabbed the edge of her apron to make a pocket for the potato to land in. Except her hand grasped air. She wasn't wearing an apron. The tips of her ears flamed as her jaw dropped. She blinked at the potato, which stared at her from the dirt.

"I knew it." Duke slapped his knee and hooted. "I knew you were a woman."

Her lip trembled as her mind scrambled for some excuse for why her hands responded that way. No thoughts formed. Panic scratched the back of her throat. No words came out, only a few dreadful tears. Blasted tears. She clamped her mouth shut and swallowed the rest of them back.

Duke jogged off. His laugh trailed him, mocking her.

She'd ruined everything.

A potato. How many times had Loreen tossed her potatoes from the garden? How many times had she caught them in her apron? The memory of her sister whistling twirled around her as Duke's laughter faded. How could she have let her guard down? She fisted the fabric of her trousers. She'd fooled many people, but not Duke. He'd suspected from the beginning. Some actress she was. Surely, right now he was telling her superiors. Soon, everyone would know, and the only part she'd play was the one of the girl who'd disgraced her family.

Chapter 7

Suburb of Wilmington, North Carolina
Present Day

Ivy should be thankful she'd escaped with her life. This heavy "should" hung like a thick drapery in her mind as she opened her eyes to a new day. She rolled over and felt Austin's side of the bed. Still warm. He must have just gotten up. The rattle of dishes siphoned gratitude from her soul. Her ever-attentive hubby was preparing breakfast for her. Why wouldn't she be grateful?

Her hand trailed to her trim waist. So what if she'd never have a baby? She could be happy. *They* could make a life for themselves. A family of two, like Everly and Zach. Her sister didn't need children to feel complete. Neither did she.

Only this ache wasn't merely from her body's recovery. Her heart throbbed. No womb. She had no womb. Cancer had sliced her dreams from her body.

She shook herself from the depressive thoughts. Time to find a new dream.

After propping a pillow behind her back, she pulled her computer onto her lap and brought up the search bar.

She'd heard enough stories from foster parents to know her anxiety made that an unhealthy option for her. It was an admirable and meaningful calling, but not realistic in their case. Surely, there was something else. Another way.

She typed in "other ways to be a parent" and scrolled through the results. Adoption. Foster care. Adoption. Respite foster care. Adoption.

Perhaps they could consider adoption. It didn't matter if the child wouldn't have her DNA. She could still be a mother. Right? But her insides writhed at the thought of a baby holding no resemblance to her mom. She'd always imagined looking into her little girl's face and telling her how much she looked like her grandmother. It'd be a way to keep her mother with them, a way to keep their family line alive.

That shouldn't be important. Not when there were children who needed a home.

So why did it feel important?

She needed to get over it. Play the hand she'd been given instead of wishing for different cards. Her curser hovered over an adoption link. It wasn't like she was committing to anything. Only finding more information. No harm in that.

Something at the bottom of the page snagged her attention. The word *surrogacy* stood out like a beacon.

She clicked. Devoured the article. Did a separate search and dug into several more sites. Her scalp tingled. What if this was possible? She didn't have a uterus, but she had eggs. She and Austin could have a baby. A beautiful mix of both of them. They could keep her family line alive. She could be a mother to a child with her eyes and Austin's nose. Or would it be Austin's eyes and her ears?

Austin entered the room, coffee in one hand, omelet-laden plate in the other. "Good morning, mi amor." He stilled and studied her. "What's up? I haven't seen you look this excited since before …"

She winced at the truth that didn't need saying. Her wedding should have been the most exciting day of her life, and yet the diagnosis had left a dark cloud looming overhead. Hope hadn't pierced the darkness since she'd gotten the doctor's concerned call.

Austin deserved so much more than that.

She patted the spot next to her. "Sit. I have something to show you."

He deposited her breakfast on the side table and joined her, the hint of a smile warring with his caution.

She met his piercing eyes. "I've been having a"—she swallowed—"hard time with the loss of my womb."

His face sagged. "I know."

Of course he did. She couldn't hide anything from him. She took his hand and squeezed. "I might have found a way for us to still have a family."

"Ivy—"

"Hear me out." She squeezed again, harder this time.

"We've talked about this."

She yanked her hand away. "Not about this, we haven't." They'd discussed adoption. Fostering. Even the Big Brothers Big Sisters program. But not this.

When he opened his mouth, she turned the computer toward him before he could shut her down again. "Surrogacy." She gestured to the screen.

He leaned forward with furrowed eyebrows and browsed the site.

She put a hand on his bicep. "We could hire a surrogate and have a baby that's genetically ours."

He puffed out a breath and clicked a few times, then turned the screen back to her. "Average cost is thirty thousand dollars to pay a genetic carrier."

Desperation clawed at her chest. "We could take out a loan." Great. Her voice sounded whiny and desperate. Definitely *not* the way to win Austin over.

"We'll be paying on your hospital bills for two years, Iv. It's going to take every bit of excess in our budget to get those paid off."

She picked at a loose thread on the comforter. "People take out thirty-thousand-dollar loans for cars. This would be for our baby. Isn't that far more important?"

He pushed his glasses up the bridge of his nose. "It's not about that. It wouldn't be fiscally responsible."

She threw her hands up. "Ugh. I hate when you use that word. Fiscal. Who says that?"

"Bankers do. I do." He stood and raked a hand through his hair. "I knew what I was getting into when I married you, and you knew what you were getting into when you married me. I'm never going to be okay with making an unwise financial decision, Ivy." He stepped toward the door, then paused. "We can revisit this in a few years." His expression softened with this truce, but her heart couldn't accept it.

Years? How could she wait years? Heat flashed in her chest. "I'm surprised you allowed me to get cancer treatment. It would have been more fiscally responsible to let me die."

His nostrils flared. "That's unfair."

"You're unfair." A voice in the back of her mind said she was being completely irrational, but she couldn't stop. She flung a pillow from the bed onto the floor by his feet. "Everything about this is unfair. I'm twenty-four years old. All I ever wanted was to get married and have babies. Was that too much to ask?"

His frown dipped. "I'm not your enemy."

"Who is?" She wiped her now-running nose with the back of her sleeve. "God?"

"Cancer," he said at the same time.

She dropped her gaze and studied the rose-patterned comforter. Cancer, of course. Not God. Never God. He was for her, not against her. Why had she said that?

With a shuddering breath, she took a drink of coffee but spit it back into her cup. It was cold.

She needed a hug, needed Austin to wrap his arms around her, kiss her hair, and promise her everything would be okay.

She opened her mouth to say as much, but he'd already left the room.

She stomped to her keyboard and pounded out Tchaikovsky's Fifth Symphony as tears plunked the keys.

~~

My phone pings as I round the last corner of my running route. With my house in sight, I slow to a jog, then a walk. Pain stitches my side. The good kind that comes with a strenuous workout and toxins flushing from the body. The only kind I don't push away.

When I pull my phone from my jacket pocket, I'm greeted with an email notification.

New records hit on Ancestors List.

I pull the site up and log in before my feet hit the front porch. It takes me a minute to find what the email referred to. The whirring of a blender assaults my ears when I step inside.

"Post workout smoothie?" Zach slides a glass of green frothy goodness across the island.

I plop onto a bar stool. "In a minute."

He returns to blending as I click one final time and reveal the ancestral record.

Henrietta Frontenac, born 1841

My shoulders sag. Not sure how this could be of any help. This relative of ours lived far too long ago to reveal anything of significance regarding Ivy's health struggles. Did they even know about cervical cancer back then? I check to see if it lists any information on how she died. Nothing. But there are other names here.

Loreen Frontenac, Gretchen Frontenac, Charlotte Frontenac, Mildred Frontenac, Beatrice Frontenac

Were those all sisters or other relatives? Sheesh. That's a lot of girls. At least one thing has remained the same throughout the years—the Frontenacs know how to have girls.

I scan the page for who created the entry about Henrietta. Perhaps it's a relative I can connect with for more information. Cassaundra Walt. The name is unfamiliar, but that doesn't mean much. I click on it and formulate a quick message explaining our situation and desire for information.

Zach rounds the island and sits next to me, smoothie in hand. "What're ya looking at?"

I set my phone down and sip my breakfast. "Ancestors List."

He rolls his eyes. "It's a wild goose chase. Give it a rest."

In the condensation on my glass, I write Ivy's name with my finger. "But if it could help my sister …"

He takes my hand and caresses my thumb with his. "It can't. No amount of information is going to fix what happened."

"I know." I take a drink. In doing so, I erase half of Ivy's name. My lip wobbles.

"Oh, honey." He strokes my cheek. "Cancer happens. It sucks, but it happens all the time to all kinds of people. You can't prepare for it. You can't research your way out of it. And discovering some hidden family medical history isn't going to prevent a recurrence."

"Still." The next sip is harder to swallow. Zach has never been anything other than logical and practical, but what I wouldn't give for a bit of unfounded optimism.

He stands and massages my tense shoulders. "I love your sister—"

I snort. "You tolerate my sister."

"No," he teases, "I love Poison Ivy. I do."

I tamp down my laughter to let him finish.

"But I see how her high stress levels affect you. I don't want you to take on her anxiety, babe. It's not healthy. There have got to be boundaries."

"There are." Aren't there?

His thumbs dig deep. "Really? What?"

Boundaries. What boundaries have I set with my sister? Nothing comes to mind. That must be because nothing is needed. Best to turn this around on him.

"What do you think should be in place?" I shimmy my shoulders to signal I'm done with this massage. He's hit a sore spot.

"You have better things to do than search ancestry sites for random health history, for one."

I quirk a brow, but he's not looking at me. "Better things to do? Like what?" Our pristine house glints in the beam of sunlight cascading through the window. Minimalist décor means little upkeep. It's clean. Peaceful. Uncomplicated.

"Your physical therapist license. When you're certified in acupressure, you're going to be much happier at work."

I shrug. That was the idea, but a niggling in my gut questions whether this additional success will satisfy me. "Digging into the ancestry site isn't interfering with my studies. I'm on track to get my license. It's not like I need to study every moment of every day."

A long pause, and his teasing returns. "What about gardening?"

The brat. He can't pass up an opportunity to remind me that I couldn't keep a plant alive if my life depended on it. I look for something to throw at him, but there's nothing within arm's reach. Instead, I lunge at him. I'm not sure if I'll slap him or tickle him when my hands make contact, but it's all in good fun. He catches my wrists and kisses them in the sensitive spot that makes my knees go weak. In seconds, I'm on the ground in a ball as he goes for the other ticklish spot on my neck.

I'm laughing so hard I can't catch my breath when my phone rings. Zach grabs it from the island. His smile dissipates. "It's Ivy."

I sober in an instant. Zach hands the phone over, and I sit hugging my knees to my chest, hoping beyond hope this isn't more bad news that will rip our world farther apart.

"Ivy?"

"Everly, it's me." Austin's voice.

"What's up?"

"Ivy's … Can you come over? She's not doing well. I've tried to comfort her, but I think I'm only making things worse."

"What's going on?"

"She's in the fetal position on the floor. I can't get through to her."

"A panic attack?"

"No, I don't think so. This seems more like grief."

"Did something happen?"

"No, not really."

"Austin?"

He sighs. "We had a little argument about hiring a surrogate. We can't afford it right now, not with the hospital bills."

Of course, he would say that. "I'll be right over."

I ignore Zach's dramatic sigh as I rise from the floor. I send him an apologetic shrug while I grab my keys and purse from the hook by the door and rush to the car.

Twenty minutes later, I burst through Ivy's front door. I don't have to ask where to go. My feet angle toward the extra bedroom my sister dreamed would become a nursery someday. When she first showed me the house, I endured nearly an hour in this room as she mapped out where a crib and changing table might go and which colors would look best on the walls. I forced out a promise to paint after she learned the gender of her would-be baby. She'd spoken of her watermelon belly filling stylish maternity shirts while I rolled paint onto the walls.

Those dreams died with the cancer.

She's right where I knew she'd be, balled tight as a roly-poly in the corner where the rocking chair was supposed to go. Three steps and I envelop her in my arms. We huddle on the floor together as her body racks with sobs. I have no words, but it's okay. None are needed.

My mother's plea reverberates through my brain. *Take care of Ivy.* Only I can't make this right. I can't undo this pain for her. Mom would understand, right? I'd do anything for my sister—anything to keep my childhood promise—but I'm at a loss here.

Instead, I kiss Ivy's hair. I squeeze her shoulders. I allow something I rarely grant permission for—I let tears trickle down my cheeks.

Forcing a smile when Ivy spoke about a future pregnancy was difficult, but I managed. I've had much practice ignoring—or avoiding—this ache inside. This situation, however, is a whole different level of hard. Helplessness yawns like a chasm I can't breach. Perhaps my tears are also for myself. I am defeated. After all my striving for success, I've failed at the one thing that truly matters. I can't protect my sister.

Ivy lays her head on my shoulder and speaks through sniffles. "A solution was so close. Sometimes, I hate him."

I press my lips into a line to keep from smiling at her dramatics. Two months into marriage and she hates her husband? I'd chide her if I couldn't relate to her frustration. We both married men very different from ourselves. I twirl a strand of her hair and say, "You don't hate him."

She groans. "I would if I didn't love him so much."

I can't help but chuckle at that.

She presses her palms against her eyes. "Why is he standing in the way of the one thing I want most?"

I open my mouth to encourage her to be patient, but I redirect. "Was it a hard no?" Perhaps there's a glimmer of hope for her idea.

"Rock hard."

Hmm. I adjust my approach. "He's looking out for your future."

Austin and Zach are alike in that way. Forward thinkers.

She drops her hands into her lap and wrings them. "What's our future without children, Ev? If neither of us has any, family gatherings will be just the four of us forever. When we're gone, that's it. No more of our family line. No trace of Mom or Dad."

There's more that she could say, but she won't. She knows better than to bring it up.

I tug the strand of hair. "Hey, I'm not *that* bad to hang out with, am I?"

Her frown remains. "You know what I mean."

I do.

We sit in silence for a good five minutes before Ivy speaks again. "Ev?"

"Hmm?"

"I was thinking …" She chews her lip as her fingers fidget at a frantic pace.

"What?"

"I can't. It's too much to ask. I could never—"

"Out with it."

Her face twists as if it's painful to force the words from her mouth. They seem to drip from her lips in slow motion. "You could be my surrogate."

I concentrate on what she said, willing it to make sense. Surrogate. Someone who carries someone else's baby for them. I could be Ivy's surrogate. I could carry Ivy's baby for her. Why is this not computing? My head tingles much like a foot when it falls asleep.

Ivy's eyes widen, and she shakes her head. "Sorry. I shouldn't have said that. You could never face pregnancy."

Pregnancy. I could get pregnant with Ivy's baby. A pang shoots through my chest, followed by my mother's words: *Take care of Ivy.*

I place a hand on her arm. "Wait." My voice trembles as I say, "Tell me more."

Her face lights up. She turns to me, sitting cross-legged. "I don't have a uterus, but I have eggs. We could create an embryo through IVF and implant it into your womb. You'd carry our baby for us." She winces. "It's a lot to ask with your history. But I think Austin would go for it if we didn't have to pay a stranger. Maybe we could pay something—"

"No, of course not." I wave her off. "If I do this, I'm not charging you."

"It's a lot to ask," she says again.

She's not lying.

I remember how difficult it was for me to even attend Jessica's baby shower. I purchased the present already gift wrapped so I wouldn't have to look at it. Could I honestly go through nine months of pregnancy? Hope leaps from my sister's eyes and latches onto my soul. *Take care of Ivy.* I've said I would do anything for her. Did I mean it?

Her eyes moisten again. "You're my only hope."

Goodness gracious. Zach will strangle me if I make this kind of commitment without discussing it with him first. No doubt he'll spout something about boundaries. I'm eighty percent sure he'll talk me out of it. I'm seventy percent sure I want him to. But I say, "I'll think about it." How can I not do that much?

Ivy's arms wrap around my neck, and all air deflates from my chest as she squeezes hard. When she pulls back, she's glowing. "I can always count on you."

Maybe she can. Maybe she can't. The jury is out.

~~

Ivy ignored Austin's curious stares until she closed the door on Everly's retreating form. Then she spun around, did a happy dance, and flung herself into her husband's arms.

"Whoa. What's going on?"

She laughed at the wariness in his voice. He probably thought her crazy. One minute, she was weeping on the floor. The next, she was dancing in the living room. Welcome to living with a female.

"Everly's going to be our surrogate." She clapped, hugged him again, then planted a kiss on his cheek. "Well, probably. She said she'll think about it, but I'm sure she will."

His forehead wrinkled. He placed his hands on her shoulders and met her eyes. "Slow down. What?"

"I asked Everly to carry our baby, and she said she'd think about it. She wouldn't charge us. Problem solved."

He puffed out his cheeks and paced four steps away, then back to her. "Financial problem, possibly, but mi amor, this could cause a host of other issues."

Heat flared in her chest. She planted her hands on her hips and stared him down. Why did he have to see problems around every corner? She had enough anxiety of her own without him adding to it. Couldn't he be happy for her? For them?

He threw his hands up. "You and your sister are very different people. How are you going to agree on the specifics of having a baby? On a birth plan?"

"I don't care about that. As long as we get a healthy baby."

"Oh, you'll care." He pointed a finger at her. She had a mind to bend it backward. "Believe me, you'll care quite a bit the first time you two disagree about something."

"I won't."

"You're blinded by the possibility right now. When you come down from the cloud you're floating on, things will get real."

She narrowed her eyes. "Why are you so negative?"

"Not negative. Realistic." He approached with cautious steps as if she might bite. Smart man. He took her hands in his and brushed soft kisses on her knuckles. "I'm not saying we shouldn't pursue this. But we should think long and hard about it before jumping in. You'd be putting your relationship with your sister on the line."

What if Everly said no? Things might never be the same between them. Had they already crossed that bridge?

Light dawned in Austin's expression. "Wait. I just remembered something I read. I don't think your sister would be eligible. To be a surrogate, you have to have had at least one previous successful birth."

Oh, there was so much her husband didn't yet know about her family's past. Things Everly had made her promise never to tell. But Austin was her husband, and Ivy couldn't keep this back. She gave a solemn nod. "That won't be a problem."

Chapter 8

IT IS WITH PLEASURE THAT I TAKE MY PEN IN HAND
TO INFORM YOU THAT I AM WELL AT PRESENT AND
GETTING FAT AS A PIG!

SEP. 29, 1861, HENRY DEDRICK

Garysburg, North Carolina
May 1861

The commanding officer had kicked her out. How utterly humiliating to stand before the men who'd berated her, disgust pooling in their eyes. So much for earning their respect. The officer told her to put on a dress, but she didn't have one—and he didn't either—so she'd donned the civilian attire she'd worn on the docks the day Summerland had recruited her.

And now? She wandered. She couldn't go home. She'd rather die on the side of the road than return home in shame. Let Pa and her sisters believe she'd fought bravely in battle and given her life for Southern freedom. She could not slink up the hill, look them in the eye, and tell them she'd failed. They still had debt to repay.

She could find her way back to the sea, become a roustabout again, and send home wages that way. It was better than nothing. Far better than dying of hunger.

She'd stowed crackers in her rucksack and broke pieces off when her stomach complained too loudly. Best not to exhaust her supply. Who knew when she'd make wages again? She'd sent everything she had to her family.

Her steps dragged, as did her spirits. If only she'd been wiser.

She stilled. The steady clomp of marching sounded in the distance. A regiment? Her regiment? She bit the inside of her cheek. She didn't have a regiment any longer. Good thing she'd kept her distance from the chaps. No hard goodbyes. No friendships lost. Nothing lost but her pride.

The thud of boots approached. She craned her neck to see. Yes, down that hill a line of soldiers marched in her direction. She squinted. The officers didn't look familiar, at least from what she could tell. She leaned against a tree and waited for their approach. Soon, they paraded past her.

She fell in line next to a chap. "Where you headed?"

The soldier kept his gaze trained in front of him and spoke in short, even bursts. "To Virginia. Interested in joining?"

"Actually, I am."

The man nodded to the front of the line. "Talk to McGuffy. He'd be happy to have you."

"Thanks."

She jogged ahead and walked backward, offering a salute. "Colonel McGuffy?"

"Yes?" His dark brown hair did not match his scruffy white beard. Deep lines creased the edges of his eyes, and more lines extended from his nose to his mouth like trenches.

"Interested in enlisting, sir."

"Excellent. Fall in line. We'll process you in Virginia."

As she scurried to the end of the line, she caught another soldier's gaze as she passed. Her chest hitched with a jolt of something familiar she couldn't place. The soldier's eyes held steely determination, yet a softness. Fierce grit, yet something tender underneath. It was like looking into a mirror, except the blond hair and blue eyes staring back at her didn't match her own. What was it, then, that passed between them? Henrietta shook her head. She hadn't time to contemplate it. She had a job to do.

She had to fool an entire company of men, for good this time. No more playing it safe. She must be one of the boys. If that meant smoking, so be it. Drinking? Count her in. She'd do whatever she had to do to fit in, whatever the cost. She couldn't afford to waste another opportunity. She must drop everything feminine in the dust like that wretched potato and take on the nature of a man.

~~

Dearest Loreen,

I've joined a different company. Enclosed is updated information on where to send any letters. The change in units came with extra pay. Please use the money enclosed for shoes and clothes for everyone who still needs them. And food, of course. Stock up on dry goods and preserves. I wonder what the house sounds like at night without the rumble of hungry bellies. I hope it's peaceful and happy despite this ugly war.

Please don't fret over my safety and well-being. If you only knew how boring army life is, you would rest much easier. We drill and jaw around much of the time. Nothing as spectacular as you probably picture. At home, I had so little to eat that I resembled a fence post. Here, I've grown strong, and I'm well-fed. Many of the soldiers complain about the rations, but they're consistent, and they fill me. It's more than I've had for years. We might sleep in tents, but most nights, I'm sheltered from rain and wind. The uniforms might be ill-fitting, but I'm fully clothed and have sturdy boots. Most of these fellas don't know how well they have it or what destitution is like. I feel safe here. If anyone can understand such a strange statement, it's you. You do understand, don't you?

*Give my love to the girls and Pa. Write again
soon, and tell me how everyone fares.*

*Yours Truly,
Henry*

What she'd first thought was the worst thing that could
have happened to her turned out to be a delightful twist of fate.
In Virginia, they mustered her into service with merely a
glance at her teeth and offered her another sign-on bonus.
Another fifty dollars off to her family. No one questioned
where she came from or where she'd been going when she'd
found their company on the road. She couldn't believe her
luck.

Her loud, obnoxious tentmate, Ralph, spent too much time
gabbing about himself to pry into her affairs. She ached for
Loreen.

Escaping from Ralph's snores into the night air, she
padded toward the woods to relieve herself. The moon
shimmered upon the dusty path as crickets chirped, enveloping
her in their chorus. To her left, a branch snapped. She froze.
Only a large animal would make such a loud sound. A bobcat?
She held her breath and waited.

Seconds later, blond hair peeked around the corner of an
oak, illuminated by a moonbeam. Henrietta's heart rate slowed
as recognition dawned. The soldier she'd spotted that first day.

The man's slender hand flitted to tuck a strand of hair
behind his ear. Strange. Feminine. What if it wasn't a man at
all?

Sneaking off to the woods wouldn't be uncommon, as the
latrines were filthy enough to ward off a number of
conscientious men. But that dainty hand.

The dim lighting illuminated only half of the soldier's
face. Hard to tell, but were the lines around the soldier's mouth
more delicate? Were those eyelashes finer? What was it about

this person that called out to her with a siren song of camaraderie? Could it be?

She swallowed. "What are you doing out here?"

The soldier frowned back at her. "I could ask you the same question."

Henrietta bit her lip. "If I were to throw a potato at you, how would you catch it?"

Raised brows were her only answer.

She tried again. "What's your name?"

"Michael."

Michael? What was a feminine counterpart to Michael? She scuffed her boot in the dirt. "Michael, as in Michaella." Oh great. She sounded as ridiculous as Duke.

Was there a shift in the shadows, or did the color drain from Michael's face?

By golly, she was right! The soldier before her was a woman. A sister-in-arms. How could she reassure her?

"My name's Henry Frontenac." She stuck out her hand. Michael only stared at it with wide eyes. Allowing her voice to resume its natural tone, she continued, "People back home call me Henrietta."

The whoosh from Michael's lungs brushed Henrietta's face. A trembling, calloused hand clasped her own.

"People back home call me Miranda."

The edge of Henrietta's mouth crept upward. "That's a far cry better than Michaella."

Miranda breathed a laugh. "You about frightened me to death."

"I apologize. I had to know."

"You won't tell?"

"Not as long as you don't."

"Deal."

As they shook, relief coursed through her. She wasn't alone.

~~

The next morning at breakfast, Henrietta sought Miranda out. Being known was like oxygen, and she was starving for another breath. Her new friend's countenance lit as Henrietta neared. Miranda stood from her bench and waved Henrietta over.

"Henry, let me introduce you to my *cousin* Wyatt." Miranda gestured to the stocky giant of a man beside her with a handlebar mustache.

The way she emphasized the word cousin told Henrietta the relationship was a ruse, but what was its true nature? Were the two … married? The thought brought a snigger to the surface, and she worked to tamp it down. But truly, Wyatt dwarfed the young woman at nearly twice as tall and three times as wide. What an unsightly pair.

Henrietta dipped her head in greeting. "A pleasure to meet you."

"You as well." The soft-spoken timbre of his voice didn't match his stocky build.

"Want some coosh?" Miranda asked, holding a ladle full of the brown gravy-like substance made of bacon and cornmeal.

Henrietta warmed. How splendid to have a friend to share a meal with. "Sounds mighty nice."

Miranda dished some into a bowl and handed it to Henrietta. Questions swirled in the air between them, begging to be asked. Who was Wyatt to her? How did Miranda go about not getting caught? Had she had any close calls? Had she told Wyatt about Henrietta?

But she couldn't think how to voice any of these out in the open. Here, they shared a commonality, possibly a world of similarity, yet it had to remain hidden. Was there any chance Henrietta would be able to get Miranda alone later to discuss their shared secret?

"Wyatt was surefire desperate to enlist for this war. Couldn't sign up fast enough." Miranda cut him a side-eyed glance laced with annoyance. "I *had* to see what the fuss was about. Keep an eye on my dear cousin."

His face reddened, and his gaze dropped into his bowl.

Henrietta studied the two of them. "Oh, I see."

Keeping him on a lead rope, was she? They must be married. How had she gained such gumption? In the paper, female soldiers who followed their husbands into battle were lauded as brave, noble, and romantic. Perhaps not all wives did so from the motivation of undying love.

Miranda's hand lingered a bit too long on Wyatt's arm. Henrietta scanned the area. Did no one else notice this blatantly feminine display? She hadn't flaunted her femininity, and yet she'd been caught. How unfair for Miranda to stomp on caution and not be found out.

Miranda turned her full attention to Henrietta. "So, why did you join?"

No use fibbin' about that one. "For the money."

"Oh dear." A frown dimpled her chin. "You know what the Good Book says. The love of money is the root of all evil. Be careful, Henry."

Henrietta snorted. "I've never had enough of it to develop deep feelings."

"But the devil walketh about as a roaring lion—"

"Leave the man alone, Mir-Michael." Wyatt's voice applied gentle pressure. "He doesn't need your church lesson about money."

So he didn't know. Good. Or maybe he was keeping up the ruse like she was.

Miranda huffed. "You'd gamble all yours away if I didn't prevent you."

Wyatt stiffened. "It's convenient that you're here, then, isn't it?"

Oh my. What had she walked into? Ma and Pa had never quarreled. These two sparred like those quite familiar with the game. As much as she had longed for a friend, she didn't relish coming between such fiery darts. And a religious fanatic? No thank you.

She finished off her last bit of meal, then stood, bowl in hand. "Thank you kindly for breakfast. I'll see you around." She headed toward the sinks.

When footsteps crunched behind her, she didn't turn. How could she get herself out of this mess?

"Henry, wait." Miranda touched her shoulder.

She slowed her pace, and the two approached the camp sinks together.

"I apologize for Wyatt." Miranda handed over her dish and pumped the spigot handle.

For … Wyatt? The poor chap had hardly said a thing.

"I love the man, but it's as if he has no moral compass. Heaven only knows what temptation he'd fall prey to if no one were here to remind him of the Lord's ways. Dens of iniquity these camps are." Miranda shuddered.

Henrietta rinsed the dishes under the stream of water, clamping her mouth shut. If she had to choose which of them to befriend, she'd choose Wyatt.

Miranda ceased pumping and wiped her palms on her trousers. "You do know of the Lord and Savior, Jesus Christ, don't you?"

Henrietta swallowed. "I do." She knew Him well. Knew how her mama had loved Him. And how He'd betrayed her. Betrayed them all.

Miranda's teeth gleamed with her wide smile. "Good."

No. He wasn't good. Of that much she was certain.

~~

Henrietta scanned the area before stepping out of her tent. She only made it four steps before Miranda's blonde head popped into view. Ducking behind a tent, she held her breath. Avoiding Duke had been easier than dodging that woman. Mrs. Holier Than Thou had a hound dog's nose for sniffing her out. Maybe Henrietta could evade her by cozying up to the menfolk who were known as the biggest sinners in camp. She normally avoided the crowd that formed on the west side, though she'd have to be deaf not to hear their jeers and curses as they gambled together each evening. Now she headed straight toward them.

A chap waved his hat overhead. "Winner of this next round gets four dollars."

Henrietta's ears perked. Four dollars? What for?

She neared the place where five men stood in a line. A race? The announcer counted down from three, but at the declaration, "Go," instead of running, the fellows stuffed their cheeks full of tobacco. They chomped, brown juice dribbling from the corners of their mouths, as those around them cheered.

Once again, the announcer counted down. "Three, two, one, spit."

Streams of tobacco juice glided through the air. Two judges crouched low and conferred on a winner. "Contestant number three. You won."

The cheers of the majority mixed with the complaints of the other contestants.

"Beuford, do you want to double the pot?" the announcer asked.

The winner wore a dopey grin. "Sure do."

There went the hat in the air again. "Eight dollars for the next round's winner."

Henrietta's hand shot up before she could think the whole thing through. Eight dollars? There wasn't much she wouldn't do to earn over half a month's pay in an instant. Loreen and Gretchen had shoes, but not the rest of the girls. Surely, eight dollars would buy three mighty fine pairs.

"You there." The announcer pointed in her direction. "You in? What's your name?"

"Yes, sir. Henry."

The man guffawed as he held his hat for her to place money into. "Don't sir me. I sure ain't your commanding officer."

The guys around him chortled.

She pulled a dollar from her billfold. Good thing she'd brought cash, just in case. Thankfully, the announcer didn't seem to notice how her fingers trembled as she dropped the money in the hat. He handed her a sticky wad of tobacco.

She'd smoked her first cigarette when she'd arrived at this camp. Chewing tobacco couldn't be much different, could it? What if she wasted an entire dollar on a foolish scheme? That'd be akin to stealing food from her siblings' mouths. But if she won …

She'd have to win.

Taking her place on the line, she inhaled deeply and squared her shoulders.

Three. Two. One. Chew.

Following the other contestants' lead, she stuffed the wad between her cheek and lower gum and immediately strangled a gag. Her eyes watered as she forced her jaw to work. Oh, how it burned. And the taste. She might as well have stuffed a rodent into her mouth.

She couldn't think of how horrid it tasted or she'd retch. Instead, she had to focus on keeping her jaw moving. She'd pretend she was talking to Loreen. What if she only had a few minutes to talk to her, to relay all that had happened since they were last together? She imagined herself jabbering on, wrapping her mind around words and picturing her sister's face instead of the juice building in her cheek.

"Three. Two."

She hadn't finished relaying all she had to say, but she shifted her focus. Aiming at a spot far past the judges, she narrowed her eyes.

"One. Spit."

She expelled the disgusting stream of juice and held her breath as it flew. Did it surpass her neighbor's? Hard to tell.

"Contestant four. You won."

Contestant four? She was contestant four! Her mouth parted, and the tobacco wad nearly fell out. She pointed to herself to make sure.

The announcer walked to her, eight fat dollars in hand. He quirked a brow. "Do you want to double the pot?"

Double the pot. Sixteen bucks. Mighty tempting. But what if she'd only had beginner's luck? If she had to admit to her sister that she'd had eight dollars only to lose it on a fool's bet, she might sink into the ground.

"Nah. I'm done for today." She spit the wad into the grass.

Groans and complaints rose around her.

She forced a smirk. "Don't worry, fellas. I'll beat ya again next time." Pocketing the precious cash, she sauntered off.

A figure in the distance stood with arms crossed as if waiting for her. Oh no. Not—

"Henry Frontenac. What do you think you're doing?" Miranda's horrified whisper pounced on Henrietta as she breezed past.

"Earning a pretty penny to send home to my family." If she didn't make eye contact, would that deter Mrs. Holier Than Thou?

Miranda fell into step beside her. "Tell me you weren't"—she dropped her voice—"gambling."

Fine. "I wasn't gambling." Easy enough to say if it would keep the lady off her back.

"Thank heavens." She paused mid-stride. "You sold a personal item to one of those men, then?"

As if she had anything of value to sell. Instead of scoffing, though, she nodded.

Lying was just one more sin to add to her ever-growing list. Good thing Miranda's God didn't pay a lick of attention to such things from the likes of Henrietta.

Chapter 9

Suburb of Wilmington, North Carolina
Present Day

I call Zach on my way home and ask him to cover for me at the office a while longer. Our schedules are light this morning, so it's doable. I will miss my favorite client, Mrs. Martina, but I should make it in before Laura Abrams arrives. She's a gem.

The hum of the refrigerator is the only sound that greets me when I barrel through the front door. Quiet. Our house is always so quiet. Ivy's right. If neither of us has children, it'll be like this forever. Is that truly what I want?

I drop my purse and keys on the couch and make a beeline to the bedroom. I pull the lone desk chair into our walk-in closet and stand on it so I can reach the top shelf. My fingers stretch until they grasp the petite box. After bringing it down, I reverently blow the dust from the lid and carry it to the bed. Three deep breaths and I lift the lid and pull out the single thing inside. The tiny hospital bracelet looks fragile in my hand.

Baby Girl Alexander. March 2, 2007.

My heart pinches. I never gave her a name.

It wasn't mine to give. She wasn't mine to hold on to.

I can remember how it felt for my teenage body to expand like a balloon. What it was like to take midterms with swollen ankles and an aching back. How I'd lay with my hand on my stomach as my belly convulsed with her hiccups. She'd nudge my side, and I'd nudge back, like a game.

Everyone told me not to get attached. I tried.

I failed.

I never got to see her, hold her, tell her goodbye. It was easier that way. Or so I thought. The decision doesn't seem as solid now.

Can I do it again? Grow a child in my womb only to give her away? I run the bracelet in between my fingers.

Maybe I can if I don't have to go back to a sterile room with the nurses telling me I can't eat or move my body like I feel I need to. When I was seventeen, all I knew about birth had come from watching my mother's home births. In the hospital, I broke rules I didn't know existed. Nurses scolded me like a naughty child. Told me to get back in bed, the most painful place to be. The doctor taunted me for not wanting an epidural. The memory of him leering at me and saying, "How do you like the pain now?" haunts me to this day.

When I relayed the traumatic experience to Zach, he didn't blame me for wanting my tubes tied. My doctor needed more of a push to do the procedure, but Zach stood by me from the start. Before he even proposed, he'd accepted that we'd never have children.

Will he accept a pregnancy for my sister? My sister who knows little of this pain, who thinks it's in the past. That I've moved on. Exactly what I've convinced her to believe.

The memory of Ivy's birth surrounds me like an embrace. Mom invited me to be there. Such a privilege for a ten-year-old.

The house was serene. Soft music lilted in the background. Candles flickered. It was like a magical world. The scent of lavender hung in the air. Mom was in the birthing tub, swimsuit top and skirt on, hips swishing from side to side. The water rippled as she hummed. Her hums got deeper, stronger, louder. She rasped out, "It's time," and the midwife flew into action. In two long strides, she was at the tub. She obscured my view for a moment, then lifted out this pink, wriggling miracle.

It was as if time stood still when I looked into her eyes. She was perfect, and she was mine. As soon as Daddy cut the cord, I begged to hold her. Mom had me sit on the couch, then the midwife brought her to me. My heart leapt toward this baby. My baby. My sister. It was the perfect night, and I knew I wanted to have ten babies, and I wanted to birth each one at home, just like this. Once the midwife helped Mom from the tub and did some things with her, Mom and Dad snuggled together in bed, Baby Ivy in between them. I crawled in the middle, not willing to be separated from my sister. I stayed on Daddy's side, careful of Mama. We fell asleep like that, a perfect family.

That's what I want. Not glaring fluorescent lights and beeping machines. Not flustered nurses and rude doctors. Maybe a picture-perfect home birth will help to heal the trauma inflicted by the horrendous hospital birth. Perhaps, if I do this for Ivy, the part of me that's been stuck for nearly two decades can begin to move on.

Heart throbbing, I kiss the bracelet before returning it to the box and the box to the closet shelf. On my way out the door, I text my sister.

I'll do it on one condition.

She replies seconds later.

Anything.

I have a home birth.

I can nearly smell fumes of anxiety transmitting through the phone as I watch those three little dots and wait for her return message to appear. And wait. And wait.

Okay.

As much as she fears anything naturally minded, that concession must have cost her a great deal. Still, I won't allow my heart to soften. This will cost me too. It might cost everything inside of me. But if I don't do it, it will inevitably cost my relationship with my sister, and that's too high a price to pay.

A lump of air catches in my chest as I pull into the parking lot of Moore Chiropractic. I've moved forward without my husband's approval or even his knowledge. How will Zach react?

~~

Ivy's thigh pressed close to Austin's on the love seat in the fertility clinic's office. Traffic noises filtered in from the street, melding with the air-conditioning's soft whir. On a matching sofa across from them, Everly and Zach sat far too rigid for a couple with a chiropractic practice, their mouths pressed into firm lines. Ivy laced her fingers with Austin's and offered him the only smile in the room.

A petite Asian woman in a pantsuit breezed in and offered the excitement the room had lacked. "Hello! I'm Dr. Diction. Which one of you is the prospective genetic mother?"

Ivy's hand popped up. "Me." She made introductions.

Dr. Diction offered a hearty handshake to each of them before settling into a chair centered between the two sofas.

"Today's visit is a consultation only. No one has committed to anything." The doctor's gaze locked onto Everly's. "I'm here to go over the process and answer any questions you might have, as well as bring up some things for you to consider you may not have thought through yet."

Zach and Austin nodded in unison, both with pronounced frowns.

"Our role here at New Life Fertility would be to take Ivy's eggs and Austin's sperm to create embryos. How many embryos will depend on a variety of factors, but at the end of the process, we'll hope for at least three or four viable little guys."

Austin stiffened. Was it due to the possibility of four children or multiple losses?

Dr. Diction turned her attention to Everly and Zach again. "If you choose to proceed as a surrogate, there will be a few tests you'll need beforehand to ensure your body is good to go. Then we'll choose the date for implantation and work backward from there. Progesterone shots two weeks before the implantation, estrogen prior to that, and birth control before that to align your cycle and thicken the uterine lining."

Everly shifted in her seat. "How long before we know if it worked?"

Good question. Ivy's pulse thrummed as she waited for the answer.

"We'll do a blood test ten days after implantation and again forty-eight hours later. If the HCG numbers are trending positively, you can proceed like a regular pregnancy. Although, you'll continue taking estrogen and progesterone until your tenth week."

Ivy leaned forward. "I can choose my own OB?"

"I can have a home birth?"

Ivy's and Everly's simultaneous questions tangled in the air. Ivy winced. Yes, of course. It wouldn't be *her* OB, and she'd agreed to no OB at all. Everly would choose a midwife for her home birth. A dangerous home birth for Ivy's precious baby. How could she have agreed to that? How could Everly have asked it of her? The two of them, above everyone, knew the risks. Bile rose in her throat. She swallowed it.

Zach shifted his jaw, his eyes brooding.

Dr. Diction's gaze ping-ponged between the two sisters. "After we confirm a healthy pregnancy, you are free to proceed however you see fit. New Life Fertility will be out of the picture."

"What about the costs?" This from Austin.

"Great question. A financial counselor is reviewing your insurance information. She'll be in shortly to go over your benefits with you."

The set of Dr. Diction's shoulders reassured Ivy that this was possible. They could do it. They could work together to bring a life into the world. She squeezed Austin's hand.

"What other questions do you have?" Once again, Dr. Diction angled toward Everly.

Ev leaned forward. "Can you explain those tests you mentioned?"

As the doctor explained about a mock embryo transfer, saline sonogram, and HSG, Ivy watched her sister's face for any hint of hesitation. Ev would go through with this, wouldn't she? She had to. If she backed out now … Fire leapt in Ivy's chest. She doused it with reassurances. Everly wouldn't deny her. Not when this meant so much.

When the doctor finished answering Everly's question, Austin asked how the IVF process worked. It sounded straightforward. Give her the dotted line. She'd sign right away.

"There are other considerations you might need to discuss." Dr. Diction folded her hands in her lap. "We'll need you to sign a legal document stating what will happen to the child if Ivy and Austin were to die, God forbid, during the pregnancy."

Ivy startled. "Excuse me?"

"However unlikely, the law requires us to be prepared for the possibility. The child will be placed in foster care when born if there's no alternative plan. For families who hire a stranger to be a genetic carrier, they might choose an adoption plan to avoid that possibility. Many couples who choose a family member as a carrier choose to have them raise the child in case of tragic circumstances."

Oh. Ivy's hands turned clammy. "Of course, Everly and Zach would raise the baby."

Everly's eyes widened. "I don't know—"

"You'd let her go into foster care?"

"I don't know." Everly groaned and covered her face with her hands.

Zach wrapped an arm around her shoulders and shot Ivy a look she couldn't decipher.

Dr. Diction jumped in. "You don't have to decide right away. This is only a consultation."

"Ivy," Austin hissed near her ear, "give your sister a break."

She pursed her lips. Of course. Everly had to feel overwhelmed. The conversation had gone from carrying Ivy's baby to raising her in sixty seconds flat. Anyone would feel bulldozed. Especially someone who swore she never wanted children.

Ivy might be the only one left in the world who believed Ev didn't mean it. Not really. Not in her core. How many times in their youth had the sisters dreamed of getting their large families together for holidays and birthdays? There was a time when Everly swore just as vehemently she wanted ten little ones running around someday. A hard few years after Mom's death and a heart-wrenching pregnancy later, her sister had done a one-eighty. And Ev called *her* dramatic. Everly swore she was fine now. Healed from that experience. If it was true, Everly had to still want children, didn't she? What if this surrogacy was just the thing to unlock the dormant desire inside of her?

"Absolutely," Ivy croaked out. "You don't have to decide right away. And if you decide you wouldn't want to raise this child, we would be okay with an adoption plan." *Lord, forgive my dishonesty. I want to be okay with whatever You have in store.*

Austin raised a brow at her but said nothing. Was that overkill? Perhaps she should have stayed silent.

Everly's eyes remained closed while she massaged the spot in between her eyes. Probably a pressure point. Zach studied his wife with a furrowed brow. What did he think of all this? Tight-lipped in public, Ivy would presume he didn't hold many opinions if Everly didn't spout otherwise. Apparently, the man could be quite vocal when alone with his wife. How intimidating to think his brain was churning, but Ivy had no clue to its inner workings.

Dr. Diction broke the awkward silence. "If you decide you want to proceed, the next step will be a social work consult for both parties, separately. Our practice requires this whether you are choosing a known surrogate or hiring a stranger."

Ivy asked, "What is that for?"

"How much does it cost?" Austin's question came at the same time.

Ivy pinned him with a glare. Why did he have to focus on money? He shrugged. She could imagine him saying something about being fiscally responsible.

Dr. Diction's warm smile reoriented them back to her. "The social work consults are performed by independent social workers who charge various rates according to their own practices. We have a list of recommended practitioners, but you'll need to contact them to see about cost. You'll pay them directly."

She nodded to Ivy. "As for why we require this, we want to make sure everyone is fully aware of what they're getting into and is psychologically capable for the task at hand."

Austin adjusted his glasses while emitting a frustrated huff. "A legal maneuver. A way to cover yourselves."

Seriously? Was he trying to embarrass her? Ivy gave him a subtle nudge in the ribs.

Dr. Diction conceded with a tilt of her head. "In a way."

Everly's gaze snagged Ivy's from across the room. Eyes now open, clear, and focused, they zeroed in on her as if she were a bullseye.

"I'll do it." Everly's voice sounded calm and confident.

Ivy scooted to the edge of her seat. "What?"

Zach's mouth dropped open as he placed a hand on Ev's shoulder.

"I said, I'll do it." She nodded and stood. "Are we done here?"

The doctor's hands fluttered around. She looked as flustered as Zach. "The financial counselor will be here in a moment to go over—"

"Can you email us the information?" Everly spun Mom's ring on her finger.

"Yes, but—"

"Then I think we'll be going. Thank you." Everly reached across the space to shake the doctor's hand.

"Wait a minute, Ev. We need to talk about this." Zach stepped to block her path.

She patted his chest. "We will. We'll talk in the car."

He didn't smile as he gave a cursory goodbye to everyone in the room. With his jaw clenched, he stepped out the door. Everly followed him out but turned back before closing the door.

"I'll do it. Carry your child. Raise your child. Whatever you need. I'll do it."

Then she was gone.

~~

On the ride home, the tension in the car is so thick, it's hard to breathe. The confidence I displayed back in the office dissipates under my husband's seething. In the twelve years we've been married, we've weathered our share of storms. I don't doubt for a minute we'll come through this one intact, but the question remains of how battered we'll be at the end of it.

As an only child, Zach can't understand the bond I have with my sister. I remind myself of this every time he makes an Ivy joke or dig. He doesn't get it because he can't. How can I fault him? Plus, his parents adhered to the "stop crying, or I'll give you something to cry about" adage. Not everyone was raised by hippies. I must give grace.

I take a deep breath as I prepare for the verbal torrent I can predict with more accuracy than our meteorologist predicts summer storms.

He grips the steering wheel with white knuckles. His jaw shifts. He punches off the radio like an exclamation mark. Here it comes.

"We're partners, Everly. A team. That's what you agreed to when you said, 'I do.' We stood before the pastor, and we promised ourselves to each other. We promised it would no longer be Zach doing life for Zach and Everly doing life for Everly, but we'd do life together as a team."

Images from our wedding day flash through my mind. My beaded lace dress and braided crown updo. Zach in his swoony tux. My redemption day. The day the Lord gave me beauty for those ashes of my teenage years. But in every mental picture of that day, I see someone else as well.

Ivy's there too. My sister stands beside me in her lilac chiffon dress, my maid of honor. Ivy giving a tear-inducing toast. Ivy at the piano, playing the music during the ceremony, then again at the reception as Zach and I dance together for the first time as man and wife.

Yes, I agreed to make a new life together with my husband, but I never promised to abandon my sister. The words burn my tongue, but I know better than to speak them. Doing so would only add fuel to the fire and lengthen the argument. If I want peace, I must hold my tongue.

He continues, "You're acting like my feelings don't matter. Like I'm some extra, nonessential pawn to the game you're trying to play."

I can't let this one go. "I'm not playing a game."

"Well, I certainly feel nonessential. I'm supposed to watch your body grow with a baby that's not mine for nine months? What's in it for me? Do we at least get compensation out of this?"

I gape at him like a fish. Did he really just say that? When I find words to voice, they're hot with indignation. "Do you realize how selfish you sound?"

He throws a hand in the air. Our car veers into the neighboring lane, and a jeep honks. Either Zach doesn't notice or doesn't care. He spits out sarcasm. "Selfish. Of course."

I cross my arms. "It's not like you even want a baby of your own. Why do you care?"

He stares straight ahead with both hands on the wheel, suddenly the safe driver of the year. "Maybe I do."

I rear back. "What?"

"You heard me."

"Who are you?" My seat belt is choking me. I pull it away from my throat. "You knew before we married that I didn't want kids. You said you were perfectly fine with it."

"Doesn't mean it was my first choice. Doesn't mean I wouldn't want a child."

I speak through clenched teeth. "Stop the car."

"What?" We're barreling down a four-lane road with strip malls on both sides.

"Stop the car. Let me out."

"I'm not going to let you go traipsing into—"

"What? A shoe store and a coffee shop? Let me out."

"Fine." He makes a right at the next light and pulls into a parking lot. My door is already open before he shifts into park. "I'll wait in the car while you cool off."

"I'll call an Uber."

"Ev, you're being ridiculous."

I snatch my purse from the seat and shoot him a glare. "Just wait until I'm pregnant." Then I slam the door and march off.

I've thrown four pairs of shoes into my cart before I consider texting an apology. It truly was ridiculous to flee from the car as if he were a masked murderer. He's my husband, and I love him. But has he secretly wanted a baby all this time? Have I kept him from a desire of his heart? I don't want to be the bad guy here. Much better to sling the slimy guilt onto him. He's the one who would charge my hospital-bill-laden sister to carry her baby. Sure, Zach. Let's make a quick buck on Ivy's misery. Despicable.

My fingers hover over my phone. I can't let the sun go down on my anger, but there's still a good four hours left of daylight. It won't hurt to wallow in these feelings for a while longer.

As I put the device away, it dings. An email notification fills the screen.

> Cassaundra Walt replied to your message on Ancestors List.

Here we go. Maybe I can prove this is not a wild goose chase. I click on the message.

> Hi, Everly,
>
> I understand you're interested in learning more about females who fought as

soldiers during the Civil War. I'm happy to share what I know. I did a dissertation on the subject in graduate school, and I'm currently working on a book that includes the stories of a half dozen female Civil War soldiers. Ask away, and I'll answer as best I can.

Cassaundra

What in the world? I squeeze my eyes shut, then blink them open and read the message again. It doesn't make any more sense the second time. She must have messaged the wrong person. Got her wires crossed. Why else would she think I was interested in female Civil War soldiers? I shake my head. Women fought in the Civil War? Who knew?

Thank goodness Zach isn't reading this message over my shoulder. I wouldn't want to hear his snide remark. I shoot back a quick reply.

Cassaundra,

Thanks for getting back to me, but I think your message was meant for someone else. I'm not looking for information about female soldiers. I'm trying to find information on Henrietta Frontenac, who, apparently, was a relative of mine. If you have further info on Henrietta, specifically how she died, please message me back. If not, I wish you the best on your book.

Everly

Maybe Zach is right. This ancestry search is pointless. What else is he right about? Setting boundaries with my sister? Perhaps I should work on that if for no other reason than to protect my marriage. It's unraveling right in front of me.

Chapter 10

AS LONG AS YOU ARE SO GOOD A GIRL AND
IMPROVING IN YOUR WRITING I SEND YOU $2.00
DOLLARS TO BUY A PAIR OF BOOTS FOR THE WINTER
AND TELL MARTHURE IF SHE WRITES ME A LETTER I
WILL SEND HER $2 MORE.

SEPT. 27, 1863, MICHAEL LALLY

Stafford, Virginia
May 1861

> *Dearest Loreen,*
>
> *I am safe and well.*
> *I came into extra money and am enclosing it with this letter. Please make sure you have plenty of food stored. Have you found a job yet? Has Gretchen shown herself competent to tend to the household? Is everyone healthy and safe?*
> *I haven't received a letter from you in some time. I hope everything is okay.*
>
> *Write soon.*
> *Yours Truly,*
> *Henry*

If Loreen truly knew what her sister had been up to, she might faint dead away. Henrietta pasted on a grin even as her insides quivered. Ralph motioned at her from the pub's doorway, beer in hand, his head tilted in the direction of a table full of men, already half drunk. "C'mon, Henry. Join us."

She had to do it. Of course, she had to. Blend in. Be one of the boys. Not give them one reason to see her as an outsider. But Lord help her, she'd never tasted a lick of alcohol in her life. Hopefully, her bravado wouldn't falter.

She took a step forward, but Miranda put a hand on her arm. "Surely, you're not going to go drink with that brood." Miranda's scowl panged her chest.

"I have to," Henrietta whispered. "I've got to fit in."

Miranda's gaze spat fire toward the pub. "Don't you know what kind of debased filth goes on in those establishments? Drunkenness. Wretched language. Gambling. Have you no morals?"

Henrietta frowned. "I can't afford morals. I've got to take care of my family." She shouldered past Mrs. High and Mighty toward the den of sin. The nerve of the woman. To think Miranda had seemed of like heart and mind, a sister to turn to and confide in. But she would only judge Henrietta for her choices. Well, she didn't need that. She could make it fine without female camaraderie.

Ralph waved her over, beer sloshing out of his mug, weaving like a Virginia fence. "You comin'?"

"Don't mind if I do." That sounded convincing, didn't it? Hopefully, he couldn't tell that she walked toward him on shaky legs.

"We just finished a mean game of blackjack. About to start another." Ralph winked.

"You don't say? Deal me in."

Blackjack? How did one play blackjack? She'd picked up on the game of poker by watching men play the past couple of months, but she hadn't a clue about this game. She'd better catch on quick.

Ralph stopped to introduce her to several men he knew. By the time she got to the table, the others had already started the game. Good. It gave her time to watch and dissect the rules.

A burly man with a wiry mustache slid a glass of whisky in front of her. Lantern light glinted off the dark amber and seemed to mock her. It dared her to prove her mettle. She wrapped her hand around the glass, her palm sweating at the touch. Her younger sisters' cries for more food echoed in her ears. For them. Henrietta would do anything for them. She lifted the liquor and sloshed down a gulp. Bitterness greeted her. She forced her mouth into a straight line instead of a wince as it burned her throat.

Laughter echoed around her. Someone must have said something humorous. She joined in. A man with a curly beard reaching nearly to his navel slapped her on the back and ordered another round. He spoke with a cigar hanging from the side of his mouth. "One battle is all it will take to send them Yanks running."

"That's right." This from a young buck who looked more child than man. "One Reb can whip ten of them Yanks. When're they gonna let us at 'em?" The boy bounced in his seat like a spring sat underneath him.

"Soon enough, Jeffrey. Soon enough."

Wiry Mustache Man offered her a cigar. Why not? If she could smoke a cigarette, she could handle a cigar too. He lit it for her, and she puffed. Her nose, her eyes, her chest flamed as she struggled to hold in the cough that would expose her as a novice. She managed to merely wheeze as her eyes watered. The smoke scratched her throat, but she couldn't let it show. She exhaled and joined in more laughter.

Another glass appeared in front of her. She downed it with more confidence this time, the camaraderie of the men drawing her in, pulling her close. See? Who needed Miranda? She had friendship right here.

It was hard to pay attention to the cards when conversation and bantering flew back and forth between the men. Her shoulders relaxed, and she leaned back against her chair. When they offered her another glass, then another, she partook without hesitation. Why had she resisted for so long? It felt good to be a part of the group. She belonged here, same as the rest of them.

"What about you, Henry?"

Henrietta blinked back at Curly Long Beard. What was the question?

"How are you finding army life?"

Her mouth spread in a smile. Ah, this was an easy one. "Sure beats washing petticoats."

The rowdy group quieted. She gazed around at the men's confused faces.

"Washing petticoats? What in the blazes are you talking about?"

She squinted. What had she said? Why were they looking at her like that? Realization sunk into her stomach with the liquor she'd consumed. She straightened as her mind scrambled to come up with an excuse for her fumble. Her pulse throbbed in her ears.

"It's a saying we have in North Carolina." She attempted to smile, but her mouth twitched.

The man across from her folded solid arms over his chest and frowned. "I'm from North Carolina. Never heard that saying."

Ralph leaned forward, elbows on the table, brow knit. "Are you saying you laundered clothes for a living before the war?"

"No, no." She spat out her denial, then swallowed. "My sisters did."

Every eye studied her. If only she could disappear. Ralph tilted his head, daring her to continue. She pushed through the cloud enveloping her brain.

"I had to help occasionally. So they could finish in time."

Wiry Mustache Man leaned close. Smoke from his cigar swirled in her face. She coughed. Perhaps too feminine a cough. "By golly, you're a woman." He sat back, disgust splayed on his expression.

She forced a laugh. "What?"

Ralph's eyes widened. "No. It can't be. Henry, you can explain this, can't you?"

"Explain it? Have him—or her—prove it." Curly Long Beard began unbuttoning his shirt.

Jeffery still bounced in his seat, but his grin had faded. "Prove it? How?"

She knew how, and her blood cooled.

Curly Long Beard's eyes glinted at her in challenge. "Every man here, unbutton your shirt." He exposed his curly haired chest.

Jeffery complied, then the others followed suit. She fiddled with her top button, dread pooling. She was trapped, and they knew it.

Curly Long Beard smirked at her as if he'd caught a coon in a trap. "You ain't doin' it 'cause this ain't a peep show."

"This is ridiculous." She stood and stumbled toward the door. "I don't have to answer to you."

"No, but you'll have to answer to the colonel."

She barely made it out the door before she retched. From across the street, Miranda raised her brows. Was she concerned? Or haughty? It didn't matter. Henrietta wouldn't be around long enough for it to make a difference. She made it halfway down the street before the first tear fell.

~~

Henrietta's spirits finally lifted when she neared Fort Monroe. She'd been wandering, looking for another regiment to join since being kicked out of her last one two weeks prior. She could go home, but humiliation prevented her from taking that route. That and the debt they still owed to the doctor. When she returned to her family, it would be as the heroine they imagined her to be. Not as a failure. And all their needs would be cared for.

As she wandered, she solidified new rules: She would smoke. She would even chew tobacco. But she would not, under any circumstances, drink again. Ever. There had to be a way to fit in without allowing alcohol to loosen her tongue and impair her judgment.

Good thing she'd sent that letter home prior to being kicked out. Loreen would be less likely to worry having received word all was well. All was not well, but perhaps it would be soon.

She'd been waiting for a letter from home for so long, and she'd have to wait even longer. She had to send Loreen the new information about where to reach her, then how long would it take to hear back?

Was everyone faring well? Without information to the contrary, she would imagine it so. She'd picture the girls running around fat as hogs with soft, new, bright-colored dresses. Loreen was likely working behind a store counter, showing women swaths of fabric and measuring out cups of oats. Gretchen was probably corralling the younger ones, persuading them to do their chores and to help with the gardening and housework. And Pa? Try as she might, she couldn't picture him any different than she'd last seen him. So much for her vibrant imagination. Convinced all was set right at home, she pushed forward.

A few civilians she'd passed a while back said a regiment was stationed at Big Bethel Church near Fort Monroe. She'd enlist with them and not blow her cover a third time. After she stopped twice to ask for directions, the air of anticipation drew her toward the church like a moth to a flame. The atmosphere sparked with excited tension. Each soldier she passed didn't merely walk. They bounded forward, eyes alight, posture upright. A battle must be imminent. Henrietta's heartbeat turned feral. This is what they'd been waiting for, training for. Was she ready?

Signing up proved simple as the colonel was too busy with battle plans to fret over the qualifications of a willing participant. With nary a second glance, he issued the command to work on building the earthworks overlooking the creek.

"What's the story?" She forced her shovel into hard dirt, then glanced at the soldier next to her.

"The Federals control Fort Monroe. Lee's nervous. It's a threat to Richmond. We've got to stop them from advancing."

"Think they're about to make a move?"

"Any day now."

Any day. This war would flip from hypothetical scenarios played out in each soldier's imagination to a real battle any day now. She swallowed. Pushed a grin to the surface. "We'll be ready for 'em."

"Absolutely." The soldier stopped shoveling long enough to extend his hand to her. "Jacob."

"Henry." She gave his hand a firm shake before returning to her work. She studied the amount of dirt on his shovel compared to hers. Her strength had grown in the past couple of months, and she could perform hard labor for long hours without wilting. Still, Jacob had her beat, shoveling nearly twice as much as she'd managed to. She had to keep up. Prove she was as capable as everyone else and could carry her load.

Dust coated her mouth as remnants of the pile she'd dumped clouded the air. It caked her fingernails and likely her face. Two soldiers came with logs to add to the earthworks.

"Thanks, Francis. Jesse," Jacob said.

Henrietta's glance snagged on the two soldiers wedging a log into place. It was a sense she trusted more now, a knowing that spread through her gut and lodged in her chest. She didn't have to question how she knew, what gave it away, whether it was the shape of their profiles or the slightness of their forms or something in the way they carried themselves. It didn't matter how. What mattered was letting them know she knew and she, too, was a sister-in-arms.

She let her shovel fall. Brushed her hands on her trousers. Stepped toward the pair with a welcoming smile and an outstretched hand. "I'm Henry." She blinked at them, trying to communicate with her eyes all she could not say.

The tall, lanky blonde crinkled her nose as if annoyed to be distracted from her task. A wisp of hair danced across her forehead, and she brushed it away and moved to tuck it behind her ear, only it was far too short to do so. A telltale sign. Had no one noticed this tendency before? Surely, this wasn't the first time she'd done so. "Francis." The blonde managed a puny, polite smile and curt handshake before returning to her task.

The brunette was shorter and a bit stockier with unruly wavy hair. Longer hair would flatter the woman nicely, bringing out her cheekbones. She hefted the log into place, face reddening with the effort, before extending her hand to Henrietta without making eye contact. "Jesse."

"Nice to meet you. Are you siblings?"

"No." Jesse kept her gaze on the ground while picking up another log. "Childhood friends."

"Hmm." She added a wink, then returned to shoveling.

This need inside of her for companionship must be fierce indeed to cause her to keep reaching out. She should shut herself away where it was safe. But the loneliness echoed like a cavern inside her. Mama would have told her to talk to the Good Lord, would have said He was always listening.

Mama was dead. As dead as her God. It was all up to Henrietta now.

~~

Her attempt to put the ladies at ease must have done the opposite because for the past few days, they seemed to be going out of their way to avoid her. Every time she tried to draw near to them, they headed in the opposite direction. She could take a hint. She'd scared them away. Now, as sleep eluded her in the predawn hours, her mind traversed through ways she could reveal her identity to the women. How could she catch them alone? What could she say to allay their fears?

A steady beat in the distance caused her heart to leap into her throat. She sat up. "What was that?"

Jacob rubbed his eyes and shifted on his bedroll. "What?"

In the stillness of the night, it came again. A drumroll. "That."

She scrambled out of the tent and stared into the distance. Stars twinkled. Crickets chirped. A faint breeze rustled tent flaps. All looked to be well, but a chill shivered down her spine and into her toes. All was not well. War was finally coming for them, creeping closer and closer like a monster hovering in the shadows. Like Old Man Meager.

Jacob emerged behind her. "Magruder's issuing the alarm. Time to gear up for battle."

Goose bumps prickled her skin, and she rubbed her arms to subdue them.

As murmurs signaled others were awakening, fear attempted to snake its way through her. She was about to see the elephant, a term the men used when someone encountered their first battle. What would circumstances force her to do? Could she pull the trigger and vanquish the life from another human being? What if she were the one left writhing in agony?

No. She could not focus on these what-ifs. She had to take the neck of this serpent of trepidation and strangle it. She must focus on Loreen, Millie, Bea, Charlotte, and Gretchen. On what—or who—had brought her here in the first place. She closed her eyes and let her sisters' faces float before her. She could do this. And she would. For them. For Pa. For their future.

~~

At three in the morning, she marched as one of six hundred North Carolinians down Sawyer Swamp Road to Little Bethel, hauling three cannons. When a woman met them on the road and informed them that over four thousand Federals marched their way, they turned back toward the fortifications at Big Bethel. There, they waited behind the earthworks they'd erected, improving the structure with sassafras boughs. Henrietta bit her nails to the quick.

At nine in the morning, the Yanks marched into view, star-spangled banner waving overhead. Their bayonets glinted in the hot sun as their footsteps clomped in rhythm like a heartbeat. Her stomach threatened to empty its contents. Then, a Parrott shell whizzed overhead and plummeted through a man a few yards away. Henrietta's body stiffened. A man was dead. The beginning of battle. A shiver coursed down her spine. Instinctively, she touched her ring finger. No ring. Loreen had it now, and Henrietta could draw strength from it no longer.

Perhaps she should pray. No time for much more than a *Help us, Lord.* Would it suffice when far more fervent prayers had failed? She'd have to wait and see.

Shells shrieked overhead as she dodged. Time to shoot as she'd been trained to do. Her finger trembled as she pulled the trigger. Her body jolted with the kickback. She'd done it. But she couldn't reflect on this initiation. A Yankee regiment advanced, firing a volley. Fire rained all around. Heart hammering her ribs, she dodged again. She needed to reload. Her teeth chattered as she used them to tear open the cartridge. She fumbled when dumping the powder into the barrel, spilling a third of the contents.

The stench of sulfur twisted her stomach, and smoke burned her eyes. She'd scoffed at those who'd said the female constitution wasn't up to the atrocities of war, but she'd wager many of her comrades would prove the naysayers right. How did the other women fare? How were Jesse and Francis handling this? Every impulse screamed at her to flee, but that wasn't an option. She had to follow this through. And she had to stay alive to do so.

The exotic Zouaves—in their blue, collarless jackets with red trim, their vests, and their baggy, red trousers—acted as sharpshooters, firing muskets from the refuge of an abandoned house and blacksmith shop. She'd be mesmerized by their fancy attire if they weren't aiming at her. Nerves abuzz, she watched as five men from her company leapt over the earthworks armed with hatchets and matches, intent on setting the house ablaze. They dashed toward the structure. A volley boomed. They dropped to the ground. Other men scrambled, but one of them—oh no, not Jacob—did not get up. He sprawled flat on his back, blood pooling under his head, arms extended to his sides.

Henrietta's knees shook as she stared at the bloody figure in front of her. She'd never seen someone alive in one blink, dead the next. Not a man she'd spoken with. She shook herself from the trance, but even when she looked away, bloodstains filled her vision. What was wrong with her? This was war. Of course, men died. Many would die, and she might be one of them if she didn't snap out of it.

Fellow soldiers rushed past her. What had she missed? She tugged on a man's tattered sleeve as he attempted to dart past her and implored him with her eyes for answers. He waved her forward. "To the swamp. We're to be sharpshooters."

"Sharpshooters?" What in tarnation? They weren't trained as sharpshooters.

He merely jerked a quick nod and hurried away. She raced after him. And tripped.

Her hands flew out to catch her fall, but the blow still knocked the wind from her. She worked to heave air into her lungs. A hand grasped hers and pulled her to standing. Her gaze tangled with the forest-green eyes of a tall, muscular, brown-haired man. Her knees wobbled, and she stumbled over a clump of dirt. Cheeks heating, she looked down and hastened into a jog to cover her second fumble. What was that? When she saw that man, she felt a twinge of … attraction? Oh dear. What was wrong with her?

No time to ponder that. She had to move. Maybe later she could contemplate running into the most handsome man she'd ever seen.

She rushed to join her company. When the Yankees cheered and crossed the creek, the Rebs fired volley after volley at them. Henrietta fought to keep her mind clear of everything save shooting, reloading, and shooting. She couldn't think of how she was a murderer. If she did, she'd start shaking again.

A stifled moan stole her attention. It stood out among the incessant cacophony of battle. It sounded not quite masculine. Francis and Jesse? She had to check. Keeping her rifle aimed ahead, she searched for its source. She stepped to her left once, then again. She had to be close.

There. Behind that tree. She ducked behind the trunk and nearly stumbled over Jesse's feet. The woman lay on her side, face contorted in pain, hand pressing against her thigh. A crimson ring of blood encircled her palm. Francis stooped over her, eyes wide and searching as if a bandage would appear in the dirt.

"You're injured." Henrietta's statement hung between them like stale air. The women merely glanced at her before returning their attention to the blood-soaked leg. "Let me see."

She dropped to her knees and lifted Jesse's hand for only a moment before pressing it down again. Blood oozed from a deep wound. This wasn't a graze from a rogue bullet. The enemy had hit his target and taken her down.

She leaned over Jesse's pale, sweat-dampened face. "Let's get you to the medic."

"No." The word burst forth from both women.

Henrietta frowned and cocked her head to Francis. "Sure, we can do it. I'll support her from the left side, you support her from the right."

"No." Francis pressed her lips together in a thin line. "We can't."

Realization dawned. Going for help would risk exposure. They didn't want anyone to find out their secret. Henrietta took a step closer. "Listen, I understand. I'm your sister." She put a hand on Francis's shoulder and waited for the word to register through the panic. She should use her natural tone of voice. "Your sister." There.

Francis's mouth parted. Her lower lip trembled. When she spoke, her voice came out raspy. "Then you know why she can't see the doctor."

"Yes, but …" Henrietta's gaze dropped to the blood-soaked trouser leg. "She's at risk of infection. At risk of," she lowered her voice to whisper, "death."

Francis shook her head. "I won't let anything happen to her."

Goodness, couldn't the lady understand? By refusing medical help, she could be signing her friend's death certificate. They could always come up with another plan if the army kicked them out, but only if they were alive. Henrietta straightened and channeled the authority she'd used as the eldest sister when directing her younger siblings. "She needs a doctor."

"No!" A stomp accompanied Francis's scream. The woman was as stubborn as her little sister Mildred when demanding her way.

Henrietta clenched her jaw. "Fine." She spun from the scene. If they wouldn't let her bring Jesse to the doctor, she'd bring the doctor to Jesse.

Chapter 11

Suburb of Wilmington, North Carolina
Present Day

Ivy sipped her venti caramel macchiato as she waited for the elevator to open to the second floor. A glance at the reflective surface showed nothing amiss. No one would be able to tell that her life was about to drastically change. She managed one deep breath before a *ping* rang out, and she stepped into the bustling office.

"Ivy, there you are." Carol stood from behind her desk and waved a frantic hand over her head. "We need you. Seven-car pileup on the freeway. Victims have filled urgent care to the brim all morning."

Good thing she'd opted for a large coffee. "I'm on it." The busy morning would keep her mind off her personal life. Off waiting for an official commitment from Everly. She had almost asked Austin to order one of those phone lockers to keep her from pressuring her sister for an update.

She stepped into the office she shared with two other medical transcriptionists to find Bridget already hunched over her computer, headphones muffling her ears. Her fingers flew over her keyboard. Cherry was MIA. Nothing new there. She rarely rolled into the office until ten thirty or eleven.

Bridget blew out an exaggerated sigh. "Thank goodness you're here. It's a madhouse today."

"Heard there was an accident." Ivy placed her purse in the drawer, switched her computer on, and settled her headset on her head.

"That and four moms went into labor at the same time."

"Ooh, we've got babies?" Ivy waggled her eyebrows.

"Two were born. They're in the queue. One's having complications. Still waiting on the other."

Complications? Ivy's pulse skittered. If only she could choose *not* to transcribe that report. But no. First in, first out. The three of them transcribed for all offices in their small medical building: a radiologist, pediatrician, OB, and urgent care. Any of them could receive and need to transcribe reports from any office. While they all had their preferences, rarely did they have the luxury of choice.

But she *could* pray. *Please, God, don't make me go there. Not today.* This whole thing with Everly was dragging up memories. Throw a traumatic birth into the mix and Bridget might have to peel Ivy off the floor.

Deep breath. Anxiety would not win this morning. Fully-caffeinated and confident Ivy had shown up for work today.

The first report in the queue came from urgent care and had to do with contusions from glass fragments. Nothing too gory. The second from pediatrics. One of the Palmy children tested positive for influenza A. Hadn't another one of their children gotten the virus last month? Did the family even vaccinate for the flu? Ivy shook her head.

"What are you mumbling to yourself?" Bridget asked.

Ivy's neck heated. She'd said that out loud? "Nothing."

Bridget snorted a laugh. "Uh-huh."

Ivy finished the report in record time.

"Guess who's in the radiology queue?"

"Who?" Before Bridget could answer, Ivy scanned the list and found the culprit herself. "Tommy Ronato."

"You mean Tommy Tornado?"

"What'd the little daredevil do this time?" Last time, he'd jumped from a tree limb into an inflatable swimming pool, breaking his forearm.

"Took a skateboard down concrete steps and busted his head open." Bridget tsk-tsked. "Some kids."

"Some parents," Ivy mumbled. Why couldn't his parents get a handle on him?

Bridget made a strange sound in her throat, but before Ivy could ask her what *that* meant, an urgent request lit the queue. Ivy took it and hurried to transcribe. Parents had raced a sweet toddler to the urgent care with symptoms of an asthma attack. By the time they arrived, however, the boy was unresponsive. She needed to finish transcribing the records before the ambulance reached the ER so the medical staff there could know exactly what was going on. Adrenaline pulsed through her during these high-stakes situations, but these also filled her with purpose. Her job was important. She might not be a doctor, but she played an important part in saving lives.

After she submitted the report, she busied herself for the next hour with a string of minor injuries from the accident, followed by routine pediatric appointments. Her phone buzzed in her purse, safely secured in the desk drawer. Had Bridget heard it? Ivy normally kept it off, but she'd been waiting for Everly to confirm her desire to proceed with the surrogacy. She'd do it, wouldn't she? She'd said she would, and Ev pretty much always followed through with her word. But Zach …

Austin, the pessimist, was banking on Zach's veto.

Bridget continued to type away, seemingly oblivious. Ivy slipped her phone into her pocket, then excused herself to the restroom. Once safely in a stall, she pulled out her phone and checked the text. Her shoulders slumped.

Want to lose 25 pounds in 3 weeks? Try our Happy Hormone program. Guaranteed results. Thousands of happy customers. Click for more info.

"No, I don't want to lose twenty-five pounds in three weeks, Mr. Spam Texter." She deleted the text and blocked the number. "I'd love to gain twenty-five pregnancy pounds in nine months, but that's not going to happen."

Her eyes stung with the threat of tears, and she pinched the bridge of her nose. So much for keeping all thoughts of personal business away from the office. She couldn't make it through the rest of the day like this. Waiting. Wondering. She had to know for sure. Everly'd had enough space. With trembling fingers, she typed a quick text before she could second-guess herself.

Would appreciate an update.

Seconds later, Everly replied.

Update on what?

Seriously?

On what you've decided. Do you think you'll go through with the surrogacy or not?

Three dots appeared, then disappeared. Again. And again. Finally, a text came through.

I said I'd do it, didn't I?

Yeah, but …

What about Zach? He didn't seem on board.

More like adamantly opposed. What had she ever done to him for him to dislike her? He'd always been civil but never warm or friendly. What did Everly see in the man anyway? He was not the kind of guy Ev had dreamed of marrying when they were younger. Then again, not much remained the same from her sister's childhood dreams.

Don't worry about him. I've got you. I promise.

Really? If only texts could convey tone of voice and subtext. Would Everly resent her choice, or was she giving her womb willingly, without reservation?

Ev sent their favorite *Gilmore Girls* GIF. Ivy's hand covered her heart. They were good. Everything would be all right. And she was going to be a mother!

She stuffed her phone into her pocket and banged out of the stall. In front of the mirror, she put both hands on her cheeks and whispered, "I'm going to be a mom!"

How surreal. She should celebrate. But first, back to work.

When she reentered her office, Cherry looked up from her desk.

Ivy offered a smile. "Good morning, Cherry."

Cherry studied her. "What's up with you?"

"What do you mean?" Ivy slid into her chair, biting back a grin.

Bridget studied her as well.

"I know." Cherry waggled a finger in the air. "You're pregnant."

Ivy's ears flamed. "What? Why would you say that?"

"You're glowing, girl. That's it, isn't it?"

Ivy pressed her lips together. Cherry was new to the office and was clueless about Ivy's health crisis. Bridget didn't even know the specifics. Transcriptionists were the gossip queens of the medical field, and there was no way Ivy wanted details of her personal life floating around for everyone to inspect. But it would feel good to tell somebody.

"Okay, kind of."

Cherry's left brow arched. "How can you be kind of pregnant?"

"My sister agreed to be my surrogate."

Ivy's hands fidgeted and flailed as she explained the story. Would they think her crazy? Perhaps she was. Everyone said not to mix business with family, and here she was diving into a much deeper partnership. So many things could go wrong. But her relationship with Everly could withstand any trial. Couldn't it?

She finished the explanation and shrank under their perusal.

"Wow." Bridget's smile looked forced. "How exciting for you. Good luck."

Cherry whistled. "Man, your sister must be a saint."

Inwardly, Ivy cringed. What could she say? "Yeah, she's special."

Special didn't even begin to describe Everly, but the fan club pledge had grown a bit stale over the past decade. Since neither Mom nor Dad was here to sing Ev's praises, that left Ivy. Except no amount of accolades would ever convince her sister she was enough. Everly was intent on repaying a debt she didn't owe. No one could talk her out of it. Maybe … maybe that's why she'd agreed to this.

The thought took some of the edge off Ivy's excitement.

"Well, good for her," Cherry said. "And you. Good for you both."

With that, all three ladies returned to their work. A child got a bead stuck up her nose. Another broke his wrist from falling off a trampoline—the death traps. The pediatrician suspected a mild peanut allergy for one patient. Poison oak for another.

"Oh no." Bridget gasped and covered her mouth.

"What?" Ivy and Cherry asked in unison.

"Audra Bennet lost her baby."

The words on Ivy's screen blurred. "No. It can't be." Her voice came out in a raspy whisper. "She was in labor. Had a healthy pregnancy. Full term."

"Stillborn." Bridget's hands encircled her neck as if she had choked on the word. "Mom's in critical condition."

The edges of Ivy's vision darkened. Air. She needed air. The chair wheeled out from under her. It only took a moment for confident Ivy to find herself huddled underneath her desk as her coworkers reminded her how to breathe.

~~

I roll my hips from side to side on my ergonomic balance ball chair as I wait for the social worker to start the Zoom call. I'm in my office. Zach's in his. We both logged in on separate computers despite being yards apart. We've blocked off our schedules until ten this morning, giving us an hour for this mandatory social work consultation. It's the next thing to check off our list for this surrogacy.

Zach has his screen off, which is just as well. I don't need to view his scowl. I've seen it enough the past week. We're at an impasse, but it's my body. I'm free to give it as I choose. His protests fall on my deaf ears. He'll come around.

I twist Mom's ring on my finger. Has he agreed to cooperate for this consult so he can tell the social worker he disapproves? If so, there may be trouble. He wouldn't, would he? He rarely airs grievances in front of others. I should be safe. My hands move to massage my earlobes, but I stop myself. My camera is on, and I shouldn't let on that I'm nervous.

An upbeat chime sounds from my screen, and a woman with silky black hair appears. Her blazer touts her as a professional, but the T-shirt underneath, spouting a peace symbol, immediately puts me at ease.

"Hello, Everly and Zach. I'm Gale Deare. Nice to meet you."

Gale leans slightly to her left, and her eyes scrunch a bit as we greet her. She's sizing us up. Has to be. What does she see?

"Zach, I'm going to need you to turn your camera on. There'll be no hiding here."

A straight shooter. Nice. As long as she doesn't call *me* out.

Zach's frowning face appears.

"That's better." Gale gives a satisfied nod. "Now, do you two understand the purpose of this consult?"

My fingers twist in my lap. "To make sure we're not crazy?"

She chuckles. "Well, there's that. But it's mainly to ensure you've thought this through, and you're prepared for the journey."

"Okay." Do I sound as unsettled as I feel?

"First, why don't you tell me what brought you here? Why do you want to be a surrogate for the Hartgroves?" Her hand rests casually under her chin as if she's settling in for a good story. This will be a short one.

"She's my sister." I shrug. Do I need to say more?

Gale's nod prods me to continue, but words fail to materialize. I fight the urge to make eye contact with Zach. We usually partner well in the game of verbal catch, but he'll be no help here. I open my mouth, then shut it again.

"Ivy had a hysterectomy due to aggressive cancer." Zach's voice comes so unexpectedly that I startle. "She's unable to have children. It's been her dream since as long as they can remember. My wife—" He clears his throat. "My wife has always been the supportive type. Loyal. The kind of person you can count on in a crisis." I shudder as his gaze locks onto mine. "This is Everly being Everly."

Maybe he understands more than I've given him credit for.

"What a lovely tribute to your wife, Zach."

I wouldn't have been surprised if he threw me under a bus for the way I've treated him. Instead, he's responding with understanding. I moisten my lips. Nod. It's not enough to express my gratitude.

"I won't ask if you're nervous about this adventure. Anyone would be. I want to know what you're most worried about. Zach, you go first."

He shifts in his seat. "I don't really have a part in this whole thing."

Gale's brow lifts. "How does that make you feel?"

"I don't know." He taps a pen on his desk. "Everly's always had a close relationship with her sister, but this … I'm completely left on the outside."

"Do you worry your connection with your wife will weaken?"

I lean in. My face looms on the screen as I wait for his answer.

"Yes."

My heart drops.

"Everly's my world. I'm afraid of being shut out."

Regret clogs my throat. Zach has only wanted to draw close to me, yet I've pushed him away. This man who's been my sunrise fears being left in cold shadows. I would leap up and rush next door to hug him, but Gale's voice brings me back to the task at hand.

"Everly, how do you feel hearing this from your husband?"

"Surprised." It's the only word I can manage to say, though a dozen other thoughts swarm my brain.

Gale smiles as if this is a good answer. "Zach, it sounds like you value your relationship with Everly and desire to remain as connected as possible during this process. Correct?"

He nods in a way that shows he's too choked up to speak.

"Everly, do you think you can make your connection with your husband a priority throughout this surrogacy?"

I haven't a clue what that looks like, but I agree without hesitation. I can and I will.

"Good." Gale shifts and leans to her other side. "Everly, what are you most nervous about?"

"The birth," I spout. But that needs explanation, or she'll think I'm a sissy with a low pain tolerance. "I had a traumatic hospital birthing experience when I was seventeen, which is why I told Ivy I want to do a home birth this time around." I bite my lip. Is this too much to divulge? We're supposed to prove to this lady we're fit for this task, yet something about her makes me want to open the vault of my heart. "But my mother was having a home birth and she died. My baby sister died too. I was fifteen." I wince. I shouldn't have divulged that. "It wasn't the home birth's fault." I scramble to justify my birthing choice. "Home birth is statistically as safe or safer than hospital birth. My midwife will be licensed and experienced. There's no reason why I should have to go through another horrendous hospital birth."

Gale's head tilts. "You'd be terrified by a hospital birth, but you're also nervous about a home birth, is that right?"

I blow out a breath. "Yeah. I guess so. The baby's got to come out some way, though."

"True." She smiles. "There's a lot to unpack here. Have you seen a therapist to explore these traumatic experiences?"

Zach's brows lift a fraction. I can hear a dozen past conversations where he's asked me to do just that.

"No."

"I'd recommend you do so. No one should have to wade through such muddy waters alone." She flips a few pages in front of her. "It looks like I take your insurance if you'd like to see me for continued therapy. It could be in person."

Zach's voice breaks into the conversation. "That'd be great."

I meet his eyes across the screen. Those golden orbs ask me if I'm going to fight him on this too. For over a decade, I've proclaimed that I've moved on from my messy past without looking back. I've quoted Philippians 3:13: "Forgetting what is behind and straining toward what is ahead, I press on toward the goal to win the prize for which God has called me."

Zach has reluctantly agreed to let it lie, but he used to beg me to talk about it with someone. It seems this is his open door.

I moisten my dry lips. He's finding a way to make peace with me carrying my sister's baby. How can I deny him the one thing he's asking in return? "Okay."

I will do two things for two people I love. Which one will cost me most? The birth now seems the least of my worries.

~~

Ivy let herself in Everly's front door, nasty kombucha in hand. "Hello. It's me."

Zach waved from the couch. The screech of basketball shoes on a hardwood floor sounded from the TV. "Ev's in the bedroom."

"Got it." She made her way through the hallway and pushed open the primary bedroom door.

Her sister was bent over a yoga mat in the downward dog position.

"Trying to relax?" Ivy set her purse and the drink on the dresser.

"Look at the size of that needle. I'm terrified." Everly rose and pointed to the bed where a capped needle lie. "Thanks for coming. Zach took one look at it and said no way."

Ivy sat on the edge of the bed. "Aw. Sweet man. He can't stand to inflict pain on you."

The corner of Ev's mouth tipped up. "Good thing you have no trouble."

"Har har."

Everly sighed. "I already drew the progesterone oil into the syringe and switched out the needle. All you need to do is insert it."

Ivy picked up the needle-capped syringe. "Where does this go? Right in the butt?"

"Upper right quadrant."

"Ready to get it over with? I brought you a disgusting reward for when we're done."

"Kombucha?"

"You've got it."

"Let's go." Everly came to the edge of the bed, lowered her leggings to expose the right spot, and leaned over. "You sure you know how to do this?"

"Of course. I gave myself shots in the stomach, remember? To stimulate my ovaries to produce eggs." She'd heard these progesterone shots were far more painful, but the basic concept was the same.

"There should be an alcohol wipe."

Ivy found it. "Yep. I'll get you lidocaine for next time. It will help." She disinfected the area, glanced over the instruction pamphlet, and uncapped the needle. "Here we go." She counted to three, then administered the progesterone. "One down. How many more to go?"

"Five before the implantation, then nine or ten after." Everly straightened, her face lined with pain. "Give me my kombucha, woman."

Ivy handed it over. "We're getting close. Three viable embryos. Genetic carrier on the final stretch of prep." What would they do if three wasn't enough? What would they do with the extra embryos if Everly got pregnant on the first try?

All the potential problems swirled in Ivy's mind. So many variables she had no say over. Like the social worker had said during their consult, "Welcome to parenthood." She needed to get used to not being in control.

Everly sipped her fermented drink with the same satisfaction Ivy would have slurped on a milkshake. On the bed next to Ivy, Ev's phone pinged. Ivy checked the notification.

"Email from Ancestors List."

Everly's gaze snapped to the phone. "Is it a new hit?"

Ivy shook her head. "Message from Cassaundra Walt."

"Oh." Everly lowered herself to sit next to Ivy, but then popped back up. "Ouch. I'll stand." She waved toward her phone. "You can read it. She sent me a strange message a while back that I think was meant for someone else. Haven't heard from her since. Doubt she has any info."

Ivy pulled it up and read it out loud.

Everly,

I apologize for the misunderstanding. When you said you were looking for information on Henrietta, I assumed you were doing so because she fought in the Civil War disguised as a man. That's what most people who contact me are interested in. I do have a ton of info on Henrietta. I've been slow in uploading it to the site, but I'll get there eventually. It might be easier to video chat. Would you be up for that? In the meantime, here are a few pictures of her. One is of her as a soldier, and the others are of her after the war. The other woman in the third picture is her sister Loreen.

I look forward to hearing from you.
Cassie

Ivy looked at an open-mouthed Everly. "What? We have a relative who fought secretly in the Civil War?"

"I want to see the pictures." Ev sat next to her, apparently no longer focused on the pain in her behind.

"Oh man," Ivy said as she pulled the first picture up. "She fought on the Confederate side. Bummer."

Everly shrugged. "If our whole family is from this area, it makes sense. People in the South fought for the South."

"Yeah." Still. Not exactly something one could brag about. She studied the woman before her. How could anyone have mistaken her for a man? Had short hair been enough to fool people? "She looks feminine to me."

"I was thinking the same thing. How could she have kept her gender a secret from all those men?"

"You're going to connect with this Cassie lady, right? I want to hear more."

"I guess so. It doesn't help with our original purpose, but it's interesting."

Ivy pulled up the next picture. In this one, Henrietta stood to the side in a plaid day dress. A long, dark braid hung down her back. She looked into the distance as if a promise hung there.

"She must not have died in the war, then," Everly mused.

Ivy held Henrietta's picture next to her sister's face. "You look like her."

"Do I now?" Everly struck a pose similar to Henrietta's.

"You do. You could play her in reenactments."

"I'll look into that." Everly nudged Ivy's arm. "Let's see the last picture."

Ivy pulled it up and sucked in a breath. It was like looking in a mirror. Henrietta and her sister Loreen looked eerily similar to them. "Wow."

"Crazy."

In the picture, Henrietta's arm rested protectively on Loreen's. Something on Henrietta's hand caught Ivy's eye. She gasped. "Ev! She has your ring."

"What?" Ev pulled the phone closer to her face and squinted at the image. She brought her hand up. The sapphire gleamed back at them. "Oh, my goodness. It *is* Mom's ring."

Ivy grasped her sister's hand. "Message Cassaundra back. Whatever the story here, it's *our* story, Ev. We were supposed to find out about this. Set up the video call and make sure I'm on it."

Chapter 12

I EXPECT TO ARRIVE AT HOME THROUGH STORMS AND HURRICANES. I EXPECT IF I NEVER MEET YOU ON THIS SHORE OR NEVER SEE YOUR FACE ANYMORE, I EXPECT TO MEET YOU IN HEAVEN, GOD BEING MY HELPER.

NOV. 24, 1863, SERGEANT SIMEON A. TIERCE

Manassas, Virginia
July 1861

Both women glared at Henrietta as they left the regiment. She huffed. What about a thank you for saving Jesse's life? *Jessica's* life. But no. Despite the doctor's admonishments, they felt she would have pulled through fine without intervention. Fools.

It didn't take the doctor long to learn Jesse's secret. When he exposed her gender, Francine confessed as well. As much venom as they spewed at her through sharp glances, Henrietta expected the duo to rat her out as well, but they didn't. They probably didn't want her tagging along with them.

Their rejection twisted her gut. The Confederate victory didn't do a thing to lift her spirits. She'd set out to do something noble, and they labeled her a traitor. She'd thought she'd found a sisterhood, but they'd snubbed her. Perhaps she fit in better with men than she did with women. Once again, she was alone in a world of men. But the one man she longed to set eyes on again was nowhere to be seen.

That green-eyed soldier must have been from a different regiment. Or had she hit the ground so hard she'd hallucinated? Perhaps he was only a figment of her imagination.

What she wouldn't give to have a cup of tea with Loreen. How exciting it would be to chat about her mystery man. To have someone, anyone, she could confide in, share her burden with. Being unknown was so lonely. Hollow. The knowledge that the only people who could see past the facade were miles away, far beyond reach, tightened inside her, curling into a tight ball in her chest.

She could act tough. She *was* tough. Far more capable than what most people gave women credit for. But she had the niggling sense she wasn't meant to be strong alone. She wandered into the woods, heart aching. Branches snapped under her feet as sun filtered through the trees. Many from her company busied themselves burying dead Union soldiers, but she hadn't the capacity. She needed to gulp life-giving air before she lost herself completely.

Should she try praying? God hadn't been too kind to them in the past few years, but maybe He'd give her a listen. On account of Mama, if nothing else. She had nowhere else to go. Everyone who loved her felt a world away. Her attempts at friendship had failed. Death crept close enough to touch, and she needed something, someone besides herself.

"Lord," she whispered. "Send me a friend, will You? Someone who trusts me to know them. Someone I can trust to know me." She swallowed against the swollen feeling in her throat. "In this horrible mess of war, show me something good."

~~

Henrietta reclined under an oak at Manassas. The sun filtered through the leaves, casting dancing shadows on the ground. The way the shadows flitted about made her think of her sisters. What were they doing right now? Their last letter indicated full bellies and warm blankets. Did they have enough money? Could she quit soldiering and return home? She could find other employment as a female, if need be. But what if Millie got sick again? What if Loreen couldn't find work? They could end up in the same place they'd started. The possibility of hunger clawing at her again shook her to the core. Weren't they only one disaster away from starvation? No, she couldn't quit.

Out of the corner of her eye, she glimpsed a soldier walking toward her, shoulders hunched as if he carried a great burden. Time to put thoughts of home aside and be sure her masculine mask was firmly in place.

The soldier crouched beside her. Stuck out his hand. "Hello. I'm Bernie."

As she took his hand, his breath hitched. He searched her face. She examined his. Or … hers?

"Bernie," the soldier repeated, then whispered, "Bernice."

Bernice? Had God heard her prayer after all? This had to be the friend she'd asked for. Panic welled in Bernie's eyes. Oh dear. Henrietta had yet to reciprocate their shared secret. She leaned forward and whispered her name, revealing her true self.

~~

Dearest Henry,

Goodness, you move around a lot. I'd only just sent you a letter when I received yours saying you'd switched regiments again. Please stay put for a time. It will make it easier for us.

Word reached us of the Battle of Big Bethel. Were you a part of it? I still shudder to imagine Yankees shooting at you. If only there was another way.

I finally secured a job at the general store in Faison. I've only begun working, and it's hard to keep up with all there is to learn. Mr. Sawyers is a grumpy fellow and nearly every word he speaks to me is a cross one. I fear he'll fire me for some infraction or another before the week is through.

A few days ago, I fumbled the scoop and spilled sugar on the floor. I thought for sure I was done for there, but after giving me a stern talking to, he told me to make sure I came on time the next day. It's a dreadful long walk to town, and I must awaken before dawn to arrive on time. I miss Ma more than ever.

At first, I applied for a position as a nanny. I purchased a new dress and arrived looking as prim and proper as I'd ever been. The clothes and shoes weren't enough, however. One look at me and the matron could tell I was lower class. She stuck her nose in the air and said they'd already filled the position, only they hadn't. It was listed in the paper again the next week. Some actress I am. I can't fool anyone into thinking I'm someone other than who I am. A poor, foolish girl with a bright, brave older sister.

Again, I beg you to stay safe. You are our family's anchor. Without you, we'd be tossed to bits at sea.

Yours Truly,
Loreen

~~

Rags in hand, Henrietta trekked through splintered woods. Heat and humidity strangled the air. Sulfur from the battle clung to her nose. She'd fought bravely today, but never had she needed more courage than now. Bernie had lost her baby, the baby she hadn't even known she was carrying but desperately wanted. And it was Henrietta's job to comfort her.

She froze, the image of Mama's lifeless body pummeling her. Henrietta had attended Charlotte's and Bea's births, as young as she was. Those had been happy occasions.

Millie's birth had been altogether different. As the night wore on, Mama's cries had grown increasingly weaker, more breath than sound, until, with a strangled cry that might as well have come from an animal as from a human, Mildred slid into the world, and Mama slid out. If only she'd pleaded with Mama to fight to stay with them instead of blindly agreeing to take her place.

Henrietta shook herself from the memory. A couple of yards ahead of her, past a few trees, her friend mourned. A child. A mother. Loss was loss. Affecting different corners of the heart but bruising just the same.

Bernie's wail pierced the air, ricocheting off the trees, reverberating in Henrietta's core. With a fortifying breath, she strode toward her friend.

Bernie held a miniature infant in her palm. Fragile. Bloody and devoid of fine details. But very much a baby.

A lump formed in Henrietta's throat. "Oh, Bernie." She fell to her knees as tears brimmed in her eyes. She dropped the rags and instead cradled her hands under Bernie's. She had no words to ease this burden. She could only lend the support of her hands and tears.

Mama would have spouted hope of heaven, telling Bernie she would see her child again. Should Henrietta at least say those words, even if she didn't quite believe them? Perhaps Jesus was cradling the babe in His arms. Maybe He looked kindly upon such innocent ones and only turned His back on those who displeased Him. People like her.

The child deserved to be buried. Her stomach soured at the thought of some animal feasting on her. Bernie needed the assurance that her child rested in peace.

Henrietta broke the hushed cocoon. "We can bury her."

Bernie could only nod.

Henrietta stood and brushed off her knees as she surveyed the ground around them. She scuffed at rocks and sticks with the toe of her boot. "What about here?" She pointed to the base of a pine.

"Sure."

Heavy footsteps approached. The women locked wide-eyed gazes. Bernie's fingers closed around her stillborn child, and she lowered her hand to her side.

"Who's here?" A battle-worn man assessed her. His full beard and hair were tinged gray from smoke, and his uniform bore the marks of the fight.

"Just us, sir." Henrietta saluted. "Private Henry Frontenac and Private Bernie …"

"Reisenfeld," Bernie answered.

"Are you injured?" He studied Bernie with a piercing gaze.

She looked down at her bloody uniform and nodded.

His brow furrowed as he peered at her. "Your color looks good. I'll fetch a doctor."

Bernie shot Henrietta a panicked gaze.

Henrietta put a finger to her mouth and waited for the man to retreat. Then she bent close and whispered, "Let's bury the baby right quick, then we need to get out of here before a doctor comes looking. We'll head to the creek and get you cleaned up and back to your regiment."

"Okay."

Henrietta dug at the thirsty ground with a stick until it was deep enough to keep scavenging animals away. Bernie lay the miniature form inside. Both women pushed dirt to cover the child.

Should she pray? It was the least she could do. Maybe God would hear, not for her own sake, but for the babe's.

"Lord," Henrietta prayed, "look over this precious child. Welcome this baby into Your kingdom."

"They're right back here." The booming voice made it clear this vigil was over.

Bernie gasped. "Do we run?" She glanced around wildly.

"They'd see us."

Bernie clutched her friend's arm. "What do we do?"

"There's nothing we can do." Her season with this regiment was finished. Time for another switch. "We fess up."

"Fess up? And get sent home?"

Henrietta patted Bernie on the back. "It'll be all right. Trust me." She stood.

The gray-tinged man appeared, accompanied by a young man with spectacles carrying a doctor's bag.

"Oh my." The doctor peered down at Bernie over his glasses. "What's the nature of your injury?"

Bernie gaped like a fish.

It was time. Henrietta spoke up. "This soldier is uninjured, sir. We are Private Reisenfeld and Frontenac, two soldiers who fought bravely today in the heat of battle." She squared her shoulders and lifted her chin. "Two female soldiers, sir."

~~

Henrietta swished down the street, her skirt ruffling with each movement. Oh, how heavenly to be in feminine attire again, if only for a little while. She swayed her hips, relishing the freedom of being herself. Of not having to hide.

Beside her, Bernie's frown proved her far less delighted by the turn of events.

"Are they still watching?" Bernie whispered.

Henrietta glanced over her shoulder. Greenman's scowl was barely visible in the distance. "Greenman is."

Bernie groaned. "Is he going to watch until we get to the station? Why didn't he carry us over his shoulder and put us on the train car himself?"

That would have been interesting. Henrietta chuckled.

"I don't know what you think is so funny. We've been kicked out of the army! Put in lady clothes. Sent home. I'm disgraced." Bernie hung her head. So dramatic.

"First time, I take it."

"First time what? Getting kicked out of the army?"

"Yes."

"Yes, it was my first time. You?"

"Third." Henrietta explained how they could enlist with another company. How she'd done it before. They'd get to serve together. A picture of Jesse and Francis flitted through her mind. They might have snubbed her, but they'd had each other. How nice for them.

Now she had someone to share soldier life with. Once again, she had a sister. A sister-in-arms. Not that Bernie could ever take Loreen's place. But the presence of someone who *knew* her and enjoyed her company was a godsend. Did God send her this blessing? Had He turned His face to her yet again, after all these years?

How dangerous to hope for such a thing. Far safer to presume it luck. But with the breeze caressing her face and these few moments free of pretense next to her new friend, hope sparked inside her just the same.

~~

Dearest Loreen,

I apologize for yet another move on my part. I am now serving with the Eighteenth Mississippi. Please use the enclosed information when writing me from here out. I will try not to switch regiments again as I know it has confused you.

I have good news. I've found a friend, a soldier like me who goes by the name of Bernie. It has been delightful to have someone to confide in, someone who sees me for myself.

I'm sure you've heard of the Battle of Manassas. It was brutal, but once again, I made it out unscathed. Don't you worry. Our troops are high-spirited and a bit drunk on the victory. Things around here have settled down. The war will soon end, and I'll return to you fit as a fiddle and full of lively tales.

How's the job going? How is Gretchen managing at home? How's Pa? Please tell me of the people I love.

Yours Truly,
Henry

Sharing a tent with Bernie was a dream come true, almost like being home again enjoying late-night chats with Loreen. Only the Eighteenth Mississippi's camp in Leesburg wasn't nearly so private. Even in the seclusion of their own tent, they had to keep up the ruse. One never knew who was listening.

After their victory at Manassas, things had eased up. There were fewer drills. More free time. Bernie and Henrietta lounged against a tree, observing others throughout the camp and talking of life back home.

Bernie picked at a blade of grass. "What are your plans after the war?"

"Plans?" Henrietta spun her hat in her hands.

"Yes, silly. I want to expand the farm. We have Tunis sheep, but I want to bring Marino sheep in. Hermann wants to grow the herd too. What about you? What are your dreams for the future?"

Dreams. She released a humorless chuckle. "I've never thought about it."

Bernie turned to face her, one brow raised. "Never?"

Henrietta shrugged. "I've never been able to think past my next meal. But now …" She scratched the back of her neck. "My belly is full."

"Full?" Bernie tilted her head.

Her laughter held mirth. Her friend didn't know how good she had it. "Yes, full." She shifted and pulled an acorn from under her leg. "My family is taken care of. I'm safe and cared for."

Bernie nudged her. "Safe? We could get called into battle at any moment."

"I've never felt safer than I do here." How could she explain it? Bernie had never stared starvation in the face. Hunger had stolen her sleep. An old memory surfaced, and Henrietta gasped.

"What?"

"Old Man Meager is gone." Her voice was merely a whisper.

"Who?"

She grabbed Bernie's hand before she could think better of it, then dropped it as if it were a hot coal. A quick glance around showed no one was paying attention. Thank goodness. "When I was little, there was a beggar in our town. We called him Old Man Meager." She shuddered. "He was a gaunt man, yet somehow imposing. His clothes were full of holes and smelled something awful. All the children feared him and told stories about him."

Henrietta leaned closer to her comrade as if sharing a grand secret.

"Some said he used to be a wealthy landowner, and he lost everything because he was too greedy. One boy swore Old Man Meager roamed the streets begging for coins because he was greedy still, and if you didn't give him any, he'd suck your soul from you."

Bernie covered her mouth. "Oh dear. You didn't believe him, did you?"

"I was young. I didn't know what to believe. Once, he rattled his cup at me, and I had nothing to give. I told him as much, but he kept asking. He said he'd come back later. That I should go home and get something for him."

"So, why'd you say he was gone?"

"Because he hasn't plagued my nightmares since ..." When was the last time? "Since I met you." Laughter bubbled from her. "He's gone. I'm free."

Bernie smiled. "Good riddance."

Henrietta brushed her hands together as if brushing off Old Man Meager's presence. Of course, if she went home, he could come back. He probably would. One more reason to stay. With Bernie as her friend, the pull to leave had waned. She tossed her hat a few yards away, then returned to her spot. "Maybe I *can* think about what I want for my life. For my future."

"Now you're talking. If you could do anything, have anything, what would it be?"

Henrietta picked up an acorn and lobbed it through the air. It landed in the hat.

Bernie nodded her approval. "Good shot."

"Thanks." She picked up another acorn. "I think it'd be right nice to settle down and have a family." If only she could do so with the green-eyed soldier who'd consumed her thoughts most days. She sighed and sent the projectile flying. Another perfect shot. "I'm too old, though. With so many chaps dying in the war, it'll be slim pickings." And she'd never see that handsome man again.

"Twenty-one isn't *too* old." The forced cheerfulness in Bernie's tone did little to convince her.

"I think I must settle for a different dream." But what?

Chapter 13

Suburb of Wilmington, North Carolina
Present Day

I smile and shake hands with a dozen people as I attempt to leave the church's sanctuary. Every three steps, someone stops me. Some ask how Ivy is doing. My sister attends Austin's home church, but I added her to the prayer chain here, so they're invested. Some have a chiropractic question. Others only want to say hi. No one knows my body is preparing to carry a child. We've kept our plans to ourselves. Regardless, it won't be a secret forever. The implantation is next week.

I finally break free into the lobby where I cast a glance over my shoulder. Zach is trapped in conversation with Mr. Montgomery, an older man with sciatica. I snicker and make a beeline for the restroom.

I cringe inwardly as a line comes into view. As I wait, it occurs to me that Cassaundra hasn't contacted me about setting up a Zoom meeting. Perhaps she's inundated with emails. Surely, she'll respond soon.

I'm not sure why it matters, why I'm invested in some distant relative. But it feels like there's a secret to unlock here that will unleash freedom within. So, I wait.

"Great sermon, wasn't it?" Eileen asks, tucking a piece of hair behind her ear.

I smile. "Excellent." Only, what was it about again? How could I have forgotten when it's only been a few minutes? If it were a week later, pregnancy brain might apply. Is there such a thing as pre-pregnancy brain? My thoughts have been scattered.

"I love what Pastor said about how God wants to redeem our past, and how nothing we've done can thwart His purpose for our lives."

He said that? I should have paid more attention. It sounds like the sermon was meant for me. "So good," I say, putting a hand over my heart.

"Sometimes, I wonder if the way I chased drugs before I turned to Jesus will haunt me forever. But He truly has saved me to the uttermost, as it says in Hebrews."

Despite my best efforts to keep a straight face, my eyes widen. Who would have thought Eileen, of all people, had a past like that?

A response evades me.

In front of Eileen, a young mom jostles a baby on her hip. The little girl whimpers and points in the direction of the café.

"Someone's hungry." Eileen leans toward them and coos.

The mom's cheeks flush pink. "Grandma usually spoils her with a cookie after service." She turns her attention to her child. "But Grandma isn't here this week, is she?" Under her breath, she adds, "And I really have to go to the bathroom."

The line inches forward. The mom is next to enter the restroom. She turns to us sheepishly. "Could one of you hold her while I go?"

My hands tremble.

Eileen says, "Of course, dear."

But as we step inside the restroom, two stalls open at the same time. It's Eileen's turn too. The mom must have taken Eileen's offer as a collective one because she places the child in my arms.

I sputter, "O-okay."

Except it's not okay. I can't hold this baby. Sure, I might be getting ready to house a baby in my body. Birth a child into the world. But I can't hold a little girl in my arms as if I were a … mom.

Can children smell fear? Apparently not because chubby fists cup my face, smushing my cheeks. I can't help myself. I laugh. Bounce her a little.

"Hi, sweetie."

The mom's voice calls from a nearby stall. "Her name is Laurie."

"Hi, Laurie." I coo at her as if it's the most natural thing in the world. "Aren't you a cutie?"

As if on cue, she pulls on her headband, sporting a huge pink bow, and yanks it onto her face.

"Uh-oh." I struggle to right it with one hand while holding her in the other arm. She foils my haphazard attempt in seconds. "She doesn't like this headband," I call out.

The mom laughs. "Not at all. I can't quit buying them, though. They're so cute."

She's not lying. If I had a little girl, I'd probably buy the huge bows too. A pang squeezes my heart. *If I had a little girl.* I did, once. What had she looked like at this age? Did her adoptive parents dress her with gigantic bows and frilly dresses? I'll never know. My throat constricts. There's so much I'll never know about the child I had when I was seventeen.

A wave of loss laps over me. This is why I refuse to think about it. It's why I've refused counseling all these years. Talking about this tremendous loss will dredge up these horrible feelings. And for what? I can't go back. Can't change what happened. Why did I agree to meet with Gale? Our first session is a week after the implantation and dread already tightens my muscles.

Laurie spots my ring and grabs for it.

"You like this?" I hold my hand up for her to inspect. She attempts to bring my finger to her mouth. "No." I laugh. "You can't eat it."

If I had a little girl, I'd have someone to pass this ring down to as my mom passed it down to me. Mom said it's been in the family for generations. As it stands, I guess I will need to pass it down to Ivy's child. That shouldn't pain me, but it does.

Maybe I could find her. I attempt to fling the thought away the instant it enters my brain. There are too many obstacles to that curious hope. If I ever did find the child I placed for adoption all those years ago, it's not like she'd want to meet me. Even if I only wanted to pass the ring down to her, why would she want such a memento from a stranger? Heck, she might be angry with me for abandoning her. She'd probably fling Mom's ring into the ocean and never look back. No. A preposterous idea.

Laurie's mom exits the stall and washes her hands. "You're a natural." She beams at me. "She normally doesn't allow anyone unfamiliar to hold her without crying."

Strange. She hasn't cried once. Not even a whine.

I'm still holding Laurie as I exit the bathroom in front of the mom. The urgency with which I'd headed there is gone. I don't want to let her go, even for my turn in a stall.

I make a funny face, and Laurie laughs. A glorious sound. "How old is she?" I ask.

"Eleven months."

"She's precious." I should hand her back, but I need to hear that giggle again. I roll my eyes and stick out my tongue. There it is.

"Ev?" Zach's voice slams into me from across the foyer.

My gaze snaps to his, and I shudder at the toxic brew of hope and pain pooling there. He wants this. His wife as a mother. His child in my arms. His longing is nearly palpable.

I plop Laurie back into her mother's arms and rush back into the bathroom before I choke.

~~

Ivy watched the screen as the doctor inserted the embryo into Everly's womb. Fascinating. She could actually see her baby. Well, the embryo was so tiny, it wasn't visible. But she could see the little air bubble they inserted next to the embryo, showing they found the right spot.

How could big lives start so small? It was a miracle. No doubt about it. Once again, she thanked the Lord for modern medicine and the ability to create a life in this unconventional way. It wasn't what she'd envisioned, but it was her chance.

Jesus, let this little life make her home inside of my sister. Three embryos had survived, so they had two more chances after this. But God forbid they should need them. Everly did all things well. Surely, she could incubate this baby without a loss.

Ivy was sick of losses.

"How do you feel?" Dr. Diction asked.

"Good," Ivy said. Heat climbed her cheeks. She hadn't been asking her.

Dr. Diction chuckled. "And you, Mrs. Moore?"

"Fine." Everly smiled. "This was the easiest part of the whole process."

"Good." The doctor took out the catheter and snapped his gloves off. "No heavy lifting or strenuous aerobic exercise for three days. Afterward, you can resume normal activity. No restrictions. We'll see you in ten days for a blood test to see how things are faring." She narrowed her eyes. "I tell everyone this and hardly anyone listens, but I highly suggest you *don't* take a home pregnancy test. Too many false negatives."

Everly nodded. "Got it."

Ivy shifted in her seat. How could she wait a whole ten days to see if the pregnancy had taken? She'd go crazy.

"All right." The doctor stood and shook Everly's hand, then Ivy's. "I wish you the best of luck. We're going to flush the catheter to ensure the embryo didn't hitch a ride back.

Then, Mrs. Moore, you can get dressed and use the bathroom. I'll walk Mrs. Hartgrove to the lobby."

That was it? So much prepping for such a short procedure. It felt a bit anticlimactic.

Ivy followed the doctor into the lobby where Austin and Zach waited.

Austin popped up at the sight of her. "How'd it go?"

"Great." A relieved smile found its way to her lips. "Smooth as silk."

"Good." Austin broke into a grin.

Zach stood and shoved his hands in his pockets. "How's Ev? It didn't hurt, did it?"

"Not at all. She's great." She'd taken everything like a champ. Not a word of complaint, not even about the full bladder she had to have for the procedure. "She'll be out in a minute."

"I'm glad." Only he didn't look glad. Not even a hint of a smile. Ev hadn't spoken of Zach's thoughts about the whole thing. Had his position changed since their initial consultation?

Ivy explained the ten-day wait and the doctor's instructions not to take a home pregnancy test.

Austin nodded. "Makes sense."

Yeah, but that didn't mean Ivy wouldn't convince Everly to take a test anyway. Just to see.

Austin pulled her into an embrace and kissed the top of her head. "We did it," he whispered in her ear.

Her smile wobbled as she looked at him, then over at Zach's frown.

~~

I'm mixing in my yogurt starter six days after the implantation when Ivy bursts through the door. Her hands are overflowing with bags and … a bucket?

"What's all this about?" I wave to her supplies.

"I'm here to clean your house."

I arch my brow. "Clean my house?" Where did this come from?

"Yeah, so you can rest."

I turn my attention back to making homemade yogurt. "I don't need rest. Try again in a few weeks." By then, we'll have confirmed the pregnancy, and symptoms might start to set in.

Ivy drops her stuff on the kitchen counter. "You're carrying my baby. The least I can do is clean for you."

I shrug. It's not worth arguing.

"Plus, I brought this." She pulls something from a bag and slides it across the counter. A pregnancy test.

"Ivy, you know what the doctor said." I pour the milky mixture into my crock pot. Delicious, creamy yogurt will be mine in thirteen hours.

She waves me off. "Yeah, but he was only concerned about false negatives. If it comes out negative, we won't get discouraged. But if it comes out positive …"

"I don't know." I'm not exactly eager to ride an emotional roller coaster.

She bites her lower lip. "Think about it while I clean." She takes the bucket full of supplies and disappears down the hall.

"I don't need you to clean!" I yell after her. "The doctor said regular activity."

She peeks her head around the corner. "Would it kill you to put your feet up for a while?"

"Maybe," I tease.

She disappears for only a moment before popping her head in the room again. "No word from Cassaundra?"

"Nope." I've checked my email every day, but so far, nothing.

"Hmm. Busy woman." Ivy vanishes again.

I water my sad, yellowing aloe vera plant and plop on the couch. There is that documentary on organic produce I've been meaning to finish. I pick up the remote.

From across the room, the pregnancy test winks at me. What would it hurt? Doctors must err on the side of caution. It doesn't mean it's necessarily bad to check for ourselves to see if this crazy scheme is working.

No. Better not.

I turn the television on and find the documentary. As it starts, I try to pay attention, but my mind wanders. What if I'm not pregnant? I'll have to go through the whole process again. What if I am? Morning sickness was a beast with my first pregnancy. Will it be so this time around as well? Grief may have contributed to the knots in my stomach last time. Perhaps now that I've learned how to stretch and breathe through stress, it won't take me down.

I roll my neck from side to side. How will that other-level tiredness affect my ability to work at the office? What about my studies? Silly how I haven't thought this through before. I thought I'd counted the cost, but I've left some factors out. I blow out a breath. One step at a time.

A noxious odor wafts to my nose. An artificial lemon scent? I shoot up from the couch. *She wouldn't.* I stalk toward the smell. Ivy is stooping over my toilet, wearing yellow rubber gloves and scrubbing like her life depends on it.

"What are you doing?" It's a ridiculous question.

Her brow lift tells me as much. "Cleaning."

"With Lysol?" I spit the word out as if it's a curse.

She leans over and studies the bottle. "Yeah."

"Ivy, you know I only clean with all natural products. Baking soda and vinegar."

Her face scrunches as if she's disgusted. "But it's your bathroom. You've got to pull out the big guns here, right?"

"No," I sputter. "Anything that touches your skin leaks into your bloodstream in less than thirty seconds."

She waves her yellow hands. "Hence, the gloves."

"Those toxic chemicals rest on every surface, Iv. They're"—I almost say *carcinogenic* but stop myself—"not safe."

Ivy rolls her eyes. "Of course, they're safe. Hospitals use these cleaners. You need to get over yourself. I want my baby to have the healthiest environment to grow in."

Heat climbs my neck. "The healthiest? Ivy, those cleaners are poison. You're trying to poison me." I almost add *and your baby*, but that creates too cruel of a picture.

Her gloved hands fist. "That's ridiculous."

"Studies prove—"

"For every study you can show me saying natural cleaners work best, there's two that prove it takes chemicals to eradicate germs."

I huff. The nerve. She's wrong. There's a ton of research to back up my approach. Her studies are likely paid for by Big Pharma or Lysol itself. How dare she barge into my house and shove chemicals at me? There might be smoke coming out my ears.

Ivy's face is red and tight, but she lowers her voice. "It's not worth fighting about. Stress is bad for the baby." She pulls her gloves off and dumps them onto the counter. "Where's the vinegar." Her tone is laced with disdain, but I ignore it.

"I'll get it." I stalk out of the bathroom, mumbling, "but I can clean my own house."

Is this what the next nine months are going to be like? My sister hovering to make sure things are to her liking? I cringe. What's next? She'll probably forbid me from drinking raw milk and demand I follow the outdated food pyramid. She seems to forget I'm healthy and fit. I've done fine navigating life my crunchy way. I won't bend to her misguided whims. I'm doing enough for her already.

As I procure the vinegar from the kitchen cabinet, my thoughts traverse to my long-lost daughter. It irks me to have had no control over her upbringing. She'd be seventeen now.

Do her parents let her drink soda and eat processed desserts? I shudder. If she were with me, she'd know about proper nutrition and how to listen to her body to tell her what it needs. If she were with me, so many things would be different. Would I still work, or would I homeschool?

I shouldn't allow my mind to go there, yet thoughts of the child I gave up pull stronger than gravity. Busyness will keep sorrow from taking me down.

I return to the bathroom to find Ivy has tucked her cleaning supplies inside her bucket. She takes the vinegar from my outstretched hand with a pout. My shoulders relax. This isn't worth fighting about. After all my sister has been through, I hate to see her sullen, even if it is for a ridiculous reason. I throw her a bone.

"I'll take the pregnancy test."

Her face instantly transforms. "Really?"

"Yes."

I retreat to the living room only to find Ivy on my heels. I startle. "You don't plan on following me into the bathroom, do you?"

Is her indignant expression because of my sassy tone or because I want to pee on a stick in peace?

She crosses her arms. "It's my baby."

This I know. Despite my crucial role, this child isn't mine. This is not about me. That shouldn't send a pang of longing through me, but it does. Traitorous emotions. I don't want to be a mother. These feelings don't make sense.

"I'll come right out, and we can wait for the results together."

Her mouth twists, but she nods.

When I exit the bathroom, stick in hand, we sit together on the couch. Though we're supposed to wait ten minutes for the results, our eyes zero in on the minuscule window. I can't look away. One dark pink line stares back for a full four minutes before a faint second line joins it. It's so dim, I blink to ensure I'm not imagining it.

Ivy squeezes my knee. "That's a line, right?"

"I think so."

Her breath hitches. The line darkens.

"Definitely," I say, then turn to her and grin. "We're pregnant."

Ivy wears a mask of bewilderment, as if it's too good to be true, too good to believe. "We're pregnant?" she whispers in awe. Then something snaps into place, and she catapults to her feet. "We're pregnant!"

She jumps up and down, clapping, and I can't help but join her. This dream of her heart is coming true.

"Thank you, Everly." She wraps her arms around me and kisses my cheek. "Thank You, God."

I start to tremble. This is really happening. Before, it was a vague possibility in my brain. Now, it's a reality in my body.

"You okay?" Iv asks.

I smile and say, "Of course," but I don't believe it. I've started something I'm not sure I want to finish.

Chapter 14

YOU ... CANNOT BEGIN TO REALIZE WHAT WAR IS. ...
NO HOUR OF THE DAY PASSES THAT THE HEAVY
BOOM OF THE CANNON IS NOT HEARD, AND THE
SCREAMING OF THE SHELL AS IT FLIES THROUGH THE
AIR, AND ITS FINAL THUNDERING EXPLOSION AS IT
BURSTS, SCATTERING ITS DEATH MISSILES IN EVERY
DIRECTION.

NOV. 18TH, 1863, ELY S. PARKER

Leesburg, Virginia
November 1861

Dearest Henry,

How do you fare? I pray you're well. While I'm working at the store, the war is all I hear about. None of the news is good, though mothers and sisters hold out hope the best they can. I may not have to abide the gossip much longer, unfortunately.

Mr. Sawyers gave me one last warning. I arrived late again and in quite a disheveled state. The hens got loose that morning, and Gretchen and I both went in search of them. Did I even tell you we'd purchased hens? Two of them. We enjoyed fresh eggs for two weeks before I awoke to find the fence knocked down. At first, I thought it must have been from the girls at play, but when we couldn't find the fowl anywhere, I had to conclude that passing soldiers had taken them and butchered them.

I hate this war. It's made thieves of the most moral of people. Or perhaps what Mama used to say about sowing and reaping is true. You stole a chicken to feed Mildred, and now marauding soldiers stole two hens from us. Maybe that's the way of it. The justice of God or what not. Either way, I don't like it. It feels like we'd just gotten a step ahead only to fall behind again.

You'd tell me to hold my chin up, wouldn't you? So, I shall stop boohooing and remember all you're going through for us. We miss your stories and your plays. We miss you. Come home to us swiftly.

Yours Truly,
Loreen

Henrietta folded Loreen's letter with a grunt. Would her sister never answer her questions? How frustrating to wait for weeks unto months and still be left wondering exactly what was going on at home. No word of Pa at all. No word of how Gretchen was managing the home in Loreen's absence. And what was this about Loreen's job being in jeopardy? From the sound of it, her sister had arrived to work either late or disheveled more than once. How serious was the shopkeeper about letting her go? Had they stocked up on food?

To think they'd had hens. Had the thieves been Confederate or Federal? Both armies took liberties, but it would smart something fierce to find out her own people had taken from them. Was it God's justice? That would be another reason to steer clear of such a God. Even if He did answer her prayer for a friend.

She needed to write back. Only what was there to say? She couldn't burden her sister with details of Ball's Bluff. How they'd watched in horror as the Confederates chased the Yanks off the bluff into the river, shooting them as they fell.

Best not to tell Loreen how Bernie had nearly died at the end of a bayonet, saved only by Henrietta's bullet. She'd killed the man who'd nearly murdered her friend. If Loreen knew how close her death had been, she'd not be able to sleep a wink. No. Those particulars were best kept secret.

She pulled out paper and tapped her pencil.

Dearest Loreen,

I am well. Bernie and I are great friends and have made it through the Battle of Ball's Bluff together. We'll come through this war just fine.

I'm sorry to hear about the hens, but if you bought a pair before, you can do it again. Use the enclosed money for that purpose. It was a mighty smart idea. I'm proud of you.

Focus on getting to work on time and in tip-top shape. It's a decent job, one I hope you'll keep.

Please answer the questions I've asked in my previous letters. I long to know more of home.

Yours Truly,
Henry

~~

A warm April breeze tickled the nape of Henrietta's neck as she stepped forward to sign the next two years of her life away. She picked up the pen and focused on writing *Henry*, not her real name, as well as erasing any trace of feminine flourish from the scrawl. There. Done. Thank goodness for this security. Two more years of guaranteed pay, if the war lasted. She'd been waiting for such assurance ever since they arrived in Richmond a month ago. Waiting was all they'd managed to do since Ball's Bluff in October.

She turned to find Bernie, who hadn't been quite so eager to find a place in line. But her friend would reenlist, wouldn't she? Her throat constricted at the thought of Bernie departing for South Carolina and leaving Henrietta alone again. This sisterhood was a precious commodity. If she had to go back to being completely unknown, she might suffocate.

There her friend was, loafing by a cluster of trees. Henrietta pulled at her collar and forced a deep inhale as she meandered to Bernie. All would be well. Of course, Bernie would reenlist. She hadn't found her husband yet and had no reason to call it quits.

At least Bernie had a husband to find. Once again, Henrietta imagined that green-eyed soldier who'd helped her up in the heat of battle.

"Henry, you're blushing. Why?" Bernie's gaze sparkled.

Could she share about the man who had monopolized her thoughts? Of course, she could. This was Bernie. Her closest friend. "Don't tease me." Henrietta looked around to ensure they were alone, then dropped her voice. "I was just thinking about a soldier I saw once who I thought was right handsome."

Bernie laughed. "What's the harm in that?"

Henrietta shook her head. What a ridiculous question.

"Look," Bernie whispered, "you said yourself, since your needs are being cared for, you can finally think about your future. Maybe that includes finding a fella to settle down with."

"Hogwash." She could never form an attachment disguised as a man. And even if she could, even if she found the soldier she dreamed of, it would be unwise to fall for a man doomed for the front.

Perhaps she was overreacting. It had only been a flutter in her belly. Nothing much. Maybe it didn't mean anything. She'd never given more than a passing glance to the opposite sex. That didn't have to change. She needed to keep her focus on providing for her sisters and let nothing distract her.

"You don't have to do this." The earnestness in Bernie's voice snaked through her defenses. "You needn't risk your life in battle to provide for your family. There must be another way. Besides signing away the next two years of your life, I mean."

Did Henrietta's expression look as hollow as she felt? "Too late."

She'd already signed the papers. Her family might be in better straits than before, but without Pa's income, their situation remained precarious. They still owed the doctor money, and another sickness could leave them desperate again.

She pushed a smile to the surface. It wouldn't do for her friend to feel sorry for her. Bernie had enough problems of her own. No need to add Henrietta's burdens to her already laden shoulders.

She would put all thought of the opposite sex out of her mind, at least until after the war. Or until after some of her sisters were well-situated with beaus of their own. By then, she'd be an old maid, far past marriageable age. Would she need to live the rest of her life as a man to earn a livable wage? God forbid. What she wouldn't give to twirl in a skirt, free of ill-fitting trousers.

That night, Henrietta and Bernie lounged against a tree. She maneuvered her back against the bark to scratch a persistent itch along her spine. Orange and yellow flames danced above a nearby campfire, nearly hypnotizing her with their movement. She could let her mind go numb, her heart too. Not thinking, not feeling, just floating in this space of the unknown. If Bernie left, she might crumble. And she couldn't crumble. Best not to dwell on the possibility of being alone again.

A man stepped near the fire and warmed his hands. She squinted at him. Was it … Could it be? His full lips tipped into a smile as he spoke to someone nearby. As he leaned close, the flames illuminated a trimmed beard covering his angular jaw. No, this wasn't her mystery soldier. His profile was too square. Still, he was good-looking. She willed him to turn her way. What color eyes did he have? Certainly not green. Brown, maybe, like his hair.

"Take a look at that soldier. He's a mite handsome, wouldn't you say?" She kept her voice low. "He must be new. I don't recall seeing him before."

As if sensing she spoke about him, the soldier turned and locked gazes with her. Her heart thudded as he stepped toward them. She spoke out of the corner of her mouth. "Goodness! He's coming this way."

Bernie nudged her. "Remember who you are, *Henry*." She scrambled to her feet and stuck out her hand. "Hello, I'm Bernard."

Why was Bernie acting so strange? Henrietta stood and shook his hand as well. "And I'm Henry."

"Freddy Rempart. Nice to meet you."

"Good to meet you." Bernie spoke as fast as a rabbit running from a wolf.

Henrietta studied him. His eyes were as blue as a mountain creek. Not quite as captivating as her dream soldier, but pleasant. "You're new?"

"Joined this morning. Had to take care of business back home before I could enlist." Not a moment too soon.

"Glad to have you on board." Henrietta patted him on the back. Whoa. Firm. Muscular.

"Thanks. I've been looking for friendly chaps. Seems like you're the welcoming committee."

"That's us." Henrietta roped an arm around Bernie's shoulder, pulling her close.

Bernie forced a grin. "We were about to retire for the night, but perhaps tomorrow, I can best you in a game of checkers."

Retire? Already? She opened her mouth to protest, but Bernie stepped on her toe. What was wrong with her? Henrietta slid her foot away.

"Retire this early?" Freddy lifted a brow.

"It's been a long day." Bernie's voice sounded pinched and awkward.

It wouldn't do for Freddy to think they didn't want to be around him. "We were on night patrol last night."

"Ah." Freddy nodded. "Understandable. See you tomorrow, then."

They headed toward their tent. When they were out of earshot, Henrietta whispered, "What was that about?"

Bernie glanced over her shoulder. "I know him."

Henrietta's mouth parted. "You know Freddy?"

"Yes. He was a childhood neighbor."

"What's he doing in the Eighteenth Mississippi?"

Bernie rolled her eyes. "I don't know. What are we doing in the Eighteenth Mississippi?"

"Well, he didn't recognize you. That's good."

"Not yet. But it's dark. What if the resemblance hits him when the lighting's better?" She touched Henrietta's shoulder. "You cannot call me Bernie. Call me Bernard."

"I'll try. It'll be difficult."

"We have to steer clear of him."

Of all the luck. They met a dashing man and couldn't spend time in his presence? Probably better that way. Nothing could come of it. Still … "Then why'd you offer to play him checkers?"

"I didn't want to appear suspicious."

"Don't you think it'll be a bit suspicious when you don't make good on your offer?"

"I haven't thought that far ahead."

Henrietta's laugh came out as a snort. "This will be a fun game of cat and mouse."

Sleeping that night proved difficult. Had she been tempted to flirt? She barely recognized herself. It'd all started with haunting forest-green eyes. What did she think? If she couldn't have him, she'd flirt with any other good-looking man? This was not the time to develop an interest in men. She draped her arm over her eyes, blocking out the glow from the full moon. How had she gotten herself into this mess?

~~

Henrietta didn't see Freddy again until dinner the next day. While she made coosh out of bacon and cornmeal, Bernie split more wood for the fire with the knife the boys liked to call an Arkansas toothpick.

Freddy loped up to them, stretching his arms over his head. "Hiya, boys."

Bernie gave a tight smile. "Hello, Freddy."

Henrietta would give him a warm welcome if Bernie wouldn't. She waved and patted the stump next to her, ignoring Bernie's glare. Yeah, they were supposed to avoid him, but they couldn't turn him away now that he was here. Might as well learn more about him.

"So, Freddy," Henrietta said, "where are you from?"

He leaned forward and laced his fingers together. "Corinth, recently, but Charleston originally."

Henrietta sat forward. "How interesting—"

"What made you move?" Bernie stopped chopping wood and turned the knife over in her hands.

He smiled. "Don't tell me you're a South Carolinian."

Bernie nodded. "From Honey Hill."

"It's a splendid state. I'd be there still if not for my wife. She hails from Corinth. We live there to be near her family."

Married? Henrietta sighed. Of course, he was married. How could such a stunning man not already be hitched?

"Any children?" Bernie asked.

He straightened. "One boy. Two years old. Buster."

Bernie sounded pained. "Congratulations. You must be proud."

"Proud as can be." His chest puffed out. "How about you? Married? Children?"

Bernie shook her head.

He turned to Henrietta. "You?"

She scoffed. "Not me." Never her. All the good men would be long taken by the time this war ended and her family was situated. She'd better get used to the idea of spinsterhood.

"Well, it will come."

No, it wouldn't. But that wasn't his fault. Henrietta slid coosh onto two tin plates. "Want some?" she asked Freddy.

"No, I'm all right. I'll have my slave cook me something in a bit. He's laundering my clothes at the present."

"Suit yourself."

The women picked at the meal. Disgusting. She'd gotten distracted for the second time of late, her thoughts swirling around men.

"You burnt the bacon again," Bernie mumbled.

Henrietta forced a chuckle. She couldn't let on that Bernie's comment rankled. She cast a glance at Freddy. "Aren't you disappointed you passed? Bernie and I take turns cooking. You'd have a better meal tomorrow." She lifted her fork to her mouth, then paused. *Bernie.* She'd called her friend Bernie.

"Bernie, you say? Is that what you go by, Bernard?"

Oh no.

"That's right." Bernie's gaze remained on her plate.

He tilted his head. "I used to know a Bernie."

"You don't say." Bernie picked up her knife, tugged a long branch in front of her, and began trimming.

"It was a girl, actually. Bernice, I'd guess, though I never heard her called anything but Bernie. Plucky little thing." His voice took on a reminiscent air. "She wasn't afraid to get her hands dirty, that's for sure. Caught frogs and lizards. It was nearly like she was one of the boys. Her parents had the hardest time teaching her to be ladylike."

Bernie hacked at the branch with her knife.

"You remind me of her, actually."

Bernie's head yanked up.

"Something about your eyes."

A gasp rent the air. Crimson bled through Bernie's trousers at her right thigh. Henrietta stood, plate and fork clattering to the ground. Bernie had cut herself with the bowie knife. Freddy and she huddled around Bernie.

Henrietta knelt in front of her. "Here. Let me see."

Bernie's leg shook as she stretched it out.

"I'll fetch the doctor." Freddy started to jog away.

"No!" Bernie gritted out. "I'll be fine. I don't need a doctor."

His brow furrowed. "What do you mean? You have an injury. Of course, you need a doctor."

"No." Henrietta firmed her voice. "We can take care of it. Fetch us bandages, will you?"

"No, I won't. I'm going to get the …" He looked back and forth between them, then zeroed in on Bernie's face. He blinked. His jaw dropped. "Bernie?"

"Please don't tell," Bernie whispered. Her eyes pleaded with him.

"Bernie?" he repeated, his voice raspy.

She nodded.

"What are you doing here?"

"Fighting for the one I love."

Henrietta stepped close to him and put a hand on his arm. No romantic tingles accompanied this touch. "Now, please go fetch bandages so she can continue to do it."

He shifted his weight from foot to foot, clearly torn. His jaw worked from side to side. Finally, he shoved a hand through his hair and turned to go.

"Do you think he went to get bandages, the doctor, or the colonel?" Bernie bit her lip.

Henrietta shrugged. "I don't know, and we can't worry about it now. Let's take care of this wound."

With a wet handkerchief, Henrietta wiped away excess blood. Bernie pressed the handkerchief to the wound to stop the flow. A few minutes later, Freddy returned with bandages.

"Thank you." Henrietta met his concerned gaze. He looked as if he might run off and tell on them at any moment. They weren't in the clear yet. She needed to ensure his allegiance. "Can you help me get her to our tent?"

Henrietta hooked her arm through one of Bernie's, and Freddy hooked his through the other. With their support, she managed to limp to her tent.

"Stand guard, will you?" Henrietta asked Freddy.

He nodded.

Inside the tent, Henrietta helped Bernie undress, then she wrapped the bandages around her wounded leg. Once her pants were back on, Bernie lay down. Henrietta lifted the flap and went out.

Freddy's deep voice shook. "So, are you a-a—"

"Am I a woman, you mean?" Relief coursed through her at his question. Relief? Shouldn't she be terrified to confess?

"Yes. I guess that's what I mean."

"I am." Her answer rushed out of her like a gust of wind. Freedom. She couldn't help but smile.

His face clouded. Not the response she was looking for. Was he thinking of snitching on them? She and Bernie were in a good place here, together. Who would enlist Bernie if she got kicked out? No one would want her with an injured leg. Henrietta had to reassure him.

"But I'm a fine soldier. Bernie and I both are. We fought in Manassas and Ball's Bluff, and we'll fight in whatever other battles we face. Don't you think that because we're women that we're not up to the task."

"I don't know what to think."

"Just don't say anything. We've worked real hard to get where we are. Let us be. Please."

When he looked into her eyes, camaraderie bound them together. It wasn't romance, as she had once hoped. Not the gaze of star-crossed lovers, but the bond of two people who cared for an injured comrade. Two people who counted Bernie as a friend. They would protect her. Fight for her.

Henrietta ducked into the tent.

Bernie's worried voice floated through the air. "Do you think he'll tell?"

"No. Most decisively not." She'd never had a brother before, but she had one now.

"How can you be sure?"

"I have a sense about these things." She dropped onto her blanket. "He's handsome. Too bad he's married."

"You're something else. You didn't have to confess, you know. He'd be none the wiser if you denied it."

She shook her head. How could she describe how good it felt to let her secret loose? "I'm proud of who I am. Wish I didn't have to hide it from anyone." She rolled onto her side and propped onto her elbow. "Can you imagine a world where society acknowledged women as brave and strong instead of merely docile and dutiful?" A world where she'd never have to hide.

"What a world that would be."

Chapter 15

SISTERS SHARE A BOND UNLIKE ANY OTHER—
THORNIER, BUT ALSO TENDER, FULL OF POSSIBILITY.

JOY MCCULLOUGH, BLOOD WATER PAINT

Suburb of Wilmington, North Carolina
Present Day

Fatigue pulls on my limbs as I climb from the car. If I can make it to the sofa, I'll collapse there until Zach carries me to bed. I've been wanting to check back in with Cassaundra to make sure she didn't forget about planning a Zoom meeting, but that will have to wait. I'd forgotten how pregnancy can make one inert. Actually, I don't remember feeling this tired ever in my life. Maybe I did with my first pregnancy, but time has softened those edges. The only thing that still sticks out to me is the otherworldly feeling of my baby when it kicked inside of me.

My neighbor, Mrs. Avendale, is watering her plants and having far more success than I've ever had with vegetation. I wave to her and drag my feet toward my front door.

"Everly, dear, how are you?" Mrs. Avendale smiles at me. An enormous straw hat covers her puffy white hair.

"I'm good. You?" The response leaks out without thought. Good is relative. I'll be far better when I'm horizontal.

"Fine, fine." She shuts the spray nozzle off and shuffles toward me. "I've been wondering, can you teach me how to make your banana bread? I've tried my hand at it a dozen times, and it never turns out like the heavenly loaf you brought me a few months back."

The sweet lady lives alone. I haven't seen any visitors in longer than I can remember. I've tried to be a blessing to her throughout the years, bringing homemade treats and sitting to chat. Loneliness surrounds her like a thick cloud. I make a point to dissipate it whenever I can.

"Sure." I angle fully toward her as if to reassure her I don't want to flee, though the sofa calls to me. "I'd be happy to share my recipe."

Her smile falters. "That's just it. You already gave it to me, but I can't seem to get it right."

I gave it to her? Oh yeah. I did. "Almond flour can be a bear to work with. How about I come over sometime and we can make a loaf together?"

Her countenance brightens. "That would be lovely. How about now?"

It's my smile's turn to falter. I catch myself and force the corners of my mouth back up. "I'm not sure ..." I don't have the energy right now, but I'm kidding myself if I think tomorrow will be different. When does pregnancy fatigue lift? In the second trimester? We could try a baking date in a few months.

"I have all the ingredients."

I scramble for an excuse that will not reveal my pregnancy. I don't want to talk about this odd arrangement. Not yet. Not until I have to. *Lord, help me out here.*

Go.

Seriously? God wouldn't expect me to do something so impossible.

Those who wait on the Lord will renew their strength.

As I argue with God, Mrs. Avendale looks on expectantly. I shouldn't fall asleep at four in the afternoon anyway. It would kill my sleep cycle. I cast one last longing look toward my front door and concede. "Sure. Sounds great."

Mrs. Avendale yanks the hat from her head. Her hair is flat on top but billows at the sides like clouds. "Wonderful! Let's get to it."

As I follow her inside her house, my feet no longer drag. Her home's charm draws me in. She has a thing for cows. Miniature cow figurines grace her bookshelf, side tables, and the top of her old-style box television. A black-and-white splotched rug covers her living room floor. We've had discussions previously about her idyllic childhood on a farm. After my last visit, it took everything in me not to run out and buy a dozen chickens and a goat. How amazing would fresh eggs and goat's milk be? Zach issued a firm veto.

Now the desire to be a homesteader rises in me again as I follow her to the similarly decorated kitchen. True to her word, browning bananas and almond flour sit on the counter.

As we measure out and mix ingredients, I prod her to talk again about her younger days in a simpler age. "Back then, there weren't all these distractions." She waves her hand in the direction of the television, which is just out of sight. "Technology takes away from what's important."

"Which is?" I prop my elbows on the island, leaning in.

"People. Family." Her shoulders stoop. "My biggest regret is not having children."

I suck in a breath. For all the conversations we've had, we've never discussed her immediate family. I'd assumed she had grown children somewhere. "You and your husband never ..."

She shakes her head. "I had one miscarriage early in our marriage and never wanted to try again. It seemed too much to risk the heartache of another loss." Her gaze floats to the ceiling as if she's imagining another path her life could have taken. When she meets my gaze, it's with conviction. "If I had it to do over, I would have tried for another." She chuckles sadly. "Then maybe I'd have children and grandchildren to visit instead of bugging my next-door neighbor."

I put my hand over hers. "You're not bugging me."

It's true. I've forgotten I was tired. The simple act of baking amongst conversation has revitalized me. It's almost like God knew what He was talking about.

When we pull the banana bread from the oven an hour later, it's perfect. She cuts it in half and sends the other portion home with me, encircled in plastic wrap. I try not to cringe as I picture chemicals leaching into my food.

As I give her a hug and let myself out, her words seem to trail me. Will I one day be an elderly lady with such regrets? I'll have a niece who can visit. The baby growing inside me nearly guarantees I won't be completely alone. This does little to comfort me.

~~

Ivy studied her GPS. She'd missed her turn, but the app was rerouting. Stupid one-way city streets. If Everly were seeing a normal OBGYN, this prenatal visit would be far easier to get to. It'd probably be in a towering medical building next to the hospital. But no, Everly *had* to insist on a midwife. All checkups until the last month of the pregnancy would happen in the midwife's home. In her *house*. Ivy shuddered. Must be nice to be able to work from home. Unfortunately, this lady lived in a confusing neighborhood.

Her cell rang, and she pushed the button to accept.

"You coming?" What was it in her sister's tone? Not frustration that Ivy was running late. Something else.

"Almost there."

"Oh, okay. We'll wait for you before getting started."

Nice. The two of them were probably swapping recipes for elderberry syrup. "Thanks. I'll be there in a minute."

She disconnected and slowed to a crawl so she didn't miss the next turn. A few minutes later, she pulled into the driveway of a house that resembled Snow White's cottage, complete with an arched wooden door. Flowers of all kinds and colors dotted the sides of the cobblestone pathway. And here she thought this experience couldn't get any odder. She half expected a dwarf to step out from behind the bush.

Her timid steps to the front door proved she was out of her element. As she knocked, she squared her shoulders. She had to appear confident and knowledgeable. Peeking in her purse, she made sure her list of questions was in tow.

The door opened to reveal a short woman with a round face and springy blond curls. She grinned wide. "You must be Ivy."

"That's me."

The woman stepped back to allow her inside.

"I'm Wanda. Come on in. Everly's right through there." She gestured to a sitting room to the left.

Everly waved at her from an overstuffed green couch that seemed too close to the floor. Ivy joined her.

Wanda sat across from them on an equally low matching love seat. "It's so good to meet you both. I'm glad you've chosen me as your midwife."

Ivy held back a snort. *She* certainly hadn't chosen this.

"Everly and I were going over common questions people have regarding home birth. She asked if she could have a water birth." Wanda and Everly smiled at each other. "The answer is yes, of course."

Bile rose in Ivy's throat, and she fought to keep her expression neutral. "In a bathtub, or …" If Ev would be having the baby in a tub, there was no way Ivy wouldn't scrub it with every chemical known to man.

"I don't recommend bathtubs, though there have been a couple of times that's accidentally happened." Wanda laughed like she'd told a massive joke. Like exposing a newborn to germs was no big deal. "But I recommend she rent a birthing tub." She picked up a flier from the side table and handed it to Ivy.

Everly scooted closer to see. "You'll purchase a birth kit that will include most everything you need. If you two decide on a water birth, the tub rental information is there." She pointed. "And you'll need to purchase a liner for it as well."

A liner. At least that was more sanitary. Ivy stared at the picture of the inflatable blue birthing tub. Shadowed memories rose to the surface. "Is that the kind Mom used?"

Everly nodded. "It looks nearly identical."

How in the world could Ev sport such a serene look on her face when talking about such things? This entire idea was ludicrous.

Ivy thrust the paper at Everly and sat straighter. "What about the risk of infection with a water birth? I read that because blood and fluids are part of delivery, the baby could open her eyes and mouth underwater and be exposed to bacteria."

Everly's eyes narrowed, but Wanda seemed nonplussed.

"Complications with water birth are rare, and I take every measure to ensure safety." Her tone radiated kindness and understanding. "I've been a certified midwife for over fifteen years, and I've never had a baby have adverse effects from a water birth. In fact, the benefits have been proven in several studies. Shorter labors, lower pain scores, less tearing—"

"Many doctors have expressed concern." Ivy shifted in her seat.

"Yes, they have," Wanda conceded. "Just as they have expressed concern about home birth, in general. And yet"— she spread her arms in front of her—"many other doctors believe there's no increased risk. I can email you several links to different studies showing the safety of home birth."

"Okay. Sure." Not that they'd convince her.

Wanda went on to explain what prenatal visits would look like. Weight check, listening to the heartbeat, a urine test.

Ivy interrupted. "What about an ultrasound?"

"Good question." Wanda reached for another flier. "It's entirely up to you if you'd like to have an ultrasound. Some women do, some don't. You can go to a 3D/4D ultrasound facility like this one." She handed Ivy the paper.

The lifelike image that stared at her took her breath away. "Wow," she whispered, tracing the baby's nose and cheeks.

Everly leaned over to see. "Technology sure has come a long way from those grainy 2D photos."

Ivy's throat clogged with emotion. Someday soon, she could see *her* baby like this, in vivid detail. After a minute or so, she blinked and refocused. "But are these diagnostic?"

"Depending on the facility you choose, you can have a diagnostic ultrasound done if you wish. Some only do the fun 3D and 4D ones. Others do both."

"But you don't require them?" Ivy let her sister have the paper.

"Nope. It's up to you."

How irresponsible. "How will you know if something is wrong?"

"I can tell a lot by the baby's positioning and heart rate, along with Everly's symptoms." Her smile remained soft. "Even with an OBGYN and a hospital birth, there are no guarantees. Are you a believer, Ivy? A Christian, I mean."

Ivy straightened. "Yes, I am."

"Then you know the importance of relying on the Lord and trusting Him each step of the way."

What could she say? To continue to press with a hard line of questioning would only make it seem like she *didn't* trust the Lord. And, of course, she did. She could trust God and ensure the safest circumstances possible at the same time.

Everly broke the uncomfortable silence. "So, appointments every month until the end, right?"

Wanda angled toward Ev. "Correct. At around week twenty-eight, we'll do a visit every two weeks. During the last month, we'll move it to once a week. Those visits will take place in your home."

Ivy held back from taking out her list of questions. Maybe she could come across as conversational instead of as a doubting Thomas. "How long did you say you've been a midwife?"

Everly cleared her throat. When Ivy glanced to make sure she was okay, Ev skewered her with a glare.

Wanda didn't seem to notice. "It'll be sixteen years next month."

Ivy leaned back against the fluffy cushion. A relaxed posture would appear less confrontational. "And what kind of training do midwives need to be able to legally practice?"

Everly sat forward and planted her hands on her knees. "Why don't we get started? Ivy has to get back to work."

Wanda's gaze swung between the sisters in a knowing way. "Sure, we'll get started. Ivy, I'll send you a link explaining the midwifery requirements."

Ivy forced a return smile. Did Wanda think she couldn't look up information online? She'd already done her research, of course. Her question was intended to verify Wanda was indeed legal. How else could she do that besides asking to see her certificate?

Wanda led Everly to a scale in the corner and weighed her, then handed her a disposable plastic cup and directed her to the bathroom. While Ivy waited, she studied a bulletin board full of birth announcements. Dozens of babies' faces. Handwritten sentiments of *Thank you, Wanda!* and *We couldn't have done it without you.* Okay, so this did make her feel better. Each card displayed was a successful home birth. All these families had a positive experience. Her baby would be fine. *She'd* be fine.

If only her stomach would take the hint and unknot.

When Everly emerged, cup in hand, Wanda slipped into the bathroom to test the urine. Everly came to stand next to Ivy. "I could pinch you," she whispered.

"Why?" Feigning ignorance was her best defense.

Ev rolled her eyes. "Stop being difficult. You're stressing me out, and that's not good for the baby."

Point taken. "Fine."

Wanda reentered the room. "Everything looks great. I think I have everything I need from those forms you filled out, Everly. I'll see you in a month."

That was it? "What about hearing the heartbeat?"

"We'll do it next visit." Wanda's tone relayed sympathy. "This early, it's hard to hear it with a Doppler, and I don't like to worry my moms. Next month, we'll have a better shot."

Ivy bit her bottom lip. She'd told Ev she wouldn't be difficult, but she had to know. "How can you be sure the baby is fine without hearing a heartbeat?" An OB would probably do a vaginal ultrasound to ensure all was well.

Everly answered before Wanda had a chance, her tone far less gentle. "If something were wrong, I'd likely be bleeding or at least have symptoms. I feel great, the urine test is good. Everything's fine."

Wanda nodded as she led the way to the front door. "Call me if you experience any troubling symptoms, Everly, or if you have any questions." She looked to Ivy, including her in the invitation.

"Thanks." Everly stepped outside.

"Yes, thank you," Ivy echoed.

Once the door closed, Everly nudged her. "Don't you dare call and pelt her with the third degree."

Ivy adjusted her purse strap. "It's my—"

"Yes, I know. It's *your* baby. I can't stop you, but I'm begging you to let it rest."

"Fine." Ivy leaned in and hugged her sister. "Talk to you later."

She'd taken three steps toward her car when Everly's murmur reached her ears. "Can't wait."

~~

I cross my ankles and straighten as Gale breezes into the room. Our first counseling session last month was more of an introduction. We talked mostly about my relationship with Ivy. I offhandedly mentioned Zach's irritation with our sisterly bond, and Gale pounced. I walked away from the session with newfound compassion for my husband's lack of understanding and a strong dose of gratitude that Gale hadn't broached the subject of my teenage rebellion.

It's doubtful I'll be so lucky today.

"Nice to see you again." Gale's easy smile proves her comment genuine. As if the payment I'm offering for her services isn't the only reason she wishes to be in this room with me.

"You too." My knee bounces, betraying my desire to flee.

We spend a few minutes in easy conversation. She asks if I've heard back from "the female soldier lady." I'd briefly mentioned the situation last visit.

"Actually, yes. She messaged me asking what times work well for us to have a Zoom meeting. Apparently, her computer crashed, which is why she hadn't responded earlier."

"Wonderful. Let me know how it goes," she says before shooting an arrow at the bullseye of my fears. "Today, I want to talk about the child you placed for adoption."

My palms sweat. "What about her?"

Gale relaxes in her chair, her perceptive eyes boring into me. "Tell me about the pregnancy, the decision to place her for adoption, and how you felt afterward. All of it."

I swallow. All of it? "I don't like to talk about it."

She smiles knowingly. "Which is exactly why you need to."

When I don't speak right away, she waits. Her gentle expression says *Go ahead. I'm listening.*

Okay. Here goes nothing. "When my mom died, anger consumed my life. I went off the rails for a bit." I rub my hands on my jeans, but they remain clammy. "I'd spent my life until that point following all the rules. A perfectionist, I guess. Maybe just a typical firstborn. But Mom's death shook me. What was the point of walking the straight and narrow if she wouldn't be there to see it?"

Gale nods for me to continue.

"Ronnie had been after me for a date, teasing me about it for months, but I never gave him a second thought. He hung out with a different crowd. A wild one. After Mom died, he asked again, and my resistance snapped."

I snap my fingers for emphasis. "We started dating, and I got into the party scene. Drinking, pot, sex. Trying to forget. Dad didn't know what to do with me. He was drowning in his own grief while trying to single-parent a five-year-old and a wild teen."

I take a cleansing breath and let it out slowly before continuing. "When I found out I was pregnant, Ronnie bailed quicker than a getaway car. He said he only pestered me for a date because some of his friends dared him to corrupt Little Miss Perfect." I point to myself. "He kept me around because I was easy. The second it got difficult, he fled."

Gale tilts her head. "How did your father react?"

I shudder. "I was scared to tell him at first. Kept my growing belly hidden under baggy sweatshirts for as long as I could. When I finally told him, he flew into a rage. Demanded I place the baby for adoption and finish high school." He'd broken Mom's favorite lamp when he'd slapped it from the table. It would have hurt less if he'd slapped me.

Gale's voice breaks into the memories of that encounter. "Did you want to raise the child?"

There's a question. "I-I …" My throat is tight and hot. I gulp from my water bottle. "Ivy and I both dreamed of households full of children. She was so young and naïve. I guess I was too, before …" I twist Mom's ring on my finger. "But I thought it was for the best, to give my baby to another couple to raise. I understood where Dad was coming from. Agreed with it, even. Until she was born."

Tears clamor for release. This is a safe space to let them fall, but for some reason, I resist. "The birth was horrendous. I'd always envisioned having home births like Mom, but with her death so fresh, of course, Dad insisted on a hospital birth. I had no idea what I was getting into. They wouldn't let me eat. Once, the monitor slipped down on my belly to where they couldn't hear the heartbeat, and they freaked out. Made me get in bed. Wouldn't let me move."

My hands shake. "My body was telling me to move, but they forced me to remain on my back. They mocked me for wanting a natural labor."

Gale's forehead creases. "That's horrible. How did you feel?"

"Trapped." I bite my lip. "Ashamed. To them, I was a dumb kid who'd gotten herself into trouble. The condescending way they talked to me and talked about me while I was right there … Then they whisked the baby away. I never held her. Never said goodbye."

My insides quiver. I can't do this, can't dwell on that horrible experience. I shake my hands at my sides as if to shake the memories off. "Anyway, good came out of that nightmare. After the birth, I gave my life to God." I force a smile. "Beauty for ashes, you know."

Gale's eyes narrow. My attempt to brush the trauma aside and focus on the good must not have fooled her. "Are you sure you did? Give your life to God, I mean."

I bristle. "What do you mean? Of course, I did. I became a Christian after giving birth to my daughter at seventeen."

She puts a hand out as if to reassure me, but her expression remains skeptical. "Oh, I don't doubt your salvation. But from my vantage point, it seems you gave *part* of your life to the Lord back then, and you're living with *some* of your life surrendered to Him today. You may want to ask yourself if you've given Him your entire life, your entire heart. Have you given Him your wounds? Have you given Him your womb?"

A shiver climbs my spine. My wounds? They are laid bare for Him to see. As for my womb … I place a hand on my stomach. "Obviously, my womb is not my own."

Her light chuckle banishes some of the heaviness in the room. Surely, she can see I'm not holding anything back. But then, she leans forward and pins me with her gaze. "But you had your tubes tied, correct?"

I nod. We went over this last time when we spoke about the strain it's caused to my marriage.

"Is that because you don't want to relive your past traumatic experience?"

My cheeks flush. "Is that unreasonable?"

She shakes her head. "Not unreasonable. But not healthy either." She taps her pen against her chin. "What would happen if you got pregnant with your own child? Let's explore the worst-case scenario and the best-case scenario."

My gut churns. What's the point of talking about this? Can't we leave well enough alone? I throw back my head with an exasperated sigh. "I don't know."

One glance at Gale proves she's not going to let me get away with that.

"Okay." She claps her hands together in a prayer gesture. "Let me propose that in the worst-case scenario, you are forced to confront the negative feelings you've buried for so long."

I fight an eye roll. Aren't I doing so right now?

Her brow lifts. "You disagree?"

"I disagree that confronting memories is the worst that can happen. Yeah."

"So, what is it, then? What's the worst that could happen?"

My answer comes on the back of a growl. "I could lose her. I can't lose another baby."

Gale nods thoughtfully. "You fear loss. That's understandable. You've had your fair share of losses."

I can no longer keep tears locked behind stinging eyes. It's understandable. I'm justified. Can we end the session?

"Will you not be 'losing a baby' in a way when you hand this child"—she nods to my belly—"to your sister?"

I vehemently shake my head as tears dampen my cheeks. "No. It's not the same." I touch my belly again. "She's not mine." She'll never be mine. I remind myself of this several times a day.

"You might consider she'll always be a part of you. And that's okay."

My body convulses as emotions I've locked inside for over a decade rush out. I'm a snotty hot mess. Gale passes me a box of tissues. Smoldering anger that she's forced me to tread the terrain I've long avoided melts into blessed relief as the knots in my neck and shoulders loosen.

Maybe she's right. Perhaps I've been living all this time half surrendered to God. Maybe I haven't given Him all of me, haven't given Him permission to tend festering wounds. Perhaps my freedom lies on the other side of my fears. I only have to allow Him to walk me through it.

Chapter 16

OCT. 3, 1862, GEORGE OSCAR FRENCH

Harper's Ferry, West Virginia
September 13, 1862

A twig poked Henrietta between the shoulder blades as she lay on her back in the woods near Harper's Ferry. Church bells sang a sweet melody, eerily out of tune with the growing unrest. Their Confederate force of 2,700 soldiers waited for the coming attack of 16,000 Federals. No reinforcements were coming. Armies were amassed at Leesburg, readying for one great battle while leaving them to fight another.

Hunger gnawed Henrietta's belly. Their food stores were far away at Manassas. No food. No water. Though the Potomac flowed a mere two miles away, they couldn't reach it without being shot. How were they to fight in such a state? Her boots had holes in them. Ironic, considering she'd been so intent on her sisters getting shoes.

"Here, have a smoke." Freddy passed her his pipe. "It will help quell the hunger pangs."

She raised a brow. Surely, banishing the ache wasn't as easy as puffing on a pipe. If so, she'd have become a smoker years ago. He inched the pipe closer to her. Couldn't hurt. She took it.

Bernie came into her line of vision, something green in hand. Henrietta coughed and smacked Freddy's shoulder. "She's back."

"I found corn." Bernie plopped on the ground between them. "It's raw, but it's something. Had to go to a barn three farms down to find any. Heard the Yankees are busying themselves at the river. Shouldn't be long."

Henrietta handed Freddy his pipe back in favor of the proffered corn. She yanked off the green stalk. "They've been saying that for hours." She winced as she bit into the raw corn. "All the farmers left?"

"Not a one to be seen. They'll return to demolished gardens."

Freddy gnawed on his cob. "The least of their worries."

The kernels of hard corn fell into her belly like pebbles. Her stomach cramped, the hunger only intensifying at the meager offering. She licked her dry lips. "You sure there's no water?"

Bernie shook her head. "Not a lick."

A branch snapped to Henrietta's left. She craned her neck to see who approached and shuddered. Old Man Meager? It couldn't be. Her vision hazed. She vomited onto the bed of dried, brittle leaves.

"Henry, you okay?" Bernie rubbed her back.

Her head swarmed with visions from her nightmares. Hadn't she banished that old beggar? How could he have followed her here? He wasn't real. Of course, he wasn't real. Only a hallucination brought on by lack of food, water, and rest. It was a wonder the whole company wasn't seeing things. But if she wasn't careful, she was more likely to die by the hand of this ghost than any Yankee. One could not afford to be distracted in battle.

"I'm fine." No one would believe her reassurances when she sounded so woozy. She cleared her parched throat and tried again. "I'm fine."

"Here." Freddy maneuvered a log to its side. "Sit here."

She glanced around before she did so. No old beggar. Nothing to fear except for the approaching Federal army.

~~

Henrietta's arms trembled as she hoisted the rope, along with nearly a hundred other soldiers. This time, the trembling wasn't from being half frozen, as they were each night in their light summer clothes without blankets or fires. Her muscles quavered from being pushed to their limits. A few more heaves and they'd succeed in securing the big gun near the top of Maryland Heights. After almost four days of this, of carrying wheels and axles up the steep mountain one at a time and working together to pull the cannons up, they'd almost reached the summit. Victory was so close she could taste it. It would be the only thing she'd tasted since the battle had started.

Bullets zinged to her right and left, but she couldn't react. She had to focus her energy on not collapsing. Pulling her weight had never meant so much as it did right now, palms scratched raw with the rope's pressure.

With a screech, a shell hit the large boulder a few feet away from her. Shards of rock flew in all directions. One sliced her cheek. She grimaced. Her grip on the rope faltered for a moment. She sucked in a breath as ooze trailed down the side of her face. A swipe with her shoulder did little to alleviate the annoyance. But that's all it was. An annoyance. She hadn't been shot. She needed to ignore it and summon her strength to help hoist this cannon.

Except her cheek burned. She couldn't keep from attempting to rub at it with her shoulder again. As she did so, something on the ground caught her eye. In a pile of rocks lay … an onion peel? Her mouth watered. Stomach clenching, she inched toward it. Yesterday, some men had come upon meat skins the Yanks had thrown away. They'd scrambled over each other to devour them. One soldier had walked away with a black eye from the tussle. Henrietta hadn't gotten there in time to stand a chance. The same had happened over a crust of bread early that morning. But here was an onion peel only Henrietta knew about. She had to keep it that way, not let on to this precious treasure. Once they secured the gun, she could devour it without competition.

"Almost there." Bernie, standing a mere five yards away, sounded as if she spoke through gritted teeth.

Freddy's face gleamed beet red with exhaustion and sweat. "Heave ho."

With one last pull, the cannon crested the mountain. Bernie collapsed on her back, chest heaving as Freddy worked with others to secure the weapon. Henrietta's gaze drifted to the onion peel. Had she thought to keep it all to herself? Her friend looked half dead on the rocky cliff, and she'd considered eating while Bernie went hungry? *God, forgive me. Is this who I've become?* Of course, war changed people. She'd never dreamed it would change her. Not like this.

As casually as she could, she bent to retrieve the peel. Cupping it in her hand, she broke it into three pieces. She brought Bernie her third.

"Here, friend. Eat," she whispered.

"What?" Bernie rasped. "Where?"

"Shhhh. Just eat." She discreetly delivered Freddy his piece, then rejoined Bernie, sitting in the dust.

Covering her mouth with her hand, she chewed her piece of the peel. How bizarre that a castoff could seem like a feast, but the hint of flavor was a bonus. Henrietta closed her eyes for a moment and remembered Ma chopping onions for stew. They'd laughed at her watery eyes. Henrietta had helped with the carrots. Loreen with the potatoes. What precious memories.

"Thank you." Bernie sounded as if she were about to cry.

Henrietta met her misty eyes. "You're welcome."

"I was about to give up. This is hopeless. I'll never find Hermann." Exhaustion encircled her words.

A glance around showed no one paying them any mind. She squeezed her friend's hand. A brief touch. A needed one. "Don't give up. You never know what tomorrow will bring."

Orders came: Drive the enemy into the river.

Not again. Not a repeat of Ball's Bluff. With wide eyes, the women stood and headed toward the river, guns poised to shoot. By the time they arrived, bobbing heads filled the river.

"Return and surrender." Officers issued the Confederate command to the floundering Yankee soldiers.

Henrietta ticked off the seconds in her mind, internally pleading with the swimmers to come ashore and surrender. Only they did not. Dread pooled.

"Shoot them." Their orders. Not to be disobeyed.

Shots rang out and bullets splashed the river. One by one, floating heads sank. Henrietta's finger trembled on the trigger that she could not bring herself to pull. But why not? They'd asked for it, hadn't they? They were given a choice to live or die, and they'd chosen death rather than surrender. Martyrs, all of them, for their cause. She would likely be doing them a favor.

But she couldn't do it.

It was one thing to shoot at someone who was shooting at her. The instinct to kill or be killed wasn't hard for her to justify. Shooting the defenseless, however, proved an entirely different matter.

She didn't have to war within herself for long before it was over. An eerie stillness settled on the heights. Time to cart the wounded to hospitals, bury the dead, and secure the prisoners. They'd won. Where was the elation of victory?

Detailed to help bear the wounded, she wandered the field in a daze. Bloody clumps littered the sand. The woods looked as if a plethora of rats had gnawed on the trees, as splintered as they were by shot. Hundreds of dead were piled under the bluffs. She walked among the bodies, looking for signs of life.

She met glassy stare after glassy stare. An unnatural bend of the leg or turn of the neck. Her stomach roiled.

"Pray with me," a man rasped.

She turned.

A young man, damp black hair plastered against his pale face, blinked up at her. Finally. A sign of life.

She knelt beside him. "Can you move? Where are you hurt?"

He shook his head. "Pray with me."

"I'll get a conveyance. Get you to a hospital."

He hooked a finger toward her in a slow, laborious movement. "Not going to make it." Ragged breathing punctuated his assessment. "Pray with me."

A burning sensation rose in her chest. Confound this dreadful war. All the death and misery. And now, this man wanted her to pray him out of this world? Who was she to do so? Her gaze swiveled in all directions. There was no one else. No pastor or priest. A finger to his pulse proved he didn't have much time.

"Heavenly Father, be with Your precious son as he passes from this life into Your loving arms." Henrietta nearly winced with the words. Loving arms? How could she speak such words that were so far from what she believed? God's arms for her had been cold and distant. He'd walked out on them and left them alone, left her to fend for herself and take everything on her shoulders. She forced the rest of the prayer out through a clenched jaw and a bitter heart. "Wrap him in comfort and peace. Amen."

"Amen." The soldier tapped her chest. "Take my … Bible. Here." His words drifted on labored breaths.

Henrietta unbuttoned the soldier's jacket and found a Bible tucked within an interior breast pocket. "You want me to send this to someone? Your parents or sweetheart?" Would he live long enough to relay the details?

He shook his head. "No. You."

"Me?" Henrietta pointed to herself.

"Keep it."

She had no use for a Bible, but no way would she tell a dying man that. She bit her lip to ward off tears. Who was this person? Who would grieve his death? "Thank you."

One final shuddering breath, the ghost of a smile, and he was gone.

~~

Henrietta and Freddy loafed on a bench in Winchester. Townspeople walked past and soldiers milled about.

Henrietta yawned. "I'm bored stiff."

Was it truly boredom, or ugly grief over missing her friend? The Eighteenth Mississippi had been resting and recruiting in Winchester ever since the Battle of Sharpsburg where Bernie had found her husband Hermann. Now, he convalesced in a home-turned-hospital in the city, and Bernie waited on him night and day. Henrietta had all but lost her friend. Gone were the days when it was only the two of them. Bernie had achieved her goal.

Henrietta should be happy for her friend. It shouldn't bother her, but the loss hollowed her gut.

Freddy stretched his arms over his head. "Tomorrow, we'll head out to Fredericksburg. Never thought I'd say I was itching for another battle, but …"

She wasn't disappointed to have missed out on the Battle of Sharpsburg. They'd fought at Harper's Ferry, then marched all night to Antietam Creek. By the time they'd arrived, many were too exhausted to fight. Bernie and Freddy had gone into battle and found Hermann. If only they'd stayed back with Henrietta, things could continue between them as normal. How horrible for her to think such a thing.

Change was inevitable. In war. In life. She'd better get used to it.

Even Freddy had lost his slave, Jimmy. After the man risked his life for Hermann, Freddy had let him go free and clear. A repayment of sorts.

Thankfully, their regiment was about to move on. Bernie would march forward with her into another battle while her husband continued to recover. They'd both signed up for two years more service. At least they had that long together.

Across the street, two women in Jeff Davis bonnets haggled over a sack of salt. "I can't wait to get out of here."

This town stank of disease. Every home had been commandeered as a hospital. Devastation faced them around each corner. Once they moved on, they could try and forget the massive losses Sharpsburg had inflicted. There was no forgetting while here.

Freddy stood and turned toward a crowd of soldiers forming. "Let's go see if there's information about our orders."

"Sure." She followed him past a few drunken Rebs and some convalescing soldiers leaning heavily on canes during their afternoon walk. Excitement sparked at a familiar face— Bernie. It had been days since they'd spoken at any length. Her friend strode out of Hermann's hospital and toward the officers' headquarters.

Henrietta called out, "Where you off to, Bernie?" She smiled, rocking back on her heels and stuffing her hands inside her pockets. "Did you hear we're about to move to Fredericksburg? Thank heavens. I've had my fill of lollygagging around this place."

Bernie shook her head, her expression shadowed.

Unease niggled. "What?"

Bernie looked at her as if she'd lost use of her faculties. "I can't leave Hermann. I've got to talk with Griffen."

"Oh." She wanted to stay here? Dread clutched Henrietta's chest. Of course, Bernie wasn't coming with the army. This was the end.

Bernie pushed her way through the circle of people surrounding Griffen. What was she doing? This defied protocol. On trembling legs, Henrietta crept to the outer edges of the surrounding crowd. She cringed but couldn't keep herself from watching as Bernie requested furlough to continue caring for her "Uncle" Hermann. What a lost cause. No way Griffen would grant it, not with all the men they'd lost at Sharpsburg. If only Henrietta could stop Bernie from making a fool of herself. But what could she do? Create a distraction, perhaps. But how?

Disdain dripped from Griffen's voice. "Let the physicians and nurses tend to our wounded. Your uncle is in expert hands. I can't grant you leave when the Confederacy needs you."

Henrietta willed Bernie to walk away with dignity. Hermann could convalesce here and request a transfer to the Eighteenth when he recovered. The sister-like bond between Henrietta and Bernie would never be the same with Hermann in the mix, but at least they'd be together. "Hold your head up," Henrietta whispered under her breath, "and walk away."

Instead, Bernie remained planted in front of Griffen. "Please. My uncle and I are very close." Uh-oh. A feminine lilt snuck through the desperation in her voice.

Griffen scowled. "Look around you. Everyone here has left a loved one to fight for the cause. Every soldier has sacrificed for the South. If I were to make an exception for you, I'd have to make an exception for everybody, and we'd have no infantry left. We are not issuing furloughs."

"Walk away," Henrietta whispered again.

But no. Bernie threw herself at Griffen's feet, groveling. "Please! I beg of you. I beg of you."

Silence descended. Henrietta's breath stuttered. Had her friend lost her faculties? This behavior was far from proper for a soldier and sure to have consequences.

"Gather yourself together, Reisenfeld."

She gritted words out through clenched teeth. "I can't. Not without my uncle."

Griffen's face reddened. "I'll have you written up for this."

How embarrassing. This was Bernice, who had marched into battle with utmost bravery and held her emotions in check even as her heart broke over the passing of her unborn child. Couldn't she maintain dignity here?

Tears glistened on Bernie's cheeks as she shouted, "I'm a woman!"

Henrietta gasped. What was Bernie thinking? Murmurs and whispers leapt all around.

"You mean to tell me we've had an illegal female soldier in our company this entire time?" Griffen's hands clenched at his sides. "Disgraceful."

Henrietta's pulse raced. Would they question her as well, since she tented with Bernie? This was the first place she'd felt settled, the first place she'd been known by someone and still accepted. *Please, God. Don't make me find another company.*

"Roger, Sambold, escort her to the magistrate." He skewered Bernie with his gaze. "You, young lady, are going to jail."

Jail? Mouth agape, Henrietta watched as the two officers hoisted Bernie up and toted her, begging and pleading, down the street toward the jailhouse.

"What's happening?"

Freddy's voice behind Henrietta made her jump.

Her hand flew to her chest. "Bernie confessed to being a woman. They're taking her to"—the last word stuck in her throat—"j-jail."

Freddy's eyes widened. He lowered his voice. "Let's get you away from here."

Good idea. She shouldn't be left gawking at the scene on trembling legs as if her world had crumbled beneath her. Even if it felt like it had. Keeping a low profile was essential if she didn't want to end up behind bars as well.

She kept glancing over her shoulder as Freddy escorted her to an uncrowded street corner. The Eighteenth Mississippi would move on to Fredericksburg without Bernie. Would she ever see her friend again? Not likely.

Loss pummeled her, and she stopped to suck in a breath. Bernie had been like a sister to her, yet the feeling hardly seemed mutual. Her comrade had dropped her like a soiled rag. Of course, she would do so. It was only right. If Henrietta had a beau, she'd feel the same way. Surely, she'd put him first, above other friendships. Bernie hadn't meant any malice.

But that assurance didn't lessen the sting of being left behind. Of being discarded.

Mama hadn't meant to leave her behind either, yet she had.

At least she had Freddy with her. His face bore lines of his distress on her behalf. He was a decent chum, even if he couldn't understand the unique challenges of being a woman in this war.

They plopped onto a bench. Her head still reeled, and her chest ached as if she'd marched for hours.

Freddy frowned at her. "Will you be okay? I've got to go tell Hermann what happened." Without waiting for her to respond, he strode off, leaving her alone.

Chapter 17

Suburb of Wilmington, North Carolina
Present Day

Ivy and I sit at her dining room table, laptop settled between us as we wait for the Zoom call to start.

Austin sets two hot mugs of tea in front of us, then pulls mine back a fraction. "Wait, can you have tea?"

Ivy's eyes widen. "Oh, right. This kind has caffeine. You'd better not. I think we have chamomile in the back of the cabinet."

I fight an eye roll. "This is fine." Picking up the mug, I hold it in front of my face and allow the steam to give me a mini–spa treatment.

Ivy scoots her chair back, no doubt ready to rush and brew me Sleepytime. "But the caffeine—"

"Is safe in moderation."

"I don't think so."

I place a hand on hers. "My midwife said I could even have a coffee a day. This is nothing."

"I'd feel better if you—"

"Fine!" I plunk the mug down, and hot liquid swishes onto my hand. "Ugh." I suck the offending tea off my knuckles. Ivy probably worries those few drops will poison the baby.

Austin sweeps in and, with the voice of a kind customer service rep, he says, "I'll get you the other kind."

Before either of us can respond, the laptop screen lights with Cassaundra Walt's face. "Hello? Can you hear me?"

I flash her a practiced smile. "Yes, we can hear you."

"Oh, good. This is a new computer. I couldn't tell if I had everything set up correctly."

Ivy scoots her chair closer to mine so her face isn't cut off on the screen. "Thank you for meeting with us. I'm Ivy."

"Nice to meet you." Cassaundra's gaze cuts to me. "And you're Everly, right?"

"Yes."

She looks younger than I anticipated. Her blonde curls are pulled back with an olive-green headband. She wears the same color of T-shirt with USA emblazoned on the front. "I apologize this has taken so long. My old laptop died, and I'm just getting situated. Thank goodness I backed up my files." She shuffles through several stacks of paper on her desk. "So, you want to know more about Henrietta Frontenac. That was her maiden name, actually. Her married name was Henrietta Grimes."

Ivy folds her hands demurely in front of her. "Apparently, she was a relative of ours on our mother's side." She shrugs. "That's all we know."

I hold my right hand in front of the camera. "Well, that and she had a ring nearly identical to this one."

Cassaundra whistles. "She sure did. Might it be the same one?"

"That's what we were wondering." I put my hands in my lap and finger the smooth stone. "Our mom left it to me in her will, but she never said where it came from."

Cassaundra's face sobers. "I'm sorry for your loss."

I nod but wave her off. "It was a long time ago. She was pregnant with our baby sister, and we lost them both."

"That's one thing you and Henrietta have in common, unfortunately. Her mom died while birthing the youngest Frontenac girl, Mildred."

Ivy's soft intake of breath matches my own.

I squeeze her hand. "How many children were in the family?"

"Six. All girls. Henrietta was the oldest, then Loreen, Gretchen, Charlotte, Beatrice, and Mildred."

Ivy leans forward. "Girls far outnumber boys in our family too."

"Interesting." Cassaundra picks up a paper from the middle stack. "My research shows Henrietta was born in 1841. She started working as a laundress at fourteen. She was fifteen when her mother passed away, and she took on far more responsibility in the home."

My grip on my sister's hand tightens. Henrietta lost her mom at fifteen—the same age as me? A shiver tickles my spine.

"A railway accident left her father injured three years later, in 1859. That's when she became the sole breadwinner for the family."

I do the math. "So, she was twenty at the start of the war?"

"Yes."

"And she dressed as a man and went off to fight for the South?" Why would she abandon the family that needed her and rush off to some grand adventure? Perhaps she was some kind of Southern patriot.

"Not exactly." Cassaundra's eyes spark with interest. "First, she went to work at the docks at Wilmington, North Carolina. A Confederate recruiter found her there."

Ivy's forehead wrinkles. "Why would she do that?"

She stole my question.

"Money," Cassaundra says in a matter-of-fact tone. "The Frontenacs grew up in dire poverty. Men earned far more than women back then, and there were many mouths to feed. In some cases, the army offered a sign-on bonus as well as the promise of a regular paycheck."

Understanding dawns. "She did it for her sisters."

Cassaundra nods.

"She risked her life for them." My hand caresses my barely blooming belly. "She gave up her own life for theirs."

Ivy's gaze drops to my hand. A flicker of hurt crosses her face. I prop my elbows on the table.

"True." Cassaundra studies the paper in front of her. "Of all her sisters, she seemed especially close to Loreen."

"The second oldest?" I clarify.

"Yes. Loreen would have been seventeen at the start of the war."

So, the girls were four years apart, much closer in age than Ivy and I are.

"The two of them wrote letters back and forth while Henrietta was away." Relief passes over Cassaundra's features. "There it is."

She holds a paper to the screen that shows a grainy black-and-white picture. "I'll email you a better copy. This is Loreen at the general store where she worked during the war. Do you notice anything about her hand?"

I squint. An oval? A ring. "Is that Henrietta's ring? Or another one just like it?"

"No telling. I couldn't find any pictures of the family before the war. Afterward, though, it appears Henrietta had the ring on, and Loreen didn't."

"Must be the same one," I muse.

Ivy cuts a glance to my finger, one I can't decipher. "Looks like they shared it."

Is she still hurt because Mom left the ring to me? I was the oldest, after all. Far more able to take good care of it than a five-year-old. Did Ivy hold a grudge? No, I must be misinterpreting her expression. I'd better be because there's no way I'm giving it up.

I clear my tight throat. "I take it she didn't die in the war. Do you know much about her life after?"

Cassaundra shakes her head. "Not much. Most of what we know comes from letters passed between Henrietta and Loreen during the war. There are also sparse military records that confirm there was a Henry Frontenac in several different regiments."

"She moved around?" I ask.

"Had to. Several times, her superiors discovered her gender and booted her out. When that happened, she enlisted somewhere else."

"Persistent." I smirk.

"Stubborn," Ivy retorts. There's a coolness radiating from her. Why? Was it something I said or is it due to the information we're learning?

I scoot slightly away from her. She's not exactly making me feel welcome. I focus on Cassaundra. "What do the letters say?"

"You can see for yourselves. I'll email them to you. It's not my top priority, but eventually, I'll also get them uploaded to Ancestors' List."

"That would be wonderful." I lean forward.

Ivy smiles, but it looks forced. "Yes, wonderful. Thank you."

Cassaundra regales us with what she knows about Henrietta's time in the army. It's too much information to process at once. Something about the Eighteenth Mississippi, Harper's Ferry, and Big Bethel.

And wait … "Did you say Gettysburg?"

Cassaundra shuffles more papers. "I'll send you all of this. It's a lot to take in."

Oh, good. "Thank you."

"Feel free to contact me with any questions that arise while you dig through the details, but is there anything I can answer now?" She sets the stack down and folds her hands on top of it.

Ivy shifts in her seat. "Do you know anything more about Loreen?"

Cassaundra sighs. "Not other than what the letters reveal, but that doesn't mean there's not more out there." She offers a sympathetic shrug. "My expertise is female Civil War soldiers, so I've only researched Loreen as she relates to Henrietta. The book I'm compiling highlights a dozen such soldiers. Bernice Reisenfeld, Willow Forrester, Charlotte Adams … Well, I won't bore you with those details."

"It sounds like a fascinating study," I say.

"I think so, but then again, I've always been interested in history." She gestures to the bookshelves behind her, presumably filled with books about historical people and events. After she confirms my email address, she promises to send us all she has regarding our relative.

We thank her for her time and log off. I release a long exhale. "Crazy, huh?"

Ivy says, "Yeah," but her slumped shoulders prove she's less than amused.

"Is something wrong?"

My question is ridiculous. Of course, there's something wrong. But she shakes her head. "No."

Right. I could press, and perhaps I should, but I don't want to ride Ivy's emotional train. As the adrenaline from the call fades, my limbs weigh heavy. Sleep beckons me. "I'd better go." A yawn stretches my mouth.

"Yeah. Okay." Ivy's arms wrap around herself as she stands, making her look small and fragile.

I give her a side hug, shout goodbye to Austin, and let myself out the door before she can come right out and ask for Mom's ring. I've given my sister my womb, but I can't give her this. Gale's words about partial surrender attempt to crowd my mind. I shut Ivy's front door harder than I intend to. Classical music emanates from what must be Ivy's keyboard inside. Whether she's angry, hurt, or anxious, I can't focus on her right now. I'll concentrate instead on the story of one heroic woman braving battle to save her sisters.

~~

Ivy's sour mood persisted as she shouldered her way onto the crowded elevator. The man standing next to her smelled of motor oil, salami, and sweat. She fought back a gag. When the elevator opened at the floor below hers, a teenage boy with scraggly hair stepped on her toes. She flinched, and her digits reddened, contrasting with the beige strappy sandals.

This was an indiscretion she could justify being annoyed by, unlike last night's conversation with Everly. So what if Everly could identify with the heroine in their relatives' story while Ivy mirrored the needy one? What did it matter if everyone praised her sister for her altruism? Ivy would get her baby. That's what mattered.

She continued to tell herself this, but her bruised heart still smarted. She was tired of living in Everly's limelight. When people heard the story of how her child came to be, they'd forever gush over how selfless Everly was. Which was true, of course. But if Everly was labeled *selfless*, did that make Ivy *selfish*?

Ebony and Ivory contrasted as much as they complemented each other. Why'd Mom have to name them after that song? People would forever compare Everly with Ivy. And she would always come up short.

She trudged into her office.

Cherry eyed her. "What's got a bee in your bonnet?"

Ivy forced a smile. "Nothing."

Cherry rolled her eyes and refocused on her computer. "Full queue this morning. Jump in and help."

"I will." Ivy managed to speak this with only half the sass she felt. Was moodiness some strange secondary symptom of being an expectant mother without pregnancy? She'd read adoptive parents' blogs. Some claimed pregnancy symptoms despite the lack of hormone involvement. Might it be the same with those using a gestational carrier? She'd feel far better if she could blame this crabbiness on something.

Give thanks in all circumstances. The Scripture accompanying yesterday morning's daily devotional resurfaced in her brain. Gratitude. Yes. That's what she needed. If she started listing everything she had to be thankful for, would her rogue feelings get in line? She could fill pages with her blessings. She should do that after work.

She placed her headset on and signed into the queue. Her first task was to transcribe a well check from pediatrics. Her next was a broken finger from radiology. The routine tasks pushed out all thoughts of everything not right in her world.

An hour later, she finished transcribing another routine pediatrics visit and pulled up the next result from radiology. All breath squeezed from her lungs as she listened. Words and phrases reverberated in her head. *Near drowning. ICU. Unresponsive. Eight-month-old. Fluid in lungs. Possible brain damage.* Her fingers trembled as she typed.

A sweet baby, clinging to life by the thinnest of threads. How must those parents feel? Did guilt claw at them? The report didn't detail how this accident happened. Only that the precious boy was underwater for at least five minutes. Heat warmed her belly. Indignation at how parents could be so negligent warred with the fear something like this could happen to her child. How must that mother feel watching her son lying limply in a hospital bed?

Oh, Lord, let this never be me. Keep my baby safe. Don't let anything happen to her, ever.

The petition didn't sit well in her soul. She prayed for God to keep her child in a bubble so her little girl—she assumed it was a girl—would never experience pain or loss. So that *she* wouldn't experience pain or loss. The song Mom had played for her as a child flitted to her memory. *All night, all day, angels watching over me, my Lord.*

That's what she wanted for her child, constant angelic protection. The Bible spoke of angels. Of God's protection. Yet, Ivy had gotten cancer. Yet, she had lost her womb. Yet, her mom had died when she was only five. What did God's protection truly mean?

In this world, you will have troubles.

If only she could take a permanent marker and black out that sentence from the Bible. How could God promise troubles and protection at the same time? Why?

Bridget's voice broke through her tangled thoughts. "Ivy, you okay?"

Ivy's fingers had stilled on the keyboard, the recording long finished.

"You're white as a ghost. Don't tell me you're going to have another breakdown." Cherry's voice lacked sympathy.

No. She couldn't give in to the panic. She must calm down. Her response came out more as a squeak. "I'm fine."

The women took her word for it, turning back to their tasks. Ivy closed her eyes and breathed deeply. She was okay. Her baby, her family … everything was fine. The child in ICU, though, wasn't. She needed to get his report in pronto.

Everly had started going to therapy. Perhaps it was something for Ivy to consider. Her baby deserved the best version of her. This bound-by-anxiety Ivy wasn't it.

She sent the report, then paused to send a quick text to her sister.

> Can you give me the contact info for your counselor?

~~

In church on Sunday, Zach and I end up sitting directly behind Laurie and the woman I've been thinking of as

"Laurie's mom" since my last encounter with the duo. An older woman with sparkly silver strands interlaced throughout her shoulder-length hair sits next to them. Laurie's grandma, I presume.

The mom holds Laurie over her shoulder, and the baby offers me sweet, milky smiles throughout most of worship and the beginning of the sermon. Adorable. What's the pastor talking about? I'm clueless, lost in baby euphoria.

Zach seems distracted too. His gaze cuts to Laurie every minute or so, and he offers her goofy grins. Laurie's eyes light up at his antics. Man, Zach would be a good father. A niggle of guilt slinks into my gut at the thought that I've deprived him of this. Ivy's body is to blame for her situation, but *I've* done this to us. My choices. My fear.

Laurie grows restless and starts to fuss. The grandma takes her and exits the sanctuary. The absence settles around me like a tangible presence. I keep looking over my shoulder at the double doors, waiting for them to come back. Odd how I can pine for a baby I barely know.

Or perhaps not odd at all. Familiar.

Memories of the days after my child's birth assault me. The weight of depression had plastered me into bed for weeks. Months. Dad's plan had been for me to place the baby for adoption so I could finish high school, but I didn't finish. I couldn't. How could I function in life without my very heart? Everly Alexander, once a shining, straight A student, now turned into a high school dropout. Nearly a year passed before I found the strength to face the world and get my GED.

My knee bounces rapidly as I attempt to push the memories aside. Laurie. I need to see Laurie again. Maybe the grandma will let me hold her. I excuse myself, whispering that I'm headed to the restroom, and hunt for the baby who has stolen my heart. Or perhaps my sanity.

The duo isn't hard to find. The grandma paces through the lobby, jiggling Laurie and shushing softly.

"Need any help?" My cheeks flame with my offer. How forward and presumptuous of me.

"Oh, hello. Do you want to hold her?" Her gaze drops to my belly. "You can get practice."

My baggy dress must not hide my pregnancy as well as I thought. I hold my arms out, and the grandma transfers Laurie to them. "Hi, Laurie," I coo.

Grandma's eyes crinkle with her smile. "Ah, you've met our little angel?"

"Briefly."

"I'm Glenda, Naomi's mom and Laurie's grandmother."

Naomi. Now I can stop referring to her as "Laurie's mom" in my head. "It's nice to meet you. I'm Everly."

Laurie seems to have forgotten she was unhappy. She's fixated on my ring again, attempting to wiggle it off my finger.

"Wow. You're a natural." Glenda offers a knowing head tilt. "You're going to be a great mother."

Ugh. This is why I've tried to hide the pregnancy thus far. What am I to say to this? I'll grow weary of explaining the situation to every person who comments. But this is my church family, not strangers on the street. I'll see them again when my waist is thin and there's no baby in my arms. I can't avoid the topic forever.

"Actually, I'm a gestational carrier for my sister." I look at my belly, then shift my attention to Laurie. Two babies on whom I have no claim. "This is her child."

If it's possible for Glenda's features to soften further, they do. "That's wonderful. What a special thing for you to do for her." Her mouth opens, then closes twice, as if she's contemplating whether to speak more or not. "So, no children of your own?"

Her question lodges a thorn in my chest. I can't speak. I shake my head instead.

"Well, if you ever do have children, I'm sure you'll be an excellent mother."

Laurie cups my face with her pudgy hands. I bring my nose to hers, and she giggles. Then she blows a raspberry, showering my face with her saliva.

"Oh dear," Glenda says, but I laugh and blow one right back.

"She's a blessed little girl to have a grandma like you," I say.

I never knew any of my grandparents. They weren't keen on my parents' hippie ways. The division from my extended family bothers me more and more as I get older.

"I try to help as much as I can. It's not easy being a single mother. Naomi needs backup."

I nod as if I knew this information all along. In reality, I'm processing the fact that Naomi is walking a difficult road. One I would have walked if I'd kept my baby. Maybe it would have been possible to do so. How different would my life look if I had?

"It's Naomi's birthday today, and we'd planned on going out to eat for lunch to celebrate. Only I'm not sure Little Miss will cooperate." Glenda wiggles a finger at Laurie, who grins impishly. It's so cute my heart might melt.

"You'll behave, won't you?" I speak to Laurie in that exaggerated tone that somehow comes instinctual to everyone around babies. Odd how natural it is for me to slip into something I've never had the opportunity to practice.

Laurie tugs at a lock of my hair. I pry it from her fist while scrunching my nose. She giggles.

"If you ever need me to babysit, I'd be happy to." The offer tumbles from my lips before my mind can catch up. That's got to be the stupidest thing I've said all year. Me? Babysit? These pregnancy hormones must be clouding my judgment. Spending more time with Laurie will only cause the ache in my heart to loom larger.

"How kind of you." Glenda opens her arms to take Laurie back. I must have overstepped. Stupid mouth. "We'll keep that in mind."

The moment Laurie leaves my arms, I yearn to hold her again. The weightless, empty feeling of holding nothing pulses through me. What do I do with my hands? The way they hang limply at my sides feels wrong. I cross them around my middle. Still awkward. I need to get out of here. My smile twitches as I wave goodbye to the little princess. "I'd better head back. It was nice meeting you, Glenda."

"You too, dear."

I take two steps toward the sanctuary before I remember I said I was headed to the bathroom. Best to make a stop there so I don't lie. As I'm washing my hands, Naomi steps through the door.

I meet her eyes in the mirror. "Happy birthday," I blurt out.

Her eyes widen a fraction.

"Your mom told me."

"Oh … thank you." Her smile appears genuine, but the awkward way she shifts her weight must mean I've made things weird.

I should go, but my mouth runs off without me again. "I admire you for caring for your daughter." That didn't come out right. It's akin to saying *you're doing a great job breathing air*. "I mean, your love for her is obvious. Good job, Mama." I'm still facing the mirror instead of her. My hands are clean, and yet I'm too vulnerable to turn around and look directly into her eyes. It's as if she could see into my past.

"Thank you," she says again, but this time her words thicken with emotion.

"Of course," I say.

This is too much. Too much *feeling*. Too much remembering. I dry my hands and bolt from the room.

After church, Zach and I stop by the store, and I grab a belated birthday card. There are dozens of sentiments I could write in it, but I simply sign my name. I page through the church directory and find Naomi's address. As I drop the card in the mail, I say a prayer for this mother who is doing what I didn't have the courage to do. What I may never have courage to do, but that which I long for with everything in me. It's finally hitting me: I want to be a mother.

Chapter 18

EACH DAY, MY DARLING, TAKES ME FARTHER AND
FARTHER AWAY FROM YOU, FROM ALL I LOVE AND
HOLD DEAR.

JUNE 18, 1863, CONFEDERATE MAJOR GENERAL
GEORGE E. PICKETT

Fredericksburg, Virginia
November 1862

A gray cloud followed Henrietta to Fredericksburg in Bernie's place. Nothing was the same without her. The relief that came when no one questioned Henrietta regarding her association with the scandalous female soldier was short-lived. Perhaps being jailed with her friend would have been better than freedom without her.

Loneliness snaked through Henrietta both day and night. Freddy's kindness and the knowledge he kept her secret comforted her, but nothing compared to the sisterhood she'd found with Bernie. The sisterhood now lost.

She needed a new purpose for her days, something to help her through long hours of waiting for the next battle. The Confederate army waited on one side of the Rappahannock River, the Federals on the other. The Eighteenth Mississippi hunkered in abandoned houses in Fredericksburg, a tranquil, red-bricked town surrounded by woods. Henrietta bunked with six stinky men. Not that she smelled much better. At least she had an outhouse here. No need to slink into the woods. Frosty wind rattled bare branches, creating the town's own music.

Her chilly toes stuck out from her boots, covered by threadbare socks. They'd dug pits along the river to conceal and shelter themselves as they picketed, but so far, no movement. Perhaps the Yanks wouldn't dare make a move in this weather. At night, though, train whistles rent the air, proving the Federals were moving guns to their camp. Maybe there would be a battle after all.

Without something to occupy her thoughts, homesickness coiled around her until she could hardly bear it. Her sisters had likely grown several inches since she'd seen them last, and hopefully, they'd put on a few pounds. If only she had a photograph. Some soldiers carried such things with them. What if she was gone so long she forgot what they looked like?

As she stood in line to get rations at the commissary tent, she recounted each of her sisters' faces in her mind. A commotion distracted her.

"Heya, Bert." A few guys swarmed one of the fresh fish. The new recruit, a young kid, looked to be around Gretchen's age. Far too young to enlist. The ringleader puffed out his chest. "We're gonna need some of your cornmeal, ain't we, boys? I'd say 'bout half."

The other blowhards snickered and agreed.

The kid tilted his chin. "Get your own rations. These are mine."

"Oh, we got ours, but"—the ringleader smirked—"we get mighty hungry. You're a puny little runt. It doesn't take much to keep you going."

Henrietta stepped out of line and strode to the group. She hardened her features. "Leave him alone."

The clowns scoffed at her. "Who are you? His Pa?"

If they only knew. She pushed into their space. "I'm Henry, and I might be the one covering your sorry behind in the next battle. If you don't want me to look the other way while a Yank pelts you with a Minie ball, I'd suggest you stop pestering the new recruits."

Big Mouth threw up his hands and tossed her a saucy smile. "I ain't pestering. I'm initiating him."

She narrowed her eyes. "Skedaddle." She'd fight if she had to, even if the odds were against her.

The group walked away, mocking laughter trailing them.

She turned to the boy. "Don't let them push you around."

He straightened his shoulders the same way Gretchen used to. "I wasn't."

Sure, he wasn't. "Well, then. I'm going back in line."

She'd taken two steps in that direction when his soft "Thank you" met her ears. She acknowledged it with a slight nod.

Would the fellow who'd stood behind her in line allow her to return to her spot? Worth a try.

"Mind if I sneak back here?" She tried for a friendly air even though her muscles popped with nervous energy.

The soldier couldn't be much older than she, with blond hair draping over his eyes like a curtain. He swiped it away with the brim of his cap, but it immediately fell back. "Depends. Who's your little friend?"

He pointed to where Bert had been. Where was the kid?

She shrugged. "A new recruit. Never met him before."

He scoffed. "Then why are you takin' an interest?"

She scanned the surrounding area for a glimpse of the boy. No sign of him. Hopefully, no one gave him any further trouble. "No one deserves to be picked on."

"You aimin' for advancement?"

Is that what he thought this was about? "Not a chance. Just being a decent human being." Were those so hard to come by?

"Ah." He swiped at his hair again, then waved the men behind him forward, including them in the conversation. "Meet Mr. High and Mighty over here."

"It's not like that." She scuffed her boot at the dirt. "He reminds me of my little sister is all."

Laughter erupted from the men around her, even those she hadn't known were listening. Curtain Hair cupped his hands around his mouth and shouted, "You hear that, Bert? He compared you to a lady."

In the direction he yelled, Bert's form ducked into a house. *Please, Lord, let him not have heard that.*

They doubled over in laughter and repeated her remark as if it were the most hilarious comment ever uttered. As if being a woman was the worst insult imaginable. She pretended to ignore them. Why show the buffoons how their teasing rankled? If ever a group of men who needed female influence existed, it was this one. None of them would act half as foolish if their wives, mothers, or sisters were in earshot.

If only she could rebuke them. But one slip-up would cast her out, and now it was clear the consequences were more serious than simply finding another regiment. Was Bernie still in jail? Best not to find out firsthand. The imprisoned weren't paid, and their families often bore the consequences. No, she'd bite her tongue and let their jabs fall like bullets around her. She would not return fire.

"Psst." A sound came from in front of her.

She craned her neck to find its source.

"Psst." A man with wavy brown hair and stubble splaying his chin winked at her. A man with forest-green eyes.

Her heart pitter-pattered. It was the soldier from her dreams! The one who'd helped her stand when the wind had been knocked out of her. Her mouth parted, but she couldn't form words.

He leaned toward her, his voice low. "You can get in line in front of me if you'd like."

She pointed to herself. Ridiculous. As if he could be speaking to anyone else.

"Yes, you. I mean, if you want to get away from those numbskulls."

She nearly bounded in front of him. "Thank you." Her position gave her a staggering view of the deepest green eyes she'd ever seen. Her breath caught. Just as beautiful as she remembered. What an arresting man. Chiseled jaw. Kempt, wavy hair. Her gaze dropped to his muscular forearms. Goodness, there she went again. She puffed out her chest and put on her manliest demeanor. "I appreciate it." There. Good for her for not swooning into his arms.

He stuck out his hand. "I'm Catch."

"Pardon?" Did he say he was a catch?

Crinkles appeared at the sides of his kind eyes. "That's what they call me, anyway. From the time I caught my first catfish at three years of age."

Ah. A nickname. Stomach flopping like one of Catch's fish, her gaze dropped to his still-extended hand. Awkward. She shook it. "I'm Henry."

Oh, but if only she didn't have to be. She'd give almost anything to give him her real name and have an excuse to bat her lashes a bit.

His head tilted thoughtfully. "You look familiar, but I can't place you."

Her tongue tripped. "Y-you helped me up. A-at Big Bethel."

"Ah. That explains it." He nodded. "Admirable how you stood up for that young soldier." Flecks of gold filtered through the forest green of his eyes. He blinked, and a muscle twitched in his cheek.

What had he said? Admirable. Yes. What he'd done in the woods that day had been admirable as well. He didn't have to stop to help her, yet he'd done so.

"It's not right to bully anyone. We must have each other's backs if we want to win this war."

She forced herself to look away, lest he detect something awry. Her sisters had touted her acting skills, but she didn't trust her ability to hide the mounting attraction. But heaven help her, she turned right back toward him as if she were a compass needle and he was her north.

He crossed his arms, accentuating the muscles under his shirt. "I agree."

She needed to get ahold of herself. She couldn't afford to go weak-kneed at the thought of men. Not when her family depended on her.

The line inched forward, moving her attention to those in front.

Catch's voice lapped at her back. "I hear this next battle will be a massive one. We need every soldier focused and sober-minded."

A shiver crept up her spine. Yes, she had to focus. Needed to stay alive. She'd do her sisters no good lying dead in a ditch. Silly thoughts of romance needed to be extinguished like last night's campfire. She'd come here on a mission. One she intended to fulfill no matter the cost.

~~

From her trench along the Rappahannock, Henrietta squinted through the fog at a hazy commotion across the river. They'd been waiting nearly a month for battle orders. She trembled, though whether from the nip in the air or a premonition of doom, who could say? "What are they doing?" She'd just relieved Freddy of picket duty, coming alongside Catch.

Catch peered through his binoculars. "It looks like … Are they building bridges?"

He handed her the binoculars. She gasped. Oh no. "Pontoon bridges. They've got to be halfway finished."

How'd they manage that without being spotted? Blasted fog and darkness.

Upon relaying the information, their company rained fire on the bridge builders. This was the side of combat that didn't bother Henrietta in the least. Repelling the enemy. Protecting herself and those she cared about. She would shoot to kill if it would keep the Yankees from coming closer and killing them. Not a twinge of a guilty conscience here.

Then the Federals pointed their cannons straight at the town.

"What are they doing? They aim to slaughter civilians?" Her chest burned.

Once again, Catch was beside her. "Two-thirds of the city has got to be filled with women. They wouldn't."

The ground shook with a cannon blast. They would.

The scent of sulfur filled the air as the Federals bombarded homes and stores, streets and stables. Beams crashed to the ground as houses imploded. Smoke and dust billowed as thirsty flames licked dry lumber. Shells screeched. Women screamed. A splintered chair catapulted into the air with a blast. Another explosion thrust a bed frame into the street.

Freddy returned to her other side. Henrietta fired her Sharps rifle again and again across the river, only daring to survey the damage as she reloaded. Heaven help them. This was no battlefield. Though many of the townspeople had long ago fled, some had stayed, hoping the Confederates could hold the Federals off. Now, they fled in terror as their shelters splintered apart. What if such a thing had happened to her sisters? How would they fare? She could boil those Yanks in the heat of her anger. How dare they put innocent women in danger? Teeth clenched, she aimed and shot again and again.

"Henry?" Freddy's voice was cautious. "They've stopped. The shelling's over. You can hold your fire."

Knuckles white, she squeezed the trigger.

"Whoa," Freddy soothed. "How 'bout we go check for wounded?"

She gulped in a breath.

"Let's follow orders."

She pushed air out of her lungs. Yes. Follow orders. Check on the wounded. See who needed help. "Okay." She lowered her gun.

Freddy patted her on the back as they turned toward the smoldering town. She met Catch's gaze, filled with questions she couldn't answer.

~~

Henrietta ducked behind a house, narrowly avoiding a bullet. The Federal commander Burnside's new plan to cross the river in boats had succeeded. The Yankees climbed over the Eighteenth's ditches, despite her company's valiant attempts to club the Feds with their guns. The Eighteenth drove them back once, but the Feds regrouped and charged again. And made it through.

The Yanks chased the Rebs from house to house. Close range. Deadly combat. Nothing like Henrietta had ever seen before.

Heart hammering, she peeked around the corner. Found the soldier who'd shot at her and fired. No stopping to see if she'd made the shot. She raced to the next building. A carpenter's shop? Or what used to be before the assault on the town. Her lungs burned. To her right, Freddy aimed at a group of soldiers hunkering behind a fence. Only …

"Freddy, watch out!"

He turned toward her voice as a bullet zinged toward him from behind. He yelped and crumpled to the ground.

"No!" she screamed.

She shot at the culprit, taking him down, then raced to Freddy. His hand covered his thigh. She wrenched it away and nearly gagged.

"I'm okay. It's just my leg."

Perhaps he would be okay after a doctor amputated his leg. Maybe, maybe not. The survival rates after amputations were chancy. "Yes, you'll be all right." No need to add to his distress.

A bullet struck the ground near Freddy's head. Dust flew, coating her mouth with grime.

"Let's get you to safety." She nodded to a nearby house. "In there." It would likely serve as a hospital before the day finished anyway.

Leaning heavily upon her, Freddy limped into the abandoned house. She hated to leave him there, but the battle still raged. She'd come back as soon as she could. Make sure a medic knew he was there.

"Go," he commanded. "Fight."

She nodded and left.

Outside the protection of dilapidated brick walls, her vision swam with blue. Where were her boys? Yanks had clearly gained the ground, outnumbering the Rebs ten to one. How had the enemy pushed them so far back? A scan of the horizon showed a fellow Confederate more than two stone's throws away. The enemy was chasing them out of the city, the Rebs in full retreat. She was in a dangerous predicament, separated from her unit.

A shell nicked her shoulder sleeve. She dodged behind a tree and stumbled over a blue-clad corpse. Clean shot to the head. Hard to look at up close, but at least the fellow had died fast. No time to post vigil. She stripped his coat and slung it across her back. It wouldn't fool anyone for more than a minute, but that was all she needed. A minute to blend in and make it through the wall of Federals.

She sucked in a breath and dashed in short bursts from one landmark to another. From wall to tree to house to fence. Her focus zeroed in on a skinny Confederate a few yards away. Now, to reach him and find out the orders she'd missed. She lengthened her stride.

Bert turned, aimed his rifle directly at her chest, and squeezed the trigger. Then his gaze locked with hers. Recognition. Confusion. Horror.

The look in his eyes hit her with the force of a blow. She stumbled backward. Her back hit the hard earth, knocking breath from her. What was …? Where was …? The coat. The blasted coat. She wrenched it off.

"Henry!" Bert's anguished scream rang in her ears. "Are you okay?" He reached her, and his hands searched across the front of her uniform. She winced, but not from pain. If he only knew how inappropriate his actions were. He pulled his hands away and studied them for blood. Not a speck.

"You didn't hit me."

"What?" His mouth dropped open. "But you went down."

"I fell." She coughed. "You must have registered who I was before firing. Your aim went sideways."

He slapped her arm. "Whaddya doin', anyway, wearin' a Yankee jacket?"

"Trying to keep from getting killed." She craned her stiff neck around. A handful of enemy soldiers stormed straight toward them. "Move."

Bert helped her to her feet, and they sprinted behind a wall just in time.

"Full retreat?" She heaved in breaths. That silly fall had done a number on her lungs.

"Yeah. To the heights." The kid pulled his shoulders back as if trying to act brave. He was so young. Too young for this.

She nodded at a vision of gray in the distance. "Let's catch up."

They ran from one building to the next.

"Can't believe we lost the town." Disappointment hung from Bert's words.

"It happens." How many times had Winchester changed hands during the war? This loss didn't mean they wouldn't gain Fredericksburg back. Didn't mean much of anything. Far more concerning was whether Freddy had been taken prisoner. How well did Yankees care for wounded enemies?

In the corner of her vision, a Billy Yank peeked out from behind a barn. Aimed. Fired. Straight at Bert.

Henrietta shoved the young Reb to the ground with all her might. The thud of his body hitting cobblestone resounded a breath after the gunshot.

~~

The battle was over, the victory a shock after such a disheartening beginning. When the Federals stormed the heights, good ole Johnny Rebs blasted them good. Secured the area. Drunk on accomplishment, the men—and Henrietta—jawed around a campfire. Light and shadows danced on blackened bricks and burned rubble. Buildings left standing served as hospitals for the many wounded.

"Hey." The curtain-haired soldier, once an adversary, punched her shoulder playfully as if they were the best of friends. "I've got a new nickname for him." He pointed to Bert, then spread out his hands as if he were announcing a headline. "Scratch."

Jovial shouts of agreement sounded around the circle, helped along by a jug of whisky someone had found hidden in a cellar.

Bert lifted a lopsided smile and gestured to his nicked cheek. "It fits."

The soldier across from her hiccuped. "Tell us again. What happened?"

She resisted the urge to roll her eyes. How many times had she relayed the story? She started to shake her head, but Catch's smile snagged her. He sat on her left, so close she could sometimes feel his breath. His warmth pushed into her, chasing away the nip in the air.

"The Yank took aim, and I shoved Bert—"

"Scratch," Curtain Hair corrected.

"*Scratch* to the ground. I shot the soldier, then turned to Scratch and said, 'You okay?'"

"And he said …"

"He said, 'Just a scratch.' He turned his bloody cheek to me, all scraped up from where it hit the cobblestone."

"Remember when Henry said Scratch reminded him of his sister?" Curtain Hair asked the fellow to his other side.

The man snorted. "Bet he never shoved his sister like that."

Henrietta couldn't help but laugh along with the crowd. It was good to have something to laugh about. Even if Freddy was about to lose his leg, he was alive, and so was Bert. A different outcome and she'd be mourning instead.

"You're really something." Unlike the playful banter that floated elsewhere around her, Catch's words held a hint of awe.

She questioned him with her gaze. Mistake. He was far too close. Her mind swirled. She looked away into the vacillating flames.

"You saved two people's lives today. Freddy and Bert both would have died without you." Admiration dripped from his words.

She sloughed it off. "No big deal. Just doing my duty. What anyone would have done."

"Maybe."

She dared to meet his eyes again. He shrugged a shoulder. "I think you see things others don't."

Probably true. A woman's perspective. She reined in a smile.

Catch stood and clapped. "Somebody, get this fellow a medal."

"A medal? A medal." Murmurs erupted as the men searched through the debris around their spots for something that would suffice. "How about a trophy?" A stocky, balding man held up an empty wine bottle.

Catch tilted his head. "That'll work."

The man handed it to Catch, who presented it with a flourish. "For your courageous service, Henry Frontenac, we award you with this medal—er, trophy—of honor."

Light applause sprinkled around her. She stood and bowed. "Thank you."

His hand brushed hers as he handed the bottle over, and her face flamed.

Curtain Hair pointed at her. "Look, Henry's blushing. So humble."

She dipped her head. Maybe she should find a way to transfer companies. This was getting far too complicated. Feelings in a knot, she excused herself from the warm fire and the heat of Catch's presence.

Chapter 19

YOU MAY BE AS DIFFERENT AS THE SUN AND THE
MOON, BUT THE SAME BLOOD FLOWS THROUGH BOTH
YOUR HEARTS. YOU NEED HER, AS SHE NEEDS YOU.
GEORGE R. R. MARTIN, A GAME OF THRONES

Suburb of Wilmington, North Carolina
Present Day

Ivy approached her sister's front door, arms laden with shopping bags. When an attempt to maneuver a bag to her hip in order to twist the doorknob failed, she kicked the front door with her foot. *Thump, thump, thump.*

Everly swung the door open and studied her through narrowed eyes.

"What?" Ivy lifted a brow.

"Are these party supplies?"

Okay, she *had* told Everly she was coming over to celebrate the end of the first trimester. It wasn't a lie, just probably not what her sister had in mind. "For the love, let me in already before I drop everything on your porch."

Everly stepped back and attempted to take the heaviest bag, but Ivy breezed past her. No use putting the baby at risk by letting Sis carry anything heavy.

"I thought you'd be bringing balloons and cake."

Ivy scoffed. "Like you'd eat cake."

"I might."

"I thought you said cake icing has toxic dye in it."

Everly shrugged. "I could scrape the icing off."

So, pregnancy *was* changing her sister. Maybe she'd be less anal about all the other things she'd deemed hazardous. Like Lysol.

Ivy plopped the bags on the couch. "I thought we could celebrate by doing something else."

Everly's eyes returned to slits. "Like what?"

Ivy pulled out a box of cabinet locks and grinned. "Childproofing."

Ev did not return her grin. "Excuse me?"

"I thought it'd be a good idea to childproof your home."

Everly blinked back at her, expression blank.

"Come on. It'll be fun." Ivy wiggled the box.

"The baby is going to live with you, not me."

"I've already childproofed my house. You're going to be her aunt. She'll be over here a lot." And Ivy was not taking chances.

Everly lowered onto the couch, slow and stiff. When she spoke, her voice was flat. "Don't you think it's a bit early for this? She won't even move around for some time. We have a year before we need to worry about it."

How could Ivy explain that preparing lessened her anxiety? Ev often said she overreacted, and she was right that this wasn't needed right now. But Ivy would sleep better knowing they'd prepared a safe space for her little girl. "Humor me, will you?"

Ev's bottom lip trembled. She didn't agree, but she made no move to stop Ivy, who surveyed the room for outlets. Ivy slid an outlet cover over one slot, then two. When she moved to the third outlet, a sniffle stopped her mid-stride. Everly had wrapped her arms around herself, but it didn't suppress her shudder.

"What's wrong?" Ivy stared at her sister. Was Ev about to cry? Couldn't be.

Everly shook her head. "Nothing. I'm fine."

Hadn't they played that game enough? "No, you're not."

Ev's shoulders slumped. A sob escaped.

The box tumbled from Ivy's hand, and outlet covers scattered across the floor. In two long strides, Ivy enveloped her sister in a tight hug. "Shh," she whispered as she pulled a damp strand of hair from her sister's face. "It's okay. It's going to be okay."

A hiccup was her only reply.

"Sis, I don't understand. What's wrong?"

Everly swiped at her face with her arm and the back of her hand. "It's just …"

"Tell me," Ivy prodded while tracing slow circles on Ev's back.

"You can't do this." Ev's voice was hard. Determined.

"Do what?"

She waved her arms around. "This. You can't come here and make my house safe for *your* baby. It makes me feel like she's going to be mine. She will never be mine."

Ivy went rigid. Her chest burned. This was a bad idea. Clearly, Everly wasn't as over her experience as she claimed. What a way to relive trauma. A difficult birth. An impossible decision. A grieving heart. She had trampled on it all. How could she have been so thoughtless? How could she have asked so much from the one person who meant the most to her? Some kind of sister she was. She'd ripped Everly's heart from her chest, all because *she* had to have what *she* wanted.

She choked out a hoarse whisper. "I'm so sorry." And not just for her thoughtlessness in baby proofing. Regret welled within her for what she'd practically begged Everly to do. And for the choices that had put her in this position to begin with. If she'd learned from Ev's mistakes instead of repeating them …

"It's fine." Ev dabbed the remaining moisture from her cheeks. Stoicism replaced heartbroken anguish. As if she hadn't felt anything. As if she was incapable of feeling pain.

But it wasn't fine. Not at all.

Ivy released her, then scrambled to retrieve the outlet covers. She stuffed them back into their box, which she crammed into her bag. "Never mind about all of this. Your home is plenty safe for the time being." But she wasn't a safe person for her sister to be around.

Everly shimmied her shoulders, as if sloughing off the past five minutes. "I don't know why I freaked out. Ridiculous of me."

"No." Her sister was not getting away with dismissing her pain. "You don't have to be strong all the time."

Ev spoke in barely a whisper. "Oh, but I do."

"No, you don—"

Ev's gasp interrupted Ivy's reassurances.

"What?" Ivy's hand flew to her sister's belly. "Is everything okay?" *Please, Lord, let everything be okay.*

The ghost of a smile broke through. "Yeah. It's just …" Everly's hand rested beside Ivy's. "I felt the baby move."

"Seriously?" She pressed her hand more firmly to Ev's middle.

"You're not going to be able to feel it. Not yet. It's more like the flutter of butterfly wings than a sturdy kick."

"Oh." Everly got to experience this miracle first. Disappointment shouldn't coat her like pond scum, but it did. This was *her* baby, yet here she was standing on the other side of the barrier called Everly's womb. On the outside looking in. What would it be like to feel a child move inside of her? She'd never know.

Her hand dropped from her sister's belly.

~~

When Ivy leaves, my shoulders relax. They'd been near my ears for much of the morning. Zach's probably right. Ivy's stress transfers to me far too easily. I take on her anxiety and allow it to expand inside of me much like her child does now. I told her not to baby proof. Would Zach call that setting a boundary? Perhaps I should chalk it up as a win, but the haunted look in her eyes when I broke down and then when she couldn't feel the baby move makes victory impossible.

Her baby. I must always think of the life growing inside of me that way.

I pull out my laptop and settle onto the couch. Studying will take my mind off everything I don't want to face. Only I read several paragraphs and couldn't regurgitate a thing. My mind wanders as I go to water my now-brown aloe plant.

I didn't mean to hurt her. It wasn't even me inflicting the pain. Yet, I can't help but shoulder the burden of responsibility. My tears had rushed out because I want too much. The impossible. A second chance. A different decision. If only I hadn't let my baby go.

Zach comes in from playing pickleball with his church friends. I close my laptop and make a beeline for him. This vulnerable place inside me yearns to burrow into his arms, yet his sweat-dampened shirt repels me. I stop inches away.

"What's wrong?" He places his hands on my arms, anchoring me.

I shake my head. How to explain?

His eyes darken. "Did your sister do something?"

My words whoosh out. "No. Not at all." It's not a lie. I've done this to myself. My voice shrivels. "I just need you."

His concern is etched on his forehead, but he doesn't press. "I'll take a shower, then we can spend time together. Want to choose a movie?"

I don't, but I nod. Right now, I'd watch a shoot 'em up movie without complaint if I get to snuggle in his arms.

When he returns, emitting the scent of his tea tree oil shampoo, I'm still mindlessly scrolling Netflix.

"Find one?" He's sporting a V-neck T-shirt and jeans that fit him perfectly. My heart swells. I love this man. How'd I snag him? He's far more than I deserve.

"No. Your pick."

He studies me for a moment, his gaze tracing my face. The edges of his mouth twitch upward. "How about a dance instead?" He extends his hand. I take it and rise.

He tells Alexa to play our song. For the second time today, I fight back a tide of emotion. My hands loop around his neck, and I lay my head on his shoulder as we sway to "Easy." Every time I listen to the lyrics, it seems ridiculous that this song is ours, yet as the chorus plays, I sing along, staking my claim.

"Easy, easy like Sunday morning."

That's us. E and Z. Everly and Zach. And it's how things have always been between us … until now.

My throat constricts. *This* is hard.

"What if …" I eek out, but I can't go further. Too much to ask.

"What if what?" This man cares for me, and he wants to know what's on my heart. He always has. The concern he brought up to the counselor rises to the surface. He's afraid we'll grow apart. Will this help or hurt?

He kisses my hair. The light touch of affection emboldens me.

"What if I hired a private investigator to find my daughter." Every muscle tenses as I await his response. The chorus repeats. My movements stiffen.

"Sure." His hand caresses my lower back. "If that's what you need."

Is it? I am stuck, and this appears to be a way forward. Fear stalks me. This could be the worst idea ever. What if we don't find her? What if we do? I wouldn't blame her if she didn't want anything to do with me.

The song ends, but we continue to sway.

"Is it what you need, Ev?"

"Maybe." I swallow back a sob. "Would it be hard for you?"

Looking for a child that's not his while depriving him of one that is seems cruel. My pre-Zach life has thus far faded into the background. Now I seek to dredge up what I've managed to avoid.

"Not too hard."

I piece together what he didn't say. It will hurt him, but he'll endure the pain for me. Not much different than what I'm doing for my sister. How can I place such a burden on him? "I don't have to."

He stills and tilts my chin up. Our gazes tangle. "Yes, you do. And I'm one hundred percent behind you."

My fingers find the hair at the nape of his neck. "I'm not sure I want to rock the boat."

A laugh rumbles through him. "Too late, my queen."

Yes, I've started something I can't undo. *Lord, help us.*

~~

Ivy set a bowl of microwaved popcorn next to the letters splayed on her king-sized bed and settled next to Everly. "I've been looking forward to this."

Ev stared at the paper in her lap.

"Wait, don't start without me. You didn't, did you?"

Ev's face scrunched as she looked up. "I might have."

"Stop." Ivy swatted at her. "We're supposed to do this together. It's *our* story, remember?"

"I know, but it's intriguing, and you were taking too long."

"I had to pop popcorn."

Everly eyed the bowl. "Microwave?"

"Yeah." Was there another kind?

"I'll pass."

Rejection sliced like a paper cut. "Why? I made it for you. Gotta keep your preggo self fed."

"Microwaves are toxic. I always air pop."

Ivy rolled her eyes. "Uh, you are so annoying." She should shove popcorn down her sister's throat. "Anyway …"

Everly adjusted the pillow behind her back. "Want me to read this out loud?"

"Yes. And from the beginning." Ivy scooted closer and peeked over Ev's shoulder.

After Everly read Henrietta's letter, she handed the next paper to Ivy. "I'll read Henrietta's, and you can read Loreen's."

Yes, of course. So Everly could fully identify with the heroine, and Ivy could take on the persona of a damsel in distress. Someday, it would be nice to be the person people looked up to, the one getting the accolades instead of the needy one. But how could she argue? Everly's idea was only fair.

The letters painted a picture of a deep bond between the two women, but each one stung. Loreen was anxious and overdramatic. She had trouble standing on her own. It hit a bit too close to home.

"We can be done for now," Ivy offered. Loreen had gotten a job at the general store. They could leave off on a high note.

"Already?"

"Yes." Ivy took the half-empty bowl of popcorn and headed for the kitchen.

Ev's voice called after her. "Is everything okay?" She'd followed Ivy into the kitchen.

"Of course." Ivy dumped the uneaten food with more gusto than necessary. "Why wouldn't it be?" She stalked to her keyboard, which sat on a stand in the corner. Her fingers migrated up and down the scales.

Everly stepped close. "Would you go to counseling with me?"

"What? Like a joint session?" A shudder traveled up Ivy's backbone. What to play? Chopin's Third Sonata felt right.

Everly spoke over the music. "Exactly. I've been getting so much out of the sessions. It might be good for you too."

Ivy shook her head. "I don't think so." Though her sister had given her Gale's number, she hadn't made the call. Too risky. Who knew what memories it might unearth? She'd been rash to think she could solve her problems by talking to a stranger.

"But we both went through the same thing. *Our* mom died, sis. It affects both of us."

Fingers flying faster, Ivy bent over the keyboard. "I hardly remember her." And it couldn't affect Everly that much. She still wanted a home birth.

Everly's tone softened. "I thought since we're doing *this* together"—she tilted her head in the direction of the letters—"and *this* together"—she put her hand on her rounded stomach—"we could work through other things together."

Ivy's fingers stilled as she shook her head again. The more Ivy talked about that horrific night when her mom and baby sister passed away, the more anxious she became. Why do that to herself? She'd only dredge up a boatload of worry months before her child was due. Besides, they were moving on. All of them.

Austin entered from the game room and headed toward the fridge. "How's it going?" He popped open a Coke.

"Okay," both sisters said at the same time.

Austin's pointer finger swung between them. "It's creepy when you do that."

Ivy released a nervous chuckle. If only she could think of something to say that would effectively change the subject, but her mind had gone blank.

Everly puffed out her cheeks, then released the air with a pop. "I think I'm going to try and find my daughter."

Wait, what? Ivy pushed back from the keyboard.

"Wow." Austin swigged from his can. "On that note, I'm going to see if I can beat the next level." His gaze bounced between them. "Sounds like you ladies have plenty to talk about." He sauntered from the room.

Ivy stood, hands on her hips. "Okay, what now?"

There Everly went, twisting Mom's ring on her finger. "I'm not one hundred percent sure, but Zach thinks it'd be good for me. I'm going to bring it up with my counselor. See what she recommends."

"What brought this about?" Even as the words left Ivy's lips, she dreaded the obvious answer. Being pregnant again had to resurrect a host of memories for her sister. No one could blame her. But would Ivy's request for Ev's womb rip out her sister's heart? There was no guarantee she'd even find her daughter, and even if she did, what if the girl didn't want anything to do with her? What if she hated her?

That kind of rejection might break her sister.

And if it did, who would be there to hold Ivy together?

What a selfish, traitorous thought. How could she even think about herself at a time like this?

Everly shrugged, as if the *why* behind this pivot was of no consequence.

Ivy squared her shoulders. She could be strong for her sister. She could be brave. "If that's what you want to do, I say go for it. And if you need moral support when bringing this up with your counselor, of course, I'll be with you in this. I'll sit right next to you and hold your hand." As long as Everly remained the focus of the session, all would be well. The typical roles reversed; Ivy could be the wind beneath Ev's wings. Sure thing. No problem.

"You will?" Hope shone in Everly's eyes.

"Of course."

"Thank you." Ev wrapped Ivy in a tight hug. "That means a lot." She pulled away and went to the fridge, taking out a sparkling water. "Zach and I did our consultation over Zoom, but I've been going to her office for therapy. It's intimidating to share a space with someone who won't let me hide. Your presence will help tremendously, I'm sure."

"Yeah." No hiding. Did Ivy swallow popcorn kernels? Because it felt like they were popping in her stomach. She owed Everly this. It was the least she could do. She forced a smile. "I've got your back."

After all, that's what sisters were for.

Chapter 20

IF THERE IS ANY ONE THING THAT IMPRESSES ME
WITH FEAR IT IS THE NEWS THAT SOME ONE OF THE
DEAR ONES AT HOME ARE UNWELL.
APR. 12, 1863, H. B. FOUNTAIN

Fredericksburg, Virginia
January 1863

Cold seeped in through the house's walls, but that wasn't why Henrietta shivered. They hadn't seen any more action since the Battle of Fredericksburg. Now, they bunked in winter quarters. A moment to relax. To breathe. To wait for the Federals to make a move. Tension might not fill the air around the camp, but it filled her insides. Every moment in Catch's presence left her reeling. And at last, a letter from home.

Loreen's handwriting, normally smooth and elegant, was jagged and irregular, a telltale sign something was amiss. Henrietta sucked in a deep breath and read.

Dearest Henry,

I hope and pray you are safe and well. Reports of the Battle of Fredericksburg reached us, and as with every battle and skirmish, we wring our hands raw as we wait for word of whether you've made it out unscathed. I don't know if my nerves can take much more of this blasted war. May it end swiftly and may you come home to us.

I hesitate to write of our current struggles, not wanting to burden you when you must valiantly keep your wits about you in combat, but I fear you would never forgive me if I withheld such vital information. Our precious Mildred has fallen ill again, and she seems worse off than before. Coughs rack her body day and night. The poor dear cannot find reprieve.

Thanks to the money you've sent, we've been able to feed her well. She's plumped out quite nicely since you last saw her. The nourishing food hasn't provided relief, however. There's nothing left to do but to fetch the doctor. We haven't enough to pay the debt owed for past services as well as another house call, but hopefully, it's enough to persuade him to come.

I'll write again as soon as I know more. I pray it will be with good news of her recovery. Until then, stay safe. We love and miss you.

Your sister,
Loreen

Henrietta's hand clenched Loreen's letter. Not Millie. Not again. Her youngest sister's face appeared in her memory, shadowed by her birthmark. That beautiful rose petal's kiss set Mill Moo apart as one hand-plucked by heaven to grace their family with light. And how she had. Almost otherworldly, Millie seemed to fly while others only ran. A sprite of a thing. Hard to imagine her plump. Far too easy to imagine her ill.

Henrietta should go to her. Leave for home. How long would it take her to walk to North Carolina? Could she take a train? Her shoulders caved inward. The colonel would deny a request for a furlough, no doubt about it. If she wanted to leave, she'd have to desert. Not that her patriotism protested, but if caught, she might stand before a firing squad. How would they notify Loreen of "Henry's" death? She squeezed her eyes at the thought. God forbid. She couldn't do that to her family. The possibility of her dying in battle was bad enough. She couldn't justify perishing in such a disgraceful way.

Besides, what good would her presence do anyway? It would cut off their means of support, and for what? She was no doctor. To consider fleeing for home was selfish. Her desire to see her sisters had nearly gotten the best of her.

Drat. Why had she crumpled the letter? She smoothed it out, treasuring Loreen's uneven script. There was so much more she longed to know about things back home. Had Loreen found another job? Any prospects of a beau? What about Gretchen? How was Pa? Had he asked about her at all? Doubtful, but a flicker of hope sparked inside her, nonetheless. He had to snap out of it sometime, didn't he? And when he did, perhaps he'd return to being the father he once was. The one with a belly laugh as deep as the ocean and a listening ear as long as the river.

She pulled out a piece of paper. She wouldn't waste any time before writing Loreen back. But best not to pelt her sister with questions again. Interrogations had always overwhelmed Loreen, and when Loreen was overwhelmed, she shut down. The only thing Henrietta was likely to pry out of her sister then would be laments.

The best way to get Loreen to open up was to do so herself. Late-night chats had taught her as much. The more she would talk, the more Loreen reciprocated. This was the dance between them. Henrietta needed to hide any panic regarding Millie, as that would only send Loreen into a tither, and she needed to divulge as much as she could about herself.

Only … could she?

Until now, she'd been careful to continue the persona of Henry in all correspondence. One never knew who might read over her shoulder. But if she wanted Loreen to be honest with her, she needed to be honest as well. And she couldn't do that as Henry.

Pencil in hand, she leaned over the table to write.

Dearest Loreen,

First off, I'm alive and well. Yes, the Battle of Fredericksburg was fierce and ugly, but I made it through. It will take more than flying bullets to knock me down.

I'm sorry to hear about Millie. I will eagerly await word of the doctor's prognosis. Our Mill Moo is a strong girl. She'll pull through. Tell her when I get home, I'll race her to the creek and back. That should motivate her to regain her strength. She nearly beat me last time.

Life here is monotonous between battles. I miss my friend Bernie. I have another friend here, Freddy. I don't think I've mentioned him before. He knew Bernie from back home. He knows my secret and has kept my confidence. For that, I am grateful. He's married and has a son at home.

There are many times I've wished I didn't have a secret to keep. Never has that desire burned stronger than when I met Catch. He's the best-looking soldier here with eyes the color of fir trees. Unlike so many, he hasn't allowed himself to become unkempt while here. He keeps both his beard and his manners in check and is a man of integrity and honor. I would be taken with him if I could.

Of course, I can't.

He will remain a comrade, and not one I can confide in in any true way. Not while I'm keeping my true self hidden. But at night, I can dream.

I've written far too much. I miss our late-night talks.

Please write back straight away.

Yours truly,
Henry

~~

In May, Henrietta finally got orders to march. She had just left Fredericksburg with her regiment when word came that the enemy was headed their way. The Eighteenth turned back to hold the city against an attack from 25,000 Federals. Lord, help them! It was one thing when the Yankees didn't know they outnumbered the Rebs twenty to one. Now, though, they knew. And, confidence bolstered, they had the Confederates almost surrounded.

Hunkered behind the stone wall, Henrietta reloaded. "Why, oh why, did Colonel Griffen agree to the truce?"

When the Feds flew the flag requesting to bury their dead, the Confederate colonel agreed. But it was under the guise of that truce that the Union army had learned how outnumbered the Confederate forces truly were.

"Mercy," was Catch's only reply.

Henrietta popped her head over the wall and fired. There were far too many Yankees. What a hopeless mission. She ducked behind the wall again. "Blast mercy."

Catch raised a brow. "You're only saying that because you weren't on the receiving end."

True. But … "When am I ever?"

"Ah. A cynic."

True again. Not that it's who she wanted to be. Life just hadn't dealt her good cards. Could anyone blame her for not envisioning a glistening future?

She surveyed the pathetic number of soldiers behind the wall compared to the number who attacked. A Minie zinged past her ear. "We're either going to die or end up as prisoners."

Her throat tightened. Each breath could be her last. In all the battles she'd fought in, death had never felt so imminent. It crouched right on the other side of the wall. Its putrid odor seeped between the stones. She would miss her sisters. Watching them grow.

"A good possibility," Catch conceded. He leaned against the wall and turned his face toward her. Even covered in grime, he was the most beautiful man she'd ever seen. He reached over to grip her hand. A strong, manly shake. The grip of brothers. Comrades. "No matter what happens, we're in this together."

Oh dear. She couldn't breathe. She croaked out, "Together."

Both hands now secured on her rifle, she launched into the battle with renewed purpose. Together. They were in this together. Shots and shouts rang out. Dust and rock flew. Smoke billowed. The enemy closed in. Nearer and nearer.

"You still got that Bible on you?" Catch asked.

She patted her breast pocket. "Right here." She'd told him of the soldier at Harper's Ferry who'd given her the Bible.

"Look up Psalm 139, will ya?" He popped over the wall and fired again.

"Now?" Had he taken leave of his senses? They were in the middle of a slaughter.

"Please." Vulnerability snaked through his words.

She lowered onto her belly and pulled out the Bible. After checking the index, she flipped to the correct page and read, lifting her voice above the tumult.

"'O Lord, thou hast searched me, and known me. Thou knowest my downsitting and mine uprising, thou understandest my thought afar off. Thou compassest my path and my lying down, and art acquainted with all my ways.'"

Her heart stirred. *This* was God? The God who had walked out on her family years ago. The God who had left her all alone. The God who had left her to take care of her family by herself. The two versions of the Almighty sounded nothing alike.

"Do you believe this?" She had to shout for Catch to hear her.

"Believe what?" He turned his mud-splotched face to her.

"Believe in a God who knows you like this?" She pointed to the page.

His brow quirked. "Don't you?"

If only. Everything within her longed to be known this intimately. She was tired of hiding.

Catch ducked beside her to reload. "Okay, that was the fuel I needed. Now, help me out here, will you?" He winked.

She tucked the Bible back into place and picked up her rifle. "Yes."

The words from Scripture that seemed to ground Catch unsettled her. They swirled in her middle, stirring up questions, unearthing speculations. But she couldn't think about any of it at present. Her focus had to remain on staying alive.

The word trickled down the line. "Get out if you can. It's over."

Her heart throbbed in her neck.

Catch locked eyes with her, his tree-green gaze a canopy of safety in the madness. "Want to make a run for it?"

It was either run and risk getting shot or stay and be taken prisoner. The enemy shouted orders to surrender. Catch's gaze sharpened. Could she do this?

She nodded.

They ran.

Chapter 21

Suburb of Wilmington, North Carolina
Present Day

When Zach and I walk into church the next Sunday, Naomi greets me in the foyer. She leans forward and offers a friendly, almost hug where she pats my back but doesn't fully embrace me.

"Thank you for the card. How sweet of you."

"You're welcome." My eyes dart around the room. Where's Laurie?

"My mom told me what you're doing for your sister." She places a hand over her heart. "That's amazing. You're a saint."

I snort. "Hardly."

Zach shifts beside me. Oh yeah. Forgot about him.

"This is my husband Zach. Zach, this is Naomi. She's the mom of that sweet baby, Laurie."

"Nice to meet you." Zach sticks out his hand, and Naomi shakes it.

A glance at his unreadable expression and anxiety snakes up my spine. We've always been in sync. Able to finish each other's sentences and anticipate each other's needs. Yet, I can't figure him out now. What's going through his mind? He's uncomfortable, for sure, but why? Because Naomi mentioned the surrogacy, or is it something else? I don't have time to inspect his reaction.

"I'm going to save us seats." He kisses the top of my head and strides toward the sanctuary.

"Hey, is anyone throwing you a baby shower?"

It takes a minute for my questions about Zach to fall away and Naomi's comment to register.

"A shower?" My neck heats. I must sound like an idiot. But the thought of a shower has never crossed my mind. "For me?" I trip over the logic. I never had a baby shower for my child. This would be a first. Only it's not my baby.

Naomi's cheeks tinge pink. "Well, for you and your sister, I guess."

"I don't think so. I haven't thought it through. I guess *I* should throw a shower for my sister." Though Ivy has church friends, she hasn't mentioned any of them offering a shower. And I've spent two decades keeping most everyone at arm's length.

"The pregnant woman isn't supposed to throw a shower." Naomi chuckles. "I was asking because I'd like to do that for you. If you want me to, I mean."

I blink and force her words to compute in my brain. She radiates sincerity, but I hardly know her. "You'd do that for me?" I could kick myself. This isn't about me. "For us?"

"I'd love to."

She has much on her plate, and yet she's offering to do this great thing for two strangers. It's nearly too much. "Truly?"

She laughs. "Yes."

"Okay. If you insist." I adjust my weight to the other foot. "Thank you."

She pulls out her phone. "What's your number? I'll check my calendar and shoot you dates."

I rattle off my info. A few seconds later, my phone buzzes in my purse.

"That's me. Wanted you to have my number in case you need anything in the meantime."

"Thanks." Wow, I'm on a roll here with my stellar conversational skills.

Naomi touches my arm. "Oh, I almost forgot. I have something for you. Walk with me to my seat."

I follow numbly. Why is she going through all this trouble for me? Maybe my emotional turmoil is showing on my face, and she feels sorry for me. That must be it. I'm emitting a needy vibe. I need to rein it in, pull myself together.

We reach the aisle halfway from the front where Laurie sits on her grandma's lap. Naomi sets a hand on her mother's shoulder. "Mom, can you hand me that bag?"

Glenda bends over and retrieves a gift bag. Grinning, she hands it to Naomi. "Hello again, Everly. Nice to see you."

I return the sentiment as Naomi hands me the bag.

Suddenly, I'm back on Jessica's front porch, dreading her baby shower. The gift I brought hangs heavy like lead, full of all the emotions I've worked hard to avoid. Browsing for an organic Baltic amber teething necklace and breastfeeding supplies. Clicking *add to cart*. Choosing the gift wrap option so I didn't have to see the painful products. Then when they arrived, dumping them into a gift bag to further distance myself.

I shudder and refocus. "For me?" I ask. Possibly another stupid question, but if it's for my sister, I need to prepare myself.

"For you."

Must not be a baby product, then. It should be safe, but I hesitate to peek inside.

"Go on." Naomi laughs again.

Laurie waves her arms and squeals. So much joy in this little family that represents my alternate life. My heart twists. What have I missed out on?

They're staring at me, so I summon courage and reach into the bag. I pull out a mint-green T-shirt. I set the bag down and hold up the shirt to read the caption, *Amazing Surrogate.*

I'm making dreams come true. Little footprints adorn the middle with heart cutouts on the heels.

"Do you like it?" Naomi asks. "This way, you don't have to try and hide the pregnancy, and you won't have to explain the situation to random people."

My throat tightens. "This is the most thoughtful gift. Thank you."

"Oh, good." Her hand flies to her chest. "I was afraid I'd overstepped. I almost got the one that said *Just the Stork. Not the Mommy.* But I liked this one more."

I flinch at the sentiment on the other shirt. I remind myself every day that I'm not this child's mother. I don't need a shirt to reinforce it. "Good call. This one is perfect."

"So glad." She hugs me again. Not the awkward almost hug of a stranger, but the embrace of a friend. I guess if she's throwing Ivy and me a shower and she's bought me a gift, I can consider her such. Still, this kindness overwhelms me. I didn't need to flash credentials at her to earn her respect. Didn't need to fight to prove myself to her. She's just here, offering friendship. Are there truly no strings attached?

Guitar music drifts through the sanctuary. The service is starting. "Better get back to my husband. Thanks again." I wiggle my fingers at Laurie, then step away.

"Of course. I'll be in touch."

Warmth spreads through my chest. I have a friend. A friend with a baby. This thing I've avoided all my adult life doesn't scare me anymore. I make a pact with myself to not withdraw and to not push her away. I will embrace this friendship for however long it lasts.

~~

Ivy sat so close to Everly on the counselor's couch that their legs touched. Everly's signature essential oil scent flooded Ivy's nostrils. Here she was, ready to support her sister in the same way her sister had always supported her. She grasped Everly's hand and squeezed.

Gale smiled at them from across the room. The counselor leaned backward, almost lounging. She appeared completely at ease and comfortable in her own skin. In contrast, Everly and Ivy probably looked like they were facing a firing squad. Backs upright. Posture tense.

"I'm pleased you're joining us today, Ivy." Gale's voice soothed. "When Everly brought up the idea of a joint session, I was thankful. You two seem extremely close, and there's much to explore between you."

Ivy shifted in her seat. Much to explore between them? That wasn't the deal. "I'm happy to support my sister." Hopefully, that would clarify.

"Excellent." Gale flipped a page on her legal pad and poised her pen. "How are you both feeling about this surrogacy?"

Was it her imagination or had Everly's hand grown clammy? Maybe it was her own. She twisted out of Ev's grip and wiped her palms on her jeans.

"Why don't you start, Ivy. What emotions has this experience brought up thus far?"

Ivy's gaze dropped to the green-and-pink-checkered carpet. Emotions? No, they were here to talk about Everly finding her daughter. How could she reorient them to the visit's purpose?

She could feel Gale's gaze boring into her. Were her knees sweating? Strange. Silence stretched as she stumbled for something to say.

"Take your time," Gale said.

Could she escape instead? She eyed the door.

Gale chuckled. "You two are a lot alike."

Ivy shook her head. "No, we're not. Not at all."

Gale's brow furrowed slightly. "How so?"

"Everly's altruistic and selfless. She's always giving, giving, giving. And me? I'm the one taking, taking, taking."

Ev frowned at her. "That's not true."

"Yes, it is. You've always said you'd do anything for me. You're proving it." She waved a hand at Ev's belly. "What have I ever done for you? Made you worry about me, that's all."

"Are you talking about the cancer?" Ev angled toward her. "It wasn't your fault."

"I'm not talking about the cancer." Though, of course, that *was* her fault. "At least, not just the cancer. The bad decisions that led to the cancer, mostly. I'm surprised you don't have white hair."

Everly's posture slumped. "I've always considered it *my* fault."

"What?" How in the world could Ivy's bad choices be Ev's fault?

"I had a wild streak as a teenager right after promising Mom to take care of you. I broke that promise. If I had set a better example—"

"No. Stop." Ivy grasped Everly's arm. "I turned away from all I knew was right. I knew what was right because of you, because of the example you set for me. I'm the one who chose to walk away."

"But if I had—"

"Ev, I don't even remember your wild streak. Everything before the age of eight or nine is a blur. All I can remember is how amazing it was that you got your GED and excelled in college. Every memory I have of you overflows with integrity."

Everly's frown deepened as her brow furrowed. Had she truly lived with such weight on her shoulders?

"This is an interesting concept." Gale leaned forward. "Perhaps you've both been assuming you had similar childhood experiences, yet the difference in your ages and personalities means you perceived the same events differently." She shifted her focus to Ivy. "Why don't you relay your childhood experience to your sister, then she can reciprocate."

That made sense. Ivy nodded.

"Start with your earliest memory."

Ivy closed her eyes and sifted back through the years. "There's a flash of a memory of me sitting next to Mom at the piano. She was teaching me how to play. She had dreadlocks and she smelled like … I don't know, some essential oil, I guess, but not the same as Ev."

"Lemongrass," Everly interjected. "It was her favorite."

"Okay. Yeah." At least she had a name to go with the scent she remembered distinctly. "That's all I can recall."

She opened her eyes to find Everly staring at her, slack-jawed. "That's it? That's all you have of Mom?"

"Yeah. I think so."

Gale spoke up. "What about the day she died?"

Ivy closed her eyes again. "I remember that day, but I can't see Mom in it. Someone rushed us to the next-door neighbor's. There were sirens and flashing lights." She cut her gaze to Ev. "You held me. The old lady tried to get me to eat mac and cheese, but I wasn't hungry. Then there was a knock on the door, and Dad stood on the porch, tears streaming down his cheeks."

"Then what?" Gale prodded.

Ivy shrugged. "Nothing. It's all a blank. The next thing I can conjure up is walking into my third-grade class and finding Billy Ryan with a frog in his pocket."

Everly kept opening and shutting her mouth, as if on the brink of saying something.

Gale spoke first. "It seems like your memories of your mother's death are far less vivid than Everly's, which makes sense. You were only five, correct?"

"Yeah." Ivy pulled her gaze away from her sister to focus on Gale. "I grew up knowing a home birth killed my mother and baby sister, but I don't remember it specifically." Courage filled her, and she voiced the question that had been plaguing her for months. "I guess I don't understand why Everly's insisting on a home birth, knowing how dangerous it is."

"But that's not true." Everly's voice rose an octave. "That's not what happened."

Gale put out a hand as if to exude calm. "What is your perception of these events, Everly?"

"Mom died of a placental abruption. It can happen anywhere, anytime. Just because it happened at home doesn't mean—"

"She died during a home birth, Ev. Don't pretend like—"

"But she didn't!" Everly's voice exploded in Ivy's ears.

The room tilted slightly. "What do you mean?"

"She wasn't in labor when her placenta ruptured. She didn't die during birth."

What kind of cruel joke was her sister playing? "Yes, she did. I remember the birthing pool." Large and blue and standing in the middle of the living room. She'd forgotten to mention it, but the image had seared itself into her brain.

Everly shook her head emphatically. "No. Mom always set everything up early, just in case. But she wasn't in labor at the time. She wasn't even due for three more weeks." Ev placed her hand on Ivy's knee. "There was nothing anyone could have done. The result would have been the same if she'd have planned on a hospital birth. It had nothing to do with the home birth."

Ivy reeled. Pressure built in her temples. Had everything she'd believed for so long been false?

Gale's voice lapped over her like a gentle wave. "Does this make you feel better or worse?"

Ivy's hands trembled in her lap. All this time, she'd thought Mom's death had been preventable. She'd set out to prevent other tragedies in whatever way she could. As a medical transcriptionist. As a volunteer at their local safety fair. By gobs of research and sharing findings on her blog. She'd relied heavily on doctors, thinking that if only her mother had done the same, she'd still be here.

But now, a frightening prospect loomed above her like a dark cloud. Some tragedies couldn't be avoided. Some things were beyond human control. Beyond *her* control. She should have known this, of course. She'd gone through cancer. But in her mind, she could have prevented even that. But what could she make of a world wildly out of her control?

She answered Gale honestly. "I don't know."

~~

I flick a glance to the wall clock. Our hour is almost up, and I haven't gotten the chance to mention finding my daughter. At least I've set Ivy straight. I've known, of course, Ivy had been nervous about the idea of a home birth, but I figured it had to do with her hypochondriac tendencies. If Mom's death had been a direct result of a home birth, how could she dream I'd force one upon her? She must think me cruel.

The tick of the clock brings me back to the task at hand.

I moisten my lips. "There's something else I'd like to discuss."

Gale arches a brow. "Yes?"

What if she thinks it's a horrible notion? Can I stand to let this seedling of an idea wither and die? My pulse thrums in my ears. I won't forgive myself if I don't explore this. Here goes nothing. "I want to find my daughter."

Her other brow joins the first. "Oh?"

"Yes." I brace my hands on my knees as if it will cement the decision. "I need to know that she's okay, that she has a good life." That I didn't ruin her.

"That's fair." Her thoughtful nod prods me forward.

"I don't need to be a part of her life. At least, I don't think so." I nibble my bottom lip. "I only need information."

"Is there a reason you want only information and not connection?" She speaks as if she knows the answer already. This is a quiz I haven't studied for.

"No?" My voice lilts as if I'm asking a question. Maybe I am.

Her phone trills from the coffee table between us. She picks it up and swipes. "Unfortunately, our session is over for today."

My chest deflates.

"We should talk more about this during our next session in two weeks." She checks her calendar and throws out a date I readily agree to. "Will this be a solo or joint session?" Her gaze darts between Ivy and me.

My sister came for the sole purpose of supporting me in this, but she looks as if she's trudged through a war zone. She's dazed. Confused. Likely regretting her decision to accompany me.

"Solo," I say. No need to drag her through this again.

Something flashes across Ivy's features. Hurt? No. Couldn't be. Surprise, maybe.

"Okay." Gale's smile falters as if she's disappointed. "See you then." She stands and extends a hand to Ivy. "Nice meeting you."

Ivy returns the sentiment, and we step out of the office.

I infuse pep into my voice. "Well, that was …" The correct word escapes me.

"Something," Ivy finishes.

"Yeah, that was certainly something."

Ivy seems to snap out of whatever trance she's been under. She grabs my wrist. "Sorry, Ev. You've lived forever thinking my choices were your fault." Her forehead scrunches. "Not only is that not true, but it's also not fair. Mom should have never made you promise to take care of me. You were a kid yourself."

Goosebumps prickle my arms. She's making a point I've never let my mind rest on. It's the older sister's job to take care of the younger. Look at Henrietta. She went to war to fulfill her sisterly duty. But the sting of injustice has pierced me before. Ivy is right. It doesn't seem fair to make a fifteen-year-old pledge such a weighty responsibility.

Only … "I can't blame a dead woman for anything, especially not for ensuring her little girl would be well taken care of."

Ivy looks straight into my eyes as if she can see my soul. "You were her little girl too."

I shake my head as my throat thickens. "I was—."

"Still a child. You needed to be taken care of too. She should have asked Dad."

Should have. Why didn't she? Did she know he would crumble without her? Did she expect me not to?

My eyes sting, and I blink rapidly.

Ivy's breath catches. "You must have thought you were less valuable than me." Her hand tightens on my wrist. "Did you assume that?"

Shoot. Here we are, five inches from Gale's office and tears are dripping down my cheeks. "Of course, you're more valuable." That was why Mom wanted me to protect Ivy at the cost of everything. The cost of my desires. My needs.

Ivy's arms crush around me, and she presses her wet cheek to mine. She's crying too? Great. I made my sister cry.

"You are every bit as precious as me." She trembles against me. "I'm sorry I've been a burden to you all your life."

What? I pull back and study her face. "No. You've never been a burden."

She laughs without humor. "Poison Ivy, right?"

I wince at my hubby's nickname for her.

"I overheard Zach whisper it more than once."

"He's …" Bitter? No. "Jealous."

"You never said anything to the contrary. Never stood up for me."

I pull her into another hug. "I don't have to. It's understood. Zach could never deny my devotion to you." I loop my arm around her shoulder and angle toward the exit. Gale might be listening to our entire conversation and taking notes. The thought makes me chuckle.

"What?" Ivy asks.

"Nothing." I squeeze her shoulders. "I just love you, sis. You are the kind of ivy that adorns ancient castles. Beautiful. Not poisonous in the least."

She guffaws. "Whatever you say."

Chapter 22

IT IS NOW ALMOST A MONTH SINCE I HAVE HEARD
FROM HOME AND GEORGINA THEN SO SICK YOU CAN
IMAGINE MY ANXIETY FOR A LETTER. ... OH! HOW I
WISH I KNEW HOW GEORGINA AND ALL THE REST OF
YOU HAVE GOT ALONG.

JULY 30, 1862, GEORGE TILLOTSON

Across the Rappahannock River from Fredericksburg,
Virginia
June 1863

While Henrietta chopped firewood, she couldn't keep her gaze from drifting to Catch's muscular shoulders. The way they stretched and flexed under the weight of timber. Hopefully, she'd perfected the air of nonchalance, and to any onlookers, it would seem as if she only looked out blankly into the distance, dreaming of home. An end to the war. Decent coffee. What all soldiers dreamt about.

The loss of the town of Fredericksburg weighed on them all. Twenty-five dead in their company. Forty-three wounded. Many captured, along with their flag. General Barksdale's speech applauding their bravery didn't bolster much against such numbers. Neither did the fact that the Confederates had won the overall battle. Now, more than ever, everyone longed for an end to the madness. Even she. Even though it would mean an end to the pay that came with it. Or *sometimes* came with it. Rations and payments had been in short supply for the past few months. Still, something was better than nothing. And she'd work for free if it meant the opportunity to be near a certain handsome soldier.

When Catch turned and caught her eye, she startled and fumbled her load, nearly dropping it. Heat flushed her neck. Averting her gaze, she set the handful of logs onto the stack.

"Henry, you need water?" Catch held up his canteen.

She tilted her head in question.

"It's hot. You drinking enough?"

Ah. Best to let him think her fumble came from dehydration and not romantic notions. She held up her empty canteen. "I'm fresh out."

He jogged toward her with his canteen extended. "Here. Drink."

Her chest swelled. How thoughtful. She gulped the cool refreshment, unable to stop herself from picturing his lips upon the same place moments before. She couldn't look him in the eye lest he read her mind. "Much obliged." She offered a shy smile and nod.

"Anytime." He hurried back to his spot and continued working, giving her an unobstructed view.

Goodness, she had it bad. Heaven help her.

Footsteps sounded from behind. "Henry Frontenac?"

She whipped around. "Yes?"

A private stood, red-faced with beads of perspiration at his temples. "Someone is looking for you."

Dread pooled. "Who?" Someone from the army? Had they found out her secret?

"A lady. Says she's your sister."

The timber tumbled from her grasp. "Loreen? Loreen is here?"

As if also perplexed, his brow rumpled. "She's waiting in front of the mess tent for you."

"Thank you." She offered a nod before breaking into a sprint. What did Loreen's visit mean? *Please, God. Let Millie be alive.* Though what good was such a prayer now? If Loreen came to deliver tragic news in person, the disaster had already happened. No use pleading with the Almighty. But surely, Loreen wouldn't have left the rest of the girls in such a time of grief. What if Pa …? No. A letter would convey any news of death or sickness as Loreen was needed at home.

If Loreen *was* needed, what could have compelled her to make such a long journey? Did she do so unaccompanied? Unheard of. Dangerous.

One good thing about trousers, no matter how ill-fitting, they were easier to run in than skirts. She skidded to a stop a few yards away from the cabin being used for the headquarters. Her breath caught. Loreen. She sat facing away from Henrietta, her profile in full view. How could *that* be her sister?

Someone plowed into her from behind, sending her sprawling face-first into the dust. She coughed. Gagged at the chalky grime coating her mouth.

"Henry, I'm sorry."

Catch? He had tumbled into the dirt next to her. "What are you doing here?"

He stood, then reached out a hand to pull her up. "You left in such a hurry, so I was concerned. Wanted to make sure everything was okay."

She wiped her mouth with her sleeve. "That's my sister." She nodded to Loreen. "Don't know what she's doing here."

He brushed a leaf from his beard. "Why'd you stop?"

"I don't know. She looks so …" How could she describe it? The way the months apart had transformed the person she'd known better than herself. "Grown up." That didn't come close.

He smiled in a sympathetic way and nudged Henrietta's shoulder. "Go on. She won't bite."

No, but the news she carried might. "Come with me?" She winked to siphon the vulnerability out of her request. If only she could take his hand. Lean into his strength.

He laughed. "Yeah, we'll do this together. We took on thousands of Yanks. We can take on your pretty sister."

A pang twinged her chest. "You think she's pretty?" Her voice squeaked.

He laughed again. "Come on. Let's go."

With each step, Loreen came into clearer focus. She *was* pretty. Stunning. Good food and decent clothing had done her a world of good. Silky hair instead of brittle. Rosy cheeks instead of pale, gaunt ones. Full lips. She nearly glowed.

As they neared, Henrietta called her sister's name.

Loreen jumped up, squealed, then threw herself into Henrietta's arms. "Oh, Henri—" Henrietta pinched her sister's forearm, and she corrected. "I missed you so."

"I missed you too." When Loreen drew back, her gaze dropped to Henrietta's feet. "Oh dear. What happened to your shoes?"

"Long marches. Never mind about that." Henrietta placed her hands on her sister's shoulders. "Why did you come? Is Millie all right?"

Loreen's eyes widened as she nodded. "Oh, yes. I didn't realize … Did you think?"

"The last I heard she was ill. Then they told me you'd arrived."

"Oh dear." Loreen's hands flew to her cheeks. "Mildred's fine. She's well. The doctor gave her a tincture, and she recovered straightaway."

Henrietta shook her head, confusion clouding her brain. "Then why—"

"I got your letter." Loreen took her hands. "I had to intervene."

Got her letter? What letter?

"Don't look so stupefied. You can't be entirely shocked."

"But I am." She opened her mouth to say more, to ask more, but words wouldn't form.

Loreen's gaze drifted behind Henrietta's shoulder. Catch. He was still there, standing sentinel beside her.

Loreen's smile twitched with a hint of mischief. "Stop gaping like a fish and introduce me to your friend."

Henrietta swallowed. Her letter. The letter where she'd confessed her feelings for the man beside her. Her pulse skittered. "Catch, this is my sister Loreen. Loreen, this is Catch." At the lift of Loreen's brow, she added, "Well, everyone calls him that, anyhow. No one seems to know his real name."

"It's a secret." He leaned forward and took Loreen's hand in his own. Delicately, as if he were plucking a flower. Henrietta's chest burned.

Loreen curtsied. How could envy twist Henrietta's gut at something so simple? The freedom to curtsy. The freedom to be treated as a lady. She'd never before thought of it as a privilege, only a hindrance. Yet, she'd give anything to trade places with her sister. To be herself with this man.

"Nice to meet you." Loreen's eyes twinkled mischievously.

"Likewise." *Ugh.* A roguish smile.

She needed to put an end to this. An end to her misery. She looped her arm through Loreen's. Wait. Men didn't do that, did they? Better readjust. She tugged her sister in the direction of the woods. With a glance over her shoulder, she put space between these two people she adored.

"Thank you for making sure all was well, Catch. I'm going to speak with my sister."

He nodded and strode back to work.

Loreen giggled. "I see what you were talking about."

Henrietta quickened her pace to ensure plenty of distance away from eavesdroppers. "I did not write to you so you could come and flirt with him."

A burst of air puffed from Loreen's parted lips. "Flirt? Is that what you think I was doing?"

Henrietta rolled her eyes.

They reached a secluded grove of hickory trees. Strands of sunshine peeked through green leaves, creating a kaleidoscope of shadow and light.

Loreen wrapped her in a hug. "Oh, dear sister. I didn't come to steal him away from you. I came to entreat you to *tell him*."

"Tell him?"

"Yes. You must."

Her mind swirled. Loreen had traveled all this way to plead with her to jeopardize her position in the army? "You're not thinking clearly."

Loreen stared her down. "You are the one who has a muddled brain."

Henrietta shook her head. None of this made sense. She motioned to a moss-covered log. "Sit. Explain to me how you got here. Who's watching the homestead while you're gone? Who's taking care of the girls?"

"Gretchen is proving quite capable." Loreen's straight posture, almost regal, contrasted starkly with the girl Henrietta had left behind. What had happened to her insecure, overly dramatic sister?

"But how—"

An outstretched hand halted Henrietta's questions. "Before you fret, let me assure you they'll be fine. Pa is coming around. Slowly, mind you. But it's progress. It's as if he's waking from a long dream. He's groggy but coming into awareness of life around him."

Pa was breaking free from the fog that had encased him all these years? What else had she missed?

"Also, I lost my job at the general store." She shrugged as if this was of no consequence.

Henrietta fingered her throat. Just as she'd feared.

"'Twasn't meant to be. As fate would have it, the last customers to come into the shop before Mr. Sawyers fired me were a couple about to travel to Fredericksburg. They were looking for someone to come with them to help with the children on the journey. I volunteered." Her smile shone bright.

Relief washed over Henrietta. Loreen hadn't come this great distance alone. Millie had recovered. Pa was coming alive again. And Loreen, though currently bereft of regular employment, proved fully capable of securing a job for herself. All would be well.

"I still don't understand why you came all this way." If she'd wanted to make a point, a letter would have sufficed.

Loreen turned to face her with a serious expression. "You have laid your life down for your family, 'Etta. You've put us first always. If no one intervenes, you'll continue to do so until your last breath. I can't stand for it. I won't." She tilted her chin. "You are worth more than the money you can bring in by soldiering. Your well-being matters too."

Henrietta's eyes stung. She looked away and studied a green tuft of grass. "But you need me."

Loreen's hand covered hers, and their eyes locked. "We needed your financial support for a while, yes. To get back on our feet. Now, we need *you*. We need our sister happy and whole."

They no longer depended on the money she provided? She crossed her arms. Who was she if she wasn't the provider for her family? The one who shouldered their burdens? Blast the watery sheen overtaking her eyes. She couldn't cry.

Loreen linked her pinky finger with Henrietta's—their special ritual. "Tell him. Confess who you are and how you feel."

"I can't." Her chest squeezed at the thought. She might well faint if she tried.

"Why not? What are you afraid of?"

She guffawed. Oh, the possibilities. Getting kicked out would be the best of options. Jail would be dreadful. The thought that clenched her heart, though, had nothing to do with how the army would react and everything to do with Catch's reaction. Instead of looking at her with respect, would his expression be coated with scorn? If she confessed her feelings for him, would he reply with disgust? Such a response would taint every perfect memory she had of him. Each moment, word, and glance between them, she intended to cherish forever. His rejection would ruin it all.

A sob wrenched from her throat. "I can't."

She pressed her fist against her mouth to stifle any further displays of the emotions warring inside. Tears tracked her cheeks.

Loreen's gentle fingers wiped them away. Her lined forehead spoke of distress.

Poor Loreen. She'd traveled such a great distance to talk Henrietta into something she was incapable of doing. Henrietta had been able to face bullets, cannon blasts, blood, and gore, yet courage failed when it came to revealing her heart. How she longed to be known. How her heart trembled at the unveiling.

"'Etta, you must—"

The snap of a twig halted their conversation. Loreen's mouth snapped shut. Her eyes blinked wide. Who was there? How much had they heard?

Loreen's countenance paled as her jaw dropped.

Heart pounding, Henrietta turned. Catch stood behind her, mouth agape.

Chapter 23

Suburb of Wilmington, North Carolina
Present Day

Ivy pulled her purse over her shoulder and took a step toward the front door.

Austin's voice startled her. "Where are you off to so early? You don't have to head to work for another hour and a half, right?"

She spun around to find him standing in the hall, hands casually tucked in his pants pockets.

"You scared me."

He flashed her a wry grin.

"I'm headed to Everly's prenatal appointment. Sixteen weeks." She checked her watch. "If I leave now, I can grab coffee at Screaming Peach first." The breakfast café was nearly a half hour in the opposite direction, but she'd been craving a peach scone and vanilla latte. No one had better pastries or coffee. She was having a baby, even if she wasn't pregnant. She deserved to splurge on at least one craving.

Would Austin chide her? Wasting money on gas for such frivolity wasn't exactly *fiscally responsible*.

He shifted his jaw. "Do you plan on attending every appointment?"

No word about her breakfast choice. But he still wasn't happy.

"Of course." She fiddled with her purse strap. "Why wouldn't I? It's my baby." She winced. "*Our* baby."

He pulled his hands from his pockets and rubbed them together, like he always did when he was gearing up to go toe to toe with her.

She folded her arms around her middle. "What?"

"It's just, if I were Everly, I might feel a little …"

Cared for? Not alone in this?

"Suffocated."

She reared back. "Suffocated? What are you talking about?"

He came to her and rubbed his hands up and down her arms. "Don't get me wrong. You've been a wonderful support to her. I wonder, though, if she feels like you trust her. With the baby, I mean. Or if she feels like you're hovering."

"I have the right to hover. It's … *our* baby. I'm surprised you haven't insisted on coming to each appointment." Now that she thought about it, didn't he care about how their child was doing? She shook off his touch.

He held her gaze with his steady one. "In a month, both you and I will be at the big ultrasound. Until then, I trust Everly to keep us up to date."

But she had to know it all, firsthand. Every little detail. She would never be able to go to her own prenatal appointments with a bulging belly. This was as close as she was going to get, and she needed to be there for it. How could he ask her not to?

She searched his eyes. His gaze flicked to the floor. Oh.

"Zach said something, didn't he?" Her chest clenched.

Austin sighed. "You've got to understand, he's looking out for Everly in the same way I look out for you."

"How nice of him to protect his wife from big bad Poison Ivy." If only she could squeeze herself tight enough to offset the hurt.

Austin wrapped his arms around her, pressing his cheek to hers. "That's not what's happening. You've got to know that."

Did she? The three of them talked about her behind her back. How upset was Zach? Did he lob angry complaints Austin had to field? And why? She hadn't done anything wrong. Nothing unreasonable. It made all the sense in the world to go to every appointment. If that upset Ev and Zach, they should have thought about that before they agreed to carry her baby.

"Honey." He rubbed the small of her back. "You're not wrong for wanting to be there. But also, attending every appointment won't give you the ability to control each outcome. Everly's taking good care of our child. Can you trust that she loves you enough to do what's best for our baby? Can you allow her some autonomy?"

Her and Ev's mutual meltdown outside Gale's office resurfaced in her memory. Her sister's love had been evident then. What right had Ivy to doubt it now?

Only … "I'm sure she means well, but she's abandoned reasonable science and medicine for her hippie ways. What if she decided to do something strange, thinking it's fine when it's truly not?" The baby might overdose on vitamins or essential oils or something.

"Mi amor—"

She stomped her foot. "Don't tell me I'm being unreasonable!"

He held up his hands. "I'm not."

She narrowed her eyes at him.

"I understand your concerns. Have you talked to God about them? Why don't you skip that coffee for time in prayer."

Skip Screaming Peach? She hadn't been able to go back to bed after waking in the wee morning hours for dreaming of their scones.

"Don't pout." The corner of his eyes crinkled.

She pressed her lips together. "I'm not."

He chuckled. "I'll brew a pot of coffee and make cinnamon rolls."

Not the same, but … "Okay." There was always tomorrow.

After grabbing her Bible and favorite quilt from her room, she settled onto the giant wicker chair on their screened-in porch. The faded blue cushion, along with several fluffy pillows, provided the comfiest spot in the house. She flipped through her Bible haphazardly, reading a verse here and there, not landing on anything.

Lord, it's been a while since I've truly set aside time to dig into Your Word and listen to You. She read a daily devotional from her Bible app each day that included half a dozen Scriptures, but it felt more like she was checking something off a list than spending time with the One who loved her most. *With the cancer, then this pregnancy, I've been distracted.*

Lame excuse. *Okay, maybe it's deeper than that. Have I been avoiding You?*

The truth of how she'd pulled away from her Creator nudged her. *I have, haven't I?* Why had she done it? After all, she knew better. She'd searched high and low years ago, trying to find something that could satisfy her soul. Her restlessness only expanded. Her depression only deepened. Until she turned back to Him. Of course, only He could satisfy her heart. Why would she distance herself from Him?

Her fingers caressed worn pages. Seemingly of their own accord, they found Psalm 127, the passage she had clung to during her engagement as she dreamed of having a family.

> *Behold, children are a heritage from the Lord,*
> *the fruit of the womb a reward.*
> *Like arrows in the hand of a warrior,*
> *are the children of one's youth.*
> *Blessed is the man*
> *who fills his quiver with them!*
> *He shall not be put to shame*
> *when he speaks with his enemies in the gate.*

Back then, she'd taken those words as a guarantee she'd receive the desire of her heart. Now … certainly there were no guarantees. Her gaze traveled to the beginning of the chapter.

> *Unless the Lord builds the house,*
> *those who build it labor in vain*
> *Unless the Lord watches over the city,*
> *the watchman stays awake in vain.*
> *It is in vain that you rise up early and go late to*
> *rest, eating the bread of anxious toil;*
> *for he gives to his beloved sleep.*

Strange. She knew the verses, of course. But she'd never made the connection they were in the same chapter as her beloved verses about having children. *Eating the bread of anxious toil.*

Man, that hit home. She'd feasted on *anxious toil* until she was fat with it. She was a glutton when it came anxiety. And what had it gotten her? It hadn't stopped her from getting cancer.

She modified the verse in her mind.

Unless the Lord knits this baby together, those who wear themselves out trying to eliminate every risk and trying to ensure all is perfect will labor in vain.

Unless the Lord.

God, this really is up to You, isn't it? I can't control the outcome here. I can't bubble wrap this baby, or my heart, to ensure nothing bad happens, ever. I have to trust You ... but I'm scared. Why?

The immediate answers her brain provided—because Mom died and because I got cancer—didn't suffice. She'd weathered every negative circumstance. And still, fear held her captive.

You don't truly believe I love you.

She sucked in a breath at the clarity of God's voice. *I don't?* It seemed preposterous that after all the church services she'd attended, after all the worship songs she'd sung, after all the Scriptures she'd read, she wouldn't believe God loved her. Wasn't that Christianity 101? But knowing something in her head was far different from having it settle into the depths of her heart.

You're right. I don't. How could she fix that?

As soon as the thought came, she dissolved into giggles. Seriously? Her go-to was to try to find a way to fix her own problem. Would she never come to peace with her own powerlessness?

Okay, Lord, I can't fix this by myself. I need You to open my heart to receive Your love, to let it bury itself deep within my soul so that I know that I know that I know.

Another verse came to mind, and she flipped to Ephesians 3:17–19.

> *That Christ may dwell in your hearts through faith; that you, being rooted and grounded in love, may have strength to comprehend with all the saints what is the breadth and length and height and depth, and to know the love of Christ that surpasses knowledge, that you may be filled with all the fullness of God.*

She repeated the verse several times, making it her prayer. Peace cushioned her heart in this place. Far better than a peach scone. She checked her watch. Time to let Everly know she wouldn't be at the appointment today. The scent of cinnamon wafted to her. She'd have breakfast with Austin and share what the Lord had revealed to her and head to work at the regular time. She'd give Everly breathing room.

~~

I hang up the phone and stare out the kitchen window. Of all the strange developments. Ivy called and said she was skipping out on this morning's prenatal appointment "if that's okay." No way I could tell her how okay it was.

"Why do you look dazed?" Zach comes behind me and kisses my hair. "Is your aloe plant completely dead?"

Yes, but … "Ivy's not coming." I breathe deeply and note the scent of mangos. Zach must have varied his smoothie.

"Huh. Interesting." The way he says this arouses my suspicions.

I turn to face him. "You didn't say anything to her, did you?"

He keeps a straight face. "To her? No."

I narrow my gaze at him.

"I might have mentioned something to Austin."

My voice comes out as a whine. "Zach! Why?"

"Because her coming to your appointments stresses you out. We're going to have to hire you a personal masseuse if this keeps up."

He's not wrong. But still. "I didn't want to hurt her feelings."

"I know." He takes a drink of his protein-packed breakfast. "That's why I did it for you."

I grab the dish towel and swat him with it. "You're horrible."

He yelps dramatically. Brat. Then his arms encircle me again. "I've got to look out for my woman." He presses close and trails kisses on my neck, my ear. Tingles consume my body.

I relish being near him like this. He's been slightly standoffish since my belly started to bloom. I doubt it's intentional. Does he even realize it?

A thought sparks. "Why don't you come with me?"

"Me?" His forehead scrunches.

"Yes, you." I grab his hand and swing our arms. "We can go on a quick breakfast date afterward." If this appointment is as simple as the last, we'll have plenty of time before our office opens at eleven.

His thumb caresses mine. "I don't know. I'd feel weird being there. It's not my child."

"But you're *my* husband." I plead with my eyes. "And I want you with me." I add pouty lips for emphasis.

He tilts his head. "If it means that much to you."

"It does." I squeeze his hand.

Early on, I promised to keep our connection paramount, yet I've failed. Ivy is all-consuming. She's been in my space and on my brain. Her child is growing inside of me. There's been little room for anything else, other than the pain of my past. And Zach? I've left him on the sidelines.

Not completely. The dance we shared floats to the top of my memory. But afterward, other memories surface. Polite pecks goodnight. Him rolling to his side of the bed, and me to mine.

He hasn't touched my growing belly. Not once. And why should he? There's nothing in there for him. And yet, I used to always dream of being pregnant and having my husband caress my belly, waiting for a kick. Instead, Zach seems repelled. As long as we pretend I'm not pregnant, we're okay. It's getting harder to do.

How can I bridge this gap between us? It will take more than a breakfast date, but at least it's a start.

On the drive to Wanda's, we talk about our clients, my studies, and plans to landscape the backyard. Not once does either one of us mention where we're going and why.

When we pull into the driveway, Zach whistles. "Well, this is … different."

I giggle. "It has character."

"Character, yeah. That's what I meant." He winks.

Wanda meets us at the door and ushers us in. "This must be your hubby." She reaches out her hand to shake his.

I grin. "Yes, this is Zach." Wanda has quickly become one of my favorite people, and Zach is going to love her. Hopefully.

"Nice to meet you." He offers a wooden smile as he shakes Wanda's hand.

The easygoing vibe he had in the car has vanished. In its place is the rigidness that's his signature when he's uncomfortable. Normally, in those times, he tends to be curt. He'd better play nice here.

We sit on the sofa, and I scoot as close to him as I can. He takes the hint and wraps an arm around my shoulder.

Wanda sits across from us. "I have to say, I'm pleased you came. I know your role in this pregnancy is different, but your support remains vital for your wife."

I pat his knee. "So true."

He startles slightly. If I wasn't touching him, I'd have likely missed the reaction, but my thigh reverberates with his twitch. Has he not considered how much I need him?

"No Ivy today?" Wanda asks.

I press my lips together to hold in a chuckle.

Zach answers for me. "Nope. I'm her replacement."

I wouldn't blame Wanda for sighing in relief after enduring Ivy's interrogations, but she only nods. "Okay, then, we'll get started."

She asks a host of questions about how I'm feeling, my appetite, and my activity. "Can you feel the baby move?"

"Yes. All the time."

Zach's head swivels in my direction. "You can?"

"Yeah." I rub my belly.

"You've never said anything." What's swimming in his eyes? Betrayal? Loneliness?

What can I say? *You didn't seem interested* or *I didn't think you'd care*. Neither of those would be helpful. I shrug. "It never came up." Not hard to believe since we don't talk about this baby. Ever.

He angles toward me. "Could I feel it if I tried?"

My mouth parts. Would he want to? I mirror his position, turning toward him. "Not yet, but soon maybe?" I glance at Wanda, and she nods. "Yeah, soon."

I lock eyes with Zach again and channel all my love for him into that gaze. I can't expect him to treat this like a normal pregnancy. That's obvious. But longing to do this crazy thing *with* the man I love surges through me. No, it's not our baby. But might we be able to bond through the experience?

The silence in the room doesn't seem awkward. It's full of yearning and hope and adoration. But after a moment, Wanda clears her throat, and the bubble pops.

We both turn to her.

She stands. "Let's get your weight."

I groan. My least favorite part. I'd better be able to get back into shape after this is over. The baby weight would be one thing if I had something to show for it. As it stands, this is something I can't help but fear. What if I never get back to normal? Will this choice mar me forever?

After Wanda weighs me and tests my urine, she pulls out her Doppler. "Ready to hear the heartbeat?"

Am I ever. The excitement makes no sense. Ivy would have every right to be giddy, but me? And yet, it's proof of a miracle happening inside of me. Even if it's not my miracle, it's awe-inspiring just the same.

Wanda instructs Zach to move to a nearby chair, and I lie on the couch, exposing my stomach. She pulls an ottoman next to the couch and sits. Then, she moves the instrument around. A staticky whooshing sound fills the room, and I strain to distinguish the heartbeat.

When it comes, a laugh bubbles from me. "I hear it."

Zach's eyes widen. "Is it supposed to be so fast?" he asks.

Wanda's eyes crinkle. "One hundred and thirty beats per minute. Perfect."

"Wow. Crazy."

I close my eyes and relish what sounds like galloping hooves for a minute.

Then Wanda pulls the Doppler away and wipes my belly with a tissue. I reposition my clothing and sit up, patting the spot next to me. Zach transitions back to the couch, taking my hand and caressing my thumb with his. For the rest of the appointment, he doesn't stop.

When we're back in the car, I open my mouth to ask him where he wants to go for breakfast, but he speaks first.

"Everly, that was amazing. Thank you for inviting me." His words sound sincere, but he's averting his gaze, and there's a thickness in his voice. Is he … tearing up?

"Of course. You're always welcome." I cover his hand on the gearshift with mine. It might be better not to press, but I can't stand not knowing. I keep my voice gentle. "What are you thinking?"

He shakes his head.

"Please?"

When he glances at me, his eyes are moist. My breath hitches.

"I … I want that, Ev. I've tried not to. I've prayed for God to take away this desire for children, but …" He rubs his chest. "It's here. It won't go away."

It's my turn to avert my gaze. This is why I shouldn't have pressed. I should have changed the subject to omelets and yogurt. Why did I insist he come along? Looks like I've stoked a smoldering fire into full flame.

Now, I'm leaning against my car door, hands clasped in my lap. Without realizing what I was doing, I've pulled away.

Hurt flows though his voice as he says, "You asked."

Stupid me.

"I don't want to pressure you. I *won't*. But it's hard to have this desire and never speak about it."

"I understand." And I do. My heart breaks for him. For me. For all that will never be.

"Do you think you could ever reconsider?"

I almost blurt out *no*, but I clamp my mouth shut instead. He's not asking for a commitment. He's asking for a possibility. Gale's words come back to me. *Have you given Him your womb?* I've resolved to live surrendered to the Lord, and so far, that's meant tiptoeing into emotional waters I haven't wanted to go near. Having a child myself seems like an Olympic-level feat after such difficult baby steps. Still, is it right to limit what God *might* do in me in the future?

I take a shaky breath and reply, "Maybe." It's all I can give right now.

Zach releases a whoosh of breath that ends in something like a laugh. He takes my hand and kisses my knuckles. "Praise God." He grins at me as if I've promised him the world.

I wait for the familiar dread to swirl inside me like it does whenever I consider what it would be like to have children. It doesn't come. Instead, the word *maybe* reverberates like a gong.

~~

Ivy rolled her neck from side to side. Good thing she'd had time with the Lord this morning. Work had been grueling, a nonstop grind. How would she have coped if she'd had to face it without spiritual fuel? When she'd broken for lunch, a voicemail from Everly waited for her. The appointment had gone well, the baby's heartbeat strong. And Zach had gone with her. Maybe that was another reason the Lord had redirected her, to make room for her brother-in-law.

She checked the clock. Only one more hour until she could go home. She could do this.

She pulled up the next transcription in the queue, praying it wasn't another case of the flu. Imagining the germs infesting the doctors' offices around her really put her trust in God to the test.

"Oh, good," she muttered to herself. This one was from OB. Routine pregnancy checkups were her favorite to transcribe. They were a reminder that her baby would continue to grow and develop. At sixteen weeks, her baby was the size of an avocado. Amazing to think that one day she'd be watermelon-sized. In a month, they'd be able to see her on an ultrasound.

Okay, time to focus.

As she listened to the doctor's accented voice, her fingers flew over her keyboard. A case of multiples. As she continued listening to the visit, however, dread crept up her limbs. Three embryos were growing inside of this woman, but she didn't want triplets.

> *Mother expressed concern with carrying three fetuses to term. After I went over the risks, mother elects to terminate embryo number three.*

"No." Ivy's choked cry filled the modest office.
Bridget turned to her. "What's wrong?"

She shook her head, unable to put such horror into words.

Cherry abandoned her desk and hovered over Ivy's shoulder. "Gracious. I don't blame her. Twins will be difficult enough, but triplets? I'd rather have a root canal on all my teeth."

Ivy spun around to face her, mouth agape. "I can't believe you said that."

Cherry shrugged. "Guess I'm not a kid person."

"It's a baby." Ivy pointed to her screen. "They're going to kill a baby. Do you know how many women can't have children? How many would give anything to house three growing babies in their womb?"

Cherry threw her hands up. "Whoa. Didn't mean to offend." She backed up a few steps, then returned to her desk. As she placed her headset back on, she mumbled, "Someone doesn't believe in women's rights."

Ivy clenched her jaw to hold back a retort. Women's rights? What about the baby's rights? Why couldn't everyone see that stopping a beating heart was wrong, no matter how large or small the heart?

This wasn't anxiety whooshing through her. It was righteous indignation. An altogether different feeling but every bit as strong.

If only not typing the words would render them null and void. She'd stop this atrocity by refusing to transcribe the appointment if that were the case. But she couldn't do anything to change the situation.

A wave of nausea rose as she transcribed every dreadful line. What she wouldn't give to snatch that baby from death and carry it in her own womb. Her throat burned. She'd never experience the joy of feeling a baby move inside her. She could only watch as her sister's belly grew. Of course, she was thankful. Abundantly thankful. But there was still loss intertwined in her story, and every so often, it pricked her anew.

Lord, You are acquainted with my grief. He understood without her having to justify her emotions. With Him, she could just be. Just feel. She didn't have to force cheerfulness when sorrow battered her heart. *Thank You, Jesus.*

As she came to the end of the recording, her fingers protested finishing. She cringed at the thought of sending this through. But what could she do?

Pray.

Of course. Instead of worrying, she would pray for this woman to have a change of heart. Paging up to the top of the report, she noted the woman's name so she could make the prayer more personal. Shawna Spring. She closed her eyes and lifted a petition to heaven for Shawna and her babies. If God could turn Ivy's heart back to Him, if He could redeem her sister's life, He could certainly intervene in this situation so Shawna didn't regret her decision for the rest of her life. Of course, He could. But would He?

A desire to purchase a gift for the triplets surged through her. Was that from the Lord or from herself? Maybe it was like a step of faith. But did she have the faith to act?

Chapter 24

Across the Rappahannock River from Fredericksburg,
Virginia
June 1863

Catch's eyes searched hers. "You … You're …"

Though Henrietta couldn't seem to force herself to move, Loreen stood. "Henrietta is my sister," she stated, with far more confidence than Henrietta had ever heard her possess.

"Y-your … sister?" His gaze combed over her as if taking stock of all he knew and putting it together with Loreen's words. What was that flash of emotion in his eyes? Disbelief? Hurt? Betrayal? Her lip trembled.

He ran a hand through his hair. "You're a woman."

She nodded.

He turned and stalked away a few steps, only to march back toward her. "Your name is Henrietta?"

"Yes." Her legs, though shaky, now cooperated, allowing her to stand. She clasped her hands. "Please don't tell." Like champagne from a popped cork bottle, her words flowed. "Griffen jailed my friend Bernie—Bernice—for soldiering as a female. Please don't rat me out. My family needs the money I provide for them." She shot Loreen a look, daring her to contradict.

Loreen bit her lip.

He paced a few steps one way, then the other. "Saints alive, Henry." He shook his head. "Henrietta. What am I supposed to do with this?"

"Just keep it quiet. Go on as normal. Freddy knew, and he never said a word."

"Freddy knew?" He crouched and dropped his head into his hands. Was he praying? If there was ever a man who did the right thing, it was Catch. And if he felt keeping a secret was the wrong move, he wouldn't do it. Couldn't. Even if she landed in jail, she had to admire such integrity.

She waited with bated breath. When he stood, his shoulders drooped with resignation. Her spirits sagged. This couldn't be good.

His voice came out hoarse. "I don't know what to do or what to think. I thought I—" He coughed. "I thought I knew you. Thought we were friends."

She took a step toward him. "We are."

He put out a hand. "Friends don't keep secrets. Not like this."

She scuffed her boot in the mud. "I'm sorry."

His mouth firmed as he studied her further.

Loreen blew out a breath. "Might as well tell him the rest."

Henrietta winced. Hadn't he already heard?

Catch's brows rose. "The rest?"

Her cheeks heated as her gaze dropped. There was no way she could look at him. She'd die. She might perish just from leaking out the words, but if she didn't, Loreen would. It would be better coming from her. "I … I fancy you."

There. If she could melt into the forest floor, that would be grand.

No response. Not even a grunt of acknowledgement. She hazarded a glance at him. He stared straight at her, as if dazed.

Loreen jumped in. "I came to convince her to tell you how she felt, seeing as she's been mooning over you like a lovesick puppy."

Henrietta shot her a glare. Lovesick puppy? How embarrassing.

Loreen paid her no mind. "'Etta is always thinking about someone else, never herself. Thought it was about time someone put her first for a change."

Henrietta gave Loreen a grateful smile.

Catch shifted his weight from foot to foot. "I don't know … I never thought … I can't—"

Henrietta put him out of his misery. "It's fine. I understand."

He didn't feel the same about her. She figured as much. They'd been friends. Even that might be ruined. Perhaps not. They might be able to repair their relationship once a bubble of awkwardness between them popped. If not, surely the loss of this friendship would be one that would stick with her always.

"I'm sorry. I need time to think." He crossed his arms over his broad chest. Of course, he'd need time to consider whether he'd turn her in or not. Catch was thoughtful, not impulsive. He'd think through the options and come to a sound conclusion. Hopefully, one that didn't include bars for her.

~~

Henrietta wiped her brow with her sleeve, then collected several logs for the fire. She stilled. What was that noise? A feminine cry. *Loreen.* Henrietta's pulse skittered. What was wrong? What was happening to her sister? She broke into a run. She'd only left for a few minutes.

"Unhand me, you scoundrel." Loreen's voice sounded clear through bouts of raucous laughter.

As Henrietta neared, the scene came into focus. A group of soldiers surrounded Loreen, each one's greedy hands grabbing at her.

Heat throbbed through Henrietta's limbs. She clenched her hands into fists. She'd take down every last one of those blockheads.

Before she could reach them, someone jumped into the fray with a punch to one man's gut, then a kick to another one's groin. Catch. She couldn't help but smile. She reached the circle in time to shove ole Curtain Hair onto his backside. She lifted her fists toward another man's face. He backed off, hands raised.

"We were just havin' a little fun." He snorted. "Been a while since we've seen a lady."

"Obviously." She spat at him. "You've forgotten how to treat 'em."

Catch wrapped an arm around Loreen's shoulders, turning her away from covetous eyes. "Are you okay?"

She straightened her blouse. Dusted off her skirt. "Yes. I'm fine."

Henrietta came around her other side. "I'm sorry. I shouldn't have left you alone." As she eyed Catch's arm draped around her sister, her gut knotted. Was this why Catch didn't return her feelings for him? Was he sweet on Loreen? They'd only just met, but there was no doubt she was the prettier of the two of them. Far sweeter and more refined. What man wouldn't prefer someone more feminine?

Catch guided Loreen to another campfire, away from ogling soldiers. "Sit here." He motioned to a camp chair.

The fire flickered with dying embers. "I dropped the firewood when I heard the screams. I'll go back and get it."

"No, sit." Catch acknowledged her for the first time since their parting in the woods. "I'll grab it. You can sit with your sister." His nod spoke of respect.

She watched him walk away.

Loreen wrapped her arms around herself. "That was something back there. Do you fight men often?"

Henrietta chuckled. "This is war, so ..."

Loreen nudged her side. "You know what I mean."

"No. Not often." She patted her sister's knee. "I'd do anything for my sister."

"I know."

Catch returned and stoked the fire. He sat across from them. His eyes locked with hers. "I've never met anyone quite like you, *Henry*." He said the name with a hint of teasing. What did he mean? Was he simply acknowledging he'd never met a female soldier before? Or confessing something more?

She leaned forward, lacing her fingers together. "Are you ever going to tell me your real name?"

She narrowed her eyes in a dare. He'd said true friends didn't keep secrets from each other. How would he respond?

A muscle in his jaw twitched. "Someday, maybe."

Would there be a someday?

Chapter 25

Suburb of Wilmington, North Carolina
Present Day

My hand trembles as I dial the number listed. After one ring, I hang up. I can't do this. I run my fingers through my hair and end up twisting it into a messy bun before I realize there are no ponytail holders. With a huff, I let my hair drop.

A glance at the clock shows only ten minutes until my next client's appointment. Ridiculous to try and do something earth-shattering in such a short amount of time anyway. I can wait until this afternoon. Or tomorrow. Or … never.

A soft knock and Zach peeks through my office door. "How's it going?" His brows lift. In the kindest way possible, he's asking if I made the call.

I shake my head. "Can't."

He comes all the way in and shuts the door behind him. I can't lose it minutes before I'm scheduled to treat clients, but my limbs shake with the pressure of holding in these giant emotions. I collapse into his arms.

With his finger, he draws a heart on my back. I wait for him to quote a Bible verse. Philippians 4:13 or one of those *nothing is impossible with God* ones. But he kisses my hair and asks, "Do you want me to make the call with you?"

"For me?" I plead.

His chest rumbles with a chuckle. "I doubt they'll give me the information if I call on my own. But I can stand right here and hold your hand as you talk to them. I'll even dial."

What a sweet man. My hero, truly. But my gaze wanders to the wall clock again. "There's no time."

He pulls back and studies me. His hands run up and down my goose-pimpled arms. "When you're ready, then."

He steps back and angles toward the door, but I stop him with a question.

"What if I'm never ready?" I bite my lip. I thought I could do this. Gale and I discussed it at length, worked through pros and cons, and concluded that this is what I wanted. But now? It seems premature.

"You will be." He crosses his arms over his chest, accentuating his muscles. He's far stronger than me in every way. His confidence in me is misplaced, yet it encourages me just the same.

Zach steps out, and the receptionist sticks her head in. "Your ten o'clock is here."

"Thanks, Angela." Saved by Mrs. Mosby. I have a valid excuse to put this off a little longer. "I'll be right out."

I take several deep breaths, shake out my arms and legs, and roll my neck. I probably look like a baseball player going up to bat. As I pick up Mrs. Mosby's chart, I accidentally knock Henrietta's and Loreen's letters to the floor. I scramble to pick them up and shuffle them back into order. When Ivy lost interest, I decided to read them on my own. I've been taking it slow, savoring them one by one. I read the final one last night but must have zoned out part of the way through because when I awoke this morning, I couldn't remember what I read. Hence, why I brought them with me to the office.

A phrase stands out to me as I return the letters to the desk. *It will take more than flying bullets to knock me down.* How did I come from such a brave heritage and turn out to be such a coward? What would Henrietta say if she could see me struggling to make a simple phone call? She knew fear, yet she raced toward her goal, mindless of the opposition.

Lord, if this is what You want me to do, give me the courage to follow through.

I step out of my office and greet Mrs. Mosby, then call her back to my exam room.

"Oh!" The older woman stares at my middle. "I didn't know you were expecting."

If only I had a dozen more surrogacy T-shirts. Explaining the situation never gets less awkward. "I'm actually carrying a child for my sister. I'm her surrogate."

"Oh, how lovely. My eldest granddaughter did that for one of her friends. A delightful experience."

It's my turn to stare. "Seriously? I've never met anyone who knew a surrogate before."

"Yes, dear. Macy was born ... let's see ..." Her face scrunches in concentration. "Must be five years ago. Calls my granddaughter Auntie even though they're not related. They've remained close."

"Neat," I say, then inwardly kick myself. Neat? What kind of response is that?

"Yes, well, it takes a special kind of person." She puts her purse down on the chair in the corner.

I have nothing to say to that, so I focus on my job. "Facedown, please."

She complies, lowering onto the table. With her face in the hole, her voice comes out muffled. "You don't have any children of your own, correct?"

My fingers examine her spine. I find the subluxation and press to realign her back. "Yes, that's right." A few vertebrae lower, I adjust again.

"I thought my granddaughter said in order to be a surrogate, you had to have had at least one successful prior pregnancy."

I still. My brain blanks. How should I reply? No idea surfaces.

"Of course," she continues, "it might vary state to state. She lives in Alabama."

She's given me an out. A noncommittal grunt will do. I can redirect the conversation, and she'll never be the wiser.

"On your left," I direct.

Her aquamarine eyes meet mine as she maneuvers. There's no guile in them, only purity and kindness. And I did pray for courage.

"No, it's true. I placed a child for adoption when I was young." No need to state how young.

"You're still young, dear." She pats my hand, then bends her right knee into the familiar position. "How hard that must have been for you."

Compassion? This is not the response I expected. I blink rapidly as I check her hips, then adjust them. To deny the truth of her statement would be a betrayal to my child. What would a little honesty hurt?

"It was very difficult." That wasn't so hard. "Turn on your right side, please."

As she does so, a torrent of words rushes out of me. "There's not a day that goes by when I don't think about my little girl. It's a pain that never fully goes away, even though I believe I did the right thing."

Mostly. I couldn't have parented her, but I shouldn't have agreed to a closed adoption. I should have fought to keep her in my life.

"I was actually about to call the adoption agency and see if there's anything I can do. To regain contact with her, I mean."

I clamp my jaw shut. What in the world? Where did that come from? I verbally and emotionally vomited on a client. My cheeks are on fire.

"What a great idea." Without prompting, she turns onto her back. I move to her head to adjust her neck. Her eyes sparkle with pride. "You are a brave woman. I wish you the best."

I hold back a guffaw. She knows not of what she speaks, but she means well. I won't argue with her.

After I finish the adjustment, I help her up. When standing, she doesn't immediately let go of my hand. "You can do it," she says. "Make the call."

Apparently, my trepidation is obvious. "Thanks. I will." It seemed like the logical thing to say, but as she walks to the reception desk to pay, I wince. Now I must call, right? I promised Mrs. Mosby.

"Dr. Moore," the receptionist calls out, "your 10:15 rescheduled for Thursday. Car trouble."

"Okay, thanks." Perhaps this is God's way of giving me the time I need. I step into my office and close the door.

I can't overthink. I have to just do it. Gale reassured me this was the best first step. Inquire with the agency. If I get nowhere, then investigate hiring a PI. But ask first. I check the number listed on a pink sticky note and dial before I have the chance to talk myself out of it again.

The woman who answers sounds kind, with a Southern drawl much thicker than my own. I take a deep breath, then rush to explain. "Hello, my name is Everly Moore. In 2007, I placed a baby for adoption with your agency. I've never asked … I mean, I haven't had any contact with … I'm wondering if there's a possibility you could give me contact information for the adoptive family?"

My heart bangs against my rib cage. I did it. I got the question out. Adrenaline surges through my body.

"What did you say your name was?"

"Everly Moore. Everly Alexander at the time."

"Please hold for a moment." Instrumental worship music replaces her voice.

Oh, the torture. How can my palms sweat this much? I count backward from one hundred, then count forward. When I reach ninety-two, the music clicks off. I suck in a breath.

"I thought your name sounded familiar. We've been keeping your letters for you in case you ever wanted to collect them. It seems we had an incorrect address for you."

"Letters?"

"From the adoptive family. They've written you twice a year, every year, with updates. There are pictures too."

I plop into my desk chair. "What?" It can't be this easy. "Are you sure?"

"I'm looking at the stack right now. Where would you like me to forward these?"

Numbly, I relay my address.

"We'll get those in the mail tomorrow, and I'll call the family about your request. What's the best way for them to contact you if they so choose?"

I give her my phone number and email address.

"Sounds good. I'll pass along your information."

"Thank you," I mumble, then hang up.

They've written me. Pictures. Updates. It's more than I can grasp. I assumed I would have to fight for the chance to get to know my daughter. Now, it seems it's been gift wrapped and handed to me.

Zach steps into my office. His eyes widen as he studies me. "You did it? What'd they say?"

I blink back at him, unable to form the words.

"Door open or closed?" He's asking if the phone call ended in the door of possibility being slammed in my face or not.

"Open." I find a smile. "Wide open."

~~

Ivy grasped Austin's hand as they sat in the waiting room. They'd arrived at the ultrasound facility extremely early. In an effort not to be late, they'd given themselves a forty-minute wait. Nothing like watching women with rounded bellies come in. They smiled sweetly in greeting, then looked at her middle. Those smiles faltered. Or perhaps she was only being paranoid.

She didn't owe anyone an explanation, but she did offer "We're waiting for my sister" to one woman who tried to make small talk by asking Ivy if she was expecting too.

When the woman replied, "How nice of you to come and support her," Ivy clamped her mouth shut and smiled. Lesson learned. Pretend to read a magazine. Don't engage.

But now that they were the only people in the waiting room, Ivy ventured a conversation with Austin. "We'll purchase the video, right? And the stuffed bear with the heartbeat?" If he even mentioned the word *fiscal* or *financial*, she might jab him with her elbow.

"Of course." He kissed her knuckles. "If there's ever a time to splurge, it's now."

Praise the Lord. Perhaps she should think of other requests while he was being agreeable.

Finally, Everly and Zach breezed through the door. Zach stopped at the front desk to check in, but Ev came straight to Ivy and wrapped her in a hug.

"Sorry we're late. I made Zach stop. I had to—" Color flooded her cheeks.

Zach stepped beside her. "She needed a bathroom break. Guess the twenty-minute drive was a bit much." He chuckled. "Welcome to pregnancy."

Ivy couldn't dwell on the fact that she'd never experience such things. Instead, she checked her watch. "You're not late. You're right on time."

Ev's brow furrowed. Zach rubbed his hands together, a sheepish smile inching up on his face. "I may have set the car clock ahead by ten minutes."

Ev rolled her eyes. "Figures."

A technician with striking makeup and short pink fingernails opened the door. "Everly Moore?"

Ev raised her hand. "That's me."

The woman waved them back. "Come on down. You're the next contestant on *Let's See Your Baby.*" She did a fabulous Bob Barker impersonation.

Everyone chuckled and followed Everly.

"I'm Pattie. I'll be doing your ultrasound today."

"This is my sister, Ivy." Ev gestured to her. "It's her baby. I'm a surrogate."

"Exciting. I love when surrogates come in."

Seriously? "You've encountered this situation before?" She'd assumed it was rare.

"A handful of times. Infertility is a beast." Pattie waved them inside a homey room. Though an exam table sat in the center, turquoise couches lined the perimeter, and pictures of sunsets adorned the walls. A mural of wispy white clouds covered the ceiling. Soothing instrumental music drifted from a speaker mounted in the corner next to a large screen TV. "Make yourselves comfortable. Everly, I'll have you hop on the table."

She did so, and Pattie picked up a tube of gel. "Do you want to know the sex?"

Ev swiveled her head to look at Ivy.

"Sure." Ivy took Austin's hand. "I mean, I'm sure it's a girl. Our family is full of girls. Hardly a male among us." She'd get to pick out frilly outfits, braid hair, paint nails. Nothing better than being a girl mom.

"Okay, then, let's meet Little Miss." She squirted gel onto Ev's exposed belly.

A grainy 2D picture appeared on the screen. Ivy squinted at the image. What was she looking at?

"I'll take some pictures, then we'll switch to 3D."

Gradually, the shape of her baby came into focus. A head. A trunk. Wiggling arms and legs.

"Do you see the heartbeat?" Pattie asked.

Yes! She did. That little flash was her baby's healthy heartbeat. Tears prickled her eyes as the sound of a rapidly beating heart flooded the room.

"Sounds perfect. One hundred and thirty-two beats per minute." Patty moved the wand around to focus on different areas.

Baby Girl moved her hands. Ivy's breath hitched. "Is she sucking her thumb?"

"Yep."

Another move of the wand and Pattie whistled. "Looks like Little Miss is Little Mister."

What? "You're kidding." A boy? Couldn't be.

"You can see right there." A curser pointed in the image. "There's one leg. There's the other. And there's something else."

Austin chuckled. "A boy. Who would have thought?" He and Zach fist-bumped.

Ivy's mind reeled. All this time, she'd been thinking of her baby as a girl. Her daydreams had involved feminine things. This would take getting used to.

"Now, lct's switch to 3D."

In a flash, her little … boy appeared on the screen. His chubby cheeks, button nose, and angelic eyes were right there, as real as if he were lying in front of them. Her heart swelled. Girl, boy, it made no difference. This was their baby.

"Remarkable." Austin squeezed her hand.

They gaped in wonder for several minutes at the miraculous sight. Then a soft sniff pulled her gaze from the screen. Everly. Tears coursed down her cheeks.

A pang of guilt shot through Ivy. She'd been so wrapped up in her own joy that she hadn't considered what this might be like for her sister. It had to bring back memories of the child she never got to hold. A glance at Zach showed his eyes misted too.

When the ultrasound finished, Everly rose and fled straight into Zach's arms. He stroked her hair and whispered something in her ear as he held her. Pattie must have mistaken their sorrow for happiness. "Life's a beautiful thing." She replaced the wand and went to her computer. "You'll get a disc, but I'll also print out some of these pictures for you."

"We want the teddy bear too." Ivy stole another glance at Ev and Zach. "Actually, can we have two?" It wouldn't be the same as being able to hear her own child's heartbeat, but perhaps it could give Everly comfort. After the baby was born, Ev would be left with nothing. Nothing but a bear.

This was such a horrible idea. They should have hired a surrogate. She'd been selfish to drag her sister into this.

"Sure, we can do two. If you'll wait in the waiting room, I'll bring everything out in a few minutes."

Everyone thanked Pattie and filed into the waiting room. A war between elation and despair raged inside Ivy. If only she could focus on her little boy without regret about Everly creeping in.

Ev put a hand on her shoulder. "Thank you." Her eyes were red and swollen, but she smiled.

"For what?"

"For this opportunity."

Ivy blinked back at her. Ev wasn't mad? She didn't regret agreeing to do this? Though her sister's expression brimmed with a whole brew of emotions, a glimmer of gratitude shined through.

"Thank *you*," Ivy returned. She'd never be able to thank her enough.

~~

I open the door to an explosion of blue. Naomi went above and beyond decorating for this baby shower. Blue streamers and balloons fill Glenda's bungalow. Naomi's mom graciously offered to host the shower, and Naomi has taken care of every detail. There's nothing left for me to do but arrive.

"Welcome." Naomi wraps me in a hug.

I hug her back, thankful for a friend. "Is Ivy here yet?"

"Yep. She's setting out the punch bowls."

I plant a hand on my hip. "I thought you said there wasn't anything to do."

She leans forward conspiratorially and whispers, "There's not. We had to come up with something to keep Ivy occupied." Her eyes crinkle. "My mom went in there and moved the bowls just so Ivy could move them back."

I chuckle. "Smooth."

"I thought so." She leads the way into the living room and gestures to a floral-patterned couch. "Have a seat. Your job today is to take it easy." She rubs my shoulder before breezing off toward the kitchen. "Oh, Ivy, that looks wonderful," she says. "Go join your sister. We've got it from here."

Ivy enters, hands fluttering to her hair and then to adjust her hot-pink shirt. It matches her lipstick. "I look ridiculous, don't I? I didn't know what to wear."

"You look great." I'm wearing the surrogacy shirt Naomi bought me and a pair of jeans. Clearly, I missed the memo our outfits mattered today.

Ivy sits, but she's fidgeting up a storm.

"You nervous?" I ask.

"Yes."

I raise an eyebrow.

"Well, this isn't exactly conventional. I'm having a baby shower, and there's no baby inside me. What are we going to do? Have people measure string to guess how big my belly is?"

I roll my eyes. "No." At least, I hope not. And I hope no one will be measuring my belly. I intend to be a wallflower, blending into the background. As it should be. "Naomi is great at these things." I have no way of knowing this, but it seems true.

What Ivy needs is a distraction. "Hey, I finished those letters."

She instantly brightens. "From your daughter! Oh my gosh, what did they say?"

I shake my head. "No, not those letters." Those ones currently remain in the oversized envelope on my nightstand. "Haven't gotten to them yet."

It's Ivy's turn to hike an eyebrow.

"I'm not ready to read them, okay? Give me time." I cross my arms over my immense belly.

"You've had seventeen years."

"I only found out about the letters a couple of weeks ago."

"Whatever." She waves her hand in front of her face. "What letters did you finish, then?"

"Henrietta's and Loreen's."

Her forehead wrinkles. She uncrosses her legs, then recrosses them. "You read them without me?"

"You didn't seem interested."

"Of course, I'm interested. I thought we agreed to read them together."

"That was before you acted weird."

Ivy huffs and mumbles, "Acted weird," in a mimicking tone.

The doorbell sounds, and Ivy jumps up and takes a step toward the front before Naomi breezes by and pats her back. "Sit. I've got it."

Ivy screws her mouth and plops back down. "I hate not being useful."

"I know." I brush a strand of hair from her face. "Don't worry. Soon, you'll be so busy you'll wish for time to sit and do nothing." I touch my belly.

She puts her hand next to mine. "I can't wait to feel her, er, him move."

I chuckle. I've made the same mistake a dozen times since we learned this baby is a boy. "Soon, I'm sure."

Jessica steps into the room, her six-month-old on her hip. "Hey, ladies."

"Hi." There we go again, speaking in unison.

I stand to hug my cousin and run a finger over Timmy's downy-soft hair. He blows a raspberry, and spit dribbles down his chin.

"Thank you, both, for your baby gifts, by the way. I'm not sure if I ever sent cards or not. My brain's been mush."

Did she send a thank you card? Beats me. We had other things consuming our minds and lives after her shower.

"He loves the teething necklace, Everly. And the travel first-aid kit was so thoughtful, Ivy."

A first-aid kit? Really? Clearly, I purchased the better gift.

"It's Baltic amber. When a baby wears it, his body heat triggers a minute amount of oil that contains succinic acid. When absorbed into the bloodstream, it helps to sooth sore gums."

Jessica's eyes glass over. I've lost her. Timmy pumps his pudgy arms up and down and laughs. We fawn over him as if we've never seen a baby before.

"He's so cute." Speaking of adorable babies … "Where's Laurie?" I call.

Naomi appears. "Currently napping, but she's bound to wake soon."

"You'll love Laurie," I coo at Timmy.

When I step back, Ivy takes my place. Off she goes, chatting up a storm, asking Jessica about sleep and feeding schedules. I'm left in the background, which is, of course, my proper place. So why this tightness in my chest? I scan the room for something to do, something to show I'm valuable as more than an incubator. But everything is in order. I lean back and allow my mind to wander.

What do those letters from the adoptive family contain? First words, maybe. First steps. First foods. All the firsts I've missed. No wonder I can't bear to open them. As if I need a reminder of everything I've missed out on.

"You run, right, Everly?" Jessica's voice breaks through the haze of my thoughts.

"Run?" I shift toward her. "Yeah, I did." I cradle my belly. "Haven't lately."

She makes an I'm-such-a-doofus face. "Of course."

"Why?" I smile warmly. It wasn't a stupid question, no matter what she thinks.

"I'm looking to lose this baby weight. Brian bought me a jogging stroller. Thought I might as well try it."

I nod to encourage her. "I love running. It releases endorphins like nothing else. But don't push yourself too hard to lose weight. You need extra calories while nursing."

Her smile falters. "I'm bottle-feeding."

"Oh." Doesn't she know how much better breastmilk is for babies? I scramble for something nice to say.

Ivy beats me to it. "Breastfeeding is not for everyone."

I nearly choke.

"Do you miss running, then?" Jessica asks.

I shrug. "Yeah, but I'm in a kickboxing class right now. It's fun."

Ivy's mouth drops open. "You're in what?"

"A kickboxing class." I grimace. There's a reason I haven't mentioned this fact to my sister.

"You're kickboxing while pregnant with *my* baby?" She spits out the word *kickboxing* like it's poison.

Jessica sits back and shifts her attention to the bowl of mixed nuts on a nearby table.

"It's fine." I wave a hand in the air. If only it were that easy to wave her worry away. "My midwife says it's not a problem."

Ivy scoffs. "Oh, well, if Snow White okays it, it must be perfectly safe."

"Snow White?"

"She lives in a perky little cottage."

Interesting. It fits.

The doorbell rings again, and more distant cousins file in. Ivy's work friends are close behind them. As are her church friends. Our workout conversation is seemingly forgotten, but Ivy will likely bring it back up as soon as we're alone again. How could anyone not adore Wanda and trust her implicitly? Of course, Ivy would find fault.

Soon, the house is filled with chatter. I blend into the background again as Ivy takes center stage. Eventually, Laurie awakens. I reach my arms out for her as soon as she joins the party. If I spend the whole time holding this precious one, maybe I won't feel left out.

Naomi announces we'll be playing the tray game. She walks around with a tray laden with baby items, then hides it out of sight. When she gives the signal, we scramble to write as many things as we can remember. It's not a horrible game, as far as games go, and I play without complaint. I lose horribly, but I wasn't trying to win.

Afterward, I wait to see what she'll make us play next, but there's nothing except cake. Someone's plate has a star on it, and they win a chemically scented candle. Good thing my plate was clear. I sigh. Thank heaven there's no measuring bellies today.

While everyone munches on red velvet cake with toxic blue icing, Ivy opens presents. She carefully pries off each piece of tape, saving the paper as if it's gold. What would it have been like if I'd kept my daughter? I'd have used all these gadgets. Well, maybe not *all* of them. Half of them probably weren't invented seventeen years ago.

When I'm about to completely zone out, Naomi draws near with a small, wrapped box in hand. "This one's for you, Everly."

"For me?" I point to myself as if she could be mistaken.

She chuckles and nudges my arm playfully. "Yes."

Ivy still holds everyone's attention as she unwraps the last few gifts. Naomi is the only one focusing on me. Good thing. My eyes well as I gush thanks for her thoughtfulness.

"Open it."

I do. No careful unwrapping here. I rip the paper off and stare at the box of herbal tea. "It's to make your milk dry up. Hopefully, it'll make the whole process less painful for you." She crosses her arms over her chest. "I can't imagine."

I can. Last time, it was torture waiting for my body to figure out I wouldn't be feeding a baby. Now, I can't keep tears from coursing down my cheeks. She thought of me. Of *me*. What did I do to deserve such a friend?

"Thank you," I rasp. "For everything."

Chapter 26

Across the Rappahannock River from Fredericksburg,
Virginia
June 1863

Henrietta floated in the space between sleep and wakefulness, men's snores mixing with visions of puffy white clouds, rolling country farms, and the faces of her sisters.

"Henrietta." One of her siblings had whispered her name. Which one? She scanned their dreamy faces. "Henry, wake up."

She snapped out of her trance and stared straight into Loreen's eyes. Her hand flew to her heart, breath coming in a gasp. "You scared me."

The edge of Loreen's mouth lifted. "You sleep more soundly than you used to."

"Work harder, sleep harder." She rubbed her eyes. "What is it?"

Reality slowly came into focus. When her tentmate, Sol, learned her sister was visiting, he offered to bunk with some chums, giving Loreen space in their tent. The two girls had a slice of privacy, but anyone could overhear them at any time. Had Loreen spoken her real name?

Loreen's smile broadened. "Catch wants you to meet him in the woods."

Henrietta catapulted to sitting. "What? When?"

"Now."

Now? Henrietta ran her fingers through her hair. What she wouldn't give to look fetching for him. But he'd seen her covered in grime and blood. If he still wanted to talk, it was a good sign, right? Unless he only wanted to relay his decision to turn her in.

"Where? How?" Any soldiers caught lollygagging after light's out were asking for a reprimand. What if a commanding officer overheard them?

"I know the spot. I'll be your lookout."

Loreen would look out for *her*? After what happened earlier, Henrietta should be the one keeping guard.

"Trust me. Catch and I worked it out." Loreen glanced toward the tent flap. "But we need to hurry. No one is watching right now."

Henrietta opened her mouth to ask when they'd come up with this plan and how, but Loreen took her hand and pulled her to standing. If this was her opportunity, she'd best not waste it. Who knew if Catch would ask to speak to her again? She brushed her hands up and down her trousers, but it did nothing to diminish the dust caked into the fabric. This was as good as it was going to get. She nodded at Loreen.

As her sister led the way, Henrietta scanned the area. Crickets and snores drifted through the air, but no movement caught her attention. Perhaps she'd get away with this after all. But how unlike Catch to break the rules. How could she bear it if he were punished on her account? *Please, Lord, let no one discover us.*

Loreen led them deep into the woods. Branches snapped under their feet. A screech owl hooted. Finally, Loreen stopped, picked up a stick, and struck a tree trunk three times. What in the world?

Three taps answered from what sounded yards away.

"Over there." Loreen pointed.

A figure leaned against a distant tree.

Loreen gave her a little nudge. "Go to him."

Henrietta glanced from Loreen to Catch and back again.

"I'll stay here and keep watch. If anyone discovers me, I'll say I came to take care of nature and that you and Catch are guarding me at a distance to ensure my privacy. I'll speak loud enough for you to hear." Another nudge. "Go."

Who was this confident woman? It couldn't be the same sister she'd left behind. Slack-jawed, Henrietta inched toward the man her heart pined for. He straightened at her approach, pushing off from the tree and taking a few steps toward her. Would the pounding of her heart wake the camp? It thundered in her ears.

"Catch?" Her teeth chattered despite the muggy air. No need to deepen her voice now. She could speak normally. Who was she kidding? She could barely speak at all.

"Henrietta." The way he breathed out her name sent tingles up her spine. His gaze perused her as if looking at her for the first time.

Her cheeks heated. How did he do that? Without words, he made her feel entirely seen. Fully known. And every bit a woman despite her male attire and dingy appearance.

"I'm   " His voice croaked, and he cleared his throat. "I'm not going to turn you in."

Oh! Her knees went weak with relief. He grasped her arm and steadied her. When she was again sure-footed, instead of pulling away, he put his other hand on her other arm. They stood facing each other, touching in a way they'd never touched before. *Lord, have mercy.*

She couldn't make out the color of his eyes in the dark, but no matter. His forest-green gaze was emblazoned in her memory. It caressed her now.

"All this time, I thought the connection between us was one of brotherhood. I felt bonded to you in an unusual way. I assumed it was deep camaraderie, the kind I've heard can be forged when you experience war with someone." He rubbed his hands up and down her arms. Her breath hitched, every nerve on edge. "But this felt different somehow. I just never dreamed it was infatuation rather than brotherhood."

What had he said? Infatuation? Did that mean …

"What I'm trying to say is, I fancy you too." He rubbed a finger over her warm cheek, her trembling jawline.

Goodness, gracious. Why couldn't she gather her wits? He had rendered her a mound of putty.

"I … uh …" She worked her mouth as if she were chewing a wad of tobacco, but coherent words escaped her.

He chuckled. "May I call on you after the war?"

She managed to nod.

He cupped her cheeks in his calloused hands. "How could I not have seen it?"

She closed her eyes and leaned into his touch. "You weren't looking."

"You're beautiful. I'm a dunce to have missed it."

Beautiful? Her? It was her turn to chuckle. "Then the whole company are dunces with you."

His lips grazed the top of her head. She swayed, and his arm looped around her waist. "Easy."

What was wrong with her? She'd faced flying bullets without wavering, but a gentle touch from this man and she nearly fainted.

He led her to the base of the tree he'd been leaning against earlier and guided her to sit. He sat beside her. "Tell me everything. From what led you to join up until now."

She did, spilling out even more than she had to Bernie. As she talked, his eyes spoke of interest and something else. Admiration? She relayed how Griffen had ordered Bernie jailed. "Then I met you."

He laced his fingers with hers. "You are magnificently brave."

She averted her eyes. "Most every soldier here is brave."

"No one here has taken the risks you have."

She tilted her head. "Except for the other female soldiers I've met, you mean."

His thumb stroked hers as his voice dropped to a husky whisper. "There is *no one* like you."

No, there wasn't. Because only she was sitting next to this handsome man.

A massive yawn came from Loreen's direction. Henrietta said, "We'd better go. My sister has had a long day. She needs to sleep."

He squeezed Henrietta's hand. "Meet me here tomorrow night. Please."

He didn't need to ask twice. "I'd love to."

He pulled her to standing. And with a parting kiss to her knuckles, he bid her goodnight.

~~

After a week of late-night rendezvous, she'd shared more of her heart with Catch than anyone other than Loreen. As he held her hand, she'd spoken about years of hunger pangs, her knack for putting on theatricals, and how she adored precious Millie. She'd even divulged how Old Man Meager still wielded power to shake her to her core.

He'd spoken of his favorite fishing pond, the sorrow of losing his younger brother to typhoid, his adeptness at growing corn, and his deep faith. He talked about God as one would a friend. What a fascinating outlook. His words breathed hope that perhaps she'd been mistaken. Maybe God hadn't abandoned her family after all.

In all their conversations, there was one thing he'd yet to divulge.

She laid her head on his shoulder as they sat snuggled close at the base of an oak. He stroked her hair. She'd bathed last night after their meeting. How delightful to not have to worry about her stench when close to him. Though she didn't smell like a lady, at least she didn't stink like a hog. Someday, maybe, he'd see her all gussied up with ribbons in her hair and a full skirt swishing around her ankles. What would he think of her then?

There was a future for them, right? There had to be.

She pulled back to look him in the eyes. "If I ask you something, you promise to tell me the truth?"

"Sure."

"What's your real name?"

He threw his head back and chuckled. "Of course, you'd ask that when you could have asked anything."

"Well?" She gripped his upper arm, solid beneath her touch.

"You must promise not to laugh."

"I promise."

"My name is Rollin."

"What's funny about that?"

"Our old hound dog was named Rollin. I was named after a hound."

She couldn't help but snicker.

He poked her side. "You promised not to laugh."

"I'm not laughing at your name." She covered her mouth to rein in her laughter. Nothing wrong with the name Rollin. It was distinguished. A fine name for a gentleman. But to share your name with a hound?

His knuckle grazed her cheek, his breath heating her neck. Goosebumps exploded on her arms. He was so close. The moonlight cast a thin beam, illuminating his full lips.

"It's my turn to ask a question." His voice went husky.

"Yes?" She couldn't tear her gaze from his mouth.

"May I kiss you?"

She hadn't breath enough to speak. Could he see her desire in the dark? She could only nod.

Then his lips were on hers. Soft. Warm. All-encompassing. She melted against him. Closer. Closer. If only she could get closer. His hands tangled in her hair while hers explored his muscular shoulders. Saints alive! So, this is what it felt like to be kissed by a man. How could no one have told her how glorious it was? Her soft moan melded with his. When he pulled back, they both panted for breath.

She rested her forehead against his and laughed.

"What?" He kissed the tip of her nose, her cheek, then her mouth again, quick yet full of passion.

She bit her lip. "I've never enjoyed being a woman more."

A cry sounded from behind them. Loreen? They both shot to their feet. After they'd fended the men off with their fistfight, no one had bothered her sister again. Not that they'd had much opportunity. She always remained close by. But what if scoundrels had assumed her alone in the woods?

Catch dashed up the hill. Henrietta followed close behind. Darkness obscured their surroundings. No raucous laughter rent the air. Only insects and rustling leaves and … Was that a bobcat's scream? It melded with Loreen's whimper.

Catch slammed to a halt, and Henrietta crashed into his strong back. She stepped back as he bent down, blindly grappling.

"It's only a bobcat. A forceful noise will scare it away, except too loud and we'll bring attention to ourselves." When he stood, he held two sticks.

Her insides quaked. A bobcat had decimated their hens once. Blood and feathers everywhere. "What if it attacks her? Eats her alive?"

A smile was evident in his reply. "They don't hunt humans. Only small animals."

Her shoulders relaxed at his pronouncement, but only a fraction.

He banged the sticks together, stomping toward the animal. It startled and stepped back a few feet, drawing even closer to her sister. Loreen yelped, and the bobcat scurried away.

Henrietta ran to her and wrapped her in an embrace. "Are you okay?"

"Y-yes." Her voice shook. "I-I'm fine."

"We should have stayed closer to you." Henrietta smoothed back hair that had fallen from Loreen's braid.

"Yes, I apologize." Catch sidled up next to Henrietta. "You were guarding us, yet we should have been guarding you."

Crunching sounds came from the direction of camp. Henrietta grasped Catch's arm. Bad idea. If someone were to discover them out here, she couldn't be touching him in such an inappropriate way. Blood whooshed in her ears.

"Is someone here?" The gruff voice sounded overloud in the placid night.

Should they freeze and hope he didn't spot them? But then it'd appear more suspicious if they were caught.

"It's me, Private Grimes with Private Frontenac and his sister."

The footsteps neared. "What in Sam Hill are you doing out here?" The outline of a man came into focus.

What was their excuse again? They'd prepared for this possibility, but all justifications left her mind.

Catch stepped forward. "Private Frontenac's sister needed to take care of … personal business. We were guarding her from a distance when we heard her cry for help."

"A bobcat frightened her," Henrietta added. Then she dared to ask, "Who are we speaking with?" *Please, Lord, not a high-ranking officer.*

"Private Jones. I was going off picket duty when I heard the commotion. Is all well now?"

Her shoulders slumped forward. Thank goodness it was only a comrade, and he didn't question their story.

"All is well," Catch answered.

"Very good, then."

As footsteps retreated, Henrietta drew her first full breath in minutes. The three of them turned and shuffled back to camp. They couldn't keep going on like this. These late-night meetings courted danger. So, it had only been a harmless bobcat. Next time, it could be a more ferocious animal. What predators were native to Virginia? Or worse, it could be a group of men intent on having their way with the only beautiful woman within miles. What if they were outnumbered and unable to fight the attackers off?

And it was only a matter of time before someone would discover them, discover *her*. Would Griffen send her packing or jail her? Would Catch get in trouble for hiding important information? God forbid he suffer because of her.

No way around it. They needed to stop these encounters. But how her heart ached at the thought of never feeling his lips on hers again.

Loreen wrapped her arms around her middle. "I want to go home."

"Yes. Of course." Henrietta placed a hand on her shoulder in what had to be a brotherly way. "Do you have an escort home?" Why hadn't she thought of that earlier? Loreen couldn't travel back by herself.

Loreen stopped abruptly. "Well, you, of course."

"Me?" There was no way they'd give her leave to travel with her sister.

"Yes." Loreen's tone spoke of exasperation. "Now that you've done what you needed to do"—she gestured in between Henrietta and Catch—"you can come home."

"Come home?" The war was far from over, and Henrietta had signed on for the duration.

"Yes. Come home. I told you the family is doing better. The wartime economy has opened more jobs for women. There's no need for you to put your life on the line to feed and clothe us. Not any longer."

"B-but …" Henrietta's desperate gaze clung to Catch's. He seemed to understand all she couldn't find words for. How the thought of being away from him sliced like shrapnel.

He searched their surroundings before taking her hand. "I'll come for you. As soon as the war ends."

She shook her head. No. She couldn't leave. They needed her here. She was a good soldier, and the Confederacy was desperate for those. Catch needed her near. Her family still needed her financial contribution. Surely, they did. They wouldn't be able to survive without her.

"Go home," Catch pleaded. "Now that I know, I'll be tied in knots any time you're in danger."

Henrietta huffed. "Do you know how many times I've nearly died?"

Loreen flinched.

"You're not invincible." Catch's voice was gentle, yet firm. "And I couldn't bear it if something happened to you." He kissed her knuckles.

Her knees wobbled, and she yanked her hand away. He couldn't do that this close to camp. Someone might see. Might hear.

"Please." The tenderness in his voice nearly undid her.

She couldn't let it. She straightened her shoulders. Balled her fists at her sides. "I'm not going anywhere." She marched closer to the row of tents. "We'll find someone to escort you home."

It wouldn't be her. After all, who was she if she wasn't the one rescuing her family from certain death? In the past months, she'd become a soldier. How could she be anything else? Anything less? How could this tobacco-spitting, card-playing, *good ole boy* return to normal life as if nothing had happened? War had changed her. There was no going back.

Chapter 27

WE ARE SISTERS. WE WILL ALWAYS BE SISTERS. OUR
DIFFERENCES MAY NEVER GO AWAY, BUT NEITHER,
FOR ME, WILL OUR SONG.
ELIZABETH FISHEL

Suburb of Wilmington, North Carolina
Present Day

Ivy stepped onto the elevator and pressed the down button. Another busy day at work. Austin had promised dinner out and a movie at the theatre tonight. She bounced on her toes as she pictured the evening out.

One floor before hers, the elevator stopped and opened. She stilled and put on a professional air. No one would know how goofy she'd been. On stepped a very pregnant woman with a sleek black braid hanging halfway to her feet. Might as well make friendly conversation, seeing as they were both expecting, even if she didn't look the part.

"Hello. Are you on the homestretch?"

The woman startled. "Me? Oh, no. Twenty weeks."

Ivy raised a brow. "Only twenty?" The lady looked ready to pop.

The woman massaged her lower back. "Triplets."

Triplets? "Shawna Spring?" She slapped her hand over her mouth. She shouldn't have said that. She could get fired for not respecting client privacy.

The woman gaped at her. "Yeah. How …?"

Ivy grimaced. "Sorry. I shouldn't have said that. I'm a medical transcriptionist with your OB's office. I saw … I saw a record of…"

Shawna's eyes narrowed. "Isn't that against the law?"

"Technically?" Ivy ran a hand through her hair. "I only wanted to pray for you by name."

Shawna's expression remained tense. "I guess you know how I freaked out when they told me I'd be having multiples."

"Yeah."

The elevator stopped at the ground floor, and both women stepped off. Neither moved toward the exit.

"I don't judge." Ivy spouted out the half lie as if grasping for straws. "Anyone would be overwhelmed by that surprise."

Shawna shifted her weight. "Well, I didn't go through with the termination. Too risky. I waited too long and worked too hard to gamble like that. Plus, my mom said she'll help."

"That's great." Ivy's shoulders relaxed. "I'm so glad."

"Okay, well …" Shawna angled toward the front doors.

"Oh! Wait. I have something for you." Ivy dug into her gigantic purse and extracted a wrinkled gift bag.

"Uh …" Shawna stared at her as if she'd grown horns.

"Here." Ivy shoved the present in Shawna's direction, then cringed. Way to creep a stranger out. "I know this is weird, but I bought these for your babies."

The poor lady's eyebrows hitched up. "Okay." She took the bag and peeked inside. "Baby blankets?"

"Muslin swaddle blankets. Three of them."

She'd felt compelled to buy them, though she hadn't a clue why. Worst-case scenario, she'd walk around with this gift in her purse for months, then end up using it for her baby. Best-case scenario …

"Thanks." Shawna lifted a slight smile before walking through the double doors.

Ivy's phone vibrated in her purse. She fished it out and answered Everly's call on the way to her car. "What's up, sis?"

"Okay, I don't want you to freak out."

Great way to start a conversation. Ivy's stomach wobbled. "Why would I?"

"My prenatal appointment was today—"

"What's wrong?" Her pulse kicked into overdrive. Something was wrong with her baby. Air. She was surrounded by it, but she couldn't get enough. Her vision hazed.

"Nothing's wrong with your boy. I told you not to freak out."

"Which is exactly the kind of thing that freaks me out." She paused in the middle of the parking lot and hunched over, planting the hand that wasn't holding the phone on her knee.

"I just have gestational diabetes. No big deal."

Ivy straightened. The ground tilted for a second, then righted itself. "You? You're like the healthiest person I know."

"Yeah. Totally unfair, but it is what it is." Traffic noises snuck through the line.

"So, what's the plan?" She'd switch to a hospital birth with an OB, naturally. And eat … How could Everly eat healthier than she already did?

"I'll check my blood sugar daily. Avoid sweets and starches."

"And?" This was the part where Ev was supposed to relay her change of birthing plans.

"And that's it. Everything will be fine."

Ivy unlocked her car and slid in. "But Snow White can't handle this. You'll have to switch to an OB. Someone who can manage complications."

Everly huffed. "*Wanda* is perfectly capable of navigating this."

"I don't think so." Ivy shook her head. "It's not safe. I'd feel better if—"

Now, a growl. "Ivy, don't be unreasonable."

"Excuse me?"

A horn sounded on Everly's end. "You act like Wanda is completely incompetent. She's not. This happens all the time, and she's going to make sure the baby is safe."

Ivy rolled her eyes. "I'd feel better if—"

"Of course you would. You'd feel better if I covered myself in bubble wrap and lived at the hospital. But I'm telling you, it's *fine*."

Rude. Unfair. "It's—"

Everly's voice hissed. "If you even say *my baby*, I'm hanging up this phone."

Fine. But just because she didn't say it, didn't make it any less true. Maybe she should try a gentler approach? Honesty might work to her advantage. "Ev, I'm scared. Terrified of losing yet another person I love. And even though I can't feel this baby move inside of me, even though I'm unable to experience bonding with him in that way, I love him. Please." Her throat tightened. "Please don't do anything that might take him away from me."

When Everly spoke, her voice had gentled as well. "I won't. But you've got to trust me."

Trust? Yeah, she was still working on that one.

Trust Me.

The gentle voice in her spirit humbled her. Trust the Lord? That was as hard as trusting her sister. Harder, maybe. Everly hadn't had any choice when Mom was taken from them so soon. Everly hadn't allowed cancer to invade Ivy's body. But God? He might not have caused any of it, but He sure didn't stop it either. Could she entrust yet another thing into His hands?

I'll try, Lord. But You've got to help me.

A scene played in her mind unbidden. In it, a hand—the Lord's hand?—sculpted a baby—her baby?—as if out of clay. Nimble fingers bent tiny knuckles. A careful fingernail patterned fingerprints. Even now, God was working. He watched over her child with a love stronger than a typhoon. The winds of that love swept over her.

"'For You formed my inward parts. You knitted me together in my mother's womb,'" Ivy whispered the words from Psalm 139 as awe overtook her.

"What'd you say? I can't hear you. It's this stupid car speaker." Ev's voice sounded overly loud, then soft again, then at normal volume.

"I wasn't really talking to you." Ivy chuckled.

"Huh?"

"Never mind. Okay, I'll trust you. Or at least try to."

"Thank you." Everly's exhale flooding the car couldn't compare to God's love flooding Ivy's heart.

~~

I sit on my back deck, coffee in hand, and Bible open in my lap. Ivy would probably pitch a fit if she knew I wasn't drinking decaf. "Lord, help my sister to not be anxious. Give her Your peace."

A niggle inside makes me shift uncomfortably. I picture Jesus giving me a raised-eyebrow look that says, *Really, Everly? Let's talk about you.* Which is ridiculous because Ivy is clearly the problem here.

I press through with my prayer. "Help her to trust You and not be afraid."

The picture of Jesus in my imagination casts a glance through the wall to where the adoptive family's letters sit on my nightstand. Okay, so I have my own issues. Everyone else has given me space to ignore them, but it looks like I won't be so fortunate today.

"Lord," I whisper, "this is hard for me."

That line has worked on Zach and Ivy. Whenever I spout it, they step back. But Jesus? He presses closer. When I close my eyes, His presence surrounds me. He's right here with me in my fear and insecurity. He speaks straight to my heart.

We can do it together.

Together. Yes. Can't I do anything with the Lord by my side? I stand, go inside to retrieve the letters, and reemerge into the sunshine.

My hand trembles as I pry open the flap. I pause and close my eyes again. "Still here, God?"

Yes, He is. *Together.* Jesus and I can do this together.

I pull out a bundle of envelopes secured together with a rubber band. Unfamiliar loopy script stares back at me.

To Gracie's birth mom.

I blink. That's me. They named my little girl Gracie. I shift through everything I've imagined about this child for years and view it through the lens of this new info. Gracie's first birthday party. Gracie learning to walk. Gracie's first day of kindergarten. Gracie's eighth grade graduation. It fits.

Now, to open the first letter. I unwrap the stack and gently peel it open. When I unfold the lined paper, three pictures fall into my lap. A newborn picture of Gracie in nothing but a diaper and purple headband with a gigantic matching flower. Laurie would hate that. I chuckle. Gracie's eyes are closed, and the ghost of a smile transforms her face into that of an angel.

The next picture shows my little girl on a month-milestone blanket with a heart surrounding the number three. Her dark hair sweeps across her forehead, longer than the previous picture. Instead of smiling, her mouth is puckered, and her expression seems to say, "C'mon. Really? Another picture."

Adorable.

The next picture is of her sitting, propped up by a couple of pillows in the back. She grins wide, her chubby hands clasped around the fabric of the blue bellbottom pants she wears. Does she want to ditch them?

I trail my finger on her face, reminding myself this version of Gracie no longer exists. It's a mirage of the past. I pick up the letter and read.

Dear Gracie's birth mom,

Our little girl is six months old today. She is such a joy. She's the light of our lives, and we're thankful every day for you and your sacrifice.

Gracie is rolling all around the house, exploring her toys, and putting everything in her mouth. She loves to play peekaboo and has the most magical laugh. She's babbling and pretending to read books. Her favorite toy is a light-up ball that plays music. Her favorite song seems to be "Head, Shoulders, Knees, and Toes."

We've started feeding her solid food. She loves the pear-broccoli blend of baby food and applesauce but hates rice cereal.

I hope knowing a little about her brings you comfort. We pray for you, that you're safe and well. Words can never convey the depth of our gratitude for Gracie and for you.

Best,
Karen and Tim

I dab my wet cheeks with the back of my hand. I can't believe I missed out on reading this so many years ago. It sounds like Gracie is loved and cherished. She's in good hands. Warmth spreads through my chest. I did the right thing, then and now. None of this—not my giving her up, not my seeking her out—has been a mistake. Nor has it been a haphazard act of chance. God's hand has been in it all. Clearly, His fingerprints are all over my life. They're all over Gracie's.

I reach for the next letter, hungry to know my little girl, but I'm prompted to pause. I did the right thing then. What about now? Suddenly, I'm unsettled about pressing on for a home birth. Ivy's worried face comes to mind. I've been fighting for what would make me feel safer, more secure, more in control. But look at me. I did a hard thing, and I didn't crumble. Instead, freedom lifts my spirit. Why did I put off reading these letters? I couldn't have known what lay on the other side of my fears. Might it be the same with this birth?

Lord, lead me.

I'm struck with the overwhelming sense that I need to give in. To surrender. I must lay my will down again for my sister's sake. I've thought the reason I desired a home birth is because it's best for the baby and mama … er, genetic carrier. I've done my research, and I can back that up with a list of facts and anecdotal stories. But it's clear that such things haven't been my motivation. It's fear, plain and simple. Fear has propelled me to run away from one scenario and toward another. And fear is never a good motivator.

What would it look like to not be motivated by fear and instead to let God's love move me?

I need to find an OB and switch to a hospital birth. This idea would have seemed ludicrous an hour ago, but now it's the only solid path forward. I've asked the Lord to guide me, and He is, straight into the valley of the shadow of death.

""I will fear no evil. For You are with me. Your rod and Your staff, they comfort me.""

I can do this. I can do anything with Jesus beside me, with me, empowering me.

I shoot a text to Wanda letting her know I won't be using her services. My nerves sizzle as I press *send*. This is the Lord, right? Or have I gone off the deep end? The wave of doubt crashes over me, then recedes as I recite Psalm 23 again.

I pull up my local crunchy mama Facebook group and ask for recommendations for an OB that's more naturally minded. If anyone knows of one, it'll be this group.

How's that for a step in a brave, new direction? Pride in such an accomplishment bolsters me. "There, God. I did it."

I expect a shot of relief, yet something still doesn't seem right. My spirit remains unsettled. "Lord, I've given everything over to You. I'm holding nothing back."

My ring glints in the sunshine. I twist it. Surely, He doesn't want me to … He can't expect me to give this up. Mom willed it to me. It's rightfully mine.

The conviction persists.

Giving Ivy Mom's ring wouldn't even make sense. She's having a boy, not a girl. Her son won't treasure a woman's ring. And me? I have a daughter. One I might be able to get to know. One I might eventually feel comfortable passing it on to.

No. God wouldn't want me to give up this ring.

I snap my Bible closed, place the letters back into the envelope, and stand. I don't have time to be ridiculous. I need to get ready for work.

Trust Me.

Ugh. Haven't I trusted God enough? Haven't I done my duty?

Complete surrender.

I growl as I stalk inside, slamming the door behind me. Who is this God who demands so much of me? Who won't let good enough alone?

In complete surrender is total joy.

"Come on!" My shout bounces off the living room walls. I stride to the bathroom and brush my teeth with such force my gums bleed. Okay, probably best not to take out my frustration via oral hygiene. I rinse my mouth out and slam my palms on the counter, staring my mirrored reflection straight in the eye.

The Everly blinking back at me looks a bit like a two-year-old throwing a fit.

I'm a good father. I give good gifts.

Can I trust that if God asks me to do something, His motivation is always completely agape love?

Lord, help me. Show me how much You love me.

Last counseling visit, Gale had asked me what my favorite thing about myself was. I'd answered with uncertainty. Maybe my perseverance? My dogged determination has gotten me far. But what's God's favorite thing about me? Does it match my own? Maybe it's that I'm willing to carry my sister's child. Might as well ask.

Lord, what's Your favorite thing about me?

The answer comes quickly, so distinct I don't question whether it's Him.

Your smile.

Really? Not my womb? Not any of my accomplishments? Not my ability to *do* for Him?

My smile? If that's true, He probably wants me to smile more … which means He delights in my joy.

I grin. Can't I follow a God like that?

Yes. Yes, I can.

I pick up my phone and send Ivy a text.

> I'm finding an OB and registering at the hospital. This is your baby, your birth. I won't stand in the way of what you want.

A couple of minutes pass as I apply light makeup. My phone buzzes. Ivy.

> Thank you.

A crying emoji.

I'll do whatever it takes to help you reunite with your daughter. Just say the word.

It's been weeks, and I haven't heard back from the adoptive family. Should I let it lie or pursue it further? The holding pattern I'm in can't last forever. I might never hear back. If that's the case, I could hire a PI or … not. I'll have to ponder this more later. Or pray about it. One thing at a time. I check my phone calendar and text back.

Thanks, sis. Can you meet me at the Wilmington River Walk tomorrow at six p.m.?

~~

Ivy pulled into the Second Street parking lot and approached the payment kiosk. There were parking lots closer to the river walk, but with such a beautiful day, walking a little would be good for her. This mystery meeting had her stomach in knots. Why wouldn't Everly tell her what this was about? She'd been so cryptic.

Maybe it was nothing. Just a desire to connect. They'd made tons of memories walking around historic Wilmington, browsing through shops, and indulging at coffee houses. Could Everly only want to spend time with her? But if so, why wouldn't she just say that?

Ivy would find out soon. She stuck the payment receipt on her dashboard and moseyed toward the river. As soon as she approached Water Street, Everly came into view. Her sister stood facing the water, elbows propped on the railing. A breeze tossed her hair to and fro. As if sensing Ivy's presence, Everly turned and searched the area. Her belly had grown since Ivy had last seen her. Ev's white T-shirt pulled taut around her middle. Their eyes met, and both women smiled as Ivy crossed the street.

"Beautiful day, isn't it?" Ivy turned her face toward the warm sun.

"Sure is." Everly wrapped her in a hug, then turned back to the river. "Henrietta stood here over a hundred and sixty years ago. Can you imagine?"

Oh yeah. She'd come to Wilmington to work the docks. "I hadn't thought about that."

"Really? History has seemed to come alive to me after reading those letters. It's not just random people. Henrietta's blood flows through our veins."

Ivy remained silent, staring over the waters also.

Everly cast her a glance. "Why did it bother you to read those letters?"

She let out a long, slow exhale. "I guess I got tired of being compared to the needy one. You're like Henrietta. The brave, strong one. The rock. And I'm like Loreen. Far too anxious and clingy. Henrietta's the hero, and Loreen is left to bask in her sister's glow." Everly opened her mouth to speak, but Ivy cut her off. "I get it. You're amazing. You always have been, always will be. I'd just like to be a little bit amazing too."

Ev's touch to her arm was gentle, yet weighty. "You didn't finish reading the letters."

Ivy freed a piece of hair that had gotten trapped in her mouth. "I will. Eventually."

The wind's rustle competed with Everly's laugh. "I'm not chiding you, sis. I said that because it's obvious you don't know the whole story. You missed the part where Loreen saves Henrietta. In the end, Loreen is as much a hero, in my opinion."

"Saves her? How?" Did Loreen become a soldier too?

"You'll have to read it. Suffice to say, if it wasn't for Loreen, Henrietta might have ended up an old maid." Ev's face brightened. "Actually, then we wouldn't be here. We're descended from Henrietta, so we'd never have existed."

Ivy tilted her head. "That's a bit dramatic, especially for you."

"It's true." Ev laughed again. "Read it. You'll see."

"Okay, I will." They faced the river again. "Is that why you wanted to meet here? To talk about Henrietta?"

Ev shook her head. "No. I need to give you something." She pulled Mom's ring off and held it in her palm. "This is yours." She tried to press the ring into Ivy's hand, but Ivy took a step back and nearly bumped into a jogger.

"No. You can't." She had fought off jealousy over that ring for years. It was completely understandable for Mom to leave it to Ev. The sting in Ivy's chest whenever her sister admired it or fiddled with it was unjustified. Still, she longed for something tangible of Mom's. She had nothing. Nothing but a few faint memories.

Ev stood sure and steadfast. "Why not? Mom left it to me, and it's mine to give as I choose."

"But why? You love that ring."

"I do. But I love you more."

This sacrifice, the affection pooling in her sister's eyes, the magnitude of all Ev had done for her … it overwhelmed her. Her knees wobbled. She crushed Everly in a hug and let her sister's strength hold her upright.

When she pulled back, she clutched the ring in one hand and fished a tissue out of her purse and dabbed her eyes and nose with the other. "Maybe we could share it? Henrietta and Loreen did, right?" Not having read all the letters, she didn't have the details.

"When she went off to war, Henrietta gave it to Loreen, who gave it back when Henrietta returned."

The ring warmed her palm. "Maybe I'll give it back to you someday."

"There's no need. I'm giving it to you without stipulation." Everly put her hand over Ivy's, then pried her fingers open. Gingerly, she slid the ring onto Ivy's finger. "Do you want to eat at Paddy's Hollow? Henrietta never made it there, but we can." Her eyes sparkled.

"Or we could grab acai bowls from Riverside Greens." Going to Everly's favorite eatery was the least she could do.

"Ooh, that sounds amazing."

Ivy linked arms with Ev, and they strolled down the street Henrietta had walked a century and a half earlier.

Chapter 28

Gettysburg, Pennsylvania
July 1, 1863

Why hadn't she gone home? As Henrietta trudged toward Emmitsburg Road, every nerve urged her to turn from this battle and flee to her sisters. Her scalp tingled. She couldn't explain the bad feeling she had about this plan, but intuition told her General Lee's command to cross the road and get to the enemy's left flank wouldn't be seamlessly accomplished.

Was the peach orchard truly unoccupied? Though Captain Johnson's intelligence claimed so, she doubted it. If the orchard sat on a knoll where much of the battle could be seen, surely the Union would have seized the best part of the field by now. The high ground was never taken without a fight.

Of course, she'd never dare voice her worries to Catch, who marched beside her. No need to demolish morale.

They reached the woods lining the crest of Warfield Ridge and stopped. As she'd feared, across from them stood not the Union left flank, easily pushed aside, but a compact line of artillery and bayonets pointed straight toward them.

"Dear God," Catch prayed.

Barksdale commanded their brigade to lie down and wait for the order to move forward. In front of them, McLaws's division opened fire. The earth rumbled under her, knocking her teeth together. The air filled with smoke. Cannons shrieked. Horses whinnied and cried as they collapsed and writhed in the dirt. Trees splintered, branches creaking as they crashed upon fallen men. The whir of guns was like the devil's hiss.

Heart pounding, nerves taut, all she could do was watch as man after man went down, exposing their company further and further.

Beside her, Catch murmured. She strained to make out the words over the tumult. "Where can I … Your Spirit?" Was he praying? "Where can I flee … presence?" Wait. She'd heard him quote this before. A Bible passage.

She nudged him with her elbow. "Speak up." If there was any chance God hadn't abandoned her, she needed to hear His words now.

"'If I ascend up into heaven, thou art there: if I make my bed in hell, behold, thou art there. If I take the wings of the morning, and dwell in the uttermost parts of the sea;

Even there shall thy hand lead me, and thy right hand shall hold me.'"

Could it be true? Might God be with them here, amongst dying men's groans. She could have sworn God had forsaken her long ago, but what if …

With her face in the dust, she ventured a prayer. *Lord, if You're there, I need You.* The small Bible pressed against her breast. *I might die today, and I'm not right with my Maker. Forgive me, Lord, for casting You aside. Forgive me for thinking I can manage things better than You.*

Mama had trusted the Almighty until her last breath. Henrietta had abandoned Him with her first trial. She'd thought Mama weak to rely on a God who did what He pleased. Now it was clear Mama was the strong one. Faith took fortitude.

Accept me back, Lord. Be my God.

Many turned to the Almighty when staring death in the face. She might not be so different. But she was tired of striving in her own strength, struggling to prove her worth. The picture Mama had painted of God was of a loving Father who welcomed His children onto His lap. Much different from Pa today, but not too far from the Pa of the past. As screams rent the air and the earth quaked under cannon fire, everything inside her wanted to climb onto Father God's lap.

Catch paused his recitation and cast her a glance. "Are you okay?"

"Yeah." And surprisingly, she was. Her pulse had slowed. An unearthly peace surrounded her like a shield. If she died today, she'd be okay. She would be with the One who had loved her all along. Who had been with her throughout her life.

For an hour or so, they waited for the go-ahead to advance and open fire. Then, when it came, they were hardly ready. But when they reached the front, it was like looking into hell itself. Dead and wounded horses littered the ground, many were missing legs. And the men! They carpeted the orchard. Bloody, lifeless men in both blue and gray. She attempted to count the cannons but gave up after seventy. She'd never witnessed more rapid firing. Her head thrummed with the deafening roar.

But there was no time to gape. No time to mourn the wretched scene. Only one task lay in front of her: kill or be killed. She took aim.

White steam-like clouds of smoke puffed into the air, sometimes obscuring her view entirely. The rotten-egg scent of artillery overwhelmed her. Men fell around her on all sides as missiles plowed up the ground. Aim and fire. Aim and fire. Her mind numbed as she fell into the rote task.

Until something caught her eye. She froze. The soldier ahead and to her left looked like Bernie. It couldn't be. But the set of his shoulders, the curve of his neck, his hair ... her hair?

Maybe the smoke had clouded both her sight and her judgment because she couldn't tear her gaze away. And the man beside the soldier ... She could swear it was Hermann. No, impossible. Griffen had jailed Bernie, and if Hermann had recovered, he would have returned to his Confederate regiment. No way they'd be fighting for the Union.

A bullet spit into the dirt inches from her foot, shaking her from her trance. She needed to aim and fire. But what if it was her friend? As the soldier across from her reloaded, the certainty settled within her. The movements were too similar. It had to be Bernie.

She turned to point Bernie out to Catch only to find him poised to shoot her friend.

"No!" She rammed into his side, sending them both sprawling into the dirt.

"What in the blazes are you doing? Trying to get us killed?" He spit out a tuft of grass.

"That's Bernie. That's my—"

"Watch out." Catch rolled on top of her, shielding her with his body, moving them both a few feet down the hill.

The ground thundered as a shell exploded nearby. Catch yelped.

Oh, Lord, no. He'd been hit? And it was her fault?

"Are you okay?" She panted, pressed under his weight.

He rolled to the side, revealing his blood-tinged sleeve. He winced.

"Shrapnel?"

"Just a scratch." His eyes crinkled with the joke and with pain. "Thank God you're okay."

Her breath puffed out ragged and uneven. "You saved my life." If he hadn't rolled her away from the point of impact, it would have lodged between her ribs.

"Anytime." He managed a wink as he stood.

She scrambled up. Where had her rifle gone? There, a few feet away. She lunged for it and turned again toward the raging battle. Where had Bernie and Hermann gone? No sign of them. With each bullet she fired, her stomach roiled. It could be her friends she hit. Blasted war.

Catch had saved her. Shielded her body with his. Why? Because he knew her secret and thought it his heroic duty to protect a woman? He'd been adamant she return home and not engage in this battle. Yet, he had to know she could hold her own. Could it be because he loved her?

A Scripture surfaced in her memory, one she'd read in the Bible covering her heart.

> *Greater love hath no man than this, that a man lay down his life for his friends.*

It was about Jesus, surely. But right now, it seemed to refer to Catch as well.

He loved her! This was a gift she dare not spurn. If he asked her again to return home until he could come for her, she'd comply.

If she lived to see that day.

~~

A chill crept up Henrietta's spine as she surveyed the landscape. Flies and gnats buzzed around dead bodies, horse and human alike. She'd fought in gory battles, but nothing could have prepared her for this. Severed limbs. Blood oozing from every possible bodily surface. The stench threatened to gag her. But here she was, intact. She'd survived. Many had not. Was Bernie one of those who'd made it? Or had Henrietta spared her from one bullet only for her to fall to another one? She might never know.

They'd spent the 3rd of July supporting artillery on Peach Orchard Ridge. Today, Independence Day, they'd held their position. Soon, they'd begin marching to Hagerstown. Would she go with them?

Nothing like narrowly escaping death to make one aware of their mortality. And to make one question why they were fighting in the first place. Some in her company spouted about states' rights. A few blatantly insisted on their right to own slaves. For her, neither of those explanations held any weight. The only thing that *did* make sense was the reason of fighting to protect their homes and families. That's the reason Catch gave. He'd joined to keep Federals away from his ma and sisters, to push back a Southern invasion.

It sounded a bit fantastical to her. As if Northerners would be a threat if not provoked by secession. But if her sisters were in danger, no doubt she'd fight to protect them. Isn't that why she'd enlisted in the first place?

She rubbed her hands up and down her arms to ward off a chill that didn't come from the temperature. Truth was that the reason she'd signed up no longer existed. She hadn't gotten pay in months, and still the girls thrived. Loreen had blossomed like Henrietta never could have conceived. Like she might not have if her older sister had been there to overshadow her. From the sound of it, Gretchen had matured too. Her sisters didn't need her here. They didn't *want* her here.

Catch came and stood beside her. "What a horrendous way to settle conflict, huh?" His gaze roamed from one end of the field in front of them to the other. She'd repaired his coat sleeve from where the shrapnel had penetrated it. A doctor had removed the debris and stitched up his arm. As long as infection didn't set in, he'd heal fine and go on to continue the Confederacy's fight.

The question remained, would *she*?

"Turn yourself in today. Please," he whispered out of the side of his mouth. "My heart might not be able to endure another near-death incident."

She worried her lip. Why not? She had nothing to prove to anyone. She'd fought bravely time and time again. Paid her dues. Been a fine soldier. If her family didn't need her here, why shouldn't she confess?

Jail didn't seem fun, and there was a possibility that's where she'd end up. Still, that threat wasn't the one looming largest in her mind. Being separated from Catch would ache like a sore tooth. Doing without the comfort of his presence was a hardship, for sure, but since she couldn't behave freely around him anyway, it didn't account for her hesitation.

No. She couldn't pretend like she held out for any reason other than fear. Fear she wouldn't know how to act at home. Fear she'd spent so long pretending to be a man she no longer knew how to be a woman. Fear that nothing would ever be the same … and fear that it would. It didn't make a lick of sense, but there it was. The truth she'd hidden from ever since Loreen had suggested she return home.

But God had saved her. Not only her life but her soul. He'd taken away her guilt. He'd replaced the need to strive for acceptance with an unconditional love that welcomed her in her weakness. And if He had been with her as she faced the jaws of hell on the battlefield, He'd be with her at home as well. Or, if need be, in a jail cell. There was nowhere she could go where His love wouldn't reach.

She turned her gaze to Catch. "You promise you'll come for me when this is all over?"

"With all my heart." His voice was so low, she had to strain to hear him. "I love you, Henrietta. I'll fight my way to you."

Her heart fluttered at his declaration. "Well, then. In that case." She pivoted and set off to find Griffen.

Chapter 29

Suburb of Wilmington, North Carolina
Present Day

The contractions start at two a.m. I slip out of bed and tiptoe from the bedroom before another one hits. No use waking Zach. It could be hours yet, or labor might stall. For now, I'm happy to pace in my living room and bounce on the birthing ball. Worship music plays serenely in the background. The moon casts a sliver of light onto our hardwood floor. A diffuser mists lavender essential oil into the air. I am at peace.

When a contraction comes, I breathe through the pain and find a sense of accomplishment in doing so. This is my *I am woman, hear me roar* moment. With my first birth, Dad rushed me to the hospital as soon as he became aware I was in pain. I won't make the same mistake this time. No way I'm calling Ivy until things have progressed significantly. She'll insist I hightail it to the hospital. I'm full term, technically, but at thirty-seven weeks and two days, Ivy will worry about low birth weight and complications.

A twinge of guilt niggles as I ponder this. Is it wrong to hide the beginning of labor from this child's mother? Then again, who knows if this will even end in a birth today. False labor is common, right? This sure doesn't feel like the same

Braxton Hicks I've experienced over the past few weeks, but I'm not an expert. I can wait a little longer before alerting Ivy.

A half hour passes, and the pain intensifies. I'm moving and breathing through it, but I've started vocalizing. The music disappears under my soft hums and moans, then resurges after each contraction finishes. They're closer together, but not to the point I need to abandon my home or wake my husband. Instead, I run a bath and labor in the tub for a while. It's not a birthing pool, certainly not as comfortable, but the water does lessen the impact.

These are my last hours with this baby. When that realization fully sinks in, I release a thunderous wail. Today or tomorrow, my womb will be empty, and so will my arms. Sure, Ivy will let me hold her baby, but he's not coming home with me. Gale was right. This is a loss. Not quite the same as handing my own child over, but eerily similar. I'm gutted. My tears plink onto the bathwater.

Zach stumbles in, his bleary eyes wide. "What's wrong?"

"I'm oka—" I start to say, but a contraction pinches my words. I clench my jaw and sway my hips as I concentrate on riding this wave.

"You're in labor?"

I manage a nod.

"Oh, baby." In a second, he's on his knees at the side of the tub, holding out a hand for me to crush. "Why didn't you tell me?"

Good question. When the pain subsides, I offer him a sheepish smile. "I wanted to let you sleep."

But is that truly the reason? If this was our baby, I probably would have woken him. If he'd shown an ounce of enthusiasm about this arrangement, I might have insisted he keep me company. Zach, though, has been clearly uncomfortable with this pregnancy. The only excitement he's displayed centers around the hope that my belly will expand again, next time with our child.

"You should have shaken me awake. We're in this together."

I bite back the sassy response of *since when* and take his hand. He strokes my cheek. Affection cascades from his eyes.

He places a hand on my rounded stomach. "Go easy on your aunt, okay, little guy?"

I chuckle. "It takes strong contractions to birth a baby. Easy ones won't do the trick."

He rubs my belly in a circular motion. Another contraction comes, and he gasps as my belly tightens. "Whoa."

I switch position, kneeling and bracing my arms on the side of the tub. He whispers encouragement until the contraction wanes, and I let out a long sigh.

His forehead furrows. "How close are they? That one seemed really close to the last."

"I don't know. I haven't been timing them since I got in the tub." But he's right. It does seem like they're much closer than before. I should probably call Ivy.

He grabs my Fitbit from the bathroom counter and holds it as if ready to time a runner. "Tell me when."

I'd laugh at his focused demeanor if I wasn't in the middle of such a momentous feat. He times the next two contractions. I have to focus harder on my breathing. There's no doubt this is real labor. "I need to move. Help me get out of the tub."

He takes hold of my arms and propels me to standing. "We need to go to the hospital now. The doctor said"

My wet hair drips in my face. "I know what he said, but it's overkill. I can stay here longer."

He quirks an eyebrow. "Do you intend on having this baby here?"

I scowl. "No. I'm just not ready."

He has the decency not to laugh, though it's clear he's exerting effort in holding it back. "Ready or not, here he comes."

Ugh. He's right. We need to go lest Zach ends up delivering Ivy's baby in the car. But it's painful to think of leaving the haven of my home for an impersonal hospital. Still, I promised. "Fine. Call Ivy, will you?"

After assuring him I can dress myself, he leaves, only to reenter a minute later with a change of clothes. I don my favorite maternity dress and Birkenstocks, then enter the living room. I eye my bag in the corner. So different from the typical bag of an expectant mother. There are no baby clothes or burp cloths. Only toiletries and a change of clothes. Ivy will no doubt arrive with a diaper bag stuffed full of baby items and probably a first-aid kit.

Zach enters, rubbing his ear. "I might be deaf now due to Ivy's squealing." He strokes his jaw. "Need anything else? Food? They won't let you eat in the hospital."

I love this man. "Cheese. Give me cheese."

He rushes to the fridge while a contraction nearly bowls me over. I brace my hands on my thighs and vocalize. Loudly.

He hurries back, eyes bugging out. "We'd better go."

This time, I don't protest. He settles me in the car, and I gnaw on an organic cheese stick until another pain hits. "Can you drive any faster?" Sitting strapped into the car is the absolute worst position.

"I'll try."

By the time we pull up to the hospital, I'd rather be anywhere but in the car. I wouldn't mind giving birth in the hospital parking lot. As long as I'm not in a car. As soon as Zach puts the car in park, I spill out of my door.

Before I can register what's happening, Ivy is at my side, grasping my arm with one hand and rubbing my back with the other. "How are you doing, sis?"

Austin appears with a wheelchair. "Here you go."

I'd respond, but I seem to have lost my voice. Nothing comes out but a moan as I double over.

Ivy and Austin settle me into the wheelchair, and Austin pushes me inside. Ivy holds my hand. "Zach's parking the car. He'll be right in," she assures me.

Why don't I want an epidural? I had reasons, but I can't remember them. Drugs would be delightful. Is it too late to change my mind?

We're in an elevator, going up. Then we're out and approaching the triage desk. Austin does the talking, telling how far apart my contractions are and how long, or at least the last stats Zach relayed. I brace myself for an onslaught of florescent lights and bossy nurses as Austin follows the attendant into a room.

I blink, delightful surprise fluttering in my chest. The room is lit with a soft glow. Instrumental music plays from the speaker. The warm colors give the place a comfy feel. And there's a birthing ball in the corner.

"Hi, honey." The nurse who enters has curly red hair and looks like a much older version of the little orphan Annie. Or perhaps Lucille Ball. "I looked at your birth plan and saw you want a natural labor, and you'd like to be able to move around as much as possible."

I nod and prepare for a rebuke.

"Good for you." She smiles sweetly. "Let me get vitals on you and baby and check your cervix. Then you can move around if you'd like."

Seriously? Her kindness renders me dumbfounded. My last hospital birth was full of ridicule and disdain. Can it really be so different?

I told you to trust Me.

I can nearly see Jesus's wink. Could this thing I've feared for all these months be the very thing that brings healing from my past?

I lay on the bed for only a few moments before the nurse releases me to get up and either walk the halls or use the ball.

I opt for the ball. I'm seven centimeters. Almost there. And I'm still allowed to labor how I see fit. Gratitude fills me.

Ivy, Austin, and Zach fill the room but give me tranquil space. They speak soft encouragement. Ivy feeds me ice chips. I'm surrounded by support and love. Amazing.

Knowing I'm so close helps me push through the intense contractions. When I feel pressure, I ask Zach to get the nurse. It's time.

~~

Ivy had never been prouder of her sister. Holding Everly's hand as she pushed, Ivy told her as much. Each hand squeeze caused Mom's ring to bite into her flesh, but she wouldn't dare complain. Zach dabbed Ev's forehead with a cool washcloth, his expression one of wonder. Clearly, she wasn't the only one impressed. Austin, however, looked like he might throw up.

The doctor gave an encouraging nod. "One more giant push should do it. When the next contraction hits, give it all you've got."

Two breaths later, Everly crushed Ivy's hand and yowled as she ushered their little boy into the world. He scrunched his face, and a robust cry filled the room.

Instant love flooded her heart. He was the most beautiful thing she'd ever seen, even slimy with wrinkled feet. Ivy moved to the foot of the bed, arms outstretched.

The doctor wiped him with a towel and held him up for all to see. "Hold on a minute, Mama. Who's cutting this cord?"

Austin stepped forward. "I am."

A nurse handed him scissors, and he snipped, untethering their child from her sister, then the nurse whisked him away to check his Apgar score. Oh, Everly. For a minute, Ivy had completely forgotten about her. Forgotten to thank her. Congratulate her on a job well done. A glance to the head of the bed showed Zach and Everly engaged in whispered discussion. Tears streamed down Ev's cheeks. Should Ivy interrupt?

But then, a nurse placed her little boy into her arms. So light and tiny, he stared at her with a look of wonder. What was this giddiness bubbling up inside her? This wave of otherworldly affection heating her chest? This was what it felt like to be a mother. Unbelievable. Undeniably a miracle. She couldn't take her eyes off him.

Austin rounded the bed and stood next to her. He put his pinky finger into their son's hand. Her breath caught as their baby grasped it. Just a reflex, of course, but it felt like much more. Like he was staking a claim on his father. Like the three of them were meant to be together.

Austin wore a dopey grin. "He's beautiful."

"So beautiful," she agreed. She studied him. Tufts of downy hair stood on end. He had her nose, but Austin's square chin. "Does our first choice of name fit, you think?"

Austin tilted his head to the side. "Yeah. I think it does."

They'd kept their list of possible names to themselves, saying they'd wait until he was born to decide on one. Now, she nearly burst with the announcement. She turned to Everly. Her sister wore a frown, an almost pained expression. Her hair was plastered to the sides of her face due to sweat. Maybe this would give her comfort.

"His name is Evan Henry." Ivy offered a tentative smile. "It's as close as we could come to naming a boy after you."

Ev's lip trembled. She opened her mouth, then shut it. At a loss for words?

"Do you want to hold him?" As much as her arms and heart protested the thought of giving Evan up, even for a minute, it was only right.

Everly nodded, and Ivy placed him in her arms. He immediately turned his head back and forth.

"He's looking for milk," a nurse said. "He can smell it."

"Oh no, Evan," Everly cooed. "Your mama will feed you." She traced a finger along his profile. "He's adorable."

He began to whimper, and Ev shifted him toward Ivy. "You can have him back." Her words held weight. A somber quiet filled the room as Ivy took him into her arms. She only got to hold him for a minute before a nurse took him from her again to recheck his vitals and wash him. Maybe a home birth did have its benefits. Less interference. More time to bond. Still, she had no regrets.

With her arms empty again, she was free to embrace her sister. Awkwardly, she leaned over the metal railing and held Ev as tight as she could. "Thank you." Those two words couldn't contain the explosion of gratitude Ev deserved.

"You're welcome."

~~

I should be sleeping while I can, yet I'm staring at the hospital ceiling, listening to the low hum of rolling carts and beeping machines. On the couch next to me, Ivy snores softly. Evan sleeps soundly in his crib next to her. Every time I've attempted to doze off, his soft rustles or murmurs shoot me wide awake. Ironic how I'm the hypervigilant one in this scenario. That's a role I would have typecast Ivy for. Oh, well. Best for her to sleep while she can. Tomorrow night, I'll snuggle into my own bed and experience no interruptions while she begins her lifetime role of mom.

I can't stop thinking about Gracie. I've read all the adoptive family's letters several times. Each time, I've pictured her at the various stages they described. It's as if I empty a bottle of sand and watch it sift through my fingers, unable to capture a single grain. Why did the family never get back to me? Are they opposed to me contacting Gracie, or is she unwilling to dive into a relationship with a stranger who shares her DNA? I thought the letters would bring me closure, but this ache to know her has only intensified.

A soft knock sounds at the door, and a nurse shuffles in. She places her hands under the hand sanitizer by the door, and it whirs as it dispenses clear gel. I have a long list of reasons why hand sanitizer is unhealthy and damaging, but strangely, I don't cringe. It's good they're taking precautions to keep Evan safe.

"It's time for baby to eat." Her voice is sweet and soothing. So different from the nurses I experienced with my last birth.

Ivy's eyes flutter open. She sits up. "Already?"

The nurse chuckles. "Yes, ma'am. Good job sleeping when the baby is sleeping, but this early, we don't want him to sleep past three hours."

Ivy nods and stands as the nurse unwraps him from his swaddle. Her hands must be cold because Evan shivers, then meows his distinctly newborn cry. Ivy prepares his bottle, then settles to feed him as the nurse checks my vitals and pushes on my stomach.

When she leaves, I roll on my side and study the two lovebirds. No doubt Ivy is besotted, and the way Evan blinks up at her, I'd swear he is too. My chest squeezes.

"So," Ivy says without breaking eye contact with her son, "how was it? The hospital experience, I mean."

I pause before answering. I haven't told Ivy how long I held out before coming here. If she doesn't ask, I won't tell. It's like I experienced the best of both worlds. I had the comfort of laboring at home and the supposed safety of delivering in a hospital. I would have thought I'd despise the latter, but I didn't. I offer an honest answer. "It was … different than I expected."

"How so?"

"Everyone was nice. Accommodating. Encouraging."

Ivy's brows scrunch as she glances at me. "And that's a surprise."

She doesn't remember how bad it was. She was too young. "Compared to last time, yes. A shocker."

"I'm sorry they weren't kind to you before."

"Not your fault." And, actually, it wasn't mine either. No matter what mistakes I'd made, I didn't deserve to be treated that way. Strange how this is just dawning on me after all these years. "But this time was different. I think it's been healing, in a way. This new experience is like a salve coating the wounds of the old."

It's almost like God knew what He was talking about when He asked me to trust Him. Like He had my good at heart the entire time. I smile.

"So …" Ivy's voice is hesitant. "Do you think you'll have another of your own? Since this experience was a good one?"

Wouldn't that make Zach happy? "Maybe," I say.

It's the same answer I gave Zach before, except then, on a possibility scale of one to ten, I was at a two. Now, I'm probably hovering between seven and eight. Maybe I can have a tubal reversal and see what happens. In that case, if we end up childless, it won't be because of my own stubborn fear.

Ivy must be content with my answer because she drops the subject. She burps Evan and changes his diaper. It's bittersweet watching her settle into the role of mother. My little sister. A mom. Wild.

The next morning, Ivy and Austin place Evan's car seat in their car, wave, and drive away. Zach pulls our car around and helps me into the passenger's seat. I leave the hospital without a baby. Again.

Chapter 30

Gettysburg, Pennsylvania
July 4, 1863

Griffen's face drained of color. "You're telling me you've been fighting for the Confederacy all this time as a … a … female?"

A glance to her left showed Catch standing ramrod straight and unflinching. Her moral support.

She couldn't cower. She laced her fingers together behind her back. "Yes, sir."

The colonel ran a hand through his wavy hair. "Why are you telling me this now?"

"Because I'd like permission to leave, sir. For home."

He mopped his brow with a dirty handkerchief. "I could have you jailed for this."

She swallowed. "I know."

"I suppose you do." His gaze raked her from head to foot. Was he wondering how she could possibly be a woman or how he'd missed the signs all along? "Were you acquainted with the woman who confessed to the same crime in Winchester?"

"Yes, sir." Probably best not to admit that Bernie was a good friend.

Griffen looked over her shoulder toward the battlefield. "We lost almost a hundred men in this battle. Nearly the same amount of men are missing. Perhaps this great misfortune will work in your favor." He let out a deep sigh. "I don't have it in me to face any more destruction today. I won't have you jailed."

Her shoulders sagged. Thank God.

"You must promise to return home posthaste. Where do you hail from?"

"North Carolina, sir. North of Wilmington."

He opened his mouth, likely to inquire about how she'd ended up with the Eighteenth Mississippi, but then he closed it and shook his head. He looked around, and his gaze settled on Catch. "Private, find a wounded North Carolinian bound for home and have him escort Miss Frontenac."

"Yes, sir." From the way Catch's mouth twitched, he had to be fighting a smile.

Griffen returned his attention to her. "See if you can find a proper dress."

"Yes, sir."

"And don't draw attention to yourself." He waved his hand in front of him. "Off with you, then."

She and Catch both saluted, then marched away. They converged in the woods.

"As soon as you're wearing a dress, I'm going to kiss you nice and proper."

Her face heated. How glorious to not have to hide their affection for each other. She was free! Free to love Catch. Free from the army. Free from the danger of war. May she never have to point a gun at a person again. If only Catch could avoid such peril. She'd fret every day until he came for her unscathed.

Her thoughts turned. She'd get to see her sisters and Pa again. Get to return home. She'd finally discover who she was without the brave façade of a soldier. A shiver tingled her spine. Was she ready?

~~

Henrietta crested the small knoll, and her home came into view. The rickety porch was missing a step and a few spindles, but other than that, her home stood tall and welcoming. Like a parent ready to embrace a prodigal daughter.

Hens clucked in a pen to the side. Their washbasin sat in its usual place in the yard, front and center. Voices lilted from inside. But something was different. Odd. Her breath caught. Where was Pa? His chair sat empty.

Dear Lord, let him not have passed away. She picked up her blessed skirts and ran down the path and up the porch stairs. She banged open the door.

Her sisters sat around the table, bent over bowls. Their heads jerked her way. Eyes widened. Jaws unhinged. And in the space of two breaths, arms wrapped around her.

Loreen beamed at her. "Welcome home."

"'Etta, you're back!" Bea nearly squeezed her breathless.

Charlotte almost knocked her over. Gretchen fingered her shoulder-length hair, far longer than when she'd left, but shorter than its previous length. And Millie? There she was, lifting her arms.

Henrietta picked her youngest sister up and twirled her around. "Mill Moo, you have no idea how much I've missed you." She held Millie close and kissed her head.

"I've missed you the mostest, 'Etta."

"Nuh-uh," the others protested.

Laughter bubbled from her. These precious ones meant more to her than anything else. And here they were, safe and sound. And far taller and plumper than before. They'd fared well, but what about her father?

Her gaze searched each corner of the one-room cabin. No sign of him. "Where's Pa?"

Loreen's eyes flashed with surprise. "At work. Didn't I tell you?"

Work? Their father had gotten a job? "No. Where?"

"The factory. With so many of our men off at war, even women can work there now, though I'll save it as a last resort."

"I can't believe it." Shock froze her in place. What had gotten into Pa? And if he had gotten a job, perhaps the need for her to get one wasn't as urgent. "I've missed out on so much. I don't know where to start with my questions."

Loreen threaded her arm through Henrietta's. "There will be time enough for that later. Come eat."

Gretchen rushed to grab a bowl and ladle something savory from the pot. Henrietta took her place at the head of the table. When Gretchen slid the bowl in front of her, her eyes misted. "Is this Ma's lentil stew?"

Loreen sat beside her. "Sure is. I've gotten right good at fixin' it."

She took a tentative sip and flavor exploded on her tongue. Wonder of wonders. Loreen had learned how to cook. "Mighty fine."

She opened her mouth to ask if Loreen had found a few jobs, but the younger ones pelted her with questions before she could voice any of her own. What was it like being a soldier? Where did she travel to? Did Virginia have different animals or trees? Did anyone suspect her? Was she scared?

She chuckled and regaled them with slightly embellished tales. She'd hide the terrifying parts deep inside and give them a good story.

"How's Catch?" Loreen asked.

Henrietta nearly choked on her stew.

"Catch? Who's Catch?" Gretchen asked.

Loreen's barely-there smile spoke of a held confidence. She hadn't immediately spilled Henrietta's secret to her family?

"A friend." Her whisper came out hoarse. Catch was the best friend she'd ever had and so much more. If he died before the end of the war, how would she be able to carry on? She'd been brave in facing her own demise, but to be separated from the man she loved, knowing the threat he faced? This was something else altogether.

As if reading her thoughts, Loreen hooked a pinky through hers. No matter what, they had each other. She'd get through with the help of her sisters.

Strange how she'd set off to save them, yet it was Loreen who'd saved her. Saved her from regret and loneliness. Saved her from striving for something no longer needed. Henrietta was back here not because the war was over but because Loreen valued her.

Conversation picked up around the table. More questions. The younger girls had learned to sew, and they showed her their creations. Patchwork dresses and an apron. Henrietta clapped and praised them.

When night fell, she tucked Millie and Bea in and joined Loreen on the porch. They sat in rickety chairs and watched fireflies light up the inky sky. Finally, Henrietta could speak freely. "Tell me everything."

Loreen blew out a breath. "Where to start?"

Easy question. "When did Pa get a job?"

"Oh. Right after his brother died."

Henrietta straightened. "Dad had a brother?"

"Of course. You knew that." Loreen chuckled but sobered when Henrietta didn't join in. "I thought you knew. Uncle Horton. You've got to remember him."

Uncle Horton? She'd never heard the name in her life. As far as she'd known, Ma and Pa were both alone in the world. No relations to speak of. "No."

"You have to remember him." An edge of frustration snuck into Loreen's voice. "What did you used to call him? Old Man something …"

Henrietta's breath hitched. It couldn't be.

"Old Man Meager. That's it." Loreen snapped. "You and the other children your age used to whisper about Old Man Meager."

Scooting to the edge of her chair, Henrietta studied her sister's face. No trace of teasing. "Old Man Meager was a beggar who'd demand coins from us when we were in town."

"Yes. That was Uncle Horton, all right."

Confusion swarmed her brain. "We were related to him?"

"I don't understand how I know this, and you don't. When Grandpa Frontenac passed away, he left the farmstead and just about everything else to Pa's older brother Horton. Pa was spittin' mad with jealousy. Then, our uncle got too friendly with the drink and lost everything. All of Pa's family inheritance."

"Pa never said a word about them being brothers."

"Didn't he?" Loreen tilted her head. "Come to think of it, our neighbor Mrs. Mayhew might have told me the story. That would make sense. Pa shunned his brother. Didn't want anything to do with him after everything that had happened."

Henrietta reeled. It was like she'd been looking at her childhood through a broken telescope. This revelation had replaced the jagged edges with a smooth, clear lens. "Did Pa attend his funeral?"

Loreen nodded. "We all did. Went together as a family."

Henrietta's throat burned. When was the last time they'd done anything as a family? And she'd missed it.

"Pa broke down and wept like a baby. Said he wished he hadn't allowed bitterness to steal his relationship with his brother."

"Hmm." She tried to picture it, Pa weeping at a gravesite. The man's frown was far more familiar than his smile, yet a flagrant display of emotion was hard to imagine.

"The next day, he got up with the sun and headed to Warsaw to find a job. Someone in town told him of a factory in Wilmington that was hiring. He stays there throughout the week and comes home Friday evening through Sunday."

Ah. That explained why he'd yet to make an appearance. She'd have to wait two more days to meet this new version of Pa.

She swatted a mosquito away. "So, Old Man Meager is dead." She'd been so focused on the fact he'd been her uncle all along that this piece of information hadn't sunk in. "I reckon I can stop being afraid of him."

A laugh escaped Loreen, and she covered her mouth. "I'm sorry. That was disrespectful to the deceased. But truly, you were still afraid of him as a grown woman?"

Henrietta shivered. "Had nightmares about him most nights."

"Well, I'll be." Loreen patted her hand. "Guess you can sleep easy now."

They remained on the front porch and talked half the night. Loreen had found a position as a tutor. Ironic, since none of them had ever been to school. Mama's book learning had done them good. Gretchen had done well at managing the household and laundering for the few in town who could still afford it. The girls had expanded the garden, and under their tender care, it flourished. They sold excess produce in both towns on the weekends.

Loreen's glowing review of how their family had fared without her sluiced her with waves of unease. How could her sister have said they needed her? Clearly, they didn't. Where was her place? She barely remembered how to be a woman, and now anything she did would encroach on another's role.

"Maybe I'll go to Wilmington and work at the factory with Pa." She could do so as a man, if needed, but Loreen had said they hired women now.

Her sister glared at her. "Not a chance. We just got you back. We'll hog tie you if you attempt to leave us again."

A smile threatened to emerge at Loreen's familiar dramatics. But uncertainty weighed it down. "Then where's my place?"

Loreen hooked their pinkies together again. "Right here with us." The ring Henrietta had given her glistened in the moonlight.

Lord, I've forgotten who I am in this space. Show me, Lord, and guide my steps.

Chapter 31

Suburb of Wilmington, North Carolina
Present Day

Ivy settled Evan into his bassinet and padded into the kitchen in her fuzzy-slipper-clad feet. She cinched her robe tighter and reached numbly for a K-Cup of coffee. It was Austin's first day back at work, and though every inch of her exhausted body called out for another hour of sleep, she had a mission to accomplish.

Once her Keurig started, she flipped through the notebook she'd left on the kitchen table. She didn't have much to go on. All Ev had relayed was that her daughter's name was Gracie, and her adoptive parents were Karen and Tim. Good thing Bridget's uncle was a PI. Though she couldn't afford to hire him, he'd given her tips, and they'd ended up narrowing down the Karen and Tim couples within the state to ten.

She couldn't be sure the adoptive family resided in the state of North Carolina, but the picture they'd sent of Gracie at an outing to a zoo looked eerily familiar. The structure in the background seemed to be from North Carolina Zoo's Honey Bee Garden. But she might be mistaken. There could be hundreds of honeybee hives in zoos across the country. Even if it was taken at the state zoo, it didn't mean the family lived nearby. They could have visited from anywhere. Still, hope percolated inside of her.

Her nerves buzzed as she picked up her phone and dialed the first number. This. Was. Terrifying. But after everything Everly had done for her, she could brave it. One ring. Two.

Three. A voicemail came on, and Karen Drakesport announced her name in the appropriate spot. Here went nothing.

"Hello, Karen. My name is Ivy Hartgrove. I'm calling on behalf of my sister Everly Moore. She placed a child for adoption seventeen years ago and desperately wants to reconnect with her daughter, Gracie. If you are the Karen we seek, please call me back." Ivy listed her number. Her hand shook as she hung up.

What were the odds Karen would return the call? If she hadn't responded to the agency relaying Ev's request, why would she respond now? Such a long shot, but one Ivy had to take.

"One down. Nine to go." She crossed the first number off the list and wrote *voicemail* next to it. She repeated the spiel to four other voicemails, then crossed the numbers off, each strike with a harder line than the one before. Perhaps eight a.m. on a Monday was a horrible time to call. She might have better luck in the evenings, but in addition to that being Evan's fussiest time of the day, Austin would be home. And he probably wouldn't approve of her valiant mission.

On the fifth call, Karen Tremble answered, sending Ivy's pulse into overdrive. After a minute of conversation, however, the woman told her she'd never adopted. At least that call resulted in a clear answer.

Call number six went straight to a full voice mailbox. Since she couldn't leave a message, she made a note to try back later. Call seven rang and rang. No voicemail. No answer. Another note to try again. She reached voicemails for calls eight and nine. So much for a breakthrough today. She should have stayed in bed.

She sipped her now-tepid coffee, lacking the energy to reheat it. If she laid her head on the table, she might fall asleep right there.

A Beethoven ringtone belted through the quiet kitchen. She shot to attention, snatched her phone, and answered, not bothering to check who it was. "Yes?"

"Hello, this is Karen Barkey returning your call."

Adrenaline surged through her. "Yes?"

A long sigh. "My husband Tim and I have an adopted daughter named Gracie. Did your sister go through Maple Grove Adoption Agency?"

"Y-yes." Her voice trembled. She pressed her fist to her mouth to suppress the whimper—or sob—threatening to erupt. She'd done it. She'd found her niece's family.

"We've sent letters all these years and never received one in return. You can imagine how your sister's change of heart takes us by surprise." Karen's tone was kind but guarded.

"Of course. That's understandable." A good surprise or a bad one? She hadn't come this far to reach a closed door. "Everly had much to work through, but now she's eager to have some kind of contact with Gracie."

"We got a voicemail from the agency but hadn't come to any conclusions on how to respond. What would contact look like?"

Good question. "Just something. Anything. You take the lead. Everly would be delighted with whatever you feel comfortable with." Hopefully.

A dog's bark filtered through the line. "And your sister is … stable?"

"Oh yes. Very." She couldn't blame Karen for her reticence. How were they to know Everly wasn't a drug addict or alcoholic? "She's married and is a doctor."

Okay, maybe Ivy had belittled the title of Dr. Moore for her sister, not valuing chiropractic. But Everly had earned the title through study and perseverance. And it went a long way toward proving her respectable.

"We'll talk to Gracie and see what she's comfortable with. Should I call you back at this number?"

"Please."

They said polite goodbyes, and Ivy hung up. Her arms shook as she came down from the adrenaline surge. "Please, Lord, give Everly the desire of her heart."

~~

I hang up, set my cell phone on the counter, and press my hands to my cheeks. What did I do? Unbelievable how I had the courage to make that call.

The front door opens. I finished that conversation just in time. Zach barrels in, workout towel draped on his neck, face glistening with sweat.

"Good run?"

"Excellent." He grins. "When do you think you'll be up for joining me?"

It's been two months since I gave birth. The OB gave me the all clear to resume normal activity. Since I never explained the surrogacy situation to people in my kickboxing class, I've avoided returning post-pregnancy. Too many questions. But running again would be a good step toward normalcy.

"I don't think I could keep up with you. I need to rebuild my stamina."

He dabs his face with the towel. "I can go at your pace."

I wave him off. "I don't want to slow you down. I'll probably start with power walking and a light jog."

It's not like we always used to run together. Most of the time, we worked out separately. But maybe it's not about exercise. Perhaps he's hungry for connection. I've been adrift since Evan entered the world. Unsure of where I fit, my purpose. Has that affected how I relate to Zach? I may have pulled away without realizing it. But that phone call will change everything.

"I have something to tell you."

His brows lift.

"Shower first, then we'll talk." I go to twist Mom's ring on my finger, but it's not there. How many times have I done that since I gifted it to Ivy? My hands fidget.

"Way to keep me in suspense."

I bite my lower lip to rein in a smile. When I turn toward the kitchen, he snaps my bottom with his towel.

He winks. "I'll hurry."

While he's showering, I make his smoothie, pouring greens, berries, protein powder, almond milk, and ice into the blender. The machine screams as it blends. I startle when Zach comes behind me and wraps his arms around my waist. "That was quick," I say, breathless.

"I can be quick when motivated." He kisses my ear, and tingles shoot down my spine. His lips trail my neck as I attempt to pour his smoothie. I do a poor job of it, and the counter is covered with the green mixture by the time I finish and turn to face him.

He holds up the half-full cup. "Shortchanging me, I see."

I laugh. "It's your fault for distracting me."

He braces his hands on the counter, one to my left, one to my right, pinning me in. "What did you want to talk about?"

Heady desire clouds my mind. I'd wanted to talk? Oh, yeah. "I just got off the phone with my doctor's office."

His smile falters. "Is everything okay?"

"Yes." I put my hands on his biceps. "Everything is great."

He visibly relaxes. "Go on."

The words I've been holding back rush forth. "I want to go forward with a tubal reversal. I made a consultation appointment to get the process started."

His lips part. "What?"

"I want to have a baby."

His minty mouth claims mine. His hands channel through my hair as his body presses me against the counter. When he comes up for breath, I say, "I take it you're happy?"

His strong arms lift me up and set me on the messy counter, nearly knocking off my newest succulent. I cup his face in my hands and lean down to continue our kissing session. I wrap my legs around his torso. This is the passion I've missed for the past eleven months. Without Ivy's baby as a barrier between us, we drink each other in. I unwrap my legs, and he scoops me up and takes a few steps toward our bedroom, my smoothie-covered behind smearing his shirt with the green mixture.

Then my phone rings. We lock eyes. He checks the caller ID. "It's Ivy."

Whatever she has to say can wait. I won't jeopardize this moment. "I'll call her back later."

~~

Ivy huffed. "Why isn't she answering her phone?"

Bridget looked up from her computer. "Who?"

"My sister."

"Does she always answer when you call?"

"Pretty much." Ivy worried her lip.

"Wow. That's … a lot."

Maybe it was a lot to ask Ev to drop what she was doing the minute Ivy wanted to talk. But this was important.

"You going to jump into the queue, or do you need a few more minutes?" Bridget's tone clearly said *Get to work.* And yes, she needed to, but first …

"Let me just send a couple quick texts."

Bridget made a noncommittal noise and shifted her attention to her job.

Ivy pulled up Everly's text thread and typed.

> Can you meet me at the Wilmington River Walk at six?

Then she switched to the text thread that had started everything.

Six fifteen should work. Thanks.

Please, Lord, let this work.

She was a bundle of nerves all day and only made it through by the grace of God. She couldn't count the number of times she'd had to backspace due to mistyping. She finished the day with a lower queue count than normal, but hey, she'd made it through. Everly had responded to Ivy's text an hour after she'd sent it, confirming her availability, thank God. Now, for a surprise that could change her sister's life forever.

At 5:55 p.m., she stood at the same spot where Everly had given her Mom's ring months before. The wind wasn't as ferocious as it had been that day. Only an occasional soft breeze kissed her face. She alternated between staring across the river and glancing toward Water Street for a glimpse of her sister.

Finally, at 6:05, Everly neared. She'd braided her hair, and it hung over one shoulder. Her giant sunglasses hid her emotions.

"Okay." Ev smirked. "What is this about?"

She'd wanted to make sure Ev arrived in time, but now she needed to stall. "How was your day?"

"Great." Everly's cheeks tinged pink. "But you didn't invite me here for small talk. What gives?"

She needed to keep Ev talking for a few more minutes. "Why was it great? What happened?"

Ev's lips twitched as if she was holding back a smile. "Among other things, I took a huge step today."

"What?"

"I made a consultation appointment for a tubal reversal."

Wait, what? "Are you serious? That's amazing!" Ivy crushed her sister in a hug. "I'm so proud of you."

She hadn't planned this, not now. But certainty rose. She'd told herself if Everly ever had children, she'd give the ring back. Though nothing was set in stone, it was time. She may have only possessed the heirloom for a few short months, but it begged to return to its rightful owner.

She slid it off her finger. Ironic how they'd been in this very spot when the ring switched hands the first time. Maybe providential. She pressed Mom's ring into Everly's palm. "This belongs to you."

Ev shook her head.

"I won't take no for an answer. It's yours. You can pass it on to your daughter if you'd like."

Ev's eyes filled. "No, Ivy. God wanted me to give it to you."

"You did. And I'm giving it back."

A flash of red caught Ivy's eye. "We don't have time to argue about this. I've got something to tell you." Ivy took her sister's hands. "I hope you don't mind me butting in, but I did some digging, made a few calls, and there's someone I want you to meet."

Everly's furrowed brow registered confusion.

The teenager in red shoes approached, but the colored sneakers weren't needed to identify this younger version of Everly. Looking at her was like stepping back in time.

Ivy squeezed Ev's hands. "Your daughter."

Everly turned. Her mouth dropped open. "How?"

"I'll explain that later. This is Gracie. Gracie, this is Everly."

Gracie smiled shyly and shifted her weight. "Hi."

"Oh, my goodness. I can't believe—" Ev swayed. Ivy grabbed her elbow to support her. "It's really you." Tears trekked down her cheeks. "I've dreamed of meeting you ever since you were born, and now you're here."

Gracie took a step forward. "I'm here." Her hands rose and fell, as if she wasn't sure what to do with them or what came next. "My parents—my adoptive parents—are down there." She nodded to a couple standing down the river walk. "They wanted to give me space, but they'd like to meet you too."

"Of course." Ev clasped her hands together, apparently as unsure as Gracie as to what was appropriate. A handshake? A hug? "I'd love to meet them. To thank them."

A full smile bloomed on Gracie's face. "They'd like to thank you too."

Everly opened her arms. "Can I … Would it be okay to hug you?"

Without answering, Gracie stepped into her embrace.

Ivy had to keep herself from clapping.

Thank You, Lord, for restoration. Thank You for making all things beautiful in Your time.

Chapter 32

I AM PLEASED TO HEAR THAT YOU HAVE YOUR GARDEN IN SUCH FINE ORDER. I HOPE TO ENJOY SOME OF YOUR NICE VEGETABLES THIS YEAR. DON'T FORGET THE WATERMELON PATCH WHEN THE PROPER TIME ARRIVES.

JAN. 10, 1862, JAMES B. GRIFFIN

Warsaw, North Carolina
July 10, 1863

The next day, Henrietta hoofed it to Warsaw under the guise of purchasing a cut of lamb for a celebratory dinner. Pa would be home in the evening. In reality, she needed to clear her head. She'd forgotten how the activity of a full house could overwhelm a person. Army life had been raucous and busy too, but it was a different type of busy. She'd have to reacclimate to home.

And she needed to find her place.

As she walked, she prayed.

Lord, I'm more than a sister or a soldier. More than Catch's beloved. I'm Yours. Even when I turned my back on You, You didn't give up on me. Show me where to go from here. How can I be Your hands and feet?

As she neared town, a faint tinge of bacon hung in the air. Loreen had told her the day she'd headed home, July 5, the Third New York Cavalry had attacked Warsaw. They'd burned down the Confederate States Armory in nearby Kenansville the day before, then marched to Warsaw and demolished two miles of the railroad track and telegraph wire, cutting down the poles. They'd destroyed two railcars and a freight house of resin and turpentine, along with gunpowder. As they left, they'd burned a barn filled with hundreds of pounds of bacon.

The attack had shaken the girls. The Federals took thirty prisoners with them. Hundreds of slaves went along. Henrietta had never been so thankful that their family lived outside of town and had no slaves to lose. When Pa returned today, he'd have to take the Magnolia stop and walk the rest of the way. Would he be pleased to see her when he arrived? Or would she receive the same blank stare he'd given for years?

Her breath hitched as she came to the railroad tracks. The Yankees had done a number on them, all right. Twisted them up good. How long would it take to repair? Something else was new. The modest wooden building resembled a house, but a banner proclaimed it to be much more. A wayside hospital? Instead of heading into the merchant's store, she drew near to the hospital as if pulled by a lead rope.

After ensuring her short hair was safely tucked under her bonnet, she entered to find two rows of beds, a table and chairs, and a settee. Resting soldiers occupied three of the beds. Two sat at the table, mugs in hand. A woman wearing an apron over her hoop skirt, turned to her. "Can I help you?"

"What is this establishment?" Henrietta held herself erect. Though she felt more like the men in uniform, that was her role no longer. She was a woman and must act as such. "Is it a hospital?"

"Yes." The woman flashed an eager smile. "Are you interested in volunteering? We're looking for more volunteers. And donations. We'd appreciate anything you can spare." She waved a hand around the room. "We provide meals and basic nursing to weary and injured soldiers passing through. Have you any nursing experience?"

Henrietta blinked as she processed the lady's quick words. "Nursing? Not really." She'd cared for her ill siblings and watched from a distance as army doctors patched up soldiers, but she certainly wasn't an expert.

"Cooking, then? Might you be able to dish up meals?"

Providing soldiers with a home-cooked meal? What a great kindness. After existing on cornmeal and crackers for months, a hearty, warm supper might bring a soldier to tears. If Catch were injured, she'd want someone to give him such a courtesy. Only, she'd intended to find employment. A job that came with decent pay. Could she afford to give her hours away with no compensation?

Give as I have given to you.

A chill traversed her spine at the words whispered to her heart. She'd asked the Lord to show her the next steps to take. Might this be His answer?

The woman arched an eyebrow as she waited for Henrietta's reply.

Now that Pa was working, her family could survive without her income. Loreen hadn't asked her home for what she could contribute. Loreen wanted her presence, not her pay. She could do this. She could be the hands and feet of Christ to the hurting.

"Yes. I would like to volunteer. I can cook, and if someone guides me, I'm sure I can provide basic care as well."

The woman clapped. "Excellent. Thank you for aiding the war effort. I'm Martha, by the way."

"Henrietta." She smiled at the freedom of giving her true name.

She headed back home without lamb for a feast. She'd donated most of the money she came with to the hospital. But she had purchased flour to bake bread. That would be treat enough.

~~

When Pa stepped into the house and laid eyes on Henrietta, he broke down and wept. She stood stock still. She hadn't seen Pa show emotion since Ma died. She'd begun to believe he had no feelings left, only numbness. But there he was, tears running onto his neatly trimmed beard.

"My girl." He took a step toward her, and she rushed to close the distance.

"Oh, Pa." She engulfed him in an embrace. "Welcome home."

He chuckled. "You're the one who's returned. Safe and sound, thank God."

She didn't correct him, but clearly, he had traveled the long journey of despair to life.

He sniffed at the air. "What do I smell?"

"Freshly baked bread." She grinned.

"How I've missed your cooking."

Gretchen planted her hands on her hips. "Pardon me?"

Laughter filled the house. Laughter and love and belonging.

She was home.

~~

When Pa returned to Wilmington on Monday, Loreen and Henrietta walked to the graveyard. Daisies in hand, Henrietta approached her uncle's headstone. It would have been rude to show up empty-handed, but the flowers felt awkward in her hand. She'd feared this man as if he were a monster. Now, it was clear it wasn't so much Horton that had haunted her. It was what he'd represented. The ever-present fear of never having enough. His rattling tin cup reminded her of all she'd lacked. Food. Clothes. Shoes. She'd lived so many years where provisions were hard to come by. He had begged for something she didn't have to give.

She'd been so focused on what she didn't have, she'd neglected to thank the Lord for what she did have. Her family was a most precious gift, and Scripture said all good gifts came from the heavenly Father.

Her uncle had been a sad, lonely man. As she placed the flowers at his grave, she made a resolution. She would be a joyful, thankful woman. Old Man Meager was dead and gone. He couldn't trouble her anymore.

After paying their respects, the sisters linked arms and headed home. When their house came into sight, Loreen stopped.

"What is it?"

Loreen clasped her hands in front of her. "I need to return something that belongs to you." She slipped Ma's ring off her finger and slid it onto Henrietta's hand. "Thank you for lending it to me. In some way, it gave me the strength to go on without you. But now, you're back."

Henrietta relished the feeling of the cool metal encircling her finger. She could tell Loreen to keep it, but to do so seemed like denying a gift her sister was eager to give. She would receive it as intended, as a token of love. "Thank you for keeping it safe."

"Thank you for fighting for us."

She would never stop fighting for the ones she loved, though it would look far different now. She'd brandish the weapon of prayer instead of a rifle.

~~

2 Years Later

Train cars full of returning soldiers filtered through Warsaw. With each defeated man's departure, Henrietta's heart hung heavy. The South had lost the war. Did that mean she'd fought for a lost cause? No, she hadn't taken up the cause of states' rights any more than she'd worn the banner of saving slavery. She'd accomplished what she set out to do. While devastation reigned throughout the South, her family had survived. Thrived even, compared to their sorry state before the war.

Each dusty face held a story she could relate to, but the face she most longed to see was nowhere in sight. Again and again in his letters, Catch had promised to come for her. Had his affection somehow waned since she'd heard from him last? Had he forgotten his pledge? Or was he injured or worse? She swallowed hard. No. He had to have made it through.

Then where was he?

She served the last of the sweet cake she'd brought to the wayside hospital and, with one last glance over her shoulder, trudged home. She'd poured herself out for weary soldiers, but this season of service was coming to an end. What now?

She needed to write Bernie. So much had happened since they'd parted ways. Had her friend arrived safely home to her sheep farm? Would she be able to grow her flock like she'd dreamed, or had she returned to find destruction? At least she'd received a letter from Freddy. Though he might forever walk with a limp, he was alive and happy to be home.

As Henrietta neared home, she squinted at a figure sitting on a porch chair. Had Pa returned early from Wilmington? But the width and set of the person's shoulders didn't match Pa's. She sucked in a breath. Could it be?

She broke into a run. The figure stood and descended the stairs, hand shading his eyes. The closer she came, the higher her spirits soared. Catch came into focus, a grin gracing his tanned face. His cheek sported a scar, and his uniform was threadbare with a hole in the knee. Still, he was the most handsome man she'd ever laid eyes on. He rushed toward her, and she flung herself into his arms, kissing his cheek.

His laugh rumbled. "I told you I'd come for you."

She pulled back and placed a hand on her middle, catching her breath. "I waited for you at the station every day."

The sides of his eyes crinkled. "I arrived at the Faison depot a few hours ago."

Oh. That explained it. "I waited at Warsaw."

Their laughter mingled as their fingers wove together. "I met your sisters. Well, five of them. A lively bunch."

"You've already met Loreen. She's the only one missing. She and Pa."

"Ah, yes. I need to have a word with your pa."

Warmth spread through her chest. "Do you?"

He kissed her knuckles and winked. "I must ask for your hand like a gentleman."

"Oh, Catch." She wrapped her arms around his neck and nudged his head down. He captured her lips with his own, and years of waiting and longing crescendoed in a kiss that left her breathless. His strong hands cradled her head, then tangled in her long hair.

"You've never looked so beautiful." His words tingled her ears. "You make a mighty fine woman." He drank her in with another kiss. "And you'll make a fantastic wife."

Cheeks flushed and heart near to bursting, she took in Catch's rugged face and forest-green eyes, radiating sincere love.

Thank You, Lord. She'd been through fire and water, but He'd brought her into rich fulfillment.

EPILOGUE

THERE'S NO BETTER FRIEND THAN A SISTER.
MARY ENGELBREIT

Suburb of Wilmington, North Carolina
Present Day

Since I met Gracie a year ago, we've spent time together once a month, each time at a different restaurant in Wilmington. That city became full of glorious memories and laughter as I grew to know my little girl who is actually a young woman.

Maybe Gracie would like to go with me to the farmer's market sometime. My arms are full of reusable bags stuffed with fresh fruit and vegetables from my weekly trip. I can't open the door without dropping everything, so I kick it with my foot. "Come on, Zach," I murmur.

If he doesn't open this door soon, I'll be chasing dropped peppers.

The door swings open, but Zach's not the one to greet me. It's Ivy. She moves to unburden me of a bag. "What are you doing here?"

I step inside and gasp.

Balloons. Dozens of pink balloons. And crepe paper galore.

"Surprise!" The chorus meets my ears before I enter far enough to see everyone. Naomi and Glenda, Jessica and other cousins, and Gracie. My eyes mist.

"Happy baby shower." Ivy sets the bag down and slings an arm around my shoulder.

Naomi steps forward and takes the rest of my purchases to the kitchen.

"How—" I begin to ask, then groan. "This is why Zach sent me on a wild goose chase for that particular brand of tabasco sauce." A brand I couldn't find. Probably because it doesn't exist.

Laughter sprinkles the room.

The guests greet me with hugs. I hang on to Gracie longer than the others. She's at my home for the first time. God's grace and mercy overwhelm me.

I make my way into the living room and sit among family and friends. Glenda asks about the book on my side table. *Sisters in Arms: The Undercover World of Female Civil War Soldiers* by Cassaundra Walt. I tell her how amazing it is to see my relative featured there, alongside other brave women.

Evan crawls toward me and lifts his arms up. I place him on my shrinking lap. My belly makes it difficult, but we always manage.

Ivy must have had her work cut out for her in cleaning for this shower. Normally, Evan's toys clutter the floor, sticky fingerprints grace the sliding glass door, and graham cracker crumbs litter the couch. And it's wonderful. I wouldn't have it any other way.

How fitting I wore my *Dreaming of Baby* maternity shirt today. I've made no effort to hide this pregnancy. Let everyone see what God has done. Not just in my body, but in my heart and life. He's truly given beauty for ashes.

Jessica comes over from where she's been peeking at my yard through the sliding glass door. "Your garden looks great. I'm impressed."

Me too. "Naomi's been helping me." Turns out my friend has a green thumb. I wink at her, and she grins.

We chat and eat, but we do not play games, thank goodness. Ivy brings the presents to me, and I savor opening each one. Only I don't save the wrapping paper. It's finally *my* shower for *my* baby. Well, Zach helped too.

By the time the guests file out, my stomach and heart are full to bursting. What a glorious surprise. Ivy stays to clean up despite my insistence that she doesn't need to.

As she wipes the kitchen counter, her phone belts out Beethoven's Twelfth. She pulls it from her back pocket and answers. Her face lights up as she speaks to whoever is on the other line. Words like "great" and "wonderful" pour from her, then finally, she says, "Let me talk to my husband and get back to you."

As soon as she pockets her phone, I pounce. "What was that about?"

Ivy claps. "That was our surrogate. She's decided to move forward."

"Amazing." I stand and wrap her in a hug. "So, it's paid off? All your medical debt?"

"Yes! The church's donation, plus Austin's bonus, covered the rest of it."

"Praise the Lord." I squeeze tight, then pull away and smile at Evan. "You want to be a big brother?"

He squeals and claps.

Ivy hums a happy tune as she continues to clean. I lean back on the couch and sigh with contentment.

"What's this? We forgot a gift?" Ivy is holding a miniature pink gift bag from the kitchen counter.

"Oh, I almost forgot." I stand and come to her. "It's for you."

"Great news from the surrogate and a gift? Could my day get any better?" She pulls out the bright blue tissue paper and extracts a velvet ring box. When she opens it, she gasps. "What is this? A smaller knockoff of Mom's ring?"

"It's not a knockoff." I raise my hand and place my identical ring next to hers. "I had a jeweler split Mom's ring into two smaller pieces."

Ivy's jaw unhinges. "We can both have a piece of Mom?"

I nod, then take her ring from the box. She's taking too long to put it on. I slide it onto her finger. She holds her hand up to the light, beaming. We'll both have a legacy to pass on one day. One far more significant than a piece of jewelry, but the pieces signify the bigger picture well. We are a family who fights for each other, who honors one another, and who relies on the Lord's strength and love. We'll make it through whatever the future holds because we'll continue holding on to the One who's holding us. Whatever it takes.

The End

AUTHOR'S NOTE

Every new story brings new challenges as well as new joys. *Whatever It Takes* was no exception. The modern-day storyline contained both. Writing about sisters when I don't have one was something I needed to rely on the Lord for the ability to do. I grew up as an only child, desperately wishing for someone to share adventures with. My half brother came along when I was fifteen—the perfect age to babysit. I found myself coming up short when trying to portray the close sisterly relationship I yearned for as a child. (I know not all siblings are close, but some are.)

While I did some heavy leaning on the Lord for that portion of the story, I got to do some live research for another part. While writing about Everly's process of becoming a surrogate, we went through the process of embryo adoption. While these two journeys are vastly different emotionally, I "got to" go through much of the same process as Everly. From pre-med appointments and tests to make sure my body was ready to estrogen pills and progesterone shots to, finally, the embryo transfer. This novel became very personal as I set out to carry a non-genetic child in my womb.

I read many books about surrogacy, but the one that I gleaned most from was *Amazing Grace: A Story of Surrogacy and the Love of Two New Zealand Sisters*. This true story of a sister surrogate intrigued and inspired me.

As far as the historical storyline goes, I set out to show yet another reason some women chose to go undercover and fight in the Civil War. The question of *Why did they do it?* is one that fascinated me when I first learned that female Civil War soldiers were a thing. What would make a woman disguise her identity, undergo the hardships of life as a soldier, and fight in gory battles? There are over four hundred verified accounts of women doing just that, and it's suspected the true number of female Civil War soldiers might be in the thousands.

Bernie, the main character in *A Battle Worth Fighting*, did so to find her husband. Willow, in *Fall Back and Find Me*, did it to escape a difficult home situation and to prove herself. In *Whatever It Takes*, Henrietta's main motivation is to escape poverty.

There are many other reasons why women fought, but at this time, I don't plan on writing any more books in the Sisters in Arms collection.

While I tried to stick close to the true timeline of Henrietta's regiments, I did fudge the dates in a couple of places for the sake of the story. While I dated Chapter 6 as happening in May, they weren't truly mustered until June. And I dated Chapter 8 as happening in May, when they didn't move to Virginia until July. I took much of the details of the Eighteenth Mississippi's whereabouts from a book entitled *Battle-Fields of the South, From Bull Run to Fredericksburg*, written by "an English combatant," someone who fought with the regiment.

I hope you enjoyed this story, as well as the others in the Sisters in Arms collection. I look forward to exploring other stories with you.

For His glory,
Sarah Hanks

OTHER BOOKS BY SARAH HANKS

The Mercy Series
Mercy Will Follow Me
Mercy's Song
Mercy's Legacy

Sisters in Arms Collection
A Battle Worth Fighting
Fall Back and Find Me

Time Sailors Series
Braving Strange Waters

Stand Alone
Awakened to Life
New Creations

Scan to connect with Sarah Hanks.

www.ingramcontent.com/pod-product-compliance
Lightning Source LLC
Chambersburg PA
CBHW070314310726

48976CB00005B/1708